Their faces were grotesque—bearlike, but with a hint of ape as well. Heavy brows overhung their close-set eyes and their lips were curled back from yellowing teeth. Long fangs interspersed with grinding molars. They were equipped with what appeared to be black leather armor and each one wore a metal skullcap.

As he looked through the gap in the rocks, the chanting and stamping had ceased, and for a moment he thought they must have detected him.

But then they began again. They raised their spears and thrust forward as one. They emitted that terrifying grunt that he'd heard, then stamped forward so that eighty right feet slammed down onto the plain, raising a cloud of dust. Then they repeated the action, stamping, grunting and thrusting their way forward, heading for the line of rocks where Halt crouched in hiding.

Then a strange sensation came over Halt. As he watched Wargals drilling, he felt a featherlight intrusion into his consciousness.

It was faint and fleeting, but he had the vague impression that somewhere, someone was trying to speak to him—although he could hear no words. As he tried to focus on the sensation, it faded. Then, a few seconds later, it drifted back.

RANGER'S APPRENTICE

SERIES

THE ROYAL RANGER

THE EARLY YEARS

BROTHERBAND CHRONICLES

RANGER'S APPRENTICE

THE EARLY YEARS

BOOK 2: THE BATTLE OF HACKHAM HEATH

JOHN FLANAGAN

PUFFIN BOOKS

PUFFIN BOOKS
An imprint of Penguin Random House LLC, New York

First published in the United States of America by Philomel Books, 2016
Published by Puffin Books, an imprint of Penguin Random House LLC, 2017

Visit us online at penguinrandomhouse.com

LIBRARY OF CONGRESS CATALOGING-IN-PUBLICATION DATA IS AVAILABLE UPON REQUEST.
ISBN 9780399163623

Puffin Books ISBN 9780142427330

Printed in the United States of America

9 10

Edited by Michael Green.
Design by Semadar Megged.

Araluen, Picta and Celtica

1

IT WAS DARK AND CLAMMY AND DAMP IN THE TUNNEL.

Even though Halt wasn't a tall man, he found he had to stoop as he made his way along, and his shoulders brushed the rough, unlined clay walls on either side. The flickering lamp held by the miner who was leading the way cast a dim yellow light, shot with grotesque shadows.

"How far down are we?" Crowley asked from behind him. The thick, heavy air in the tunnel seemed to muffle his voice, although Halt could hear a note of nervousness in it. Crowley, like Halt, disliked cramped and confined spaces like this, preferring the clean open air of the forest and fields aboveground. How miners could work in these conditions was beyond Halt's understanding.

The miner turned back to face them briefly. "About five meters," he said. "We've been slanting down since we entered the tunnel. Not far to go now."

At his words, Halt felt the massive weight of earth and clay above them bearing down on him. His chest constricted and he had difficulty breathing. He felt his heart begin to race and paused, breathing slowly and deeply, allowing his tensed limbs and body to relax. The sooner they were out of here, the better it would suit him. Crowley, not noticing that Halt had stopped, bumped into him from behind and muttered an apology.

"Mind this shoring," the miner said gruffly, indicating the timber frames that supported the walls and roof of the tunnel. "Knock one of these loose and you'll likely bring the whole thing down on us."

The two Rangers started moving again, taking exaggerated care not to bump against the timber beams. In the distance, Halt fancied he could hear a faint clinking sound—metal on rock. For a moment he thought he might be imagining it, but the miner confirmed it for him.

"That's the lads at work," he said. "Hear them? They're widening the gallery under the walls."

He set off again and they followed, anxious not to be left out of the shallow pool of light cast by the lamp. The clinking grew louder. It didn't sound as if anyone were wielding their picks too vigorously and Halt remarked on the fact.

The miner laughed grimly. "You don't go bashing away in earth like this," he said, "else you'll have a collapse on your hands. Slow and steady does it."

Ahead, Halt could see a small circle of yellow light. As they proceeded, it became larger and brighter. Eventually, they arrived at a widened gallery, set at right angles to the tunnel. It was heavily braced with timber shoring and ran four or five meters to either side of the tunnel, forming a T-shaped intersection.

The roof was higher here, at least a meter higher than Halt's head. He sighed with relief and stood upright, easing his cramped back and shoulder muscles. He heard Crowley do the same.

"Are we under the walls?" the Ranger Commandant asked.

The miner nodded, pointing to a massive piece of granite protruding through the clay roof of the tunnel to one side. The rock was squared off and had obviously been shaped by man's hand. Timber beams were set in place all around and under it, supporting it.

"That's part of the foundation for the wall there," he told them. He held the lamp higher and they could see that the line of shaped rock continued along the gallery where they were standing. More timber shoring held it firmly in place.

The clinking sound, which had become appreciably louder since they'd entered the gallery, stopped now and a stooped figure emerged from the shadows to their left. There was really no need to stoop here, Halt thought. There was plenty of headroom. But perhaps it was a habit borne of long practice and many years spent underground in mines and tunnels.

The newcomer stopped and nodded a greeting to their guide. Then he took a few seconds to glance curiously at the two Rangers. He knew who they were—all the miners did—but belowground he was more accustomed to seeing other miners and diggers, clad in leather aprons and hoods to protect their clothes from the mud and dirt of the tunnel. These two, in their gray-and-green-mottled cloaks, with their weapons belts around their waists, were a novelty down here.

"Morning, Alwyn," he said now. "Morning, Rangers."

Halt and Crowley mumbled a reply, although how anyone could keep track of the time of day down here, Halt had no idea.

"Morning, Dafyd. Are you done?" their guide asked.

The newcomer nodded several times. "Just about. A little more digging and shoring up—say another fifteen minutes. Then we can start bringing in the combustibles."

The gallery they were in had far more supporting timber than the tunnel they had traversed to get here. Halt assumed that was because the tunnel itself was low and narrow, and roughly oval in shape, providing natural support for the walls. Here, where the open space was wider, there was a need for more frames and beams to support the ceiling, and the massive foundation stones of the wall above them, which the digging had undermined along the length of the gallery. As he thought of that, he felt his chest constrict and a moment of unreasoning fear swept through him. If he didn't check that quickly, he knew, it could turn to panic—blind, debilitating panic. Once again, he forced his tense body to relax, beginning with his fingers, hands and arms, letting the calming feeling spread through his body. He breathed deeply, slowing his breathing rate. He felt his heart hammer less stridently in his chest.

"Don't know how they get used to this," he muttered to Crowley.

Alwyn gave a short snort of laughter. "Spend your life in the mines and you get so it doesn't bother you." He gestured around the shadowy gallery where they were standing. "I started going below the ground when I was ten," he said. "This is like a big open meadow to me."

"Some meadow," Crowley said, shaking his head.

Alwyn raised his eyebrows. He knew that most people were fearful when they were in tunnels, but he and his men were used to it. So long as the tunnel was properly dug and firmly reinforced, there was no danger. He indicated the ground under the foundation stone.

"We'll pile brushwood and firewood and combustibles there," he said. "Then we'll set it alight. As it burns, it'll destroy the framing and support beams so they collapse. Then nature will take a hand and the part of the wall directly above will fall into the tunnel. Once it goes, the surrounding structure will collapse with it."

"Who'll light the fire?" Crowley asked. He and Halt had been tasked with destroying Castle Gorlan but he hoped that responsibility didn't extend to personally lighting the fire. Alwyn quickly dispelled that fear.

"Best I do it," he said. "It'll get pretty dark and smoky in here once the fire's going. Easy to lose your bearings and blunder around. I'm used to it so I'll do it."

"Good," said Crowley, the relief all too evident in his voice.

"It's quite spectacular," Alwyn told them. "Mind you, for a long while, it seems nothing's happening. Then the wall starts to subside, cracks form through the masonry, and the whole thing comes down."

"I think I'd rather be on the surface when that happens," Halt said.

Alwyn regarded him without humor. "That's definitely the place to be. Now we should get out of the way and let the crew bring in the firewood and put it in place."

Halt and Crowley exchanged a look. These men knew their job, they realized. There would be little purpose in staying to watch once they began building the fire. In cases like this, delegation was to be encouraged.

"Let's get back to the surface," Halt said, and Crowley indicated for Alwyn to lead the way.

They emerged into the bright sunlight a few minutes later, shaking the damp clay and dirt from their cloaks and blinking like moles after the darkness of the tunnel.

The fresh forest air was a welcome change after the dank, musty air they had breathed belowground, redolent with the smell of wet clay, freshly dug dirt, and the reek of smoky oil lamps.

Crowley glanced left and right, spotting locations where two other tunnels had been dug. "Do we need to inspect the others?"

Alwyn shook his head. "No different from this one."

Crowley looked a little relieved. "What about the keep?" he asked, indicating the tall, graceful tower that stood surrounded by the castle walls. "Are you treating it the same way?"

"No need for a tunnel there," Alwyn told them. "We'll set fire to it and leave it to burn. Once the timber ceiling beams and the floors are gone, the remaining stonework will be weakened from the heat and the fact that there's no more cross support." He turned and indicated a trebuchet standing twenty meters away, crouching like some malevolent prehistoric animal, its long, double-jointed throwing arm towering above them.

"Then we'll hit it a few times with that infernal machine. A couple of solid rocks crashing into the weakened structure should bring it down quite nicely."

"Nicely? Strange choice of words." Crowley regarded the castle a little sadly. "It's a beautiful building," he said quietly. "Seems a shame to destroy it."

When Morgarath, the former Baron of Gorlan Fief, had retreated to the south after his failed attempt to seize control of the Kingdom, Prince Duncan ordered his castle to be torn down, leaving the rebel baron with no potential headquarters in the country.

"It's not beautiful," Halt replied. "It's an evil place where evil things happened. I'll be glad to see it destroyed. You'll be doing us a favor," he added, to Alwyn.

The miner shrugged. He and his team had been lent to Duncan by the King of neighboring Celtica, where they spent their lives tearing silver and tin from the earth, deep below the surface.

"A job's a job," he said. "We'll be glad to be heading home again." He glanced away, shading his eyes and peering at the other two tunnel mouths in turn. "Looks like they're getting ready to set the fires there as well."

The Rangers followed his gaze. At each, they could see men dressed in the mud-stained leather clothes the miners all wore, carrying bundles of firewood and kindling into the tunnels. Close by, a third group was beginning to carry similar bundles into the tunnel they had vacated.

"Give us an hour to get things ready," Alwyn said. "Then we'll light the fires."

His manner was a little distant. He had shown the high-ranking visitors through the tunnel, as requested. That had delayed his work by a good hour or so and now he was keen to get back to it, topple the walls of Castle Gorlan and be on his way home.

"Might as well have something to eat," Crowley said, jerking his head toward the small campsite he and Halt had set up the day before.

"You do that," Alwyn told him. "I'll start organizing the fire in the keep tower."

The two Rangers set out for their campsite. As they walked, Crowley idly brushed a clump of dried clay from the shoulder of his cloak.

"I suppose it takes a certain mind-set to be a miner," he said, still thinking of the dark, airless tunnel they had so recently been in.

Halt smiled grimly. "I suppose they say the same thing about Rangers."

2

The two Rangers sat in front of their small one-man tents and rummaged through their supplies. They had a fresh loaf of bread they had obtained from the miners' cook tent that morning, and the remains of a chicken they had shared the night before. Their campfire was still smoldering—they had heaped the coals earlier that morning to keep it alight. Halt coaxed it back to life with a few twigs and lighter pieces of kindling, then set their battered coffeepot in the glowing coals beside the fire to boil.

When the water was bubbling cheerfully, he added a couple of handfuls of coffee to the pot and pulled it away from the fire to let it brew. Crowley, meanwhile, sliced the chicken quickly with his saxe, laying the pieces out on two wooden platters.

"Did you want a leg?" Crowley asked.

Halt nodded. That was his favorite part of a chicken.

"Bad luck. There's only one and I'm having it."

Halt regarded him curiously. "Then why did you ask?"

Crowley shrugged. "There was always the chance that you'd say no and then I'd look as if I had a generous spirit."

Halt shook his head. "Not likely." He took the platter that

Crowley handed him. It was piled with chicken breast and thigh meat. Crowley picked up the solitary chicken leg from his own plate and began to tear at it with his teeth.

"Best part of a chicken, the leg," he said cheerfully.

Halt glowered at him. "Don't rub it in," he said. In truth, the chicken meat he was eating was delicious. It was perfectly cooked, moist and juicy. But he would have liked a leg. He tore a chunk of bread from the loaf and wrapped it around a thick slice of breast meat. He ate several big mouthfuls, then poured himself a cup of coffee, adding a generous helping of honey to the dark, fragrant liquid. He sipped and sighed.

"This is the life," he said. "Good food, fine weather, and we can sit in the sun and watch other people doing all the hard work."

"It does have its attractions," Crowley agreed. "We've spent less comfortable times, I have to say."

Halt nodded. The previous year had been a grim time, with danger threatening on all sides. It had culminated in the confrontation here in front of Castle Gorlan, where Duncan finally brought Morgarath to heel. Halt glanced around the peaceful scene now, listening to the bees humming in the flowers and the gentle wind sighing through the treetops.

Peace, he thought. It was a condition to be cherished and enjoyed. Then he frowned, realizing that the peace was likely to be shattered at any time, once Morgarath had rebuilt his army's strength. After escaping from Castle Gorlan, where he'd been besieged by Duncan and a group of loyal barons, the Baron of Gorlan Fief had disappeared into the Mountains of Rain and Night, a rugged, forbidding and inaccessible plateau in the southeastern corner of the Kingdom. Access to the plateau was by way of a precipitous, narrow track called Three Step Pass. The pass was blocked by Morgarath's troops, so that the Araluens had no idea what he was planning.

"When do you suppose Morgarath will make his next move?" Halt asked.

Crowley stopped eating to look at him. "Is he making a next move?"

"People like Morgarath always make a next move. He won't be content to sit up there in the mountains forever. He hates Duncan. And me. And you."

"He does have a large capacity for hate. But I think he'll be quiet for a while. He lost a lot of support from the other barons when Duncan faced him. He might have blustered his way out of it, but the fact that he withdrew into the castle and then escaped destroyed his credibility with a lot of them."

"There are still some who'd like to see him King," Halt said darkly. "And far too many who are sitting on the fence, waiting to see who'll come out on top."

Crowley grimaced in agreement, then looked up. "Well, it looks as though we're almost done here," he said, pointing with the half-chewed chicken bone to the tunnel mouth, where Alwyn was standing, waving to them. "Alwyn seems to be ready to light the fire."

He tossed the chicken leg into the bushes and rose, wiping his hands on the front of his jerkin.

Halt cast a pained look after the bone. "There was still plenty of meat on that," he said.

Crowley grinned. "You're welcome to finish it off."

"After you've been gnawing on it? No thanks."

Crowley spread his hands in a gesture of surrender. "Well, if you don't want it, stop complaining."

Halt rose to join him, shaking his head. "The point is, if you take the last chicken leg, you are duty bound to eat it. All of it."

His friend's grin widened. "Life is hard," he said, without the slightest hint of contrition.

Halt snorted and they set off for the mine entrance, where Alwyn was waiting for them.

"That was quick," Crowley said. They'd been waiting less than an hour.

Alwyn pursed his lips. "We work faster when we don't have sightseers to look after."

The Rangers exchanged an amused glance. They were obviously the sightseers he had in mind. "Tact is not a quality known in the mines, apparently," Halt said.

Alwyn turned his level gaze on him. "No time for tact. Get on with the job. That's how we do it."

"And rightly so," Crowley said. He indicated the entrance to the tunnel on their right. "I take it the red flag means they're ready there?"

Alwyn nodded. There were three tunnels, set at the corners of the walls. They were standing by the middle one, so they could see the others. Both of them were displaying a red flag planted in the ground beside the entrance.

"We'll light the fires in the tunnels soon," he said. "First we'll set the keep tower burning."

"Makes sense," Halt said. "You'd hardly want to be inside the walls when they're likely to collapse at any moment."

Alwyn grunted, then put his fingers in his mouth and

emitted a piercing whistle. The gate and drawbridge were both open, and through the gap in the wall, the Rangers could see the lower section of the tower that formed the keep. There were several miners waiting there, holding flaming torches. At Alwyn's signal, they darted inside the building. After a few minutes, they emerged and jogged toward the gateway. For some time, nothing could be seen from the keep. Then smoke began to funnel out of the windows and arrow slits.

Behind them, they heard a creaking of wheels and cracking of whips. They turned and saw the trebuchet being towed forward by a team of oxen, closer to the castle walls. It had come from Araluen Fief some days before they had arrived. The artillerymen serving it halted it at a suitable spot and began to unhitch the oxen. They chocked the wheels of the towing platform and weighted the trebuchet deck with sandbags to keep it steady. Then they began to turn the windlass, drawing the short end of the throwing arm down against the tension of a twisted rope cable.

"Be a while before we need that," Alwyn said. He took the red flag planted in the dirt beside the tunnel mouth and waved it above his head, back and forth, until the miners at the other tunnels responded. Then, one of his men handed him a flaming torch and he plunged into the tunnel mouth. He stopped and turned toward the two Rangers, with the ghost of a grin.

"Sure you don't want to join me?"

"No. We sightseers wouldn't want to delay you any further," Crowley told him, and the miner turned and disappeared into the tunnel, the flickering light of his torch rapidly disappearing as the tunnel floor sloped down.

At each of the other tunnels, Halt saw a miner lay the red

flag down, then disappear into the earth, carrying a flaming torch. He glanced around, saw a convenient tree stump and sat on it.

"No sense standing here," he said. "I assume this is going to take a while."

He was right. Alwyn was gone for more than twenty minutes. The Rangers knew that it took seven or eight minutes to move through the tunnel to the gallery where the firewood had been placed.

Halt glanced to his left, seeing the miner emerging from the tunnel mouth. The man reached down and set the red flag upright again, signaling that he was done. A few minutes later, Alwyn emerged from the middle tunnel, coughing. A light cloud of smoke emerged with him. He glanced at the red flag fluttering from the other tunnel mouth and grunted in satisfaction. He planted his own flag and they all turned to watch the third tunnel. After a minute or two, a figure emerged and the red flag there was set in place.

"Now we wait," Alwyn said.

For some time, nothing seemed to happen. It was a different matter at the keep. The fire there was burning fiercely and now flame as well as smoke was pouring out of the windows and doors.

Then Halt noticed smoke rising from the ground between them and the castle, in several places.

"Ventilation holes," Alwyn told him, noticing the direction of his gaze. Then heavy smoke billowed out of the left-hand tunnel entrance, mirrored within a few minutes at the other tunnels.

"How long to go?" Halt asked.

The miner shrugged. "A while yet," he said, which was less than helpful.

Halt, who had begun to pace expectantly at the sight of the smoke pouring out of the tunnel mouth, resettled himself on the tree stump. Crowley sat on the soft grass, his back against a small tree.

Smoke continued to pour out of the tunnel mouth, becoming thicker by the minute. Inside the walls, the fire roared in the keep tower, growing in strength and violence.

"At least there's something to see there," Crowley said. In spite of Alwyn's warning, he had been expecting something spectacular at the walls—not just smoke billowing from the tunnel and the ventilation holes. At least at the keep there was the distinct impression of something being destroyed, something actually *happening*.

"Come on," the Ranger Commandant muttered.

Alwyn glanced at him. "Need patience to be a miner," he said.

Crowley shook his head in annoyance. "I'm not a miner and I have no patience. I want to see that wall come down."

And as he said so, it did.

There was a deep rumbling underground. They felt it through the earth. Then a massive crack zigzagged up the wall, from ground level to the crenellations at the top, and a section of the wall itself sank, collapsing downward as its foundations were undermined.

The crack widened and the wall either side of it began to bulge outward, breaking into two gigantic pieces at first, then those pieces breaking into several smaller ones.

With a rumbling crash, the wall fell outward, landing in a

pile of rubble. At the far corner, they heard another distinct crack and another split appeared in the face of the wall. As it came down, smoke jetted from the ventilation holes with renewed force.

At that point, the wall above the third tunnel sagged, cracked and bowed outward, crashing down with a roar like an earthquake. More smoke jetted from the tunnel mouth and the ventilation holes.

In a matter of minutes, three of the four walls of Castle Gorlan had come crashing down, breaking up into smaller pieces as they did.

Clouds of dust and smoke rose above the destroyed castle, once one of the showpieces of the Kingdom. One minute it had been there, firm and strong. The next, it had collapsed and crumbled before their eyes.

"Well," said Crowley, "that seems to be that."

3

THE MAIN HALL OF CASTLE ARALUEN WAS A SEA OF COLOR,
light and noise. Candles blazed all around the large room, in
sconces on the wall, in candelabra on the tables and hanging
from the ceilings in half a dozen chandeliers, the light refracted
and redirected by the crystal glass pendants that festooned the
chandeliers and surrounded the candles themselves.

There must have been two hundred people in the hall. All of
the barons who supported Duncan were there, along with their
ladies and their retinues of knights and attendants and their
ladies.

In the past year, there had been little to celebrate in Araluen.
Even after Morgarath had escaped justice and fled to the mountains, the effects of his plotting had continued to cast a pall over
the Kingdom. Duncan's father, Oswald, had never recovered
from being held captive and mistreated by Morgarath. After
abdicating the throne, he had held on to see his only son mar-
ried; but Duncan's wedding to Lady Rosalind Serenne had been
a quiet affair due to Oswald's failing health, and not the grand
occasion that would normally have taken place. At the beginning of the year, in a bitterly cold spell that held the Kingdom

snowbound for weeks, Oswald had succumbed to his illness. The Kingdom had been in mourning for the last two months, and Castle Araluen had been a somber place as the barons came to pay their respects.

But now it was spring, and it seemed that color and life was finally returning to the Kingdom. Duncan had declared a holiday and a feast—and he had exciting news to share.

The initial celebration had taken place earlier in the day, outside the castle, on the lawns beneath the walls, where hundreds of the common people of Araluen Fief—farmers, tradesmen and artisans—could attend.

The official ceremony was a short one. Duncan had made a brief but heartfelt speech, thanking the people for their support and obvious affection. This was all too evident in the cheers the people gave for Queen Rosalind as she stood beside her husband. The young Queen was beautiful and warmhearted, and the people loved her. Rosalind had long black hair and dark brown eyes that always seemed to hold a hint of mischief or humor. Her face was a perfect oval, with high cheekbones and a full-lipped mouth. Seen next to Duncan, she appeared tiny—slim and graceful.

When the crowd had quieted again, Duncan announced the reason for the celebration: Queen Rosalind was pregnant, and the Kingdom could expect a new heir to the throne. Baron Arald of Redmont, one of the King's staunchest supporters, called for three cheers to mark that the union of Duncan and Rosalind had been so blessed. The assembled crowd cheered so lustily that they startled the rooks that nested in the castle battlements and set them squawking and circling the castle.

After greeting the local villagers and farmers following the ceremony, Duncan and Rosalind completed their circuit of the parklands before the castle and led the knights, nobles and their ladies through the massive portcullis at the inner end of the drawbridge and into the keep, where the main hall was set up for the reception.

While the official party withdrew into the castle, tables were being placed on the lawns, kegs of ale were broached and bullocks and whole pigs were turned on spits above massive cooking fires. The celebrations outside rivaled those in the main hall in cheerfulness, and exceeded them in noise.

The festive spirit of the day gave everyone a chance to relax and rejoice, and the ladies took advantage of the opportunity to display their finery. Their gowns were a dazzling mix of yellows, blues, reds and greens. Jewelry caught the candlelight and sparkled on the ladies' fingers and around their throats in pendants and necklaces.

Not that the men were any less splendid. The barons and knights wore their dress armor, polished till it gleamed, with their colored surcoats displaying their individual crests and coats of arms. Servants circulated among the brightly clad throng, carrying trays laden with goblets of wine and ale, and fruit sherbets for those who weren't inclined to partake of alcohol.

As more goblets were emptied, the noise level gradually rose. This had a cumulative effect. The more difficult it became to hear one's neighbor, the louder people talked—which made it increasingly difficult to hear what was being said and necessitated a further rise in personal volume. Wagers were being laid as to whether the King's first child would be a girl or boy. Either one would inherit, as Araluen had no restriction on female children being heirs to the throne.

Duncan and Rosalind walked through the assembled throng, greeting those they knew and nodding to others, shaking hands and accepting the well wishes of their subjects. Duncan was a popular King.

His mother, Queen Deborah, watched the ceremony from a chair set in front of the official dais, a smile on her face. She approved of Rosalind. She was a beautiful and good-hearted woman who would make a fine consort for Deborah's son. And the Queen Mother was delighted that the people had seen through Morgarath's lies and accusations against Duncan. It was Deborah's greatest regret—and she knew it had been her husband's, too, before he died—that she had allowed Baron Morgarath to poison the Kingdom and turn the people against her son. Deborah preferred a quiet, austere hunting lodge to the machinations and pomp of the royal court, and she hadn't seen the consequences of Morgarath's rising popularity until it was too late.

Halt and Crowley were standing off to one side of the hall, in the shadows. It wasn't the Ranger way to seek attention or praise. Rangers preferred to remain in the background, observing without being observed. They had relinquished their cloaks, and were clad now in their dull gray breeches, boots and leather jerkins. Whereas the knights and barons sported dress swords, hilts blazing with jewels and bound in gold and silver wire, the two Rangers wore their workaday saxes and throwing knives supported on their broad leather belts.

Crowley studied the brightly trimmed, almost garish, outfits of those around them and glanced down at his own plain clothing. "Perhaps we should come up with some sort of dress uniform," he mused.

Halt looked at him, one eyebrow raised. "What for?" he asked. He had no interest in fine clothes. Clothes were utilitarian as far as he was concerned. In cold weather, they should be warm and waterproof. In hot weather, light and airy. And bright colors served only to make a man stand out against the background, which was never a good idea in his opinion. A man who stood out against the background made an easy target.

Crowley made an uncertain gesture with one hand, taking in the celebrations around them—the red, sweating faces; the loud voices; the music issuing from the small ensemble in a gallery above the main floor. In general, he shared his friend's preference to remain inconspicuous. But he felt there were some occasions when Rangers should be a little more visible.

"Well, for official events like this," he said. "We're like a pair of crows among the peacocks."

Halt snorted. "Peacocks are overrated birds," he said. "They're dull-witted and they make an ugly, raucous noise." He gestured at the people around them. "Rather like this lot."

Crowley smiled at his friend. "Do you include Baron Arald in that category?" he asked, indicating the burly form of Arald, who was making his way through the crowd toward them, a smile on his face. The Baron was dressed in his livery colors—blue and yellow—with a boar's head emblazoned on his right breast. His method of making his way through the crowd was a simple one. He deviated neither to left nor right, but forged straight ahead, using his broad shoulders to clear a path. A pace behind him, his beautiful wife, Lady Sandra, followed in the space he cleared. She too wore blue and yellow. In Arald's case, the colors looked martial and distinctive. His wife made them look feminine and stunning. Like her husband, she was smiling at the two Rangers.

Yet, after his first glance at the Baron and his wife, Halt had eyes only for the third member of their party, who slipped gracefully through the crowded room in their wake. Mistress Pauline duLacy was an absolute vision in a simple, sheer gown of silver cloth, which shimmered about her slim form. In her blond hair, she had a garland of white flowers.

"Crowley, Halt, good to see you!" the Baron shouted enthusiastically. His voice boomed out and several bystanders turned at the sound of it—and at his words. Most people hadn't noticed the two Rangers standing among them and now there were hurried whispers, in which the names "Halt" and "Crowley" were predominant. The two Rangers had achieved a level of some renown in the Kingdom since they had been responsible for Duncan's reinstatement as heir to the throne and the thwarting of Morgarath's royal ambitions, but this was the first time that many of Duncan's subjects had had a chance to actually lay eyes on the famous pair.

Pauline heard one whispered comment—*I thought they'd be taller*—and smiled to herself.

Now Arald was shaking hands with the two Rangers and ushering his wife forward to greet them as well.

"Lovely to see you, Halt, Crowley," Sandra said.

"And you, my lady," Crowley said.

Lady Sandra made a small curtsy, dipping at the knees while her upper body remained straight and graceful. The two Rangers bowed in unison. Watching Halt out of the corner of his eye, Crowley was a little surprised to see how smoothly Halt performed the action. He had no idea that his friend had been raised in the royal court of Dun Kilty in Clonmel.

"And you know Pauline duLacy, of course," Arald said. "My new head diplomat at Redmont."

Pauline executed a graceful curtsy in her turn. Halt and Crowley bowed again. Crowley opened his mouth to utter a greeting and was surprised when Halt beat him to it.

"It's been far too long, Mistress duLacy. A pleasure to see you again." It was noticeable that his Hibernian accent was a little stronger than normal. Pauline smiled at him, a dazzling smile that made Halt's heart lurch.

"The pleasure is all mine, Ranger Halt," she said, extending her hand. And once again, Crowley was surprised to see Halt take her hand and raise it to his lips. He didn't know that his companion had been mentally rehearsing this moment for the past day and a half.

"Delighted to see you again, Mistress," Crowley said. He was never tongue-tied around beautiful women.

"Yes . . . delighted," Pauline said vaguely, her eyes still fixed on Halt and shining with pleasure at seeing him.

Crowley grinned to himself. It was obvious that Pauline and Halt were smitten with each other and he was happy for his friend. He had no romantic attachments himself, and wasn't in any hurry to form one. But he felt that Halt, grim and dour as he was, could only benefit from the bright, sunny company of the quick-witted Courier. Mind you, that didn't mean he wouldn't stir the pot and tease Halt about Pauline whenever he had the chance.

He realized that Arald was speaking and quickly gave him his attention.

"How many do you have now?" Arald was asking.

Crowley frowned. He assumed that the Baron was talking about his efforts to return the Ranger Corps to full strength. It was a task that had been taking up most of Crowley's time in the past few months as Rangers who had been discredited by Morgarath and banished gradually returned to the Kingdom when news of recent events reached them.

"Eighteen," he replied, and saw that he had guessed Arald's question correctly. "Twenty including Halt and myself."

"Hmmm. So you're just under half strength," Arald mused. The normal Ranger complement was fifty, one for each fief.

"Yes. It's a headache working out which fiefs need a Ranger most at the moment. Some are going to have to pull double duty with the smaller fiefs," Crowley replied.

"It was a pity we lost Farrel from active duty," Arald said. Farrel was the Ranger assigned to Redmont Fief. With Arald's support, he had joined with Halt and Crowley in their campaign against Morgarath. After Morgarath's retreat from Castle Gorlan, Farrel had been leading a scouting party in pursuit of the rebels. His horse stumbled in a rabbit hole and Farrel was thrown heavily to the ground, breaking his leg in two places. He had been placed under the care of the healers at Castle Araluen, but his injury was severe and it would be months before he would be back on the active list. Crowley currently had him helping with administrative tasks and paperwork—something both of them hated. But it kept Farrel occupied and stopped him moping.

"Yes. I'm not sure who to assign in his place," Crowley said. Redmont was an important fief, second only to Araluen Fief in the Kingdom, particularly now that Gorlan had been broken up and its territories split between two neighboring fiefdoms.

"I was hoping you might give us Halt," Arald said.

Crowley reacted with surprise. He and Halt had worked closely together over the past year and it hadn't occurred to him to post him anywhere other than Araluen. But now that he considered it, it made sense. With the Corps at half strength, he didn't have the luxury of keeping two Rangers in any one fief. Halt was the pick of the Rangers, Redmont was a major fief and Arald was a senior member of Duncan's council. Halt would be just as useful as Crowley's deputy if he were based at Redmont.

"Sounds good to me," Halt said quickly, before Crowley could reply. Without turning his head, Crowley knew his friend was gazing at Pauline.

"Why not?" Crowley said, conceding. He'd miss having Halt around all the time, miss having the opportunity to twist his tail. But it was the best solution to the problem. He looked now and saw that Pauline was beaming with pleasure.

She placed her hand on Halt's forearm. "Perhaps you could ask me to dance, by way of celebration?"

Halt cleared his throat awkwardly. "I'm not such a good dancer," he said doubtfully.

Crowley felt the mischief rising within him. One last chance to twist the tail, he thought. He bowed politely to Pauline. "I'd be delighted to dance with you, Mistress Pauline."

Halt glared at him. "On the other hand, I'm not such a bad one," Halt said and, taking Pauline's hand, he led her to the dance floor.

Arald grinned at Crowley. "You did that on purpose."

The Commandant shrugged. "Sometimes he has to be pushed to do what he wants," he said.

4

THE NEXT FEW MONTHS PASSED QUICKLY FOR HALT AS HE settled into life as the resident Ranger attached to Redmont Fief.

He enjoyed the informality of the Ranger life. He was part of the senior administration of Redmont and a trusted confidant of the Baron. Yet he remained separate from the castle, preferring to live in the small log cabin set among the trees below the massive red-tinged ironstone walls that gave Redmont its name. He knew that Rangers needed to remain a little aloof from the barons, to avoid being influenced by them.

Fortunately, Arald was well aware of the Ranger's role in the fief and made no attempt to influence Halt unduly. And there was never any occasion where Halt felt that the Baron wasn't performing his duties as required. Arald was a loyal subordinate to the King and a fair and just ruler over his own territory. He accepted Halt as an important member of his team, albeit an independent one. He valued his judgment and often asked his opinion on matters relating to Redmont's administration. And his requests for Halt's opinion were more than mere lip service. Often, he acted on the Ranger's suggestions.

So their working relationship was a smooth and harmonious

one, and Halt made a point of eating with the Baron and his wife at least one evening a week. Usually, Pauline would be included in these dinners, unless she was called away on duty, which was often the case.

Shortly after Halt arrived in Redmont, Mistress Pauline had been appointed as a Courier of the first rank and was now addressed by the honorific Lady Pauline. She ranked as an equal of a senior knight such as Sir Rodney, the head of Redmont's battle school, where new warriors were trained for the King's army. Arald had great respect for her wisdom and judgment. Unlike many of his contemporaries, he didn't think her gender made her opinion any less worthwhile. In fact, he had often been heard to say that Pauline was the most intelligent and capable of all his support staff.

Halt and Pauline's relationship grew as time passed. They enjoyed each other's company and spent as much time together as their duties allowed. This was less than might have been expected. Halt could be called away at a moment's notice to tend to some problem in a far corner of the fief—a band of brigands or highwaymen preying on travelers, or a wild beast that might be terrorizing a farming community. And Pauline traveled often to other fiefs, and even other countries, such as Celtica. This was ostensibly to meet with her fellow Couriers, but also to gather intelligence and keep a general eye on the security of the fief and the Kingdom itself. In fact, the title of Courier was a deliberate misnomer. Pauline's main work consisted of intelligence gathering and, at times, espionage. The Courier service, while masquerading as diplomats, kept a covert eye on the loyalties or otherwise of the Kingdom's nobles.

Sometimes Halt and Pauline traveled together, when they

accompanied Arald to Castle Araluen for his regular meetings with King Duncan. At such times, Halt and Crowley would disappear into Crowley's office and confer, with Crowley bringing Halt up to date on the progress of his campaign to return the Ranger Corps to full strength.

"I've been assessing potential apprentices," he said on the latest occasion, four months after Halt had been appointed as Redmont's Ranger. "And I've selected six to train." He looked keenly at his friend. He had realized some time ago that, with the original Rangers scattered and banished by Morgarath, it would be impossible to bring back all of them. If the Corps were going to return to its original strength, it would have to do it by recruiting and training new personnel.

"I hope you're not planning to saddle me with one," Halt said, preempting the suggestion that he was sure Crowley was about to make.

Crowley regarded him with a bland expression. "I can't think of one who deserves such a dreadful fate."

"I'll let you know when I'm ready for one. I'm still feeling my own way."

Secretly, Crowley was disappointed, but he accepted Halt's position. The man was so skilled, so capable, that sometimes it was hard to remember that he hadn't gone through any formal apprenticeship or training himself. Of course, Pritchard had instructed him in the skills needed of a Ranger, but in a way, Halt was still learning on the job. He had good instincts for what was required, but he needed more experience.

There was a knock at the door to Crowley's suite of rooms, and Pauline entered. "The King would like to see us all," she said simply. "Arald will meet us there."

Crowley and Halt stood and followed her out.

Halt knew that Pauline had just completed a lengthy tour of the western quarter of the Kingdom, assessing the barons there. Some doubt still attached to the loyalty of four of them, and another two were definitely leaning toward an alignment with Morgarath—if the black-clad former baron ever ventured down from the wild plateau of the Mountains of Rain and Night.

The past months had been a time of peace and relative prosperity throughout Araluen. As a whole, the Kingdom had settled under the reign of its new young King. He was a popular ruler, known to be just in his rulings, not playing favorites or trying to curry favor with any group. But a dark cloud hung ominously over the distant horizon. Morgarath might not have been seen or heard from since he had slipped away from Castle Gorlan while the King kept it under siege, but he was still very much a presence in the Kingdom, made even more ominous by the very fact that so little was known of his movements.

Crowley and the three visitors met with Duncan in his office suite, accompanied by his secretary, who took notes of the discussions.

"How is the Queen, your majesty?" asked Pauline, after the usual greetings.

Duncan frowned. "She's not doing well," he confessed. "She's very weak. The pregnancy is taking a heavy toll on her."

The three visitors exchanged worried glances at this news. They had heard on previous visits to Araluen that Queen Rosalind's health was poor. But they had no idea it was as serious as this.

"She spends most of her time in her chamber," Duncan went on. "I'm very concerned about her."

Then, with an effort, he dismissed the matter of his wife's

health. "Now, on to other matters. Do any of you have any idea what Morgarath is doing up there in the mountains?" It was noticeable that he looked first to Pauline. But all four shook their heads.

"I can't get any of my people up onto the plateau, your majesty," she said apologetically.

"I know he's slipped down Three Step Pass on several occasions," Duncan told them as they sat around the large conference table in his office. "I have a company of infantry stationed on the plain below the mountains to keep an eye on him. They've seen him exit the pass, but then they've lost him. And we've lost half a dozen men when they tried to follow him."

"What do you suppose he was doing?" Crowley asked.

It was Arald who replied. "Making contact with some of the fence sitters," he said. While all of the barons had asserted their allegiance to Duncan, some were more enthusiastic than others in their support. Morgarath had been a popular and respected member of the Council of Barons. He was a champion knight and highly skilled in combat. And he was adept at flattering those he saw as vulnerable to his charm. All the barons knew that the situation with Morgarath wasn't settled, and some— admittedly a minority—were inclined to bide their time and see how events transpired between the King and the rebel baron.

Arald gestured for Pauline to speak. "Pauline, what did you find in your travels?"

The graceful Courier glanced down at the sheaf of notes in front of her, and spread a few pages out, frowning in concentration before she spoke.

"I don't believe Baron Peller can be trusted, your majesty," she said. "I spoke to my contacts in his fief and Morgarath definitely called on him six weeks ago. Apparently Peller received him most cordially."

Duncan grunted. "Peller is a pompous idiot," he said. "Always has been. He's just the type to fall for Morgarath's smooth words. He's weak and easily swayed."

"Influential, however," Arald said. "Several of the other barons owe him money. He's spent years propping up the fortunes of those who can't manage their own affairs efficiently."

"Did he know you were in his fief making inquiries?" the King asked.

Pauline allowed herself a slight smile. "I was in disguise, your majesty, posing as a commoner."

"What about Meagher and Cordell?" Crowley asked. Along with Peller, they had been some of Morgarath's more ardent supporters at the tournament.

"I think Morgarath has burned his bridges with them," she said. "He lied to them when he told them you were raiding across the border, and he was caught in that lie. He also misled them about the old King."

Morgarath had claimed that King Oswald, Duncan's father, had been ready to disown his son and instate Morgarath as his official heir. But Pritchard, the old Ranger who had mentored both Crowley and Halt, had rescued the King from the tower where Morgarath was holding him prisoner. The King had appeared on the tournament field at a crucial moment and gave the lie to Morgarath's statements.

"Men like that don't appreciate being lied to," Pauline continued.

Arald smiled grimly. "They don't appreciate being made to

look like fools, either," he said. "That would probably turn them against Morgarath faster than the lie."

Lady Pauline nodded. "Apparently when Morgarath arrived at their respective castles, they turned him away. That would seem to indicate that they're no longer aligned with him."

Duncan frowned. "Turned him away," he repeated. "But they didn't try to detain him. Nor did they report his attempted visit to me."

"There's a difference," said Arald, "between rejecting Morgarath and wholeheartedly supporting you, your majesty. They sent him packing because he'd made them look foolish. But they haven't aligned their loyalty with the crown."

"I agree. They definitely bear watching," Duncan said.

"I have agents in place doing just that, your majesty," Pauline told him. "They'll be sending me regular reports."

Halt regarded the calm, self-possessed Courier with interest. So young, so very beautiful and so efficient, he thought. There were definite advantages to her appearance. A lot of men tended to discount a beautiful woman as being no more than an ornament, a social partner. The more beautiful she might be, the less they tended to regard her intelligence or ability. Big mistake, he thought.

"Thanks, Lady Pauline. Keep me informed," Duncan said.

"There is one other matter, your majesty." Pauline's tone was a little uncertain, in contrast to her previous air of calm, almost matter-of-fact confidence.

Duncan inclined his head for her to elaborate. Halt noticed that Arald seemed interested as well. This was obviously not a point that she had raised with him.

Pauline looked at the faces around the table. "Has anyone here ever heard of a race of creatures known as Wargals?"

The silence and blank looks that met her question gave her the answer, so she continued. "I've been hearing vague rumors that Morgarath is recruiting a tribe of these creatures to act as his army."

The others exchanged glances.

"What exactly are they?" Duncan asked.

She shrugged. "I don't know a lot. As I say, it's only rumors and there's not a lot of detail. It could be completely untrue. I've tried to find out more about these Wargals, but there's very little written about them—and most of that could be dismissed as myth. What I have learned is that they are a primitive race of semi-human creatures. They're basically animals—some say they're a cross between an ape and a bear. But they're supposedly intelligent."

"A cross between an ape and a bear," Crowley mused. "That would be an awfully powerful sort of creature."

"Not the sort of things you'd want Morgarath to have as soldiers," Duncan agreed. Halt said nothing, but his mind was racing.

"This might explain why Morgarath has been so quiet for months," Arald said. "If he's recruiting and training these"—he hesitated and glanced at Pauline—"Wargals?" She nodded. "Then he may have his hands full."

"The problem is," Crowley said, "if he is doing this, he's doing it up in those damn mountains, and we have no way of knowing what he's up to."

"He's secure up there," Duncan said. "Three Step Pass is impenetrable. You could hold it with less than twenty men. There's no way anyone could get up there to see what's going on."

"I think I could manage it," Halt said.

5

Halt and the captain of the troops set to watch Three Step Pass crouched at the edge of the tree line, close to a concealed observation post where a detachment was stationed to keep watch over the entrance to the pass. Beyond the trees was a hundred meters of clear ground, reaching to the foot of the sheer cliffs that led to the Mountains of Rain and Night. The cliffs, rocky and formidable, towered either side of a dark fissure, barely three meters across. It split the cliffs to their crest. But the deep shadows prevented the two men seeing any detail beyond the opening.

"So that's the fabled Three Step Pass," Halt said.

The picket captain nodded. "There's a steep path beyond the entrance that winds up through the cliffs to the top." He paused. "Or presumably it does. I've never gone farther than fifty meters past that entrance."

Halt glanced at him. "And why would that be?"

The captain met his gaze. "Because I value my life," he said. "Morgarath has built fortifications across the pass and put his men there to stop anyone getting past. And, over the past few months, he's replaced the men with some kind of strange savage beasts. They're semi-human, I suppose, but I have to say they terrified me."

"What are they?" Halt asked. He recalled Pauline's comments about beasts called Wargals.

The captain gave an involuntary shudder. "I didn't get a clear look at them. It was dark in the pass, and after our first encounter, I was too busy running. They walk upright, but they're kind of apelike. Long claws and huge fangs. They're a real nightmare. About the height of a man but much heavier. They're covered in dark fur and they have an opposable thumb, like a man, so they can take hold of things. I took a patrol up there two months ago to test the defenses and we ran into half a dozen of these beasts. I lost two men and the rest of us barely made it back down the pass."

Halt scratched his chin thoughtfully. He studied the dark entrance to the pass and the forbidding rock walls towering on either side of it.

"There's no other way to the top?" he asked.

The captain shook his head. "That's it. The only other way is to scale the walls themselves. And good luck to you if you want to try that."

Halt said nothing for a few moments. The cliffs were granite—hard, unyielding rock that would resist any attempt to drill or cut handholds or footholds. He shaded his eyes, squinting for better focus.

At least it wasn't smooth. There appeared to be plenty of outcrops and smaller fissures that should provide purchase for a good climber. And Halt was an excellent climber.

The captain indicated the entrance to the pass. "The fissure winds up through the mountains, and the floor of the pass rises with it. The pass is rarely less than ten or twelve meters below the level of the surrounding rock walls. But the sides are smooth and slick—at least, they are in the part I've seen. I'd say they've been shaped that way so there's no other way up or down into the pass."

"Hmmm," said Halt thoughtfully. "And you've no idea what I might find at the top?"

The captain shook his head. "No idea at all. I imagine there might be some kind of guardhouse there, to accommodate the men and the . . . things . . . on watch at the pass."

"And after the first barrier, are there others?"

"Your guess is as good as mine. But I'd say yes. It would make sense to construct a series of barricades to keep attackers out. That way, if one fell, the defenders could pull back to the next."

"Yes. That makes sense," Halt said. He frowned. It was too much to hope that he would be able to bypass the first fortification, then climb down into the pass and continue to move upward unimpeded. It seemed he was going to have to climb the whole way up the cliffs.

"Well, thanks for the information," he said.

The captain made a wry face. "There wasn't a lot I could tell you," he said. "What do you plan to do?"

Halt studied the towering cliffs again before answering. At the very top, there was a flash of lightning and they heard a dull rumble of thunder.

"Place has its own climate," the captain said dourly. "And the weather always seems to be bad."

Halt allowed a grim smile to lighten his features. "They don't call them the Mountains of Rain and Night because they're a sun-drenched paradise," he remarked.

"So what are you planning to do?" the captain repeated.

Halt pointed to the west. "I'll go along the base of the cliffs until I'm out of sight of any watchers in there." He indicated the dark maw of the pass. "Then I'll climb up and see what I can see."

The captain looked at the forbidding cliffs for several seconds, trying to picture the gray-cloaked Ranger scrambling up them. Somehow, the vision always ended with the sight of Halt tumbling back down.

"That won't be easy," he said, with some feeling.

Halt patted him lightly on the shoulder. "It never is."

He moved back to where he had left Abelard waiting with the rest of the company of soldiers. There had been no need to tether the horse. He was Ranger trained and wouldn't wander off. Halt bade farewell to the captain and his men and mounted the stocky little horse, setting him to a trot as they rode away from the soldiers' campsite.

"Don't envy them their job," he told Abelard. "Sitting here in all kinds of weather, watching out for these bear creatures that Morgarath has recruited. Bored out of their brains most of the time, then facing sudden danger without any warning."

Abelard tossed his head, shaking his mane in the ways horses do.

I'm sure they'd rather be with you, scrambling up those cliffs by your fingernails, not knowing what's waiting at the top.

"You're a big comfort," Halt told the horse.

That's my job.

Realizing that he was unlikely to ever get the final word with his horse, Halt let the matter drop. As they moved farther away from the pass, and the chance that they might be observed, he urged Abelard out of the trees and closer to the cliffs, looking for a place where he might begin to climb. For the most part, the cliffs were depressingly sheer and steep.

Are you thinking of taking me with you?

"Horses don't climb." Halt nodded at the granite walls beside them.

Abelard seemed to snigger. *You could carry me. I'm not so heavy.*

"You can wait at the base of the cliff," Halt told him. Then, a moment later, he said softly, "Hold on. What's this?"

This was a narrow crack, zigzagging diagonally upward. He dismounted and moved toward it. It went quite deep into the rock face, and was a little wider than his hand. He gripped the side of it, then wedged his right foot into it and hauled himself up experimentally. The hard rock provided a firm purchase and he climbed several meters up the rock face. Leaning back, he peered upward.

"Looks like it leads up to something about thirty meters up," he said. "Could be a ledge."

Or it could be a shallow little shelf that will leave you stranded up there with nowhere to go.

"You're a real optimist, aren't you."

Just pointing out the obvious.

Halt looked around and saw a glade of trees a few meters away. Leading Abelard into them, he was satisfied with what he saw. The horse would be well sheltered here and out of sight of any passerby. As he studied the spot, he heard a trickle of running water. Following the sound, he found a small spring emerging from the rocks about two meters above ground level, and running down into a naturally formed stone basin.

"Perfect," he said. "I thought I was going to have to leave you water in a bucket." He carried a collapsible leather bucket tied to his saddle, for use on occasions like this. Abelard's training would make sure that he drank only what he needed. "I figure I'll be gone maybe three days. One day up, one day to scout around and one day to come back down. You'll have plenty of water and grass for that length of time."

For once, Abelard said nothing. Halt unsaddled him, laid the saddle across a fallen tree and then rubbed him down. He'd replace the saddle in the morning, although he'd leave the girth strap loose. He might need to leave in a hurry and wouldn't want to waste time saddling the horse. Abelard would be comfortable enough for a couple of days with the loosened saddle in place. He unrolled his bedroll and laid it on the soft grass. It was nearly dusk and he had no intention of trying to climb the cliffs in the dark. It would be hard enough in daylight.

He decided against starting a fire, although his body ached for the taste of coffee. Instead, he had a frugal meal of flat bread wrapped around a few slices of smoked beef, and smeared liberally with pickles. He washed it down with clear water from his canteen, then refilled the bottle at the spring in the face of the cliff. Abelard watched him, grazing calmly and grinding his big molars together in a constant rhythm.

"You're a noisy eater," Halt remarked.

The horse stopped grinding for a few seconds. *You should hear me with my mouth open.* Then he resumed his steady grinding.

Strangely, Halt found it a vaguely comforting noise. So long as Abelard continued to munch away at the fresh green grass, it was apparent that there was no danger nearby.

"Long day tomorrow," Halt said, and rolled into the blankets of his bedroll, spreading his cloak over the top of them. It wasn't just for the extra warmth, although that was one consideration. When he stretched out beneath the cloak, he merged into the background of bushes and grass and was all but invisible.

He listened as Abelard stopped grazing. Seeing that Halt had settled for the night, the little horse paced quietly to all four corners of the glade, stopping at each, ears pricked.

He listened to the night sounds, his ears twitching to catch them more efficiently, and sniffed the breeze experimentally, searching for any foreign scent that might indicate enemies in the vicinity. After he had covered the four points of the compass, he returned to the middle of the glade and lowered his head to graze again. The grass was good here, moist and sweet, and Abelard had learned to eat whenever he had the opportunity.

After all, a horse never knew when he might be forced to go hungry.

Halt fell asleep to the placid, comforting rumble of those big teeth grinding away.

He awoke just before first light. One moment he was asleep, the next he was wide-awake. But he did it without any sound, or visible sign. His eyes opened and that was the only movement he allowed himself.

He could see the dark shadow of his horse standing a few meters away, knees locked and dozing standing up. He lay silently for several minutes, letting his ears search the dim gray dawn around him. He could hear birds beginning their dawn chorus. That was encouraging. If there was danger nearby, they wouldn't be so uninhibited. A light breeze sprang up and riffled the upper branches of the trees around him.

His hand was on the hilt of his saxe, where it had stayed all night. Now, satisfied that he and Abelard were alone, he relaxed his grip and sat up, casting the cloak and blankets aside. The morning was chilly and he shivered, then rubbed his face with both hands, clearing the sleep from his eyes.

Abelard moved a few paces to stand over him, then lowered his head, blowing his warm breath into Halt's face.

"Time to start up that cliff," said the Ranger.

6

AFTER A FRUGAL MEAL—THE SAME AS HE HAD EATEN THE
night before—Halt began preparing his equipment for the
climb. He had a long coil of strong, lightweight cord. He knew
that it was capable of bearing his weight if necessary and he laid
it on the ground. Then he took a leather bag of iron spikes from
his saddlebags and placed them beside the rope. A mallet, its
lead-weighted wooden head muffled by several layers of canvas,
followed. If he was going to be hammering the spikes into cracks
in the wall, he didn't want the noise to ring out so that anyone
within half a kilometer would hear.

He strung his bow and slung it securely over his right shoulder, outside his cloak. Then, slinging the coil of rope across his
body and hanging the mallet round his neck on a loop of leather
thong, he patted Abelard on the muzzle, re-saddled him as he'd
planned and walked toward the cliff.

Take care.

"I plan to," he replied. He stopped at the cliff face and looked
upward. The top of the cliff was invisible from this close. It
seemed to disappear into the misty light of early morning. Still,
he didn't need to be able to see the top to know that he was faced

with a long and difficult climb. He settled his equipment more securely, then reached up into the narrow crack in the wall with his right hand held sideways, and gripped the sharp edge.

The crack wasn't vertical, but ran at an angle from left to right, so he had some downward purchase, as well as the sideways pressure of his hand against the edge of the crack. He stepped up with his right foot, turning it slightly sideways so that it would fit into the crack, then smoothly heaved himself upward, using arm and leg muscles. His left hand scouted along the rock wall until he felt a rough outcrop of rock that provided him with a secure handhold. He heaved himself a little higher, setting his left foot into the crack and gaining purchase by pushing sideways and wedging it tightly in the split in the rock. Hands, arms and legs worked together and he went up another meter.

He released his right foot and brought it up, knee bent, searching for purchase in the crack. When he had it wedged, his right hand followed, sliding up the fissure until he had it settled securely. His left foot followed. Then, when it had a firm purchase, he searched with his left hand for another hold, found it and heaved himself another meter up the cliff.

So he continued, working smoothly, never rushing, choosing his handholds and footholds deliberately and always keeping three points of contact with the sheer rock wall. He glanced down at one stage. The ground below him seemed disappointingly close. He thought he'd climbed higher. Setting his hands and feet, he leaned back slightly, looking up.

He couldn't see the top of the cliff. But he could make out the line of what he hoped was a substantial ledge, still twenty meters above him.

The fissure continued to provide him with secure hand-holds and footholds as he worked his way upward. But now he was high enough to take out a little insurance. He spied a crack in the wall to the left of the main fissure and studied it closely. The rock either side of it seemed solid and undamaged. He reached into the leather pouch at his belt and took out one of the spikes.

Hanging by his right hand and with both feet set firmly in the fissure, he used his left hand to carefully insert the spike into the small crack, making sure it was firmly set and unlikely to fall out when he released it. Carefully, he took away his left hand, ready to snatch at the spike in case it started to fall free. But it remained wedged and he nodded to himself in satisfaction. Then he fetched the canvas-muffled mallet from where it hung around his neck and drove the spike in with three sharp blows. The mallet striking the spike gave out a dull thud and not a metallic ringing that would have been the case without the canvas padding. He angled the spike so that it drove down into the crack. Then he let the mallet hang and seized the spike with his left hand, gradually transferring most of his weight to it to make sure it was solidly set. Satisfied that it was, he looped the rope around it in a loose half hitch, paid out eight meters of cord and then fastened it under his shoulders. If he slipped now, he would fall to the end of the length of rope, then be brought up short by the loop around the spike.

"So long as the spike holds," he muttered, then dismissed the thought. Worrying about the outcome wouldn't do any good. He had set the spike as firmly as he could. He didn't tighten the half hitch. He climbed on. The rope was loosely looped over the spike. If he fell, it would tighten and bring him to a halt. But left loose as it was, he could flick the small loop free of the spike when it came time for him to set another spike in place.

He repeated the action after another ten meters. As he had planned, the loose loop fell free of the first spike after three attempts to flick it clear. He hammered in another spike, looped the rope around it and climbed on.

His fingers, knees and ankles were aching from the strain of supporting his weight, particularly as he didn't have a straight-forward vertical purchase on the fissure but had to force his hands and feet to either side to gain traction. He would need a rest soon and he glanced up to see how close the ledge was.

To his surprise, he was only a meter short. He heaved himself up onto the level shelf of rock. It was less than a meter wide, but it allowed him to sit with his legs dangling over the drop and his back against the cliff wall while he took stock of his situation.

The fault in the rock face that he had been using to help climb petered out at this stage and continued no farther. But the ledge sloped upward to his left as he faced the wall and that meant it ran back in the direction of the giant fissure that formed Three Step Pass. The ledge went round a rock buttress ten meters away and he couldn't see how far it continued.

"Might as well take a look," he said to himself. A quick study of the rock face above him had showed that there were minimal handholds and footholds there. Perhaps things might be more promising over to the left.

Additionally, there was an overhang of rock directly above him and, if he tried to continue up at this point, he would have to negotiate that. He leaned out and flicked the rope, releasing the half hitch from the spike where he had looped it and bringing the rope in, coiling it as he went and draping the coils over his shoulder.

He sat for a few more minutes, taking a drink from his canteen, then flexing his cramped fingers and toes, and rotating his aching ankles. Finally, with a sigh, he crouched on the ledge, then rose to his full height. He glanced down. The forest floor looked a lot farther away now, but he could still make out the form of his horse, head craned back to watch through the trees.

Not for the first time, he shook his head in admiration of the intelligence and loyalty shown by these Ranger horses. He set out toward the pass, testing each step to make sure the ledge wasn't undermined or unsafe. Reaching the buttress, he set his back against the wall and inched carefully around the outcrop, moving sideways in the suddenly restricted space. He knew many men would have been overcome with vertigo as the ledge narrowed severely and the drop yawned below him. But he'd never been bothered by heights and went round the outcrop easily.

He smiled as he saw what lay beyond. The pass was only forty meters away and the ledge ran all the way to it. The far wall of the pass was higher than the one closer to him, so he could see the gap easily. Even more importantly, the cliff itself lost its vertical slope and slanted inward, which would make it easier to climb. And he could see that the rock face was lined with small crevices and rock outcrops, even sturdy bushes growing from the rock. They would provide him with handholds and footholds for the rest of the climb.

He made his way to the near side of the pass, moving carefully and avoiding any undue noise. The surface of the ledge was littered with loose stones and rocks, and he made sure not to dislodge any of them. Probably the noise of rocks falling down the cliff would be unheard inside the steep walls of the fissure. But he wasn't taking any chances.

Three meters from the edge of the pass, he went down on his hands and knees and crawled forward. If there was anyone, or anything, directly below him, he didn't want his head and shoulders to be silhouetted against the sky when he peered over the edge. He stopped and checked the sun's position, making sure it wasn't behind him so that he would throw a shadow into the pass. Satisfied that this wouldn't happen, he went down on his belly and crept forward, moving slowly.

A half meter from the edge, he reached back and pulled the cowl of his cloak up. It would hide the white oval of his face and break up the distinctive outline of his head. If anyone did look up, they would see the indistinct shape formed by the cowl, which could be passed off as a rock outcrop.

Not that anyone was liable to be looking up, he thought. But he had learned always to plan for the unlikely. The fact that there was no reason to look up didn't mean that somebody wouldn't, and it always paid to expect the worst.

He used his fingers and toes to inch himself closer to the edge. Then his eyes were over the rim and he was peering down into the black shadows beneath him.

At first, he could see nothing in the darkness. The sun was yet to pass overhead and light the interior of the fissure. But he could hear movement. He heard the scrape of a heavy boot or sandal on the rocks below him, and the sharp *tink* of a metal weapon or fitting hitting the rocks.

Then he became aware of a less obvious sound—a deep,

throaty grunting sound. An animal sound that made his scalp tingle.

Gradually, his eyes were becoming accustomed to the gloom, and he could discern movement below. Then he could make out the forms of those in the pass, and his heart beat a little faster. The shadowy figures weren't completely clear, but they matched the descriptions he'd been given by Pauline and the picket captain.

Dark, heavyset, covered in black fur. He couldn't make out their features but he could see they moved clumsily and awkwardly, standing erect. And all the while, he could hear the muted grunting, coming from several directions in the pass below him.

He shivered as he thought of how it must have been for the scouting party sent in to reconnoiter. Without warning, they would have found themselves confronted by these inhuman beasts. They would have been taken by surprise, perhaps frozen with fear. And that fear had cost two of them their lives.

Slowly, he squirmed back from the edge and, in so doing, dislodged a pile of rocks with his left foot. They clattered off down the cliff face beside him, bouncing off the rock to spin in the air, then hit the face once more.

He froze. The grunting from the pass fell silent. The beasts shouldn't have been able to hear the rocks. After all, they were screened by the solid walls of the pass. But they obviously had. The grunting started again, more urgent in tone now. He knew that the top of his head was still hanging over the edge and he stayed perfectly still, trusting the cloak to disguise and conceal him. He knew it was imperative that he make no movement. If anyone were looking, they would see an indeterminate shape at the top of the wall. But if he withdrew, they would see the movement and know someone was there.

The grunting continued. He began to make out different tones, as if the beasts were voicing question and answer. He breathed deeply and quietly, calming his racing heart.

Even if they were suspicious about the falling rocks, there was little they could do about it. They could hardly climb the sheer walls of the pass to investigate.

Unless they had a ladder.

At that thought, the blood seemed to freeze in his veins. He lay still, straining to listen, trying to make out what was going on below him. He heard no sound of wood on rock, which might have indicated that someone—or something, he amended—was fetching a ladder.

Eventually, the guttural discussion below him began to die away as the guards heard no further sound and began to lose interest in the matter. He waited still. Ten minutes. Twenty.

Now the grunts and growls had become more relaxed, losing the sharp edge of inquiry that had met the sound of the falling rocks. He reasoned that by now they had no ladder, or no inclination to investigate the sound, which, in any case, had not been repeated.

He waited another ten minutes. If anyone had been looking up at the top of the pass, chances were good that they had now grown weary of doing so. He worked his way backward with infinite slowness and care, a few millimeters at a time. When he judged his head was well clear of the edge, he slowly raised himself to his hands and knees. He took his canteen from his belt and allowed himself a long drink. His mouth was dry from the tension. Then, when his breathing was back to normal, he turned to face the rock wall stretching above him. This time, there'd be no using the mallet to drive spikes into the rock. He was too close to the pass. He considered moving away but the slope was less severe in this spot and the climbing would be easier. He shrugged. He'd have to do without the safety provided by the belaying spikes.

"If I fall, I fall," he said philosophically.

Somehow, that didn't make the prospect any more attractive.

7

ᘓᘓᘓᘓᘓᘓᘓᘓᘓᘓᘓᘓᘓᘓᘓᘓᘓᘓᘓ

CROWLEY KNOCKED ON THE DOOR TO THE KING'S APART-
ments and waited until he heard Duncan's voice from within.

"Come."

He pushed open the door and entered, finding himself in the
King's office. Duncan didn't stand on ceremony. There was no
anteroom or Chamberlain to delay visitors with a load of red
tape. When you were summoned to see the King, you saw the
King, not a series of underlings.

Duncan was seated at a heavy oaken desk beside one of the
windows. Sunlight streamed in, setting motes of dust dancing in
its rays. His long legs were splayed out under the desk and he
was frowning at a sheaf of papers. He made a quick notation on
one, then looked up and smiled at Crowley, waving him forward
and gesturing to a chair set opposite his at the desk.

"Come in, Crowley. Take a seat."

Crowley settled into the seat while Duncan arranged the
papers in front of him into a squared-off stack and put them to
one side. The shutters were open and there was a light breeze
coming through the window, so he placed a heavy granite paper-
weight on the sheets to stop them being scattered.

"Are you busy at the moment?" Duncan asked.

Crowley hesitated. He was the Ranger Commandant and that meant he was always busy. He had to prioritize the fief assignments. There were too few Rangers for too many fiefs, and he had to try to distribute his available men to the best advantage. Some fiefs could manage without a Ranger in the short term. But he had to remember that this was only a temporary solution and, as more men became available, he'd have to rectify it.

In addition, he was overseeing the training program for the new apprentices he'd appointed. Their mentors would train them but they had to be tested at regular intervals by an independent judge. Farrel was helping out with that. His broken leg might curtail his normal Ranger duties, but it didn't impede his ability to assess and evaluate the young men so eager to advance in the Corps.

But these were day-to-day matters and, presumably, the King was aware of them. Crowley guessed that his question pertained to any out-of-the-ordinary tasks that might have arisen. He screwed up his mouth thoughtfully, then answered.

"Not unduly, sir. There are rumors of a witch plying her trade in a small fief on the west coast. It's one of the fiefs without a Ranger at present, so I'll have to find someone to go and take a look."

"A witch?" Duncan asked. "Is she a real witch?"

Crowley shrugged. "Is there any such thing as a real witch?" he asked in reply. Then he waved a vague hand in the air. "Odds are she's just a lonely old lady who's playing with potions and spreading the rumor that she's raising demons and trolls and such."

"That's usually the case," Duncan agreed. Often, the women in question were healers, with a certain amount of skill with herbs and compounds. They would serve a village, tending the sick and usually helping to heal them. But on occasion, their ministrations were of no use and they would lose a patient. In those cases, the villagers often turned on the hapless woman, claiming that she was the cause of the illness that had struck their family member. The woman had tended to a sick person. The person had died. Therefore it was the healer's fault. From there, it was a short step to claiming witchcraft.

Sometimes, when that happened, the healer would embrace the accusation, claiming supernatural powers in order to cow the angry, frightened villagers.

"Is it serious?" Duncan wanted to know. "I can always send one of my knights to handle it if necessary."

But Crowley was already shaking his head before he was half finished. "So far it's just rumors and mumbling. It could even sort itself out. There's no real urgency if you have something else that needs to be done."

He made the last statement to move the conversation along. Obviously, Duncan had a task in mind for him and they were wasting time discussing the affairs of an old woman on the west coast.

Crowley saw that he had guessed correctly. The King fiddled with a small dagger he kept on the desk to slit open sealed documents. He seemed reluctant to speak about what he had in mind, and Crowley guessed it was a matter that was an unpleasant one for him to discuss.

"It's the Queen," Duncan said finally, and the Ranger Commandant nodded his understanding. The entire court now knew that Queen Rosalind, now seven months pregnant, was having a difficult time. She had been confined to her apartment for some weeks and spent most of her days resting in bed.

"She's not improving, and the healers say they've done everything they can. And of course, as the baby grows, things become more difficult for the Queen."

"Is the baby all right?" Crowley asked, with genuine concern. Aside from his liking and admiring the royal couple, it was important in such uncertain times for there to be a clear line of succession to the throne. Either a son or daughter could inherit, and the Kingdom needed to be reassured that—if something happened to Duncan—there was a legitimate heir ready to step into the breach.

"So far as they can tell," Duncan said, the worry evident on his face. "Of course, in these cases, nobody can be sure. But they've listened to the heartbeat through that ear trumpet contraption my head physician brought back from Toscana two years ago and they say it's strong and loud."

"Well, that's good news," Crowley said. He frowned, wondering what the Queen's health had to do with him. He had no skill as a healer and no experience of such matters. He was a young, single man. Duncan's next words enlightened him.

"Geoffrey, my head physician, thinks that the situation here might be placing too much strain on her. He thinks she might be better to get away to someplace she can rest."

The court at Castle Araluen wasn't exactly conducive to rest and relaxation. There was squabbling and bickering as people sought to gain Duncan's attention or favor, as well as constant undercurrents of possible treachery in the wake of Morgarath's machinations. And of course, there was the looming question of the rebel baron and what he intended.

All these things combined to create an atmosphere of stress and worry within the palace. Every day brought a new rumor, a new potential threat. It affected Duncan himself, making him short-tempered and irritable. And, no matter how much he tried to reassure his wife, it was inevitable that she would worry about him and the dangers that he faced each day. The uncertainty nagged at her, making it well-nigh impossible for her to relax, rest and concentrate on having a healthy pregnancy.

And all of that was in addition to the physical side of things. Even under ideal conditions, she would have been having a hard time. Her health was fragile and the demands that a growing baby placed upon her body were simply too much.

"Where could she go?" Crowley asked.

"Geoffrey recommends a health spa called Woldon Abbey, which is around fifty kilometers from here. The waters there are very beneficial and the sisters who run the abbey are highly skilled in looking after delicate patients. He says it could help enormously."

"And she'd be away from all the day-to-day rumors and uncertainty of the court," Crowley said.

The King nodded. "Precisely. I've written to the Abbess. She says she thinks they can help Rosalind get through the final months of her pregnancy—and ensure that the baby is born safely."

"How does Queen Rosalind feel about leaving Araluen?"

Duncan pursed his lips. "Naturally, she would rather stay here. She worries about me," he added with a sheepish grin. "But she's also concerned for the health of the baby and that's the most important aspect of the whole matter. If it will keep the baby safe, she'll go to Woldon until he—or she—is born."

Crowley leaned back in his chair. "It sounds like that's the answer then," he said. He was pretty sure he could see where this conversation was going. If the Queen was transported to Woldon Abbey, she would need an armed escort to protect her on the journey, and someone trustworthy in command. He thought he knew who the King had in mind.

"Did you want me to command the escort for her?"

Duncan nodded. "I can't think of anyone I'd rather have looking after her," he said. "Short of myself, of course, and I can't leave Araluen for a long period."

"It is only fifty kilometers," Crowley said.

"But it'll be slow going," the King told him. "She'll have to travel very carefully in a comfortable carriage. She can't be bounced around on rough roads and she won't be able to do too many kilometers in a day."

"What size escort did you have in mind?" Crowley asked.

The King answered immediately, which told Crowley that he had been thinking about this matter for some time. "You in command, of course. And one of my junior knights with a force of twenty mounted men."

Crowley considered. It was a reasonable escort. But perhaps a little too large. Twenty men would place an unreasonable burden on the inns and manor houses where they would stop along the way, and take time to assemble for each day's march. In addition, a group that size would draw attention to itself, and people might be tempted to try to find out the identity of the passenger in the carriage. He voiced these concerns to the King. Naturally, Duncan was most concerned with keeping his wife safe on the journey, but he could see the sense in Crowley's argument and, after considering it for a moment, he agreed.

"Ten men-at-arms under a knight," the Ranger said. "And I'd like to add some long-range capability as well. Maybe five mounted archers."

Men like Duncan—knights and warriors—tended only to think in terms of swords and lances. But when it was mentioned, he could see the value of including a force of archers.

"Another thing," Crowley added. "You could hardly afford to leave twenty men as the Queen's bodyguard while she's at the spa. Even ten would leave you short-handed. I'd leave five men-at-arms to look after her, and two of the archers."

Duncan nodded. "We need to keep this a strict secret. Nobody is to know that she's traveling to Woldon. There are still people around here who resent me and I wouldn't put it past some of them to use Rosalind to strike at me."

"All the more reason to make it a smaller party," Crowley said. "I'll pick the archers. There's no need for them to know where they're going or who we're escorting. I assume you'll select the men-at-arms?"

Crowley could easily assess the skill of the archers he'd be taking, but Duncan had a better knowledge of the knights and warriors who were in his service.

"I'll put young Athol in command of the detachment," the King said. "He's a fine leader and he has a good head on his shoulders. Of course, I'll impress on him that you're in overall command. You'll be taking any major decisions that come up."

"Let's hope there won't be too many of those," Crowley said. There was a pause as both men pictured the coming days, and the sight of the little cavalcade making its way through the countryside.

"When do you want us to start?" Crowley asked.

"Is the day after tomorrow too soon?" Duncan replied. Now that the decision had been made, he wanted to see Rosalind on the road as soon as possible.

Crowley thought for a second, then nodded. "That'll give me time to clear a few things up," he said. "And hand over to Farrel. In a way, it's fortunate that he injured himself. It's very handy having him here."

"Yes," said the King, but his tone was distracted.

Crowley leaned forward and placed his hand on the King's.

"Don't worry, my lord. I'll guard her with my life," he said.

8

⌒⌒⌒⌒⌒⌒⌒⌒⌒⌒⌒⌒⌒⌒⌒⌒⌒⌒⌒

THE SECOND HALF OF THE CLIMB WAS EASIER THAN THE INI-
tial section. The cliff sloped back now, making it easier to scale
than the sheer wall that had confronted Halt at the beginning
of the climb. And while there was no long fissure to provide him
with holds, there were plenty of cracks and faults in the granite
and small outcrops of solid rock that assisted him on the
way up.

A few meters from the top, he stopped to regain his breath
and to consider his next move. There was a thick-trunked shrub
growing out of the face of the cliff. He tested its firmness, tugging on it, and gradually placing all his weight on it. It held firm,
so he swung one leg over it and straddled it, leaning back against
the hard granite.

A fine mist of rain began to drift down. As he'd seen earlier,
the plateau had its own weather system, probably due to the
damp sea air that blew in from the southern and eastern sides.
Clouds seemed to hover over the flat-topped mountain, forming
solid gray banks, whereas to the north, the sky was clear and
blue.

The rain was cool on his head and face after the exertions of the long climb. But after several minutes, he began to grow cold. He pulled his hood up again—he had tossed it back when he left his vantage point over the pass—and huddled under the cloak. The wool material, impregnated with natural oils, kept the rain running off it. It would be some hours before the water soaked into the cloak.

He had no idea what awaited him beyond the rim of the cliff. He knew that Morgarath had left Gorlan with about one hundred and fifty troops. Presumably, most of them had stayed with him. There was every chance that Morgarath might have set guards along the cliff edge—either from the troops who had accompanied him or the new additions to his force.

"Wargals," he said softly. It was an ugly word and it conjured up an unpleasant picture of the half men–half beasts Morgarath had recruited. Halt wondered how many of them there were, and how Morgarath had suborned them to his will. There was so little he knew about the rebel baron's forces and intentions. He might be facing ten of these creatures. Or one hundred. Or more.

Halt shuddered at the thought.

He pushed back the cowl and listened, turning his head from side to side to catch the slightest sound. But he heard nothing beyond the pattering of rain on the rocks. That raised another thought. His bowstring would be wet, and that would cause it to stretch, reducing the power of his bow. Of course, he kept the string liberally coated with beeswax to stop it soaking, but even beeswax couldn't keep it totally dry. He kept spare strings inside his jerkin, but he mightn't have time to restring the bow once he reached the top. And he certainly couldn't do it here.

That meant he had lost the use of his most potent weapon, so stealth would be his best tactic. He'd have to move slowly and silently, looking carefully over the top of the cliff to see if the way was clear.

But what if it wasn't? What if he found himself face-to-face with one of these bearlike creatures?

"What if I'm struck by lightning or eaten by a lion?" he muttered. He knew he was only raising these thoughts to delay the moment when he started out for the top once more. He was rested now, and ready to move. His bow might be less than efficient, but he still had his saxe and his throwing knife.

He looked to his left, then looked upward, seeking out the handholds he would use and tracing his path over the next few meters to the top of the climb. Then he swung his left leg over the shrub, turning his body and reaching out with his left hand for a handhold. There was a tiny ledge a meter below him that would give his left foot purchase. He set his boot on it, seized hard on a rough obtrusion with his left hand, and swung his body clear of the shrub, then set his right foot on it to give him a substantial point of support. He straightened his right knee, hauling himself up with his left hand, and let his right hand trail across the rock face until he felt a narrow ledge of rock beneath it. It was barely two centimeters wide, but it was enough to give him good, solid purchase. He tested it, putting more and more weight on it, but refusing to relinquish the support he had from his right foot and left hand. Deciding it was solid, he committed his weight to it and slid farther up the rock wall.

To anyone watching, he thought, he must look like a giant gray spider, spread out on the rock. Except no spider ever moved so slowly. He continued, searching alternately for handholds and footholds, testing them for security, then committing his weight to them and heaving himself up, half a meter at a time.

His face was pressed against the rough, wet surface of the rock. Thank goodness it hadn't become slick and slippery with the rain. The granite was pocked and flawed and roughened, providing a nonslip surface for him.

A meter to go. The top of the cliff beckoned him. He paused, letting his breathing steady, and listened intently.

Nothing.

Then, plotting his next three handholds and footholds, he swarmed up the remaining distance until his head was just below the rim. He hung by his hands, his fingertips clawing into the cliff face, with his right leg supporting most of his weight, his knee bent.

Then, with infinite care, he straightened his knee, pushing himself upward, the rough rock clawing at his clothes, until his head rose above the level of the cliff rim. He paused with just the top of his head and his eyes visible above the edge and swept a look around the plateau as far as he could see.

Nothing.

A tumble of wet, glistening rocks. A few stunted, gray-leafed, twisted trees and shrubs. No men. No bearlike Wargals.

He let go a sigh of relief, then heaved himself up and over the edge, making sure that he kept low in case, somewhere, unfriendly eyes were watching. He rolled onto the stony ground, feeling sharp pebbles digging into him, and gained the cover of a large boulder several meters away.

He came to his hands and knees, then slowly raised himself behind the boulder, his eyes flicking from side to side, his ears alert for the slightest sound of danger.

Still nothing.

Rain pattered softly on the rocks. There was a wind blowing

across the plateau. But no sign of any living being. Slowly, he came to his full height and surveyed the land around him.

It was a desolate, depressing place. Boulders and large rocks were strewn willy-nilly—some individual, others piled into outcrops that stood higher than his head—interspersed by shrubs. Their twisted trunks and distorted limbs were covered in gray bark, lined and patterned with cracks and splits. None of them were taller than three meters. Many of them were dwarfed by the rock outcrops. All of them were tilted to one side—the same side. Obviously, this was due to the prevailing wind that blew in from the south, bringing the wet smell of the sea with it.

There was open space among the rocks, but nothing that resembled a track of any kind. Halt moved from behind the cover of the outcrop where he sheltered and began to pick his way among the scattered boulders, zigzagging as his path was blocked but always returning to a base course that led him due south. It was hard going. Even where the way seemed clear, the ground was littered with rough, uneven stones, some as large as apples, that turned under his feet, threatening to twist and sprain his ankles at any incautious step.

Every few meters, he would crouch in the cover of one of the larger boulders and scan the way ahead—and behind. As he progressed, his shoulders contracted and his skin crawled with the fear that someone, or something, was moving up behind him. But whenever he stopped and whirled about, there was nothing to be seen.

Then he heard the sound.

Guttural. Deep-throated. Rhythmic.

It was the sound of many voices grunting, or growling, in unison. He felt the hair rise on the back of his neck. There was something intrinsically alien, intrinsically threatening, in that sound. It was coming from the south, beyond a line of rocks at the limit of his vision. The ground rose gradually here. He hadn't noticed it earlier but now he realized that, as he was making his way through the jumble of rocks, he was moving upward, to a horizon only fifty meters away.

The grunting, rhythmic but toneless, grew louder as he continued, setting each foot carefully in the rocks and sand. And now he could hear another sound, in time with the chanting.

Footsteps. Boots or sandals slamming down in unison and in time.

"Urrgh!" *Crash!* "Urrgh-urrgh!" *Crash!* "Urrgh!" *Crash!*

So it continued, growing in volume as he reached the line of rocks. Constant. Unchanging. Menacing.

It dawned on him that he was listening to a group of people—or *things*—drilling beyond the line of rocks ahead of him. In the last few meters, he dropped into a crouch, then to his hands and knees, and scurried forward. He headed for two rocks that were standing close together, with a V-shaped gap between them. The bottom of the V was only a few centimeters wide and he placed his eye against it and peered through.

Beyond the line of rocks, the ground sloped away for thirty meters, then leveled into an open plain, some four hundred meters square. To the south and west, it stretched away to another jagged horizon of jumbled rocks. To the east, it was dominated by the solid wall of a low mountain. As Halt studied it, he could see fissures in the face of the mountain—at ground level and then higher. Watching, he caught a glimpse of movement at one of the openings and realized there were men, or creatures, in there. Smoke rose from several fires in the foreground, and he could see canvas shelters and awnings stretched out from the rocks. Living quarters, he realized. But it was the open plain that drew his attention once more. One hundred meters from his vantage point, a group of dark figures stood in formation. He estimated there were eighty of them. They were squat and powerful looking, covered in long, shaggy black hair. They stood a meter and a half tall on short hind legs. Their arms were long and apelike, with large, fingered hands and opposable thumbs that allowed them to grip the weapons in their hands—short, heavy spears for the most part, but some jagged-edged swords as well.

Their faces were grotesque—bearlike, but with a hint of ape as well. Heavy brows overhung their close-set eyes and their lips were curled back from yellowing teeth. Long fangs interspersed with grinding molars. They were equipped with what appeared to be black leather armor and each one wore a metal skullcap.

As he looked through the gap in the rocks, the chanting and stamping had ceased, and for a moment he thought they must have detected him.

But then they began again. They raised their spears and thrust forward as one. They emitted that terrifying grunt that he'd heard, then stamped forward so that eighty right feet slammed down onto the plain, raising a cloud of dust. Then they repeated the action, stamping, grunting and thrusting their way forward, heading for the line of rocks where Halt crouched in hiding.

Then a strange sensation came over Halt. As he watched Wargals drilling, he felt a featherlight intrusion into his consciousness.

It was faint and fleeting, but he had the vague impression

that somewhere, someone was trying to speak to him—although he could hear no words. As he tried to focus on the sensation, it faded. Then, a few seconds later, it drifted back.

At least, he thought it was back. It was so ephemeral that he couldn't really be sure that it was there at all. He shook his head to clear it and the feeling disappeared once more. This time, it didn't recur.

"I'm imagining things," he muttered to himself.

Unsettled, he turned away from the V-shaped aperture and leaned his back against the rocks he was sheltering behind.

And saw a quick flash of movement behind him as someone, or something, darted into the cover of a group of rocks.

9

IN AN UPPER-LEVEL CAVE IN THE CLIFF WALL, ABOVE THE ROWS of tents and awnings, Morgarath stood by a large break in the rocks that formed a natural observation window.

The drill field stretched out below him. Several hundred meters away, the squad of Wargals was drilling. Morgarath leaned against a rock shelf at waist height, studied the Wargals for several seconds, then closed his eyes and concentrated fiercely.

In his mind, he created a picture of the Wargals advancing four paces in line abreast, then wheeling to the right and advancing another ten paces, stabbing out with their spears as they went.

His brow knitted in furrows with the intensity of his concentration. He held the image in his mind, seeing the action again and again, his breath coming in short gasps with the effort he was expending. He opened his eyes, and a slow smile formed on his features.

The Wargals had wheeled to the right and were advancing, as he had directed them.

There was a wood and canvas camp seat beside him and he

collapsed onto it, exhausted. He had been developing this mind control since he had first recruited the Wargals and was gradually becoming more adept. He still hadn't learned to focus his mental commands tightly, but he was becoming more skilled.

The Wargals came to the end of the ten-pace advance he had envisioned and stopped, awaiting further direction. He took a deep breath and stood at the roughly shaped window once more. He closed his eyes and concentrated.

The boulder where Halt had seen the movement was forty meters away from him. He sat, unmoving, his head hunched low on his shoulders, resisting the temptation to lean forward and look more closely.

The watcher in the rocks—if it were a watcher—would see no sign of reaction from him, no sign that he had noticed movement and was now achingly aware, senses tautened like lute strings.

Of course, he thought, it could have been a small bird or an animal flitting into the shelter of the rocks. But he had seen no birds since he had arrived at the top of the plateau. There was no sound of birdsong anywhere in the vicinity.

A small animal then? A rabbit or a hare. Or even a large rat?

But the movement had been a meter and a half above the ground—about the height of a kneeling or crouching man.

A larger animal then? His skin crawled as he realized that it could be one of those fearsome Wargals stalking him. Even the brief sighting of the beasts drilling on the plain had imbued in Halt a sense of their implacable menace. One could be there now, watching him from a crevice in the rocks, much as he had observed the drilling force on the plain behind him. He took a deep breath. Whatever it was, whoever it was, it was essential that he showed no sign that he had seen it. He took his canteen from his belt, unstoppered it and took a deep drink of water.

He didn't really need it, but it struck him that a man who was aware that someone was watching him wouldn't relax and take a drink. He replaced the canteen in the holder on his belt. His head was tilted down but he kept his eyes up, shadowed in the cowl of his cloak, searching the spot where he had seen the flicker of movement.

And there it was again. Half a meter to the right of where he had first seen it, a face emerged from behind the rock, moving slowly. He could see the pale oval shape and felt a sense of relief. At least it wasn't a black-furred, long-fanged Wargal. It was a man. For a moment, he wondered if it might be one of Morgarath's human followers. Then he discarded the idea. If that were the case, the newcomer would surely have challenged Halt and raised the alarm. After all, he had plenty of reinforcements close to hand. But his stealthy manner indicated that he was as keen as Halt to remain unseen by the Wargals. The face slid back behind the boulder. Halt waited. Several minutes later, it appeared again, sliding out to stare at him. He remained motionless, seemingly uninterested.

The face withdrew behind the boulder.

He began counting. He had reached thirty-five when the face became visible once more. Whoever was behind those rocks, he was taking great pains to keep an eye on Halt. Perhaps emboldened by the fact that he had seemed to remain unnoticed so far, the watcher remained in the open for a period of ten seconds this time. Then, slowly, he withdrew.

And as he did, Halt acted. He grabbed his cloak, wrapping

it around him, and rolled to his right along the ground. As he rolled, he angled his body so that he could see the rocks where his observer was hiding. He covered some ten meters, then froze in place behind a row of boulders, his face hidden deep inside the shadows of the cowl.

He counted to fifteen. Then, slowly, the face reappeared from behind the rock. This time, Halt thought he could detect a sense of surprise from the watcher. The figure rose slightly, seeking a better vantage point.

Halt smiled grimly. To all intents and purposes, he had simply disappeared. Halt was skilled in the art of remaining unseen and he knew that the gray-and-green-mottled surface of his cloak would break up the outline of his body lying on the ground, making it merge into the gray jumble of rocks and boulders and dark green bushes.

Trust the cloak. Pritchard had dinned that message into him hundreds of times when he had trained with the old Ranger. Movement would be the only thing that would reveal his presence. He lay as still as the rocks around him, making his breathing shallow to reduce any movement to an absolute minimum.

The head had remained exposed for a full half minute, turning from side to side as the watcher tried to discern where his erstwhile quarry had gone. Now Halt was sure he could make out a sense of desperation and nervousness. Belatedly, the face dropped behind the rocks again as its owner sought to take stock of the situation. Halt tensed his muscles to move, but some sixth sense warned him against it and he remained where he was.

Ten seconds later, the face appeared again, turning from side to side as the watcher scanned the rocks and trees.

And withdrew once more.

Halt reasoned that this time he would have longer to act. The watcher had been surprised by his apparent disappearance. He had withdrawn, then reappeared to check once more. Now, Halt thought, he'll be thinking over what to do next—whether to move or stay put. Either way, he would remain in hiding longer than before.

And with that thought, Halt was on the move once more, staying low and scrambling on hands and toes across the rough ground. He slipped behind a tumble of rocks some thirty meters from his original position. He stopped and crouched, peering from the shadows of a large boulder toward the spot where he had seen the face.

Now the watcher appeared again, tentatively. There was a definite air of desperation about the movements now. He rose higher, so that he was head and shoulders above the rocks, peering at the spot where Halt had disappeared. Then, baffled, he sank back into hiding, and Halt was moving once more.

He came up into a crouch and half ran, angling out to the side so that he could circle behind the other man. When he was level with the rocks, he dropped into concealment once more.

Just in time, he thought, as the head and shoulders rose into view again. He was closer now and he could make out more detail. The man—for it was a man—had long, unkempt gray hair and a shaggy beard that came down to his chest. His clothes were old and ragged, patched many times. His appearance confirmed Halt's suspicion that this wasn't one of Morgarath's followers.

The man looked around, for a moment looking straight at Halt where the Ranger crouched, only twenty meters away. Halt froze, resisting the almost overwhelming urge to drop back into cover. To do that would be to reveal his position immediately.

He weathered the gaze of the other man, not moving a muscle. Then the face turned away from him to search the other side of the rock field.

Halt took the opportunity to glide another ten meters past the man's hiding spot, so that he could come up behind him unseen. So long as the stalker didn't move his position, Halt could be upon him within another couple of minutes.

Then, finally, the man left his hiding place and began to move to his left, heading straight for the rocks where Halt was hidden. His eyes were still fixed on the last place he'd seen the Ranger, and he moved sideways like a crab, crouching to remain in cover, flitting from one boulder to the next.

Halt's hand went to his saxe. He could hear the soft scrabble of the man's feet on the rocks, then the harsh sound of his ragged breathing. That, more than anything else, told Halt that the man was fearful, confused by the inexplicable disappearance of his quarry.

He moved closer, and Halt could sense he was crouched on the far side of the boulder behind which he was sheltering. Which way would he go around it? Behind it or in front of it? Would he emerge on Halt's right or his left?

He strained his ears and heard a slight movement. Good. The man was moving in front of the rock, which would bring him out on Halt's right, facing away from him. Silently, Halt slid the saxe from its sheath and tensed, ready for instant action.

A gray-haired shape emerged in front of him, crouched and peering forward. Obviously, the man was still puzzled by Halt's sudden disappearance. Halt could hear the heavy, nerve-racked breathing more clearly. He studied the man's clothes. Ragged, patched woolen trousers, feet bound in what appeared to be animal skins, laced in place with leather thongs. A short cloak, also of animal fur, hung over his shoulders. And a shapeless felt hat covered his head. The unkempt hair hung down over his shoulders.

Halt rose like a gray shadow behind him. At the last moment, the man must have heard some faint sound and he started to turn, sensing there was danger behind him.

Halt brought the heavy brass hilt of his saxe down on the back of the man's head before he could complete the turn. There was a dull, ugly thud, and the man collapsed with a small cry, his knees giving way to send him sprawling onto the coarse sand and pebbles.

He was facedown, and Halt grabbed one shoulder to turn him over. There was no resistance. The body was limp. Halt let him lie on his back and reached down to roll one eyelid back with his thumb.

He could see only white behind the rolled-back lid. The man was unconscious.

Or dead, he wondered suddenly. He'd hit the stranger a little harder than he'd intended. He rested a hand on his chest now and was relieved to feel the regular rise and fall as he breathed in and out.

Now that he had the opportunity, he studied the man's face. He was older than Halt, perhaps fifty or sixty years old. It was hard to tell beneath the tangled gray hair and beard. The face was weather-beaten and lined, turned brown by the ravages of the sun and searing winds of the plateau. The nose was long and crooked. It had been broken at some time. The eyebrows were bushy and untrimmed. It was a thin face, the cheeks sunken below prominent cheekbones.

He was unkempt and dirty, his clothes stained and patched

in a dozen places, as Halt had already observed. He was thin, his arms and legs sticklike and patterned with sinews and veins. He didn't have the look of someone who would be working for Morgarath. He looked like a beggar, a recluse, someone who slept rough and lived on his wits.

His forehead was grazed where he'd fallen facedown into the rocks. Halt seized his shoulders and dragged him till he was half sitting, supported by a boulder. Then he unstoppered his canteen and poured a little cold water over the man's forehead, allowing it to trickle down across his face.

The man twitched at the cool touch of the water. Halt placed his thumb on his bottom lip and pried his mouth open, allowing more of the water to trickle down into his mouth. Eyes still closed, the man swallowed by reflex at the touch of the water, then gulped and coughed, sitting up suddenly, eyes wide-open and filled with panic.

He tried to rise but Halt was ready for him and placed a hand on his chest, holding him down. The man's gaze steadied and focused and he studied the bearded face leaning over him.

"You're not . . . ," he began, then stopped.

"I'm not who?" Halt asked.

The man shook his head, as if trying to clear his vision further. It occurred to Halt that he might well be seeing double after the blow to the back of his head.

"You're not . . . one of them . . . ," the man said. His voice was thin and reedy, and the words came awkwardly, as if he were not accustomed to talking very much.

"A Wargal?" Halt said, and saw a quick flash of fear in the man's watery blue eyes. "No. I'm not a Wargal. But I see you know what they are."

The man nodded, swallowed twice, then gestured to the canteen in Halt's left hand. The Ranger offered it to him and he took it, tilting it over his mouth and letting water fall into it. This time, prepared for it, he didn't choke. He swallowed greedily.

"That's good," he said, a little absently. Then the eyes came back to Halt's again. "And you're not with the Black Lord?" he said uncertainly. It was obvious who the title referred to.

"His name is Morgarath," Halt said.

"I call him the Black Lord," the man replied.

Halt let a grim smile touch his lips. "It's a good name for him," he said, "in more ways than one. But, no. I'm not with him. You could say I am well and truly against him."

A glimmer of relief shone in the man's eyes. This bearded stranger didn't seem like one of the Black Lord's people, the gray-haired man thought. After all, the man had revived him and given him water, which was not what he would expect from one of the interlopers on the plateau. Of course, he had also belted him over the back of the head and sent him sprawling, which was *exactly* what he'd expect.

"Who are you?" he asked eventually, having processed these conflicting thoughts.

"My name is Halt. I'm a King's Ranger."

The man frowned. The word *Ranger* rang a bell, touched a chord of memory within him. In another life, he'd known that Rangers were men to be trusted—treated with a certain amount of reserve, mind you, but trusted nevertheless.

"A Ranger," he repeated vaguely.

Halt nodded. He thought that perhaps he might offer a comforting smile, but such an expression wasn't in his repertoire and he had the good sense to know that if he attempted one, he would end up looking something like a gargoyle. Hardly a reassuring sight.

"That's right," he said agreeably. "And who are you?"

The man swallowed several times, wondering if he would put himself at a disadvantage by revealing his identity. Then he apparently decided that he wouldn't.

"My name is Norman," he said. "I'm the hermit of these mountains."

10

"The carriage is ready, Lord Crowley."

Sir Athol was an earnest young man, who took his responsibility as head of the men-at-arms in the Queen's escort very seriously indeed. He regarded Crowley with a deep respect that bordered on awe. After the rescue of King Duncan and the events at Castle Gorlan the year before, Crowley and his partner, Halt, had gained legendary status in the Kingdom.

Crowley was finishing a light breakfast in the main dining hall. He looked up at the young face and smiled. "I'm no lord. Just Crowley will do fine if you want to get my attention."

Sir Athol shifted his feet awkwardly. "That doesn't seem sufficiently respectful, sir." A thought occurred as he said the last word. "Perhaps I could call you Sir Crowley?"

The Ranger shook his head. "I'm no knight, and that's a knight's title," he replied. "If you want to call me something, how about Ranger Crowley? That's what I am, after all."

Sir Athol considered the suggestion and nodded. It seemed sufficiently respectful. He was loath to simply call the Ranger by his first name.

"Very well, Ranger Crowley," he said, trying the mode of address and finding it satisfactory. "The carriage is ready in the courtyard."

"Let's take a look at it then." Crowley finished the last of his coffee, set down his mug and rose, taking his longbow from the tabletop beside him. He led the way out of the main hall to the entrance and descended the three steps to the courtyard.

The carriage was drawn up outside the entrance. Two gray Percherons were harnessed to its traces. He knew they had been specially selected by the Castle Araluen horse master for their smooth, matched gait. They would provide the Queen with the most comfortable ride possible.

The carriage was something new. It had been built on the framework of a normal cart. But instead of being rigidly fastened to the axles and frames, it was suspended from them by thick straps of leather, drawn tight to absorb the bumps and lurches of the rough country roads they would be traveling. Crowley unlatched a side door and looked inside. The seats were thickly padded and there were canvas blinds on the windows to keep out dust, cold weather, rain and prying eyes. On the right-hand side, a set of brackets had been installed to hold the litter that the Queen would use.

He shoved against the side of the carriage, setting it rocking back and forth against the suspension straps. It moved easily and he pursed his lips.

"Wouldn't like to travel in this at any speed," he muttered. But then, he thought, they would be traveling slowly of necessity. The Queen's condition meant that speed would be subjugated to comfort and smoothness on this journey, and the leather straps should do a good job absorbing the bumps and jerks as the carriage rolled along. He shut the door and latched it, then turned to Sir Athol.

"Let the Queen's party know we're ready to move," he said. "And summon the rest of the escort."

He looked up at the dark sky, pulling his cloak closer around him. It was chilly in the predawn, and he estimated that daybreak was two hours away. That was fine. He wanted to draw as little attention as possible to their departure from Castle Araluen. The queen's leaving had been kept a strict secret. Aside from Sir Athol, even the members of the bodyguard hadn't been told who they were escorting, although he expected that the more intelligent ones among them might have guessed.

But the carriage, with its unusual design and fittings, was obviously a conveyance for someone of high rank or riches, and since the roads were unsafe and bands of brigands roamed the countryside—a legacy of the chaos Morgarath's rebellion had caused in the Kingdom—the fewer people who knew that it had originated from the castle, the better. He wanted to be well on the way and into the cover of the trees before the sun rose.

The five archers and ten men-at-arms formed up in the courtyard with a clatter of hooves. Horses stamped the flagstones and sent plumes of steam from their nostrils as they snorted, eager to be on their way. Without appearing to, Crowley inspected the men and their equipment and nodded to himself. Each archer wore a full quiver of arrows over his shoulder and held his longbow across the saddle bow, already strung. The hilts of their short swords and daggers were visible at their waists, and a small round shield—leather over a wooden frame—was lashed to the back of each saddle.

The men-at-arms all wore chain-mail shirts under their

tunics, and their legs were protected by metal greaves from the knees down. Their swords were longer and heavier than those carried by the archers, and their shields were kite shaped and metal clad. Each man wore a helmet with a mail aventail protecting his shoulders and neck. And each one carried a long spear that, in a pinch, would serve as a lance.

There was a bustle of movement at the door of the keep tower, and the Queen's party emerged, accompanied by the King. Queen Rosalind was being carried by four servants on a thickly cushioned litter, with blankets and furs pulled up around her chin to ward off the predawn chill. She was very pale—her complexion was waxen and there were dark shadows under her eyes. Duncan strode beside her, his eyes fixed on her face, holding her hand in both of his. His look of concern was all too obvious, and he spoke softly to her as they moved toward the carriage.

She saw Crowley, and her drawn, tired features were transformed by a luminous smile. She rose against her pillows and beckoned him closer as the litter bearers paused beside the carriage.

"Crowley," she said, holding out her hand to him. "My very favorite Ranger."

She was all too aware of the role Crowley had played in foiling Morgarath's plan to discredit her husband and usurp the throne.

Crowley took the hand and bowed over it, bringing it to his lips.

"Your majesty," he said. "If you're ready, we'll get you settled and be on the road."

"Whatever you say, Crowley." She smiled. Then he relinquished her hand and nodded to the litter bearers to set the stretcher in place inside the carriage. The King put a hand on Crowley's shoulder and drew him aside.

"Take care of her, Crowley," he said. "You're one of only two men I'd trust her life to."

Crowley nodded reassuringly. "I'll guard her with my life, your majesty."

Duncan looked long and hard into his eyes. He had to look down as Crowley was considerably shorter than he was. After a long pause, he nodded.

"I couldn't ask for more," he said quietly. Then he turned away and stepped to the side of the carriage, leaning in the open window to say his final farewells to his wife. Crowley withdrew a few paces to give them privacy.

After several minutes, the King stepped back from the carriage and caught Crowley's eye. The Ranger nodded at the unspoken command.

"Sir Athol!" he called. "We'll move out." He placed his foot in Cropper's stirrup and swung up into the saddle as Athol called commands to the small force.

The order of march had been determined in the previous days as they planned this journey. Two of the archers went first, their horses' hooves clattering on the cobbles as they trotted out under the portcullis, then thudding on the wood of the drawbridge. The archers would ride ahead, staying three or four hundred meters in advance to scout the way. Five of the men-at-arms followed them, then the carriage, followed by the other five mounted soldiers. The remaining three archers would follow as a rearguard, staying several hundred meters behind the rest of the party. Crowley and Sir Athol positioned themselves on either side of the carriage.

They clattered across the drawbridge and onto the road that led down through the parklands to the forest. As the carriage crossed the drawbridge, Crowley noted that it made far less noise than a normal cart. Unlike the solid wheels of most carts, the carriage had been fitted with spoked wheels, bound with iron tires. They were more flexible than the solid, heavy circles of oak that were normally used and provided a smoother, quieter ride.

They were halfway down the sloping path that led to the dark mass of trees at the foot of the hill. Castle Araluen, like most castles, was built at the top of a rise to make life more difficult for attacking forces. Crowley turned in his saddle and looked back at the beautiful building, with its graceful spires and soaring buttresses silhouetted against the starlit sky. The world around them was silent. In an hour or so, the birds would begin their dawn chorus that would herald another day. But for now they were sleeping.

There were a few lights in the upper windows of the castle, but for the most part it was dark. He could see a small cluster of figures still at the massive gateway to the castle. One stood a little apart from the others. It was Duncan, staring after his Queen.

Crowley knew he would be there until long after the cavalcade vanished into the shadow of the trees.

The sun had risen, although here in the forest it wasn't quite so evident as it would have been in the open fields. As it rose higher and began to flood down onto the narrow forest road, the temperature rose and cloaks were taken off, rolled and tied behind the saddles.

Crowley retained his. The mottled gray-green garment was integral to a Ranger, as far as he was concerned.

In the confined space on this narrow forest road, he and Athol were riding slightly behind the carriage. He nudged Cropper to ride up next to it. He glanced in the window. The curtain had been rolled up. Two of Rosalind's ladies-in-waiting—close friends and trusted confidantes—were traveling in the carriage with the Queen, and one of them smiled at him through the open window.

"How is the Queen managing?" he asked. They had been on the road for three hours and soon they would have to find somewhere to stop and eat.

The woman glanced across at the Queen on the litter beside her, then reassured Crowley.

"She's sleeping," she said. "She's quite comfortable."

Crowley nodded. That was good to hear. Obviously, the carriage's newfangled suspension was working efficiently, smoothing out the roughness of the road.

"Let me know if she needs anything," he said. The woman nodded and he put gentle pressure on the reins, letting Cropper know that he should slow down and drop back to their original position.

Sir Athol gave him an inquiring glance and Crowley smiled. "They seem to be fine," he said. "The Queen's sleeping."

Sir Athol yawned. It had been an early start and he had slept badly the night before, nervous about the responsibilities he would face on the journey.

"Wish I could join her," he said, then immediately went red as a beetroot as he realized how that statement could be misconstrued. "I mean . . . I didn't . . . I mean to say . . . ," he gabbled.

Crowley leaned over and put a hand on his arm. "Relax. I know what you mean."

Gradually, Athol's face regained its normal shade and he made a bitter mental note to always, *always* think before speaking in future. Then he realized that Crowley wasn't paying him any attention. He had edged Cropper out to the roadside, and was peering ahead of the carriage. As he noted this, Athol became aware of the sound of galloping hooves up ahead.

"Come on," said Crowley, and he urged Cropper forward, overtaking the carriage and moving to the head of the column.

One of the two forward scouts was reining in his horse as they came closer. Athol and Crowley rode closer to the scout.

"Ranger Crowley," the man said. His tone was urgent but he had the sense to keep his voice low. "We've spotted a band of brigands up ahead. They look like they're planning to ambush the carriage."

11

HALT REGARDED THE THIN, RAGGED FIGURE WITH NEW interest.

"How long have you been living up here?" he asked. Norman's expression became vague as he tried to answer. He frowned and finally spoke.

"Dunno," he said. "Must be five years or more. I came up here after the big floods in the Mossback Valley. My house was washed away. It was the third time I'd been flooded, but before then, the house had been all right. I thought I'd head for higher ground."

It was Halt's turn to frown as he heard this. Pritchard had told him of the Mossback Valley floods. They had been the worst natural disaster in the southeast corner of Araluen in living memory.

"But that must have been eleven years ago, not five," he said.

Norman nodded casually. "If you say. Been here a long time, anyways."

"And the Wargals didn't bother you?" Halt asked.

A bitter look came over Norman's face. "Wargals was no problem. They was a peaceful folk then. Have been right up until the Black Lord took control of them. Not saying we was friends, mind you. They was shy, and they avoided contact with me. Kept themselves to themselves, and so long as I did the same, things was fine. But they was never no threat to me before."

"What about now?" Halt asked. He lowered himself to the sandy ground and sat cross-legged in front of the older man.

"The Black Lord knows I'm here," Norman said. "He doesn't want anyone spying on him or seeing what he's up to. So he set the Wargals after me to hunt me down and kill me." He shrugged angrily. "I'm not interested in spying on him, mind. Live and let live is my motto. But that doesn't seem to be the way he thinks."

"So how did you avoid them?" Halt asked, and Norman's anger was replaced by a cunning smile.

"I knows the land," he said. "I knows every path through the rocks, every cave, every tunnel, every blind canyon." He swept his arms around the bleak landscape. "These rocks and mountains are riddled with tunnels and caves and I've spent years studying them. I can come and go as I please and even the Wargals can't track me.

"Eventually, the Black Lord realized that trying to catch me was a waste of his time and gave it away. Mind you," he added seriously, "I still don't take any chances with the Wargals. I steer well clear of them. Once an idea like that has been put in their heads, they'll keep on with it."

In the background, the rhythmic grunting and foot stamping had been continuing. Now, suddenly, it stopped. Norman looked quickly at the position of the watery sun in the sky and frowned.

"They're finished early," he said. "That's not a good thing. They may have got wind of the fact that we're here."

"How would that have happened?" Halt asked.

Norman shook his head emphatically. "I never stop to ask that question. Stopping is the way to get caught. The Black Lord has lookouts in the mountains above his base. Maybe they saw us moving in the rocks." He paused. "Not me, mind you. But if you didn't know they was there, you might have been spotted."

Halt raised an eyebrow. When they were on the move, Rangers weren't "spotted," as Norman put it. But the drill session on the open plain had definitely stopped and perhaps the hermit was right. It was time for them to move.

He glanced in the direction of the field where the Wargals had been drilling. "We're wasting time. Best we get out of here now."

They moved at a brisk pace through the tumbled rocks and trackless land, zigzagging between the larger outcrops, sometimes climbing over the lower ones. At Norman's insistence, they moved in a half crouch, seeking cover from the rocks and groves of stunted trees as they went, and angling away from the drill field and the mountain where Morgarath had his base.

On two occasions, the ragged hermit led Halt into tunnels beneath the larger rocks. They sloped down, and the two men could see by virtue of a dim light that filtered through cracks in the rock ceiling overhead. The tunnels twisted and turned, and there were numerous side trails and forks in their path. But Norman seemed to know unerringly where they had to go.

On both occasions, when the tunnels returned to ground level, he would pause and scout ahead, peering cautiously round the tunnel entrance to make sure the way was clear. Then he would scamper off, threading his way through the narrow spaces between the rocks. There seemed to be no rhyme or reason to the zigzag path that he took, but he never hesitated. He was obviously following a trail that only he could see.

Eventually, they arrived at a rock wall—a sheer face of granite that towered nearly forty meters above them. The rock face appeared to be blank, and Halt hesitated, puzzled. Norman grinned at him and motioned for him to follow, leading the way to where a section of the granite stood out like a solid buttress from the cliff. Mystified, Halt followed him as he made his way down the edge of the buttress, then suddenly disappeared from sight.

When Halt reached the spot where his guide had disappeared, he saw a narrow split in the rock, invisible until you were virtually upon it. It was less than a meter wide and he stepped sideways through it, to discover a grinning Norman waiting for him in a cavern that opened up behind the narrow opening.

"This is my cave," he said, gesturing for Halt to come farther inside.

Halt stared about the cavern in wonder. It was massive. A large sandy level space stretched out on both sides, forming the floor. In the distant shadows, he could see a curved rock wall, forming a semicircle. There were several dark holes, entrances to other tunnels leading away from this main gallery.

The ceiling soared high above them, and there were gaps in what was obviously the granite wall that they had faced outside. Daylight filtered through these, illuminating the cavern with a soft, diffuse light.

"So this is where you live?" Halt said, staring about him. But Norman snickered and grabbed his sleeve, tugging him toward one of the tunnel entrances.

"No. Not here! I live through here. Come and see!"

The tunnel was dark and constricting after the light of the huge cavern. Halt followed Norman blindly as it twisted and turned, then he saw more light ahead and finally the tunnel opened into another cavern. It was smaller than the first, but still roomy and well lit. High-set cracks in the walls and ceiling allowed light to enter as in the larger cavern. Halt could see the stones of a fireplace arranged against one wall and, a few meters away, a bedroll and a rough camp chair, constructed from twisted tree limbs, with a canvas seat. Several blackened pots and pans were ranged in a line beside the fireplace, and a large wooden bucket stood a few meters away. Halt heard water trickling and looked closer. A spring ran down one side of the cavern, culminating in a shallow rock pool, then draining away as the pool filled and overflowed into the crevices and cracks in the rock floor below it.

He looked up again, studying the network of narrow apertures in the ceiling. Smoke from the fire would be dispersed through there, he thought. With so many ways for it to exit, it would be virtually invisible from the outside.

"What do you live on?" he asked, still looking about in wonder.

"Coneys and birds mainly," Norman answered. "Plenty of plovers in the rocks hereabouts. And I trap the coneys. Plenty of them too."

Coneys were rabbits, Halt knew. "You can't live just on rabbits," he said. Rabbit flesh was too lean to sustain life over a long period, although he supposed the plovers would provide the necessary fat and minerals that were missing from rabbit meat.

Norman jerked a thumb upward. "Got me a small vegetable

garden up on the cliffs," he said. "I grows greens and turnips and potatoes there. Keep myself well fed."

"I'm sure you do," Halt replied, still looking around, taking stock of his surroundings. It was a remarkable place, he thought. Roomy, airy and sheltered. And well hidden.

"And Morgarath has never managed to find you?" he asked.

Norman sneered. "He won't stir himself to look for me. Guess he figures I'm beneath him. He knows I'm somewhere on the plateau but he's learned to leave me alone. His Wargals can never find me. He set them after me a few times. But I always managed to give them the slip. These days, he doesn't bother with me. Knows I'm here somewhere, but doesn't have the time or energy to find me."

"That may change if he realizes I'm here," Halt said. "He hates me like poison."

Norman shrugged. "No way he's going to know about you," he said comfortably. "Just stay here nice and cozy and stay out of his way. You're welcome to whatever I have."

"That's kind of you," Halt said, and he meant it. "But I can't stay cooped up in here. I have to find out what he's up to—what he's planning. And I need to know more about these Wargals that he has working for him."

Norman shook his head warningly. "You go traipsing around these mountains on your own and spying on him, you'll come to no good," he said. "I know these rocks and tunnels and caves like the back of my hand. And the Wargals have lived up here for hundreds of years, far as I know. But you—you'd be a novice out there." He gestured vaguely toward the far cavern and the entrance. "You go out there snooping around and you'll be seen. And once they see you they'll come after you."

"I understand that," Halt said. "I was hoping you might help me—guide me if you like."

Norman shook his head. "Not me. Why would I want to stir up a hornet's nest just to satisfy your curiosity?"

Halt spread his hands in a deprecating gesture. "Well, you might want to get rid of Morgarath—the Black Lord," he corrected himself.

But Norman snorted dismissively. "He don't bother me. Can't find me for a start. Let well enough alone, I say."

Halt looked at the old hermit but Norman wouldn't meet his eyes. He was staring into the ashes of his fireplace. The Ranger decided to try another tack.

"Maybe you'd help me because Morgarath is planning to start a rebellion in the Kingdom and seize the throne," he said. But again Norman remained looking into the ashes and again he shook his head.

"No worry of mine if he does," he said. "He takes over the Kingdom, he won't be staying up here, will he? He'll be back in the lower country, living in a fine castle."

"Well," said Halt, "I guess I'll have to just see for myself."

This time, Norman looked up and met his gaze. The watery blue eyes were deadly serious.

"You do that, they'll kill you, sure as anything," he said.

12

CROWLEY RUBBED HIS CHIN THOUGHTFULLY. HE WASN'T altogether surprised to hear that an ambush had been laid ahead of them. The carriage was obviously an expensive vehicle and, as such, it would carry a wealthy passenger.

And the roads in Araluen were still unsafe and afflicted by bands of robbers and brigands. In the few years, the rule of law throughout the Kingdom had suffered badly, and Duncan was yet to restore it.

Exacerbating the situation was Morgarath's having weakened the Ranger Corps so badly. The Rangers would normally have led the way in keeping down such robber bands. It was one of the main priorities in Crowley's reorganization of the Corps, but so far, he didn't have the numbers of Rangers necessary to carry out the program.

Athol made a gesture down the road in the direction from which the archer had ridden and spoke in a low voice to Crowley. "Do you think these brigands know that the Queen is traveling with us?"

Crowley shook his head. "It's possible. There are spies everywhere these days. But I doubt it. Not that it matters overmuch.

They'll know that anyone in a carriage like this will be a worthwhile target."

He caught the coachman's eye and gave him a signal to halt, pointing to a small cleared space beside the road where he should take the carriage. The little cavalcade came to a stop.

Crowley turned to the scout who had brought the warning to them. "Tell me," he said, "what did you see?"

"About ten minutes ago, we heard a horse galloping on the road, coming up from behind us. It was a scout for the robbers. He went past us and a little farther down the road. That's when we saw his comrades. They rode out of the trees and he alerted them that a carriage was coming."

"Did he see you?"

"No, sir. We were riding off the road, making our way through the trees to avoid being seen. He went straight past us without a second glance. We listened to him making his report and then we withdrew fifty meters back down the road. The robbers deployed to either side. They're waiting in the trees for the carriage to come level."

"How many?" Crowley asked.

"Fifteen or sixteen," the archer told him.

Crowley inclined his head thoughtfully. The spy had seen the carriage, so he would also have seen the size of the escort. If sixteen robbers were willing to attack a force of ten men-at-arms, they must have a lot of confidence in their ability. Still, they would assume they had surprise on their side. A shower of spears from either side of the road could take down half the escort. Then a rapid charge while the remainder were confused and disorganized would probably give them a quick and easy victory.

But now their prey had been warned, the element of surprise

would be against them. He thought quickly. The Queen's health dictated that she shouldn't be put under any stress or danger. Therefore he would have to deal with these brigands where they were, avoiding any direct attack on the carriage.

"Stay here," he told Athol, "and deploy your men around the carriage in a screen, just in case these bandits get past us."

"What are you going to do?" Athol asked.

Crowley pointed down the road. "I'm going back with young Donald here"—he knew the names of all five archers, a sign of a good commander—"to discourage them."

"Just three of you?" Athol said. "Let me come with you. You might be able to use an extra sword."

But Crowley shook his head. "I don't plan on letting them get within sword's reach," he said. "Three of us should be able to manage that. But when the other two archers catch up, send them forward to help us."

He saw the lady-in-waiting he had spoken to earlier. She was looking out the window of the carriage, trying to catch his eye. He trotted Cropper over to the vehicle.

"Yes, Lady Ingrid?"

"The Queen wants to know why we've stopped," Ingrid said. "Is there a problem?"

Crowley leaned down in his saddle to look into the carriage. On the far side, propped up on the litter, he could see that the Queen was awake. Her pale face stood out in the dim interior of the carriage.

"No problem, my lady," Crowley said, with a reassuring grin. "Just some business on the road ahead that we need to take care of. Nothing for you to worry about."

But Rosalind was no fool. She knew that they wouldn't have

stopped for anything trivial and she knew the situation on the roads in Araluen as well as Crowley did.

"Be careful, Crowley," she said, her voice barely carrying to him where he sat astride Cropper beside the carriage. "I don't want to lose you. My husband needs you."

His grin widened. "I don't plan on being lost, my lady," he said. He nodded his head toward the young knight a few meters behind him. "Sir Athol will take care of things here. I'll be back in a few minutes."

"Make sure you are," she said, then, obviously exhausted by the effort of conversing, she sank back among the cushions of her litter, her eyes closing.

Crowley glanced round at Athol. "Make sure she's safe," he said quietly. The young knight turned in his saddle and began calling commands to his men in a lowered tone, positioning them in a screen around the carriage and its passenger.

"Let's go, Donald," Crowley said to the archer, and the two of them set their heels to their horses and cantered away down the road. After sixty or seventy meters, Donald held up a warning hand and they slowed to a trot. There was no sense in warning the enemy of their approach. They were coming to a sharp turn in the road, where it veered left to avoid a massive oak. Crowley saw the dim shape of the second archer waiting in its shadows. He rode close to the other man, who gave him an informal salute.

"William," he said in greeting. "What's the situation?"

The scout pointed with his bow down the road. "They're about forty meters that way," he said. "They're concealed in the trees either side of the road, but if you look carefully you can see them."

Crowley leaned down in his saddle and peered along the road, under the overhanging branches of the oak.

"Just by that blackened stump," William said, and now Crowley could make out slight movement in the shadows of the trees.

"They're probably wondering where the carriage is," Donald said.

Crowley nodded. It had been several minutes since Donald had ridden back to warn them, and they'd taken several more to get the carriage off the road and ride back to where William was keeping an eye on the outlaw band.

"Let's not keep them waiting," Crowley said, and urged Cropper out from under the trees and toward the bend in the road. "Bows ready," he said over his shoulder. But there was no need for the command. These were experienced men, seasoned fighters. Their bows were always ready.

He drew an arrow from his quiver and laid it on the bow, nocking it automatically, without needing to look. He rode out into the open, rounding the bend and facing the forty meters of straight road that led to the spot where the bandits were hidden. William and Donald rode with him, a few paces behind him. As they came onto the road, they spread out a few meters on either side, and all three halted their horses, keeping them at an angle so their way was clear to shoot.

Crowley heard a startled exclamation from the trees ahead. Then silence.

"Show yourselves!" he ordered. "We know you're there."

For a long moment, nothing happened. Then there was a rustle of movement in the trees and the bandits emerged onto the road. They were mounted on a mixed assortment of horses:

some of them shaggy farm ponies; some horses they had clearly stolen from wealthier victims. And they bore an equally assorted range of weapons and armor. Spears, of course, and axes, swords and clubs. Some had chain-mail shirts and others were protected by leather vests sewn with bronze plates, shaped like scales. None of them would be any protection against an arrow shot from an eighty-pound longbow.

The man at the front, presumably their leader, wore a pot-shaped helmet with a fringe of mail hanging down behind to protect his neck. He carried a long two-handed sword, although Crowley doubted that he knew how to use it properly. Long-swords required a great deal of strength and practice.

The bandit brandished it clumsily over his head. "Throw down your weapons!" he commanded.

Obviously, the bandits had decided they had little to fear from three lightly armed and unarmored archers. Archers, in their limited experience, were cowards—they would slink onto a battlefield, loose a few arrows, then dash to safety behind the armored lines of their armies.

"I think that's what I want *you* to do," Crowley said pleasantly. "I'll count to five and I want to see all those weapons on the road." He turned quickly to his two companions and said in lowered tones, "Shoot on four. Aim to wound if you can, but if you're not sure, just hit them anywhere. I'll take the leader."

The two archers grunted agreement. Crowley began to count.

"One. Two. Three. Four . . ."

And as he said four, he whipped his bow up, drew, sighted and shot in a heartbeat. William and Donald shot a fraction of a second after him.

Crowley's arrow hit the bandit leader in the upper part of his right arm, the force of the arrow spinning him sideways and throwing him out of the saddle. He dropped the longsword as he fell, landing awkwardly across it. He tried to rise to his feet, but the shock and the intense pain in his arm made his knees weak and he collapsed back into the dust.

William's shot hit another bandit in the thigh. The man screamed and his horse reared, throwing him. Donald's target moved at the last moment and the arrow, aimed for his shoulder, thudded into his chest. He reeled back over his horse's rump and crashed to the road and lay still.

In the time that the two archers' targets took to hit the road, Crowley had loosed another three arrows in rapid succession. Every one found its mark, and three more bandits went down. Donald and William looked at the Ranger in wide-eyed admiration. They were good shots, but this level of speed and accuracy was something else entirely.

In a matter of a few seconds, the band had lost their leader and nearly half their companions, dead or wounded. The remainder were stunned for a few seconds. Then two of them gathered their reins to flee.

"Don't move!" Crowley's voice cracked out down the road. His bow was up again, an arrow on the string. The bandits froze where they were.

"Next man to move, I'll shoot," Crowley continued. He heard a muted clatter of hooves behind him and realized that the other three archers had joined them. That made things a lot easier, he thought. The numbers were more even now.

"Throw down your weapons," he ordered. The bandits hesitated, and without warning, Crowley shot again, putting an arrow through the arm of one of the men who looked most reluctant to obey. Like his leader, the bandit was hurled sideways and lost his seat on his horse. He crashed to the ground with a cry of pain, dropping the heavy spear he had been holding in the process.

Almost before the bandits could register that Crowley had shot, he had another arrow nocked, and his gaze moved across them, seeking his next target, the arrowhead following the direction of his eyes.

There was a loud clatter as a shower of spears, axes, swords and daggers were tossed to the road.

"Now dismount and lie facedown," Crowley ordered.

The outlaws didn't hesitate. They were covered now by six longbows and they had seen that these men hit what they aimed at—particularly the one in the gray cloak, who didn't seem to need to aim at all.

Crowley urged Cropper forward, crabbing the horse so he could keep the bandits covered. The five archers followed suit. They were experienced warriors and they fanned out, making sure that each of them had room to shoot and a clear line of sight to the bandits. The small group stopped a few meters from the would-be ambushers.

"Move again, green cap," Crowley warned, "and I'll put an arrow through your backside."

One of the bandits, on the fringe of the group, had been moving surreptitiously toward the shallow ditch at the side of the road. Now he hastily dropped his nose into the dirt and remained still.

"Donald, William, take the horses' bridles and let the horses loose," Crowley ordered, and the two archers slid from their saddles and hurried to obey. Within a few minutes, the horses, urged on by hearty slaps on their rumps and shouts from the two warriors, were cantering off down the road.

Crowley now urged his horse toward a group of four bandits.

"Sit up," he ordered and the men warily rolled over and sat in the dust. "Now strip."

"Strip?" one of them said, and the arrow moved to train itself on his face.

"Strip. Lose your clothes. I want you naked as the day you were born," the Ranger told them. When they had complied, he nodded to the two dismounted archers. "Tie them up," he said. "Use the bridles and tie them back to back."

Grinning, the archers followed his orders. The former bandits were cowed under the threat of four longbows, and the certainty that if the Ranger shot, one of them would be dead.

Then Crowley repeated the order with another seven of the bandits, stripping them and lashing them back to back in two big circles on the side of the road. The rest of the band didn't need tying. They were already beyond escape. When that was done, he had his men gather up the weapons that littered the road, and the bandits' boots.

"Go and bring up the carriage now," he told William and, as the young archer turned away, he added, "Tell our passenger to roll down the window blind. This lot don't make a pretty sight."

13

⁂

THEY ATE BEFORE THE DAYLIGHT HAD FADED COMPLETELY. Norman built a small fire of tinder-dry wood that was virtually smokeless, waited till the flames died down and heated an iron pot of rabbit stew over the coals.

The food was delicious, although Halt found himself wishing that Norman had access to some salt. But the rabbit joints and turnips and greens were hot and nourishing. When they had eaten, Halt produced his small sack of coffee beans and offered some to the hermit.

Norman shook his head suspiciously. "Water is fine."

Halt shrugged, filled the kettle with the pure water from the spring in the wall and set it in the coals to boil. "Your loss," he said.

He made a small pot of coffee and sat back, resting his back against a convenient boulder, legs stretched out to the glowing coals of the fire, and sipped contentedly. They sat in silence for some minutes, then Norman began to fidget and move restlessly. Halt watched him calmly. The older man had something on his mind. Eventually, he gathered his resolve and spoke.

"Been thinkin'," he said. "T'ain't fair to let you blunder around the plateau on your own. You'll be spotted, sure as life."

Halt said nothing. He was confident in his own ability to move about without being seen. He had been doing so for years, after all. Norman, despite his bravado, was a different matter, he thought. He knew the land intimately and could lose any pursuit in the twisted, unmarked trails and tunnels among the rocks. But as for remaining unseen in the first place, Halt believed Norman was overestimating his own ability. After all, Halt had spotted him easily earlier that day, when Norman had been trailing him. The older man didn't seem to grasp one of the absolute fundamentals of remaining unseen—stillness. He had moved when Halt turned to look in his direction and that movement had given him away.

Halt suspected that the hermit was often seen by Morgarath and his henchmen as he moved among the rocks. But he presented no danger to them, and for the moment they had decided not to bother with him. Occasionally, a patrol of Wargals might come upon him and pursue him. And then, his intimate knowledge of the land stood him in good stead, allowing him to shake off any pursuit.

But if he were as skilled at remaining unseen as he thought he was, there would have been no need to evade pursuit in the first place.

"What's changed your mind?" Halt asked. Norman had been adamant that he wouldn't help when they had discussed the matter earlier.

The gray-haired man shifted uncomfortably. Then he replied.

"You go blundering about out there and they're likely to see you," he said. "The Black Lord has patrols out all the time."

"They never spot you," Halt said, although he doubted that was accurate.

Norman nodded agreement. "I know how to move," he said. "I know how to keep hidden." Halt couldn't stop one eyebrow from rising incredulously. He was tempted to remind the man that he hadn't seen Halt while the Ranger had doubled back behind him, stalked him and knocked him out. But he didn't want to insult him. He could use his help. Halt had no way of backtracking through the bewildering maze of tunnels and gullies they had passed through to get to the cave. Without Norman's guidance, he'd have to return to the edge of the escarpment and retrace his original route from there to the drill field.

"Thing is," Norman said, finally deciding to come clean, "if they see you, you'll probably lead them back to my cave here, and I can't have that."

"Ah," Halt said, understanding. Norman's decision was based on self-interest and self-preservation, not on a newfound desire to help his uninvited guest.

"In that case, I'd welcome your assistance. And I'll try not to be too noticeable." He added the last few words with a hint of a smile. Norman, however, failed to notice. Irony wasn't his strong suit, Halt decided.

"What can you tell me about the Wargals?" he asked.

Norman frowned as he considered his answer. "They're simple creatures, and once they get set on a course of action, they'll carry it through regardless of what gets in the way. The Black Lord has turned them into ruthless killers. Nothing will stop them. Or rather, they won't stop no matter what. If the Black Lord wants them to, they'll just keep attacking and attacking, no matter how many of them are killed. They are utterly fearless."

"How does he control them?" Halt asked. He hadn't heard any orders being issued while the Wargals were drilling earlier in the day.

Norman shook his head. "That's the strange part," he said. "Seems they can read his mind—and he can read theirs."

"How do you know this?" Halt asked.

"I heard two of his men talking about it. I was hunting one day and they nearly spotted me. I just had time to hide behind some rocks while they settled down for a rest on the other side. They were saying how eerie it was that he could just think what he wanted them to do and they'd do it." Norman shuddered at the thought. It seemed almost supernatural to him. "They were also talking about how the Wargals are unstoppable once he gives them a task."

Halt stroked his beard thoughtfully. In his travels, he'd seen many mountebanks and charlatans in fairs, who claimed to be able to read minds and send mental messages. The vast majority could be exposed as fakes and tricksters. But there was a small percentage where the feat couldn't be explained. Maybe some people did have that ability, he thought. If Norman was right and Morgarath really did have the power to control his Wargals this way, it was startling news. Then a thought occurred to him.

"While we were watching today, I thought I . . . felt something—as if someone was trying to speak to me."

"Ah, you felt it, did you? I used to feel that all the time. It's

Morgarath. He's sending them a message and you can sense it. These days, I hardly notice it anymore. I've taught myself to ignore it."

"How many Wargals does he have?" Halt asked.

Norman considered the question. "Must be eight or nine hundred."

Halt whistled softy. Eight or nine hundred of these fearless, implacable monsters. That would be a dangerous army to face. And of course, Morgarath also had between one and two hundred human troops.

Duncan's small standing army, by comparison, barely numbered two hundred and fifty. Of course, there were levies that he could bring in from the fiefs to swell the numbers in the short term. But they were farmers and yeomen for the most part, not trained soldiers. And he couldn't hold on to them indefinitely. There were crops to sow and harvest. The time they would spend in his army was a short one.

"I think I need to get a closer look at these monsters," he said. "We'll do it in the morning." The sooner he could gather intelligence on Morgarath's army, the sooner he, Duncan and Crowley could begin figuring out a way to beat them.

Midmorning the following day found them crouched among the rocks at the edge of the cleared drill field once more.

Several companies of Wargals were drilling in a different part of the field. Some engaged in mock combat, using wooden staffs to replace their vicious, short spears. The crack of wood on wood rang across the field.

Others practiced a steady advance to within a hundred

meters of their objective, crouching low behind their shields as some of Morgarath's men peppered them with arrows. At the set moment, the Wargals rose from their crouched position and charged. They were clumsy and heavily built but they moved with deceptive speed. Halt noticed that they often used their long arms and hands to keep their balance on the ground.

He also noticed that, the minute they charged, the archers quickly withdrew to one side. Perhaps, he thought, they didn't totally trust their inhuman allies.

All in all, it was a disquieting sight. The Wargals were powerful and fast moving. And they were disciplined, moving together in formation, each one working in conjunction with those on either side of him.

They had been observing for twenty minutes when Norman's hand closed over his forearm and he pointed to one side.

A black-clad figure on a dead-white horse was trotting slowly onto the drill field, flanked by two other riders.

"The Black Lord," Norman whispered.

Halt's eyes narrowed as he watched that hated figure. Visions of Pritchard lying still and pale at the entrance to the tunnel from Castle Gorlan filled his mind. He wanted to send an arrow speeding across the drill field and into the former Baron's heart, and his hand actually dropped to the quiver at his belt.

But the range was too great. And then the moment was gone as Morgarath turned his horse and cantered back into the compound at the foot of the cliffs. His two companions remained on the drill field, observing the Wargals and riding in a large circle around the edge of the open ground.

As they neared one group, the iron discipline of the Wargals faltered and they edged closer together, moving away from the two riders.

Norman pointed. "See that? They don't like horses."

Halt frowned. That was interesting. "Why not?"

The hermit shrugged. "Dunno. Maybe something happened in the past. Maybe it's because they haven't seen too many horses before. But they always shy away when the horses get close. I've seen the Black Lord try to drill that out of them, but so far, he hasn't managed completely. Time was they'd break and run if a horse got anywhere near 'em. That's why he has his men ride around them when they're drilling."

Halt watched, fascinated, as the Wargals slowly regained their discipline. The two riders, their task completed, edged their horses away from the first group and cantered toward the line of rocks where Halt and Norman were hiding. Apparently, they would ride in a long circle around the parade ground, approaching individual groups of Wargals to let them overcome their distaste for the strange four-legged creatures.

He felt Norman stir beside him and looked round to see the shabby hermit was rising from a crouch and turning away. He grabbed Norman's arm. The riders were only thirty meters away and they were bound to see any movement. His earlier doubts about Norman's skills were confirmed in a rush.

"What are you doing?" he hissed.

The old man tugged to get free. He was surprisingly strong. "They'll see us! We've got to get out of here!" he replied in a panicked whisper.

"They'll only see us if you move!" Halt warned him, then let out a sharp cry of pain as the old man smacked down on his forearm with a rock he'd seized from the ground nearby. Inadvertently, Halt lost his grip on the skinny arm and Norman bolted out of cover, running crouched among the rocks.

One of the riders shouted, pointing after the shaggy figure scampering through the rocks. The ground was too broken for the horses, but there was a platoon of Wargals not far away and they reacted to the shout and the pointing arm. With a concerted snarl, they started after the figure who had eluded them for so long.

Halt crouched in hiding, trying to figure out his best course of action. There were at least thirty Wargals, and he had only a dozen arrows in his quiver. He looked again after Norman's crouching figure as he flitted among the boulders and low trees, zigzagging furiously. The Wargals had spread out now among the rocks, forming a rough line, seeking to cut him off if he went either left or right. Halt's hopes rose as he saw that Norman was gaining on his pursuers.

Then the old man made the classic mistake. He looked back at the Wargals who were chasing him.

As he did, his foot landed on a large, uneven rock, which turned under his weight and sent him sprawling. He was up almost immediately, but the fall had twisted his ankle and it wouldn't bear his weight properly. It gave under him as he put his weight on it and he went sprawling again.

The Wargals snarled in triumph and redoubled their efforts. Halt could hear them barking and yipping like hounds as they closed in on the old man. Norman rose once more and hobbled away, trying to resume his flitting zigzag movement through the rocks. But the Wargals were closing in on him and he simply couldn't move fast enough. He stumbled once more, going down on one knee.

The lead pair were only a few meters away from him when Halt rose out of cover and his bow twanged twice in rapid succession.

The heavy arrows slammed into the bestial creatures. One died instantly. The other was hurled sideways by the force of the arrow strike. It snarled in agony, clawing at the arrow where it protruded from its side. The broadhead had smashed through the leather-and-plate armor that the Wargal wore and was buried deep in its torso. Death was only a few minutes away, but the Wargal continued to try to rise and reach Norman, who was now hauling himself upright once more, clinging to a boulder for support.

"It's a Ranger!" Halt heard the cry behind him and whirled about. One of the two riders was standing in his stirrups, pointing at him. He snapped off a shot and saw the man tumble from his saddle. The other immediately dropped to the ground, behind his horse.

Halt swung back to where Norman was now overwhelmed by the Wargal platoon. Halt heard the man's thin shriek of fear and pain, then the furry black creatures hid him from sight, their swords and spears rising and falling in a killing frenzy. He realized there was nothing he could do for the old man. And he was in imminent danger of being cut off from the cliff face that led down from the Mountains of Rain and Night.

He ran.

14

Norman's cries fell silent as Halt raced through the rocks for the cliff face and safety.

He could feel the uneven ground beneath his soft boots, felt rocks and stones turn underfoot, trying to bring him down. But somehow he retained his balance and ran, straining for more speed, careless of the uncertain footing and the risk of falling and injuring himself. He needed all the speed he could muster. He had to get past the Wargal line before they could cut him off from the cliff edge. He had his rope coiled round his shoulder and, if he could get a good enough lead and have time to tie it off in the rocks at the top of the cliff, he could make his escape by sliding down it.

Mentally, he took stock of how many arrows he had used so far. Two at the Wargals who had first reached the old man. And another to bring the rider down. That left nine arrows. And there were nearly thirty Wargals pursuing him.

Seeing a patch of clear ground ahead, he risked a quick glance over his shoulder to see where the Wargals were. He had gained on them. They were blundering clumsily through the rocks. They were not agile creatures and several had fallen and were limping in the rear, obviously injured.

He looked to his front again and just in time. There was a shallow gully some two meters across in front of him, filled with jagged, uneven rocks. He gathered himself and sprang over it, landing awkwardly and stumbling for a few paces. Momentarily, he was off balance, and he stretched his stride to regain his footing.

It was a mistake. By lengthening his stride, he threw himself further off balance, forcing him to increase his pace in an attempt to regain it. It was a vicious circle. The more he stretched, the faster he ran, the more he lost his balance. Finally, he could sustain it no longer. He went over. At the last moment, he let himself go and curled into a ball, rolling on one shoulder as he hit the ground, coming to his feet almost instantly. His shoulder throbbed with pain and there was a bloody graze on his cheek, but he ignored the injuries and ran, keeping a closer eye on the ground before him.

He needed to buy some time. It would take him several minutes to anchor his rope when he reached the cliff face. Making a decision, he slid to a stop, whirling to face his pursuers and whipping the bow from his shoulder.

His hands moved like lightning, plucking arrows from the quiver, nocking them and sending them on their way. In the space of ten seconds, he had dispatched six arrows and every one found its mark. The Wargals leading the charge after him went down, either dead or wounded. It was a devastating attack. The impact of the heavy arrows set them staggering before they fell. They screamed in anger and pain, or fell silently under the volley of shafts. In any other group, it would have caused panic and disruption, as the next in line saw that their turn was imminent and sought cover.

The Wargals continued without hesitation, charging past the fallen bodies of their comrades or, in several cases, bounding over them and actually treading on them and rolling them out of the way. Halt felt a thrill of fear as he faced these implacable enemies. He had two arrows left and he knew they wouldn't save him. Only speed could do that.

He turned and ran, redoubling his efforts, throwing caution to the winds and trusting to luck that he wouldn't stumble and fall. If he did, it would mean a horrible death at the hands of these snarling, yipping creatures.

Rocks turned underfoot. He slipped and stumbled several times but somehow managed to maintain his footing as he raced across the plateau.

Behind him, he could hear the snarling of the Wargals, and the sound of heavy bodies rushing after him. Several times he heard snarls of pain, followed by the sound of a body hitting the ground. The Wargals, he realized, were having just as much trouble as he was with the uneven surface.

He looked up. The rim of the plateau was in sight. To his right, he could see a solid-looking stunted tree a few meters from the cliff edge. He angled toward it. Fortunately, the Wargals were off to his left, so the change of direction gave him an additional lead. He estimated that they were sixty to seventy meters behind him. They were slower moving across the rock-strewn surface and weaving their way through the haphazard arrangement of boulders than he was. In their frenzy to catch him, they were bumping into one another and shouldering each other out of the way. It all served to slow them down and give him a greater lead.

He was a few meters short of the tree now. He unwrapped the rope from around his shoulders and passed it round the trunk of the tree. Then he took the two ends and crossed them behind his back, finally stepping over the doubled rope and bringing it up between his legs. He took a turn and a half around his right arm to give him control, then hastily backed over the rim of the cliff, paying out the rope as he went and pushing his body out over the abyss so that it was at right angles to the cliff face.

The Wargals were forty meters away when he pushed off from the cliff with his feet and allowed himself to drop eight meters or so, the rope burning as it passed around his right arm. He held it with his left hand to steady himself, then bounced out again, releasing more rope. He was now twenty meters down, with another twenty to go before he reached the wide ledge where he had rested on the way up. He glanced up and saw half a dozen brutish, snarling faces peering at him over the rim of the cliff. The rope shook as one of them grabbed it and tore at it with its fangs.

Halt let himself drop again. This time he went farther and faster, the rope burning even worse now on his arm, even through the thick sleeve of his jacket and his leather gauntlets, which protected him from the fast-sliding rope. A rock bounced off the cliff face to his right, just missing him. Then another.

He looked up again. The Wargal above had given up trying to bite through the rope. Instead, he had joined his companions in seizing rocks and stones and hurling them down the cliff at Halt.

If they had simply dropped the rocks, they would have had

better luck. But their hands and arms were clumsy and their efforts at throwing were inaccurate. The rocks cascaded past him. He saw one coming directly at his head and skipped sideways, throwing up his left arm to protect himself. He winced as the rock hit his forearm. It was painful, but it would have been much worse had it hit him in the head or face.

He bounced out again, letting out more rope and falling even faster than before.

And grunted in surprise as his feet hit the ledge after he had fallen less than two meters.

His knees flexed to absorb the unexpected shock and for a moment he dangled, off balance, in danger of falling backward off the ledge. Then he recovered and pushed himself face-first into the rock wall, as another shower of rocks and stones thudded and bounced around him. Fortunately, there was a slight outcrop just above him and any rocks that were aimed straight were hitting it and bouncing out into space.

He unwrapped the rope and released one end, pulling rapidly on the other to release it from the tree overhead and praying that it wouldn't snag. The Wargals were savage and fearless, but fortunately they were not terribly intelligent and they were slow to react to a change in the situation. Before they realized what was happening, the rope had snaked free and the end dropped over the cliff, falling down to where Halt crouched on the ledge. He gathered it in as it came, searching the rock face for one of the iron pins he had driven in on the way up the cliff. He spotted one to his right and ran to it, crouching as more rocks cascaded past him.

Then the shower of rocks ceased and he looked up to see that the Wargals had disappeared from the cliff edge. He heard their snarling and yipping fading away to his left and knew that they were heading for the top of Three Step Pass. They had realized that he had evaded them, and there was no chance now of catching him climbing down the cliff face.

Now their best course was to rush down Three Step Pass and cut him off on the ground below.

He had no idea how quickly they could make it down the pass, and he didn't waste time wondering about it. Passing the doubled rope around the iron spike, he hastily repositioned it around his body, legs and arm and dropped off the ledge, sliding down the face of the cliff in a giant bound. The rope burned his arms and inner thighs once more as he fell fifteen meters before bringing himself to a stop, his feet against the cliff. Ignoring the pain, he pushed off again. But this time the rope was cutting into flesh that was already burned and injured, and he had to stop after ten meters. He glanced down. Ten meters to go. Only a few more seconds of pain. Gritting his teeth, he let himself fall again, shoving off with his feet so that he fell in a wide arc away from the cliff.

His knees buckled as he hit the ground and he fell onto the soft grass. Abelard was watching him from a few meters away, ears pricked and alert. He lurched to his feet and staggered toward the horse. His knees felt weak and unsteady—a result of the tension of the last ten minutes. He fell against the horse, clinging to the saddle to keep himself on his feet.

He had left Abelard saddled but with the cinch loosened. He realized his mistake now as he had to waste precious minutes tightening the girth strap. Had he unsaddled him, he could have simply mounted and ridden away bareback. Then, he thought, he had never realized that he'd come sliding down the cliff face, burning his hand and thighs on the rope and with Wargals hurling rocks down on him from above.

The little horse stood steady as he tightened the straps, then Halt placed his foot in the stirrup to swing up into the saddle.

"Nothing clever to say?" he asked.

Abelard twitched his ear twice. *You never listen anyway.*

Then Halt was in the saddle and he urged the horse through the trees before he had set his right foot in the stirrup. They burst out of the grove of trees at a full gallop and he swung Abelard's head toward the northeast, and the road home.

Only to see dark figures erupting from the entrance to the pass, bounding and leaping to bar the way. Now the yipping and snarling had ceased, and the silence was somehow ominous. He realized that he had lost the race. They were across the path he needed to take.

For a moment, he hesitated, reining Abelard to a stop. The wise course was to turn away and head southwest. But somehow he knew the Wargals would pursue him if he did, driving him farther and farther away from Castle Araluen. And he had information that the King needed. If he ran, there was no telling how long or how far the Wargals would pursue him. He knew that once set on a course, they tended to carry it out. And they seemed inexhaustible.

He considered heading toward the company of soldiers set to watch the pass. But there were only twenty of them and he sensed they would be no match for the thirty powerful Wargals who were pursuing him. He was loath to sacrifice those men for his own safety. He already felt a sense of guilt over Norman's death, although, realistically, he could have done nothing to prevent it.

The thought of Norman reminded him of something the old

hermit had said. Wargals had an irrational fear of horses, a fear that Morgarath was trying to eradicate.

He swung Abelard to face the line of dark, scrambling figures, then kicked in his heels and set the little horse to a gallop. They pounded across the grass and he drew his two remaining arrows from the quiver and let fly at the nearest Wargals. Two of the creatures went down, but there were still more than twenty of them and he was now virtually unarmed. He discounted his saxe and throwing knife. In a close combat with these evil beasts, he wouldn't stand a chance. The Wargals seemed oblivious to the fate of their companions. They formed a line to stop him, raising their weapons and snarling defiance and hate at him.

Then as he drew closer to the waiting beasts, they seemed to hesitate. Several of them faltered and backed away from the line facing him. Abelard's hooves continued to pound the grass beneath them, sending clods of dirt and grass flying.

Halt leaned forward over the horse's neck and urged him on to greater speed. Abelard responded immediately, his ears pinning back and his nostrils flaring with great breaths.

I hope you know what you're doing.

"Trust me," Halt said.

And then it happened. They were barely ten meters away from the Wargals when the massive brutes panicked and broke ranks, scattering to either side with hoarse cries of terror, leaving the way clear for the pounding horse to break through their line.

Most of them ran, desperate to escape the terrifying sight of the horse bearing down on them. A few of them threw spears.

But as Halt had noticed, their clumsy hands and long claws affected their throwing skills and the projectiles went wide.

Then they were free and clear, and Halt let Abelard ease up a little, cantering smoothly toward the path that led through the forest and to Castle Araluen. He glanced back over his shoulder. The panicked Wargals were still scattered, still running headlong to escape their nemesis. Norman had been right.

"How very interesting," he said.

Oh, I don't know. I can be quite terrifying when I set my mind to it.

15

WOLDON ABBEY WAS A COMFORTABLE-LOOKING TWO-STORY building, built from honey-colored sandstone blocks. Around its upper floor, an open verandah ran, allowing patients to sit out and relax in the open air and enjoy the view. Doors leading to the numerous bedrooms lined the verandah.

The abbey was set among the trees a little way back from a small river. To one side, clouds of vapor rose from the hot spring that gave the abbey its reason for being. The water there was rich with minerals and heated by underground thermal activity. It ran out through a fissure in an outcrop of rocks, filled a pool at the base, then ran away, cooling rapidly, to join the waters of the river.

There was a level grassed section, with carefully tended flower beds, at the front of the abbey. Crowley directed the coachman to bring the carriage up to the low staircase leading to the entrance and halt there.

Three of the sisters who staffed the abbey hurried out and down the steps to meet the carriage and their royal guests. The sisters were a nursing order, not a religious one. The Mother Abbess was a tall, grave-faced woman who gave a shallow curtsy as she reached the carriage and one of the footmen opened the nearside door. Her action was enough to show deference to the new arrival, but not so much as to reduce the Abbess's own sense of authority.

"Welcome to Woldon Abbey, your majesty. I am Abbess Margrit," she said.

The Queen was awake. She had slept for the past few hours, and her color was good and her eyes bright. As the footmen reached in to lift the stretcher out of the coach, she waved them away.

"No. Thank you. I'm fine. I can walk."

She started to rise from the litter, but the Abbess held up a hand to stop her. There was no mistaking the air of command there now. And no denying it.

"Best if you're carried inside, your majesty, until we've had a chance to assess your condition."

Rosalind met her eyes and saw the light of determination there. Margrit was not a woman to deny, or to disobey. Giving in, the Queen sank back against the pillows and allowed the servants to lift her gently from the coach and set the litter on the ground, where its short legs held it clear of the damp grass.

Crowley had dismounted by this stage. As was his custom, he let Cropper's reins drop to the ground. His horse would never stray off. He approached the tall Abbess, who towered over him by a head, and smiled, nodding his head in greeting. He was a Ranger, after all. In fact, he was the Ranger Commandant, a position that ranked in many ways equal to that of a baron. He wasn't about to start deferring to any gray-haired abbess. At least, he assumed she was gray haired. Her head and shoulders were covered by a white veil, held in place by a gray band around her forehead. Her flowing robes were the same gray color, as were those of her companions.

"Good morning, Abbess Margrit," he said, then nodded to the other two sisters flanking her. "Good morning, sisters."

It was noticeable that the two junior sisters immediately chorused a greeting to him, while the Abbess, after a pause, merely nodded an acknowledgment. Crowley grinned to himself. Power games, he thought. I'm in charge here and don't forget it, the Abbess was implying.

At length, Margrit elected to speak. "And you are?" she said coolly, although she obviously knew all too well. Crowley decided not to take offense. This was her abbey, after all, and she was the authority here.

"I'm Crowley, Mother Abbess. King's Ranger," he said pleasantly.

Margrit raised one perfectly formed eyebrow. In her younger days, Crowley realized, she would have been a stunning beauty. "Then mind you don't come clumping into my abbey with your big muddy boots."

Crowley allowed the grin to show. "I'll try not to do that."

She looked at him for a couple of seconds, then dismissed him and knelt beside the litter, taking Rosalind's hand, noting her pulse, then feeling her forehead with one cool palm.

"Hmmm," she said. "Pulse is a little weak. Temperature a little high."

"We've been traveling for several days," Rosalind said in explanation.

Margrit nodded. "To be expected then. But we'll soon put

you to rights, my lady. Good, nourishing food, lots of rest and fresh air, and daily baths in the hot springs will do you and your baby a world of good."

Rosalind smiled. Crowley chipped in. "Sounds good to me. Maybe I'll stay here too."

Margrit rose from her kneeling position and studied him down the length of her elegantly formed nose.

"The abbey and spa only cater to female guests," she said archly. "I'm afraid you'd be out of place here."

Crowley shrugged. "I usually am," he said cheerfully.

No matching smile reached the Abbess's face. She made no reply, but gestured for the servants to take up Rosalind's litter and carry her into the abbey.

"We'll get settled in, my lady." Then, to Crowley, she said, "Who are all these soldiers?" She indicated Sir Athol and the men-at-arms.

You know full well who they are, Crowley thought. But he continued to smile easily. "They are the Queen's bodyguard. This is Sir Athol, their commander."

Athol, who had dismounted and come to join him, bowed deeply. "Your servant, Mother Abbess."

She sniffed. "That remains to be seen." She studied the men-at-arms, sitting at ease on their horses. "Well, you're not staying in the abbey. As I say, it's women only and I won't have a noisy bunch of soldiers disturbing the patients."

"The Queen does need protection," Crowley pointed out. This time, he didn't smile and his tone of voice let the autocratic Abbess know that this was not a matter for debate.

There was a moment's frosty silence, then Athol intervened. "We can camp down there, Mother Abbess," he said, indicating a meadow by a bend in the river about a hundred meters away. There was a grove of trees for shelter, and the ground was well grassed and level. It would be a comfortable campsite, Crowley thought.

The Abbess considered the suggestion. "Very well," she said eventually. She glanced approvingly at Sir Athol. He was young and well mannered. She found the sandy-haired Ranger too irreverent and sure of himself for her taste.

Crowley now indicated the entrance to the abbey. "Well, if that's settled, I'll make my farewells to the Queen and be on my way."

Margrit was a little nonplussed. She knew the group had been traveling all morning.

"You'll not stay for a meal?" she asked. She might be haughty and autocratic, but she was not one to be inhospitable when it came to a traveler's needs.

"Too much to do," Crowley said. "Duty calls, I'm afraid."

"Ranger Crowley is the Ranger Commandant, Mother Abbess," Athol explained. "He has a lot on his hands." In spite of herself, Margrit looked somewhat impressed as she learned of her visitor's rank.

Crowley headed for the stairs and went through the double doors. There was a large reception area immediately inside, with a registrar's table in the center and a large log fire blazing in a hearth on one of the walls. The Queen had risen from the litter and was half reclining on a comfortable settee close to the table. She smiled as she saw Crowley.

"I'll be leaving, your majesty," he said, taking her hand and bending low over it.

Rosalind allowed her disappointment to show. Crowley

had been good company on the journey—amusing, capable and reassuring at all times. She had felt safe in his care. "So soon, Crowley?"

He nodded. "I'm afraid so. The King needs me."

She pursed her lips. "I understand," she said. "He needs all his loyal officers at the moment."

Crowley went to relinquish her hand, but Rosalind seized his with surprising strength and pulled him a little closer.

"Tell him not to worry about me," she said. "I'm feeling much better and I'm sure Abbess Margrit will soon whip me into shape."

He couldn't help smiling. "That's one way of putting it. She's a bit . . . bossy, isn't she?"

Rosalind smiled. "I think she has to be. She has to keep order here—and make sure no rowdy Rangers breach the peace and tranquility."

"If you say so," he said. Then he straightened. "Be well, my lady. I'll be back for you when the baby is born."

"Thank you, Crowley," she said, smiling at the mention of the baby. She raised her hand in farewell. He bowed slightly, then turned and strode toward the door. As he reached it, Abbess Margrit was entering and he stood aside for her. She entered, acknowledging his deference with a nod of her head.

"Take good care of her, Mother Abbess," he said.

She met his gaze evenly. "Rest assured," she told him.

As Crowley mounted and rode away, a ragged figure watched from the trees across the river. He was dressed in ill-fitting, mismatched clothes that he'd snatched from a clothesline outside a farmhouse. A sway-backed mule, also stolen, stood by patiently as he watched the abbey. His eyes narrowed as he watched the

Ranger ride away. He could hear the cheerful tune that he was whistling. Unknowingly, his lips drew back in a silent snarl.

"We'll see what you have to whistle about in a few days," he muttered. He was intent on revenge. He had been one of the brigands that Crowley and his men had sent packing. As yet, he wasn't clear what form that revenge would take. But he knew it would center on the high-profile guest that the Ranger had delivered into the care of the Abbess.

A day and a half later, Crowley was back in Castle Araluen, deep in conversation with the King and his senior battle masters, Lord Northolt and Sir David. Northolt was his supreme army commander and the battle master of Araluen. He had been Duncan's father's army commander for many years, and the King was grateful to have his support and experience. But he was also glad to have David's advice. Sir David, the battle master of Caraway Fief, was the royal army's heavy cavalry commander. He was a younger man, an accomplished warrior and tactician. Best of all, he wasn't hidebound by old ideas.

"We're losing more troops every day," Northolt was saying.

Duncan shrugged at the inevitability of the matter. "It's harvesttime," he said. "I have to release them so they can gather in the harvests. Otherwise we'll all be starving in a year's time."

His standing army was a small one. In times of crisis, it was bolstered by levies from the fiefs, led by their barons. But there was no way he could keep these men under arms indefinitely. The affairs of the Kingdom still had to be attended to, and at the moment, the harvest had to be brought in and stored. That meant that hundreds of part-time soldiers had to be released to go back to their fiefs. Duncan and Northolt had tried to rotate the men released so that every group didn't leave at once. But even so, their numbers were being seriously depleted now.

"It also seems to me that some of the barons are using the harvest as an excuse. They're sitting on the fence, waiting to see how things pan out between you and Morgarath," Northolt said.

The King nodded morosely. "At least they're not actively taking his part. That would make things a lot worse."

"Things are bad enough. If Morgarath attacks now, we'll be in a bad way."

"I hope he fights the conventional way," Duncan said. "We've always avoided battle at this time of year because the harvest has to be brought in."

"Unfortunately, he doesn't have a harvest to gather," Crowley pointed out. "And he knows that this is a time when, traditionally, our forces will be weakened."

"We have fewer than three hundred infantry," Sir David said. "And even fewer cavalry. I have around one hundred and twenty mounted troops."

That was a major problem, Duncan thought. The cavalry's greatest value at a time like this was to scout for the enemy, acting as the King's eyes and bringing information about enemy movements. With such limited numbers, the cavalry couldn't perform this role effectively.

"The situation with archers is even worse. Most of them have gone," Lord Northolt added.

The Kingdom's force of trained archers came from the farms and villages, where young men trained each day with the bow. But they were the same young men who would be most needed at the harvest.

"Morgarath would know we'd find ourselves in this predicament," Duncan said. "He's seen it all before, as the commander of Gorlan Fief. Now he's on the other side."

"It depends on how his recruitment of these strange beasts is succeeding," Northolt put in. "Have we heard anything from Halt?" He addressed this last question to Crowley. Halt, naturally, would report first to him.

Crowley shook his head. "I expect to hear from him any day," he said. "If he's survived."

Duncan's forehead was creased with worry. There was a long silence in the room as they all considered the situation. Then there was a gentle tap on the door.

"Come in," Duncan called, and a young page, holding a small sheet of parchment, entered. His eyes were wide with nervousness as he found himself in close proximity to the King and the country's battle master. Duncan smiled at the boy—he was barely thirteen—and beckoned him forward, holding out his hand for the parchment.

"A message pigeon just came in, my lord," the page said, his voice breaking slightly.

Duncan took it from him and glanced at the others. "Let's hope it's good news for a change," he said. He dismissed the boy and opened the message, his frown deepening as he read. The he looked up at his three officers.

"Morgarath's on the move," he said. "His forces have broken out of Three Step Pass."

16

CAPTAIN LACHIE STUART, COMMANDER OF THE COMPANY SET to watch Three Step Pass, was sitting at a camp table outside his tent, composing his biweekly report for Lord Northolt, the supreme army commander.

As usual, there was little to report, other than the recent visit by the Ranger known as Halt, and his avowed intention to scale the cliffs leading to the Mountains of Rain and Night. Stuart hadn't seen any sign of the Ranger since he had left on this expedition, and he had no idea whether Halt had been successful or not. Glancing critically at the sheer cliffs that stretched away to the southwest, he thought the negative answer was the more likely one.

There had been a brief foray by a party of the strange bear-like creatures a few days after the Ranger had left. But they quickly returned to the pass, seemingly in panic. He hesitated about mentioning their apparent mental state in the report. It was an impression he had gained watching them as they ran pell-mell back to the safety of the pass. But in the absence of any concrete proof, he decided it was best not to mention it. Lord

Northolt wanted facts in his reports, not suspicions or conjecture from his junior commanders.

"Captain Stuart! Something's happening!"

He looked up from the half-completed report. One of his troopers was dashing through the campsite toward him, waving his arm to get his attention. The man had presumably run from the forward observation post, where a patrol kept constant watch over the entrance to Three Step Pass. Stuart rose, jolting the table and knocking his ink bottle over as he did. Hastily, he grabbed the sheets of his laboriously filled-out report and moved them out of harm's way. Then he righted the bottle and looked around for a cloth to clean up the spilled ink.

But he had no time to find one. The trooper was only a few meters away, red-faced and sweating, and his next words sent a chill of fear through Stuart.

"They're coming out, sir! Those beasts. They're coming out of the pass."

Stuart dropped the fluttering pages of the report and grabbed his sword, leaning in its scabbard against the chair he had been sitting in. He clipped it onto the rings on his heavy belt.

"How many?" he asked. It wasn't unheard of for the monsters to sortie out occasionally, and so far they had never come out in great numbers.

"We counted fifty so far. Corporal Jessup told me to come and get you."

Stuart was galvanized into action. Fifty of the creatures? And, judging by the trooper's use of the words *so far*, there were more coming. This was a major sortie. He looked around the camp. His men were relaxing, carrying out minor chores such as laundry and meal preparation. None of them were armed or armored. He grabbed the trooper's arm.

"Sound the alarm!" he ordered. "Get the company armed and have them stand to at the palisade."

Company, he thought dismissively. Normally, a company would mean fifty men. But due to the reduced state of Duncan's army, Stuart could muster barely twenty-seven. There would be little they could do if Morgarath's troops were coming out in force. The trooper ran off, boots pounding through the soft grass, shouting the alarm. Stuart saw that men were beginning to react, seizing their weapons, pulling on their mail shirts and helmets. Then he turned and ran for the observation post.

He emerged from the trees close to the camouflaged position. It was a small trench, roofed over with logs and covered in branches, dirt and grass to look like the surrounding landscape. He dashed down the shallow stairway at one end and into the dim interior. There was barely room to stand upright but he pushed his way past the three troops there to crouch beside the corporal at the observation slit. He caught his breath in shock as he saw the numbers deploying onto the open plain in front of the pass.

Corporal Jessup saw his reaction. "I've counted ninety, sir. And there's more coming."

The dark, heavyset figures were forming up in sections of twenty as they emerged from the pass. And this time, there were humans among them—members of Morgarath's force. Each group of twenty seemed to be commanded by one of these. They stood out from their troops—taller and less bulky in build. All of them wore mail armor and helmets. And all of them were armed, with an assortment of swords, axes and war hammers.

The ranks of creatures continued to grow as he watched. His throat was dry and he swallowed nervously. His small force was well outnumbered and becoming more so with each passing minute. The scene was made even more ominous by the creatures' forming up without the sort of chatter or comment that would be heard from a human force falling into line. There were occasional grunts and snarls, and from time to time a jingle of weapons. Otherwise there was an eerie silence to it all.

"Look, sir!" The corporal grabbed his arm, as much in panic as to gain his attention, and pointed to where a tall, black-armored figure on a white horse was emerging from the pass. More of the stooping, shambling beasts followed him.

Stuart felt his heart rate accelerate. This was no raid, no reconnaissance sortie. This was a full-scale attack. He swung away from the observation slit and gestured to the troopers standing behind him.

"Stay here and watch them," he ordered. "The minute they start to move, fall back to the camp and let me know. You'll have plenty of time," he added reassuringly. The last thing he wanted was for the men to panic and run prematurely before he knew what Morgarath's forces were up to.

"I'm going back to send a message pigeon to the commander," he explained. He didn't want his men to think he was abandoning them to their fate.

"What will we do if they attack, sir?" one of the troopers asked. His voice was high-pitched and querulous.

But before Stuart could answer, Corporal Jessup rounded on

the trooper with a snarl. "We fight the fell beggars!" he said. "We kill 'em till there's no more left to kill!"

His aggressive tone steadied the young trooper. He swallowed once or twice, his Adam's apple working in his thin neck. Then he took a firmer hold of his spear shaft and nodded. Stuart clapped the corporal on the shoulder.

"Well said," he told him, although he doubted they would "kill them till there's no more left to kill." It would be more like "kill them until there's none of *us* left." Crouching under the low entrance, he emerged from the bunker and ran back through the trees, his riding boots clumsy and awkward, his left hand holding his sword scabbard to prevent it tangling in his legs.

He reached the cleared ground of the campsite and looked quickly around. The men were almost all armed now and had moved to their positions by the palisade and ditch that protected the camp. He bellowed for his page and the young boy came dashing toward him, his young face ludicrous under the severe lines of the helmet that was a size too big for him.

"Fetch me a pigeon!" he ordered. "For Castle Araluen." He added the last as they had pigeons trained to home on various sites in the Kingdom. The young boy nodded and dashed away as Stuart grabbed pen and paper once more, selecting one of the small, flimsy message forms designed to go in the metal holder on a pigeon's leg. He dipped his pen in the ink, glad he had rescued the bottle before it all spilled away, and paused, composing his message. Space on the form was limited and he had to be succinct. Finally, he wrote, taking his time and keeping his letters as small as possible:

M's army exiting 3SP. Full invasion likely.

He frowned thoughtfully. Technically, it wasn't an invasion.

Morgarath was already in the country. But he needed to make it clear that this wasn't a small-scale patrol or a sortie. This was Morgarath's full force coming out to fight.

The page came dashing back, his ridiculous helmet falling over his eyes. He held a pigeon in two hands and had no hand to adjust his headgear. He tried to shrug it back. Stuart reached out and removed it for him, dropping it onto the grass. He needed the boy to hold the pigeon steady while he inserted the message in the small cylinder on its leg.

"Thanks, sir," the page gasped as the captain carefully rolled the small sheet of paper. He forced himself to work slowly. If he didn't do it carefully, the sheet wouldn't fit into the container. His hands were shaking, and at his first attempt, the sheet rolled a little off angle. It wouldn't fit that way, he knew. Nerves, he thought. He paused, unrolled the form and began again, working slowly and steadily. This time he got it right and the message slid easily into the metal tube.

He tugged the cylinder, making sure it was firmly attached. Then he took the slightly ruffled bird from the boy's hand and held it, settling it and steadying it. He could feel the tiny heart hammering against his hands like a kettle drum. The bird had sensed the nervousness of the two humans and was twitching and struggling. Stuart knew if he launched it now it was likely to fly back to its hutch and hide in fright. He slowed his breathing, stroking the little creature gently, and gradually calming it.

"You're small and frightened and not very bright," he said under his breath. "And so much depends on you."

After what seemed ages, the bird stopped struggling and settled down, cooing gently as Stuart continued to stroke its head and make soothing noises. He looked into the clear sky above them. All they needed now was a patrolling hawk to set after the pigeon—although he knew if there was a hawk in the vicinity the little bird would have sensed it and been warbling frantically while it refused to take flight.

Gently, using two hands, he tossed the bird into the air. Instantly, it unfurled its wings and began to fly. It soared up above the campsite, circled once to get its bearings, then sped off to the north.

"Watch out for hawks, little one," Stuart said. He heard pounding feet approaching and looked round to see the corporal and his men from the observation site.

"They're coming, sir," Corporal Jessup reported. "Coming straight at us."

Forcing a calmness he didn't feel, Stuart nodded. He reached down and loosened his sword in its scabbard. His shield was hanging on a low forked branch driven into the ground outside his tent. He picked it up, slid his left arm into the straps and gestured toward the men formed up at the palisade. It was constructed of heavy saplings cut down and driven vertically into the ground, held together by twisted rope at its top and bottom. Outside, there was a ditch a meter deep, with its bottom and sides lined with sharpened stakes.

Captain Stuart joined his men at the palisade, where a walkway had been built around the inside to allow the defenders to reach over the top. He felt the eyes of his small force upon him. He glanced around and saw the corporal from the observation post. He smiled at the grim-faced veteran, who nodded back. Then he raised his voice.

"Men!" he shouted. "Morgarath and his shaggy, evil-smelling creatures are on their way." He had no idea how the thickset beasts smelled, but it was a safe assumption that they would stink. And none of his men knew any better. He caught the corporal's eyes again. "Corporal! What are we going to do to them?"

The corporal drew his sword. It was a simple, brass-hilted weapon that had seen years of service. And it was razor sharp, Stuart noticed. "We kill 'em till there's no more left to kill!" the corporal shouted, and there was an answering roar from the men at the palisade. Then the men fell silent as they saw dark figures moving out of the trees.

Morgarath surveyed the battle scene dispassionately. None of the defenders had survived. The palisade had been smashed and torn down by his Wargals. They cut through the rope binding at top and bottom with axes, disregarding the spear thrusts from the defenders that came through the gaps in the fence. Then they levered the uprights apart with their spears. Finally, they used their bare hands to claw the fence down, even as they died.

The beasts then swarmed through the gap and overwhelmed the defenders, ignoring their own casualties, scrambling over their comrades' dead and dying bodies to reach the enemy. Killing and killing, even as they died themselves.

Morgarath had lost twenty-five of them in the assault. But the losses meant nothing to him. He could afford them. And this was his first chance to blood his new troops. They crouched and sat on the blood-soaked field now, snuffling and snarling to themselves as their leader walked among them, letting praise for them radiate out through his thoughts.

He stopped and called to the men who followed him. "Captains! Here!"

These were men who served him at Castle Gorlan, men who were his loyal followers for years. Previously, they had commanded his men-at-arms. Now each one would be in command of a force of eighty or ninety Wargals. The beasts had learned to understand and obey simple word commands, and Morgarath conditioned them to follow the leadership of the captains without hesitation. Now Morgarath would set them free to terrorize the fiefs and villages of the Kingdom. To burn, to loot and to kill.

His ten subordinates formed a rough half circle around him, ready for their final orders.

"You all have your objectives," he said, and they nodded, murmuring confirmation. Each one had a series of villages to raid and loot. "Strike each one quickly and without mercy. Seize their harvest, burn their houses and kill the villagers. Smash down their castles if you can." His troops had no siege equipment, but many of the fief castles were small and might be taken by surprise by a ruthless and determined group. And with eighty or ninety Wargals in each troop, they would outnumber most of the garrisons they were attacking.

"If we spread fear and destruction through the Kingdom, we will prevent the fiefs sending reinforcements to Duncan's army. They'll want to protect their own homes and villages. And not only will we starve Duncan of men, we'll starve him literally. He'll be depending on the harvest to feed his men. So we'll take it first. We'll feast while he starves."

There was a fierce murmur of approval from the men facing him.

"So spread out and sow fear and confusion in the Kingdom.

Then in three weeks, we'll rally at Twin River Forks." He named a spot a few kilometers south of Castle Araluen.

"We'll catch Duncan unawares, with his men hungry and his numbers depleted. And in a month, we will rule in Araluen!"

His voice rose as he spoke the last few words and the assembled captains cheered. The Wargals looked up curiously. Some of them stirred nervously. They hadn't understood the words, but the passion and fury in Morgarath's speech was all too obvious. The disturbance spread through their ranks. They rose to their feet and brandished their weapons, grunting and growling through their grotesque mouths.

Morgarath looked out at them and smiled. Duncan had no idea what was about to hit him.

17

Across the southern third of Araluen, as far as the eye could see, the sky was stained with columns of smoke, rising from the fiefs where Morgarath's forces were wreaking havoc and destruction. The smell of smoke was everywhere, along with another smell: the sweet, sickly, rotting smell of dead bodies—animals for the most part. The carcasses of sheep and cattle lay bloated and rotting in the sun. But here and there one could find human bodies as well—farmhands and villagers who had dared to stand and defend their property against the remorseless tide of the Wargals.

They were poorly armed for the most part and stood no chance against the savage raiders. They were killed, and their farms and villages were put to the torch.

Crops waiting to be harvested were burned in the fields—after Morgarath's army had taken all they could carry.

The small number of men-at-arms and knights who were present in the fiefs fared little better. They killed some of the Wargals, who attacked fearlessly and without thought for their own losses. But they were all too soon overwhelmed. They either died defending their territories or escaped to hide in the forests.

The barons were a little better off. They remained in their fortified castles while the tide of Wargals ebbed and flowed around them. The Wargals had no siege towers, trebuchets or battering rams, so most of the castles stood firm and unyielding. But their garrisons were always outnumbered and it would be suicide to venture out and attack the rampaging beasts.

Some of the smaller castles, with garrisons numbering less than twenty armed men, succumbed to attack by scaling ladders. Once the Wargals got inside the walls, the fate of the inhabitants was sealed. There was no surrender. The Wargals didn't recognize the word. So the surviving barons remained in their castles, husbanding their forces against attack.

As Morgarath had predicted, the presence of his marauding forces was starving Duncan of men. Whereas previously they might have returned to bolster his numbers, now they were held back as protection against an attack that could come at any time.

With their womenfolk and villagers to protect, the barons couldn't risk leaving their walls bare of defenders. A few did compromise, splitting their forces and sending half to reinforce Duncan. But many of those small parties were caught in the open by the rampaging beasts from the mountains. Fifteen men against eighty or ninety blood-crazed Wargals wasn't a contest.

And Morgarath's human commanders, adhering to their leader's orders, always ensured that one or two of the men caught this way were left alive, and allowed to escape. They quickly spread the word of how futile it was to send levies to the King's army, and the practice ceased.

"How many of these creatures does he have?" Duncan asked, running his fingers through his hair. On every side, he was staring disaster in the face as Morgarath out-thought him and outmaneuvered him. The King simply didn't have enough men to face Morgarath in an all-out battle. And that was the only way the former Baron of Gorlan would ever be defeated.

"Close to a thousand," Halt said.

"We can't fight that many," Lord Northolt said thoughtfully.

Duncan rounded on him with some asperity. "I know that! Tell me something I don't know!" he snapped. Then he calmed down. "I'm sorry, Northolt. I know you're only doing your job."

"All I meant, sir, was that at this stage, we can't afford to stand and face them. Castle Araluen is a formidable defensive position, but once Morgarath concentrates his forces again, we'd be trapped inside it. We'd find ourselves in a stalemate, unable to sortie and drive off his army. If we're to have any chance, we'll have to use different tactics, retreating to favorable defensive positions and wearing them down as they try to attack us."

"Retreating never won a battle," Duncan said heavily.

Lord Northolt nodded. "No, sir. But it's the only course left to us. At least this way we can choose the ground we're fighting on. And we'll be buying time, so that the fiefs can send us reinforcements."

"You're suggesting we abandon Castle Araluen?" the King asked.

"Yes, sir. With a small garrison. If you're not here, there's no reason for Morgarath to lay siege. He'll bypass it and come after us. Besides . . ." Northolt paused, flushing awkwardly.

The King gestured for him to continue.

"Well, sir, I doubt he'll want to damage the castle too badly. He'll want it for himself if he beats us."

The King said nothing for a moment, realizing the truth of

Northolt's words. Then he turned to Halt. "Is there no way to defeat these beasts, Halt?"

Halt hesitated, then replied. "I thought there might be a way. The old hermit told me that they had an irrational fear of horses. And they scattered when I rode Abelard straight at them. Cavalry might be the answer."

Sir David looked up with interest. But then he shook his head. "We're short of cavalry. We have barely one hundred and twenty troopers. We can't use them up in a headlong attack against nine hundred of these things."

Halt nodded. "Understood. And of course, Morgarath is aware of this weakness. I saw him trying to drill it out of them on the plateau. If he's decided to attack now, he must have succeeded to some extent."

Northolt had been studying a map of the surrounding fiefs as Halt and David had been speaking. He jabbed his finger on a spot twenty kilometers to the northeast of Castle Araluen.

"My lord, I suggest we withdraw to this position initially— the Ashdown Cut."

Halt, Crowley, David and the King gathered around him, studying the map as he explained further.

"It's a narrow valley with sloping ground either side, covered with thick forest. Morgarath won't be able to deploy his forces on a wide front. They'll be concentrated in the valley, where they'll make a perfect target for our archers."

"Not that I have many archers," Duncan pointed out. "Most of them were villagers who left for the harvest. And they haven't come back."

"We've got eighteen Rangers," Crowley pointed out. "Twenty

including Halt and me. We should be able to lay down a fairly considerable barrage."

Duncan looked at him. "Good idea. I hadn't thought of using Rangers *en masse*," he said. "I always think of you lot fighting as individuals."

Crowley shrugged. "Usually, we do. But this is a special situation."

Northolt began rolling up the map. "We should get the army ready to move as soon as possible," he said. "At the moment, all the advantages lie with Morgarath. He can choose when to concentrate his forces again and attack us. We should be ready for him."

Duncan nodded agreement. "Do it then." Then he held out a hand to stop his battle master putting the map back in its protective leather cylinder. "Just a moment," he said, as a thought struck him. "Let me see that again."

Northolt rolled the chart out again, placing small weights at each corner to keep it flat. Duncan leaned over and studied it, frowning.

"Yes. I thought so," he said at length, then tapped two locations on the map. "If we move to this Ashdown Cut you're suggesting, we'll be some distance north of Woldon Abbey, where the Queen is. That leaves her rather exposed if Morgarath sends any of his troops that way."

An uncomfortable silence fell. Halt finally broke it.

"There's no reason why he should," he said. "There's no castle nearby, and no large villages that would draw his attention."

"Still, she is rather exposed there," Northolt agreed. He glanced at Crowley. "Her bodyguard is still with her, of course?"

Crowley nodded. "Yes. But there are only seven of them—

five men-at-arms and two archers. We had no idea that Morgarath was going to start the battle when I escorted her there." He turned an unhappy look on the King. "I'd be loath to move her again so soon, sir," he said. "The journey took a lot out of her and it could be dangerous to make her travel again."

It was an awkward situation. Duncan couldn't help feeling that by moving with his army to the northeast, he was abandoning his wife to the dangers of the marauding Wargals. Yet he knew only too well how weak she was, and how dangerous another journey might be for her.

"We'll keep an eye on it," he said at length. "First sign that Morgarath is moving in that direction, get down there and get her out, Crowley."

"Yes, sir." The Commandant nodded.

Halt looked at him. "I'll come with you."

But the King demurred. "No. I want you here. You can get the Rangers organized into an archery force. And I may need you for further scouting. We really have to know when Morgarath is planning to gather his troops. He won't keep raiding forever. Sooner or later, he's going to want to attack in force. And we need to be ready for him."

Morgarath was in his pavilion, dining alone, when the prisoner was brought before him.

He was a miserable-looking creature who had appeared in Morgarath's camp, riding a sway-backed mule that had definitely seen better days. Before the Wargal sentries could kill him out of hand—as was their practice—one of the human officers had heard the man screaming that he had important news for Lord Morgarath and had interceded, clubbing the shaggy beasts away from the man with the haft of a spear. The Wargals snarled angrily at him but they backed away. Discipline had been heavily and painfully ingrained in them. None of the creatures dared to defy one of Morgarath's officers. They might snap and growl and bare their evil fangs, but they would always back down.

Morgarath looked at the shivering figure crouched before him. The man was terrified. A first encounter with Wargals had that effect, the Black Lord thought. The man kept his eyes down, refusing to make eye contact.

"Your name?" Morgarath asked. If the situation required it, he could rage and rant in a fury, but right now he knew it was more effective to speak softly. Soft his voice may be, but there was a definite undertone of menace behind it.

"Luke, sir," the wretched man mumbled. "Luke Follows."

"Look at me when you talk to me," Morgarath ordered, his tone suddenly brisk. He wanted to look at the man's eyes when they spoke. Undoubtedly, some of what he said would be lies, and Morgarath needed to see his eyes to judge that. The man named Luke reluctantly raised his eyes to meet Morgarath's icy stare. They dropped again and Morgarath leaned forward, about to issue a stinging rebuke. Then Luke raised his eyes once more and the Black Lord relaxed in his chair, slicing segments off a peach.

"Why are you here?"

Luke Follows hesitated. "I'm an honest plowman, my lord. That's why they call me Follows. I follows the plow, like—"

Morgarath raised the hand holding the knife to stop the outburst. "You may be a plowman but I doubt you're honest. In my experience, few people are."

Follows frowned, uncertain whether to proceed or not. Morgarath set the knife down sharply on the table and the man started at the sudden noise.

"More likely, you're a brigand," Morgarath said and, when Follows drew breath to deny the charge, he waved him to silence. "Regardless, that is not what I asked you. Why are you here?"

Follows's eyes darted away. Morgarath drew in his breath with an angry hiss, and the man met his gaze.

"Information, my lord. I have information for you."

Morgarath made a rolling gesture with his right hand. Taking that to be an invitation to continue, Follows took a breath and spoke further.

"I saw something at Woldon Abbey, my lord. Something important."

Morgarath snorted derisively. "Who are you to tell me what's important?" he asked. Then, seeing that his scorn had discouraged Follows's flow of words, he made the rolling gesture once more. "Go on."

"It was a carriage, my lord. A fine carriage. It brought a woman there—a fine lady. The Abbess herself greeted her."

Morgarath was shaking his head. "Woldon Abbey? I've never heard of it. What is it? Where is it?"

"It's a healing spa, my lord. About four days' ride northwest of here."

"And why should I be interested in the arrival of this lady—albeit in a fine carriage, as you say?"

Follows hesitated. He swallowed twice, his Adam's apple sliding up and down in his throat. Then he committed himself.

"I think she was the Queen, my lord."

Morgarath, for once, was speechless. He recoiled in his chair, his dark eyes burning into the cringing figure before him. Then he recovered.

"The Queen? Are you sure?"

Again, Follows swallowed nervously, wondering what would be his fate if he were wrong. But there was no going back now. He nodded several times.

"I heard them call her 'your majesty,' lord. She had an escort of men-at-arms—and one of those gray Rangers."

The former Baron's lips twisted at the mention of the hated Rangers. But if the escort had been commanded by a Ranger, this was an important person indeed.

"Is he still there?" he asked.

Follows shook his head. "He left. But the soldiers stayed. Around ten of them, there were."

Morgarath turned toward the canvas-covered doorway to the outer chamber of the pavilion.

"Plummer!" he called. "Come in here. Bring a map of the southwest."

There was a slight pause, then the canvas was pulled aside and his cadaverous second in command entered, a large chart in his hand. Morgarath gestured for him to lay it on the table.

"Woldon Abbey," he said. "Where is it?"

Plummer paused while he studied the map, then pointed to a stylized illustration of a building.

"Here, sir."

Morgarath craned to look, musing to himself. "Not near any castles or large villages. Do we have any forces there?"

Plummer shook his head. "No reason to, sir. As you said, the abbey's the only thing there. Our nearest troop would be Algar's fifty. They'd be . . ." He hesitated, studying the map and measuring distances. "Maybe five days' march away."

Morgarath thought quickly. "Send a message to him. Have him take thirty of his Wargals and make a forced march to this abbey. He can leave the remaining twenty under his sergeant to continue raiding."

"Yes, my lord. And what is he to look for at this abbey?"

"There's a woman there—a guest. I want her taken, but I want her unharmed. And he is to bring her to me."

"A woman, sir?" his underling repeated. He wanted to be sure of Morgarath's order.

Morgarath smiled at him. But it was a smile that would chill the blood.

"Her name is Rosalind, Plummer. She's the Queen."

18

DUNCAN WAS PACING THROUGH THE NEAT TENT LINES OF HIS army. His quartermaster was beside him, hurrying to keep up with the King's long-legged strides, a sheaf of reports and lists fluttering in his hands.

The King liked to be seen by his men, liked to talk to them. Many of them he knew by name and he knew that made a gigantic difference to their morale.

Mind you, their morale needed all the help it could get these days. Duncan glanced down one row of tents, perfectly aligned and with their flaps furled at exactly the same angle. The tents were set up in the parkland in front of Castle Araluen. Large as the castle was, there wasn't enough room in its grounds for such an influx of men.

"So, Abel," he said to the quartermaster, "what is our position with supplies?"

Abel didn't need to consult his papers. He glanced unhappily at the King. "I've cut rations by a quarter, my lord. In another three days, I'll have to cut back to half rations."

Duncan frowned. "That's not a lot for a man to march and fight on."

The quartermaster shrugged. "I could keep issuing three-quarter rations, my lord, but we'll be out of food in two weeks if I do. As it is, we'll barely have enough till the end of the month."

Duncan paused and scratched his chin thoughtfully. "I'll have Crowley send the Rangers out hunting," he said. "And we'll send to the fiefs north of here for supplies. So far, they haven't been hit by the Wargals."

"Aye, my lord. But they know they will be eventually, and they're sure to hold back most of the food for themselves."

"I'll take it from them at sword point if necessary," Duncan said grimly. But in his heart, he knew he would never do it. That would only alienate his people and drive them into Morgarath's camp. He would have to make do with whatever they gave him willingly.

He paused, studying a tent they were passing. The breeze seemed to be setting it billowing more than its neighbors and he knelt to look at the sliding turnbuckle on the main guy rope. He stood up, dusting his knees, and glanced around to where a sergeant was sitting inside the tent on his palliasse, honing the blade of his sword.

"Sergeant?" he called softly.

The man looked up, recognized the King and leapt hastily to his feet, remembering to keep his head bowed so that he didn't slam it into the heavy ridgepole that ran the length of the tent.

"Yes, sir . . . your majesty!" he said. He realized he was holding a naked blade in the presence of the King—a serious breach of manners—and hastily dropped it onto the straw mattress. He stepped out into the sunlight.

The King gestured for him to relax. "Stand easy, Sergeant."

Duncan looked more closely at the homely face, recognition dawning. "You're Hollis, aren't you? Noel Hollis?"

The man smiled, shaking his head slightly at the King's powers of memory and recognition. He had served with Duncan several years back, during a short border war with the Picts.

"That's right, your majesty."

"You're a sergeant now, I see," Duncan said easily. He recalled that Hollis had been a lance corporal when last they knew each other. The man was a good soldier and had obviously been rewarded with a promotion.

Hollis nodded his head, still grinning. "That's right, sir. I were a lance-jack back in the old days."

"Well, Hollis, I notice this guy rope has worked itself loose. The turnbuckle has slipped." He indicated the offending rope. The turnbuckle was a sliding piece that was used to tighten the rope, pulling it double, then twisting to create friction and hold it in place. "If any sort of wind gets up, it's likely to let go and then you'll have that ridgepole down on your head."

"Thank you, sir. Sorry, sir," Hollis said quickly. He dropped to one knee and adjusted the offending guy rope, pulling it taut, so that the canvas of the tent no longer flapped loosely. He twisted the turnbuckle, making sure it was firm and tight, not allowing further slippage. Then he stood. "These things slip eventually, sir," he said, by way of apology.

Duncan nodded. "Aye. They do. All the more reason to check them morning and night, Sergeant."

"I'll do that, sir, never fear."

Duncan grinned. "Good man. I don't have enough soldiers to have any wounded by falling tent poles." He raised a hand in farewell and turned away, resuming his long-striding inspection of the camp.

The quartermaster, caught napping again, had to skip a couple of steps to catch up. He looked up at the King with new respect.

"Do you know all the men's names, sir?" he asked.

Duncan shook his head, then smiled ruefully. "No. Although I've so few I might as well. I just try to remember men who've served with me before."

The quartermaster nodded thoughtfully. The King's sharp memory was a useful skill for a leader, he thought. He knew the men respected Duncan for his courage and fighting ability, and his grasp of tactics. But they loved him because they knew he saw them as people—as individuals, not as a mass of faceless men that he could order into battle and watch die. Duncan cared for his men and they knew it. That meant if he asked them to fight, they knew it was necessary and they'd obey implicitly.

"Your majesty! Your majesty!"

The voice reached them from the end of the tent line they had been walking down. Duncan turned and saw a young man in a messenger's uniform waving to him, half running along the lane that separated the tents, clumsy in his high riding boots. As he called out, heads appeared at the tent entrances, as soldiers looked curiously to see who was shouting for the King.

Duncan held up a hand as the youth came closer. "Calm down, Thomas," he said, and once more the quartermaster shook his head in quiet admiration. "Don't let everyone see you're excited or they'll all be wondering what's going on."

"Sorry, your majesty," the young man replied, rather

breathlessly. He came to a halt and paused to straighten his uniform, which had become disheveled as he ran searching for the King. His weapon belt had slid around so that the long dirk he carried was in the center of his back, rather than at his side. And his purse had moved to the front of his belly, where it banged dangerously at his crotch. He set himself to rights as the King waited calmly. Then, still red faced and breathless, he handed the King a message form.

"This just came in from the south, your majesty," he said.

Duncan broke the seal and opened the message, frowning as he read the text. "Find Lord Northolt, and Rangers Crowley and Halt. Have them all report to my office immediately," he said.

The messenger nodded and turned away, breaking into a shambling run once more as he headed to carry out the task. Duncan followed, striding quickly to the headquarters section of the camp, where his large pavilion was set up.

The quartermaster followed hastily, wondering if this would entail more problems for his beleaguered staff. Whatever the content of the message, it didn't appear to have put the King in a positive mood, he thought.

"Is it bad news, my lord?" he ventured to ask.

Duncan looked at him, his eyes burning, without breaking stride.

"Very bad news," he said.

The three senior officers gathered in Duncan's pavilion within a matter of minutes. Duncan was waiting for them, seated behind his travel desk, his long legs splayed out, as was his custom. The quartermaster, sensing that this meeting was above his rank, had quietly gone back to the large tents he used as storerooms. Duncan nodded perfunctorily as the others arrived and greeted him, then got straight down to business.

He tapped the message sheet he had been given. "There's a troop of Wargals to the southeast, near Sandalford Wood, who have been raiding villages and smaller castles. They've been gradually moving northwest, but now thirty of them have changed direction and they're heading north."

Lord Northolt strode to the map set on an easel to one side of the room. He studied it, finding the small wood Duncan had named, and tracing a line north with his finger.

"There's nothing there," he said. Then he looked more closely and his face fell. "Oh no," he said quietly.

"Exactly," the King said. "That course will take them to Woldon Abbey. The message estimates they'll be there in three days—possibly less."

The two Rangers joined Lord Northolt at the map, studying it intently.

"Is there anything else they could be heading for?" Halt asked.

Crowley shook his head, his lips set in a tight line. "Nothing worth their while," he said. "A small hamlet or two, with less than a dozen people in each."

"It's pretty obvious they're heading for the abbey," Duncan said in a flat voice. "My guess is, someone has betrayed the Queen's presence to Morgarath." He looked at Crowley. "Go and get her out of there, Crowley. They mustn't get their hands on her."

Crowley nodded, but shifted his feet uncertainly. "That may not be easy, sir," he said. "The trip there took a lot out of the Queen. It might be dangerous to move her again so soon."

"*Might* be dangerous?" Duncan replied bitterly. "It definitely *will* be dangerous to leave her there, with a marauding squad of Wargals on the way. How many in the bodyguard?" he asked, although he already knew the answer.

"Seven, sir. Five men-at-arms and two archers. I brought the others back with me because I knew we were short of them."

"Seven men in all," Duncan mused.

Halt shook his head. "They won't do much against thirty Wargals."

The King switched his gaze to the bearded Ranger. "They don't have to do much. They just have to buy time for Crowley to get the Queen away."

Their eyes locked for a few seconds, and Halt saw the pain and the determination in the King's gaze. The men would have to stand and fight for as long as they could, without any prospect of surrender or retreat. Not for the first time, Halt found himself thinking that he was glad he wasn't a king, or even a commander. All too often, kings had to make decisions that sent other men to certain death. This was one of those times, he knew. And he saw that Duncan was all too aware of the fact as well. He looked down. He didn't want the King to see the light of condemnation in his own eyes. He understood the necessity for Duncan's decision, yet he wondered whether he could have made it himself.

Crowley watched the two of them. Halt, he sensed, was on the brink of saying something that he would regret—that they all would regret.

"I'd better go and get Cropper saddled," he said quietly, breaking the lock between the two men.

Halt glanced at him gratefully, knowing how close he had come. "I'll give you a hand."

"Crowley," the King said, and the sandy-haired Ranger stopped, turning back to his leader, eyebrows arched in a question. "If it's not safe for her travel the full distance, take her into the woods and hide her there. Just keep her away from Morgarath's evil creatures."

"I'll keep her safe, sir. Depend on it," Crowley said. Then, jerking his head for Halt to follow, he turned for the doorway once more.

19

Halt had taken over Crowley's command tent in the camp outside Castle Araluen. Like Duncan, Crowley had a suite of rooms inside the castle, but he found it more convenient to have his headquarters close to the army camp, and his force of Rangers.

"Too many stairs to be constantly going back and forth to the castle," he had told Halt, with an easy grin.

It was a large one-roomed pavilion, with a desk in the center and a camp bed along one canvas wall. There was little else in the way of furnishings. Crowley wanted to be ready to move at a moment's notice. When the army moved out and marched for Ashdown Cut, he would probably leave the tent, table and bed behind, making do with his small one-man Ranger tent and his bedroll.

Halt sat at the table now, scowling as he studied the list of Rangers that Farrel passed to him. He hated paperwork. But it was necessary for him to get an idea of the men he would be commanding in Crowley's absence.

Nine of them he knew already, of course. They were the ones

who had joined him and Crowley as they had moved through the Kingdom recruiting a force of Rangers loyal to the King and willing to face Morgarath. Nine, he thought sadly. There had been ten before poor Pritchard was killed outside the tunnel through which Morgarath had escaped from Castle Gorlan.

But their numbers had been boosted since word had spread abroad of Morgarath's retreat to the Mountains of Rain and Night. A further nine former Rangers had made their way back to Araluen to resume their service to the King. Hopefully, more would follow. They had been scattered to other countries by Morgarath's determined persecution of the Corps. Most had been wrongfully accused of major crimes and forced to resign—and flee the country.

Halt muttered angrily. Crowley was far better equipped to assess them than he was. Crowley probably knew most of them, whereas Halt was a relative newcomer to the Kingdom and to the Ranger Corps.

He had to admit, however, that Farrel was an enormous help. Even though he was still incapacitated with a badly broken leg, he could attend to administrative work. And he was one of the older Rangers. He knew all of the returning Rangers—if not personally, at least by name and reputation. He and Halt had been going through the records and he was giving Halt a quick assessment of the men.

In most cases, the assessments were positive. That was hardly surprising as the Rangers were a handpicked group. But at least one of them had caused him to raise his eyebrows warily.

"Denison," Farrel said now, tapping the file. "He could prove to be a problem."

Halt glanced at the sheet in front of him. The man had been a Ranger for ten years. That should have meant he would be a solid addition to their small force.

"What's wrong with him?" he asked bluntly.

Farrel pursed his lips, trying to frame his answer as fairly as possible. "Well . . . he can be a little arrogant. A little full of his own importance, if you know what I mean. I sensed when he first arrived that he was wondering why Crowley had been appointed Commandant. Denison is more experienced. He's been a Ranger far longer than Crowley."

"Doesn't mean he's a better man," Halt said.

Farrel nodded agreement. "That's true. You know it and I know it. Probably Crowley does too. But don't try to tell that to Denison. Since he arrived, I've been expecting a confrontation between him and Crowley—along the lines of, *Why should I take orders from you, you jumped-up whippersnapper?*"

"And of course, I'm not only younger than Crowley and newer in the job, I'm a foreigner to boot," Halt said.

Farrel drummed his fingers on the table, trying to find a tactful way to agree. Then he decided there was no need for tact.

"Exactly," he said. "I think he'll resent it if you start bossing him around."

Halt pursed his lips. "I don't plan on *bossing him around*, as you put it. But surely he won't disobey a direct order."

"He shouldn't, that's for sure. Just don't be surprised if he does."

"Wonderful," Halt muttered. "Just what I need."

He looked up at the tent entrance as Crowley's clerk peered around. Timothy was a young man, barely out of his teens. But he read and wrote prodigiously well, and Crowley had recruited him as a clerk.

"Halt?" he said. "The men are assembled outside."

He jerked his head back over his shoulder, indicating the cleared space outside, in front of the tent. Halt had called an assembly of the eighteen Rangers he had been left to command. Crowley had spent the past week getting to know them and assessing them. Halt hadn't seen the need: That was Crowley's job and he was welcome to it. Now he had been caught out by his lack of attention.

"I'll be right out," he said. He stood, gathering the files together in one bundle. Farrel was having a difficult time standing from the low chair he had taken. Halt seized his upper arm and heaved him to his feet. Farrel nodded his gratitude.

"Thanks," he said. "I'll be glad when this leg has healed." He set his wooden crutch under his armpit and loped out behind Halt.

Seventeen pairs of eyes looked up expectantly as the two Rangers emerged into the sunlight. Halt scanned the group keenly. Half were strangers, although he had seen them around the camp over the past few days.

All were dressed in the Ranger uniform and most of them were shorter than average height—although with powerful shoulders built up by years of practice with the heavy longbows they all carried. Constant practice with an eighty-pound draw did wonders for the development of shoulder and back muscles, Halt mused to himself.

He realized that he'd been standing gawking at them for some seconds now, and they were obviously expecting him to say something. After all, he had called this meeting. He noticed one man on the outskirts of the group, leaning nonchalantly on his longbow. He was taller than the others and had a swarthy face, dominated by a large, aquiline nose.

I'll bet that's Denison, he thought. Then he finally found his voice.

"Good morning, gentlemen," he said. As ever when he was nervous, the Hibernian burr in his words was more heavily accented than normal.

There was a mumbled chorus in reply. He sensed an air of expectation in the group. They assumed they were going to hear their assignments for the next week or two. He considered what he was about to say.

They're not going to like it, he thought.

"Some of you I know already," he continued, letting his gaze travel around the semicircle of men. He was answered by nods and even grins from the group he and Crowley referred to as the originals. The remainder regarded him expectantly. They were neither friendly nor unfriendly. They were waiting to see what to make of him.

"The rest of you, I'm sure I'll get to know quickly," he said.

"What are our assignments?" one of the men asked. He was a short and rather stout character. He was going bald on top and his hair formed a wispy fringe around the crown of his head.

"I'll get to that . . ." Halt paused expectantly, holding the other man's gaze, a note of inquiry in his voice and expression.

The Ranger got the message. "Cedric."

Halt gave him a friendly nod. "Cedric. Thank you. As I said, I'll get to your assignments, but first I need to know who's who. Let's start with you." He indicated a younger man on the left-hand end of the line. "Just step forward and give me your name if you would. I hope I'll remember them. If not, bear with me."

He essayed a grin but none of them returned it. So much for pleasantries, he thought.

The young Ranger declined to step forward. There was really no need to do so, Halt realized on reflection.

"I'm Robert," he said. "Five years' service."

That's four more than me, Halt thought. Then the next man spoke.

"Bedford. Fifteen years."

And so it went on round the line, each man giving his name and length of service, Halt acknowledging each with a curt nod. Finally, it came to the taller, swarthy man at the extreme right-hand end of the line, standing back a few paces.

"Denison," he said. "Ten years."

Aside from Bedford, at fifteen years, Denison had served longer than any of the others. Halt regarded him with interest. "I'm sure I'll draw heavily on your experience and advice, Denison," he said.

Denison raised one shoulder in a dismissive shrug. "I'm sure," he agreed. But his tone was considerably less than agreeable. Halt chose to ignore the challenge implicit in the man's voice.

"And as you all probably know, I'm Halt. And I've been serving the King for a little over eighteen months now."

The Rangers shuffled their feet and exchanged glances. They seemed singularly unimpressed by his length of service. He couldn't really blame them. He cleared his throat and continued.

"As Cedric indicated, you're all wanting to know what your assignments are for the next few weeks. Well, you have one. Archery. The King doesn't have enough archers, so we're going to be his archery force. We're withdrawing to a place called the

Ashdown Cut, where Morgarath's army can only attack us on a narrow front. I figure that nineteen of us can make a pretty sizable hole in his numbers."

"Twenty," Farrel corrected him. "I might have a broken leg, but I can still shoot."

Halt grinned at him. "Twenty then. We'll take them on at Ashdown Cut, then withdraw again to another spot of our choosing."

"And what's the point of all this running away?" Denison demanded.

Halt met his gaze evenly. "We're buying time," he said. "We're chipping away at his numbers, fighting him on ground that we choose, and giving the fiefs time to reinforce us. Once Morgarath is engaged with the main army, the barons won't need to keep their men at home to defend their villages and castles. As Morgarath's strength declines, ours will grow, until we can face him and defeat him once and for all."

Most of the Rangers nodded. They could see the sense of what he said. He added something he knew they wouldn't like.

"That means I need to see how well you shoot," he said. "I know how good the nine men who've been serving with Crowley and me are. But I need to see how good the rest of you are."

Their disapproving expressions told him he'd been right. On the other hand, several of the originals made no attempt to hide their grins.

"It seems to me," said Denison, "that we're all being too frightened by these fuzzy-wuzzy creatures Morgarath has recruited." Several of the others made noises of agreement. "I say we attack him now and have done with it."

"These fuzzy-wuzzy creatures you talk about," Halt replied,

keeping his voice low to contain his anger, "are totally ruthless, totally fearless. They will climb over each other's dead bodies to get at us and kill us. I have seen them tear a man to pieces. And he has nearly a thousand of them."

That brought a few startled expressions from them. Nobody had told them so far how many Wargals Morgarath had recruited. The Rangers exchanged uncertain looks. But Denison plowed on.

"I'm more than a little concerned," he said, "that our leadership group is lacking in experience. We have a new King and a Ranger Commandant who's still wet behind the ears." He paused, and looked meaningfully at Halt. "Then there's you."

Farrel had been standing behind Halt and to the left, leaning on his crutch. Now he shuffled forward to stand level with Halt.

"Denison," he said pleasantly, "how did you spend the past eighteen months?"

Denison scowled at him. "As you know, I was forced to leave the Kingdom. I obtained employment with Baron Heinrich von Grall of Teutlandt. I was commander of his foresters."

"In other words, you were a glorified gamekeeper," Farrel sneered. "That sounds pretty dangerous. I'm surprised you weren't gored by an enraged stag."

Denison opened his mouth to reply, but Farrel forestalled him, raising his voice to talk over him.

"Let me tell you what Halt was doing while you were chasing bucks and does," he said. "Halt and Crowley decided that something had to be done about Morgarath. A lot of us felt that way, but they were the ones who did something about it. They scoured the Kingdom, searching for Rangers who hadn't run off to Teutlandt at the first sign of trouble."

Denison flushed and Halt noticed that a few of the other Rangers suddenly looked down, as if they'd found their shoes very interesting.

Farrel kept on. "They captured one of Morgarath's messengers and discovered the plot he was hatching. They rescued Prince Duncan from Castle Wildriver and sent the rest of us to capture the man who was impersonating him on the northern frontier. Then they led us all at Castle Gorlan while King Duncan and Baron Arald faced off against Morgarath and drove him back into his castle, not to mention organizing the rescue of King Oswald from Gorlan. Since then, Halt has reconnoitered Morgarath's stronghold in the Mountains of Rain and Night—something no one else has been able to do—and brought back vital information on these terrible beasts he has recruited.

"On top of that, he rides better than most of us and shoots better than all of us. He's no beginner. He was trained for four years by Pritchard. Some of you may remember him."

The newer additions to the group exchanged looks. They were impressed by Halt's credentials, as enunciated by Farrel.

"Now I, for one, am happy to follow his lead and obey his orders. And I think that goes for the rest of us who have followed him and Crowley for the past year and a half."

He paused and looked around the group. The Rangers who had campaigned against Morgarath all growled agreement. The others reluctantly signified their assent. Only Denison remained recalcitrant. He tried another tack.

"You say we're buying time until the fiefs reinforce us," he said. "What makes you think that'll happen?"

Halt smiled and pointed to the edge of the forest beneath the park. A party of armed men was riding slowly up the slope toward them. There were at least forty of them, and he could make out the blue-and-gold banners of Castle Redmont. The rider at the head of the column was unmistakable. It was Baron Arald.

The Rangers watched as the new arrivals drew closer. Then Arald detached from the group and cantered toward them. He greeted Halt and Farrel cheerfully.

"Morning, Halt. Morning, Farrel. How's the leg?"

Farrel smiled. "Hurts like blazes, sir. But it's mending. It's good to see you."

"Have the enemy gone from Redmont Fief, sir?" Halt asked.

Arald shook his head, his cheerful expression fading at the mention of the Wargals overrunning his fief.

"No. But they won't stay there long. They won't break into the castle. I've left Lady Sandra in command, and my battle master Rodney is an excellent soldier. I've brought half our garrison to join you. The others will be along as soon as these cursed Wargals have moved on." He looked around the assembled group. "Good to see we've got so many Rangers to call upon," he said. They mumbled greetings. "Well, must be off. I'd better let the King know I'm here."

He cantered away, his horse's hoofs throwing clods of grass and dirt in the air behind him.

Halt smiled at Denison. "You were wondering if the fiefs would ever send reinforcements," he said. "I'd say that's starting to happen."

Reluctantly, Denison allowed an answering smile to cross his face. "I'd say you're right," he said. He held out his hand in a gesture of peace, and Halt took it, shaking it firmly.

20

Without the encumbrance of the Queen's carriage and the need to stop continually to allow her to rest, Crowley made much better time on his return journey to Woldon Abbey.

A day and a half after leaving Castle Araluen, he rode into the clearing in the trees where the abbey was situated. As he reined Cropper in, Sir Athol stepped off the colonnaded ground-floor verandah to greet him. One of the archers was a few paces behind.

"Ranger Crowley, you're back," Athol said. There was an obvious question behind the simple statement of fact.

Crowley nodded. "We've got trouble headed this way," he said. "A band of Morgarath's creatures has changed direction and is on its way here."

"Creatures?" Athol said. "What creatures?"

"Morgarath has recruited an army of semi-human beasts called Wargals," Crowley told him. "They're like your worst nightmare."

Athol's face betrayed his concern at this news. He turned to the archer. "Where's Edmund?" he asked, then explained to Crowley, "Edmund is the other archer who's with us."

"He's scouting to the south," the archer replied. "If these beasts are anywhere within one day's ride, he'll warn us."

"Expect to see him then," Crowley said sharply. "Because they're coming." He glanced to the main door of the abbey, where Abbess Margrit had just emerged, her hands folded in front of her, in the wide sleeves of her habit. She looked calm and unruffled.

"Ranger Crowley," she said. "What brings you back so soon?"

"Morgarath's forces are heading this way, Mother Abbess. The King sent me to fetch Queen Rosalind and take her back to Castle Araluen."

There was an awkward pause as the Abbess and the two members of the Queen's bodyguard exchanged a glance. They obviously knew something that Crowley didn't.

"That could be difficult," the Abbess said eventually. "The Queen is already in labor."

"In labor?" Crowley repeated stupidly.

Margrit frowned at him. "She's having the baby. That's how these things happen."

Crowley groped for words. He had no idea how to deal with this turn of events. "Isn't it a little early?" he asked. He had the impression that the baby wasn't due for another month, at least.

Margrit nodded solemnly. "Yes, it is. And it's all the more difficult for the Queen because of it. The labor is not going well. She's very weak."

"Can I see her?" Crowley asked.

Margrit raised an eyebrow. "To what end?"

He hesitated, uncertain as to what he should say.

She continued, with a hard edge to her voice. "Perhaps you don't believe me?"

Crowley made a hasty negative gesture. "No! No! I just thought . . ." His voice trailed off and then he looked the Abbess squarely in the eye. "I don't know what I just thought," he admitted, and she nodded.

"Perhaps you should rest and have something to eat," she said. "You've obviously ridden a long way. We'll attend to the Queen."

Unconsciously, he beat the dust off his jacket, then he dismounted, realizing how stiff he was from the many kilometers he had ridden. "Do you have any idea how much longer it will go on?" he asked.

Margrit shook her head. "It's been sixteen hours already. As I said, it's a difficult birth and the poor woman is exhausted. The longer it goes, the weaker she'll become." She paused. "She may not have the strength to deliver the baby."

Crowley felt the blood leaving his face at the thought. "You mean she might die?" he said at length.

Margrit nodded somberly. "It's a very distinct possibility." She didn't believe in raising false hopes. She was a practical woman, and a realist. She went to turn away, but Crowley reached out a hand to stop her.

"Assuming she has the baby," he said, "and she's all right, would it be safe for her to travel?"

Margrit sniffed scornfully. "Only if you want to kill her," she said. "The journey here was bad enough, but in her present weakened state . . ." She didn't say anything more, but slowly shook her head.

"She can't stay here," Crowley protested.

Margrit's shoulders lifted in a shrug. "She can't travel. There's no point in our using our skill to save her here, only to have you kill her by putting her in a carriage and bouncing her along the back roads to Castle Araluen." Margrit believed in dealing with one problem at a time. The current, and most pressing, one was to help Rosalind have the baby safely. They could worry about the approach of Morgarath's forces after that was done. With that thought in mind, she turned on her heel and went back inside the abbey.

Crowley absently patted Cropper's soft muzzle while he thought through this latest development.

"Maybe I could find a place to hide her in the woods," he said, half to himself. It wasn't an ideal solution, but it was the only one he could come up with at the moment.

Athol rested a hand on his shoulder. "We could fight them," he suggested. "My men are ready to give their lives for the Queen."

"They may have to," Crowley said dully. "There are thirty of these Wargals and, from what I've heard, they're virtually unstoppable. They don't care how many they lose in a battle. They just keep coming until they win."

A flicker of fear showed in the young knight's eyes for a second, then he recovered and drew himself up.

"We'll fight them," he declared firmly. "I'm not afraid of them."

Crowley patted his arm. "Well, you should be."

But before Athol could reply, the air was split by a shuddering scream from the abbey. Both men started. Then Crowley set off at a run for the door.

He blundered into the lobby. The polished wood floors and paneled walls reflected a sense of peace and orderliness. A faint smell of incense permeated the room. There was nobody behind

the registrar's desk. Once more, the air was split by a terrible
scream. Indoors now, and even closer, they heard it more clearly
and the sound was enough to freeze their blood.

There was another nerve-rending scream, then an ominous
silence. The two men exchanged a fearful look. Then a different
sound broke the incense-tinted silence of the abbey.

A baby crying.

Instinctively, Crowley made for the door leading to the inner
rooms. As he reached it and put his hand on the door handle, it
swung open before him to reveal Abbess Margrit. In contrast to
her usual calm demeanor, she was flushed. There was a stain of
blood on her gray gown.

She composed herself quickly. She hadn't expected to be
confronted by Crowley the moment she opened the door. She
managed a wan smile.

"It's a girl," she said. "A healthy baby girl."

The baby's cry echoed through the room once more, louder
than before.

"And possessed of a fine pair of lungs," she added.

"The Queen?" Crowley asked, fearful of what the answer
might be.

The Abbess's smile faded. "She's alive. But she's very weak.
She lost a lot of blood and the birth was difficult. It'll be touch
and go if we can save her." She admitted the last with an air of
desperation.

"I want to see her," Crowley demanded, but the Abbess
shook her head.

"She's sleeping now. I'm not going to wake her so you can
bother her with a lot of stupid questions. Rest is the best thing
for her." She turned a shrewd eye on him. "And a little rest

wouldn't do you any harm either. You're going to have some big decisions to make over the next twenty-four hours and you'd better be in good condition to make them."

Crowley passed a hand over his brow. Now that she mentioned the idea of sleep, he realized how much his body craved it. He swayed slightly and she steadied him with one firm hand on his arm.

"Maybe twenty minutes," he said, and she led him forward.

"I'll take you to a chamber," she said.

"The Queen is asking for you."

The words penetrated the fog of sleep that had seeped into Crowley's brain. His eyes opened and he looked around the room, disoriented for a moment and not knowing where he was.

Then he remembered. The Abbess leaned over him, one hand out to shake his shoulder, then saw his eyes were open and withdrew it. Hastily, he swung upright. He had thrown himself on the bed without bothering to even remove his boots or weapon belt. He glanced apologetically at the dust and mud stains he had left on the coverlet.

"I'm sorry—" he began.

The Abbess waved his apology aside. "No matter."

He stood up. His eyes were bleary and he rammed the heels of his hands into them, rubbing them side to side to clear his vision. He shook his head, then looked at the Abbess.

"Take me to her."

She led him out of the small room into the corridor and past three other doors to an end room. She opened the door and gestured for him to go on. Queen Rosalind was propped up against a pile of soft pillows, in a bed by the window. Sunlight streamed into the room. Outside, he could hear the soft murmur of doves.

But it was the Queen who drew his attention, and he tried to stop the shock showing on his face. She mustered the strength to raise one hand and beckoned him toward her. She was pale, deathly pale. The flesh seemed to have melted from her bones, and she gazed at him through feverish eyes that were sunk deep in her cheeks. Huge dark shadows circled the flesh under her eyes and her cheekbones were in stark relief. The skin was waxy and had a dreadful pallor to it.

He knew straightaway she was dying.

He stepped closer to the bed, leaning down to take her claw-like hand in his. He couldn't believe how she had deteriorated since he had last seen her. It was evidence of how badly the delivery of the baby had wracked her already weakened body. Behind him, he was conscious of the Abbess watching them, ready to step in at any moment if the Queen needed her.

"My lady . . . ," he said uncertainly. Then he stopped, not knowing what to say next. He felt the weak pressure of her hand on his and her lips moved. He could barely hear her and he bent closer.

"Crowley. Why are you back here?"

He tried to smile reassuringly. "I'm to take you back to Castle Araluen, my lady," he said.

But she shook her head weakly. "I'll never make it. I'm dying, Crowley."

He started to protest, but the look in her eyes stopped him. She knew, he realized, and no platitudes or words of false cheer would help her. She saw the decision in his eyes and she nodded weakly.

"Morgarath's men are coming, aren't they?" she asked. Before he could begin to answer, she added, "Don't lie to me. I need to know." Her voice was still soft, but it held an intensity now that he couldn't deny.

He nodded sadly.

"Then take my baby to safety," she said. She began to rise on the pillows and repeated the command with more force. "Take her out of here and keep her safe. Swear you will do that!"

The effort drained her and she sank back on the pillows, her eyes closing. For a few seconds, he feared she was dead. Then her eyes flicked open, locking on his, bright and feverish and demanding.

"Swear it to me, Crowley."

He bowed his head. Then he looked up again and met her eyes.

"I swear it, my lady," he said miserably. He knew she was right. The end was very close for her and he had to get the royal baby to safety.

She closed her eyes again for several seconds, then opened them and patted his hand weakly. She smiled at him, a ghastly travesty of a smile.

"Thank you," she said weakly. "I know she'll be safe with you." This time, when her eyes closed, they didn't reopen. He could see her chest rising and falling and knew she was still alive. But for how long, he wondered.

Margrit touched his arm. "Leave her now," she said. "She needs to rest."

He nodded dumbly and allowed the Abbess to lead him from the room. At the door he stopped and turned for one more look back at the Queen.

A ray of sunlight was coming through the window beside her, from a high angle. It lit on her face and transformed it from a ghastly, pallid skull-like thing, giving it a translucent, delicate beauty.

"Good-bye, my lady," he said. At least, his lips moved with the words, but no sound emerged.

21

HALT PACED SLOWLY ALONG BEHIND THE SHOOTING LINE, watching the Rangers practice their shooting. In rapid succession, arrows whirred over the field toward the line of targets set up two hundred meters away, thudding into the canvas stretched over the tightly packed straw. The majority of shafts were concentrated in the central gold ring of the targets. Occasionally, a shooter would mutter a low exclamation of disgust as one of his shots went wide. Although none went wider than the red inner circle of the target, next to the central ring.

The Rangers' shooting was good—better than good. It was phenomenal, considering the distance and the casual way the arrows were dispatched. There was no deliberate and painstaking aiming going on. The line of Rangers simply nocked, drew and shot in one almost continuous action, sending the arrows whistling out over the field in a constant stream.

Several of the members of the small company of archers attached to the army had wandered over to the field to watch the Rangers at work. They were all carrying their bows slung over their shoulders, hoping for a chance to show these much-vaunted bowmen a thing or two. After the first few seconds, they had exchanged surprised glances and left their bows where they were. They knew they couldn't match the speed or the accuracy on display here. They had never seen so many expert archers in one spot.

Halt, who had seen their arrival and noticed their original cocky attitude dissolve, stepped away from the shooting mound and indicated a couple of spare targets at the end of the line.

"Care to join in?" he asked, with a smile.

The senior of the three archers shook his head. "Thanks, but our egos have taken too big a battering already. We'd heard about you people, of course, but we've never seen so many of you in one spot. Or such good shooting."

"Even those young ones can show us a thing or two," another soldier declared, nodding his head to the spot where the six new apprentices were also practicing. None of them could yet handle the eighty-pound longbow, and they were shooting lower-powered recurve bows over a shorter distance. But even so, they were displaying remarkable skill already.

"Well, we won't be shooting at one another when Morgarath gets here," Halt said, "and we'll want every arrow to count. Make sure you get in as much practice as possible when we finish."

"Aye, we'll do that," the senior archer said, appreciating the Ranger's friendly and cooperative tone.

Halt bade them farewell and returned to the shooting line. He put his fingers in his mouth and emitted a piercing whistle. The line of shooters all turned to look at him.

"That's enough," he said. "I've seen how good you are. No need to keep showing me."

The Rangers relaxed, lowering their bows from the shooting position and turning to face him, sensing he had something further to say. Cedric, one of the new arrivals, allowed a challenging grin to cross his face.

"You've seen us shoot," he said. "But we haven't seen you. After all, if you're—"

He got no further. Halt swung his bow down from his shoulder and, in the same motion, flicked an arrow from his quiver and laid it on the string. Without seeming to aim, he sent the arrow whistling on its way. Then another. Then another. Then a fourth, which was in the air before the first arrow had reached the target he had selected.

They could hear the rapid series of thuds as the arrows slammed into the gold central ring of the target, the fourth virtually having to shoulder the others aside as they clustered together in the very center.

There was a low murmur of approval from the Rangers, and a quiet exclamation of surprise from the three archers who were still watching.

Halt raised an eyebrow at Cedric. "Happy now?"

Cedric shook his head slowly in admiration. "I think you know which end of an arrow points outward," he said.

Halt nodded, a trace of a smile on his face. Then he became serious again.

"All right. Sorry to have put you through that practice session but I wanted to make sure none of you have got rusty while you've been away." He paused, then added, with a slight smile, "Obviously, you've all kept up your skills. Thank you for that. We will be needing them. But now we have tasks that are more suited to your other skills. We need to know what Morgarath's troops are doing. We need to know when he decides to gather them together again and head this way to confront us in force.

So we'll be heading out individually, to scout the surrounding fiefs and see how long Morgarath plans to keep up these nuisance raids and when he plans to fight us in strength."

There were nods of approval along the line of faces. As Halt had intimated, this was closer to the traditional role that Rangers played when there was an impending battle.

"I've drawn up a list of fiefs and assigned Rangers to scout each of them," he said. "Let's regather at my—or, rather, Crowley's—command tent and I'll pass them out. I want you on your way this evening."

Again, nods of approval and agreement. Then another thought struck Halt and he went on. "One more thing: Which of you have been assigned apprentices?"

Six hands went up and he met their expectant gazes.

"You've done well with them so far. They all shoot well already." The six heads nodded, knowing more was to come. "But we need them to shoot better than well. You six stay here and keep drilling them. I want them shooting morning and afternoon until their arms ache." A saying of Pritchard's occurred to him. "You know what we say: An ordinary archer practices until he gets it right. A Ranger—"

"Practices till he never gets it wrong," more than a dozen voices finished for him and he grinned, a little shamefaced.

"Oh, I see you've heard that," he said. "Well, keep them at it. We're going to need them in the coming battle and we want every arrow to count, as I told our friends the archers." He nodded to the three men who were still standing a little apart, watching.

"Now, the rest of you, let's get back to the command tent and I'll tell you where you're going."

✦ ✦ ✦

It was a sad little group that trudged back to the abbey from the small cemetery, set in a clearing among the trees. They had laid the Queen to rest in a simple grave and the Abbess had said a few words over the freshly dug earth. Even though she was not of a religious order, she seemed the most fitting to speak over Rosalind's grave.

Crowley watched the brief ceremony, staying until two of the soldiers had finished filling in the grave. Athol wanted them to level the mound and cover it with old earth.

"We can't let the Wargals find her grave," the young knight said miserably.

Crowley turned a steady gaze on him. "On the contrary, it would be better if they did," he said. "Have one of the men carve a headstone for her. Wood will do. But mark it clearly as the grave of Queen Rosalind of Araluen."

"But Morgarath's men might despoil the grave!" Athol protested.

Crowley nodded agreement. "They might. But it won't harm the Queen. She's beyond all that now. On the other hand, if they find the grave, they'll stop looking for her—and the Abbess and her nurses."

A thought had occurred to him as he remembered the earlier idea of finding a hiding place for the Queen in the woods. They could do the same for the Abbess and the other women who staffed the abbey, keeping them safe.

"We're going to need skilled healers when this is all over," he said to the Abbess an hour later when he described his idea. Somewhat to his surprise, she agreed with him. He had been worried that she might refuse to leave the abbey, staying to face the approaching enemy armed only with her powerful personality. But she understood that empty gestures of defiance were a luxury they couldn't afford.

"I'll leave Athol and one of the archers to help you," he said. "I'm sorry I can't spare more men, but the King needs every soldier he can find."

Margrit waved his apology aside. "I'm sure we can cope by ourselves."

But he shook his head. "No. You'll need them to set up the camp, and to hunt for food."

She considered his statement and nodded. "You're right. We'll be glad of their help. Now, have you considered how you'll get the baby back to Castle Araluen?"

The Ranger hesitated. Truth be told, he hadn't had time to give the matter a great deal of thought. He assumed he'd carry her in his arms while he rode Cropper. The horse had a steady, even gait that would prevent the baby being jolted and jerked, even as they traveled at speed. But now he wondered how he might feed her. He had a vague idea that babies required constant feeding. He voiced his concern and Margrit solved the problem for him.

"Take a water skin full of cow's milk," she said. "Stop two or three times a day and pour some milk into a bowl—"

"Will a baby this young drink from a bowl?" Crowley asked.

Margrit raised one eyebrow at him, her expression somewhat annoyed. She didn't enjoy being interrupted.

Crowley dropped his gaze. "Sorry."

She waited a few more seconds, making her point, then proceeded. "We'll give you some small strips of linen. Soak them in the milk and put them in her mouth. She'll suck the milk from them."

"Ingenious," said Crowley.

Margrit raised that eyebrow again. "We have done this before, you know," she said dryly.

Over the next day, Athol and Crowley scouted the area and found an ideal hiding place for the nurses. It was a blind gully in the forest, with steep, wooded hills on either side. At the end, it appeared to peter out into a blank rock wall. But on closer examination, they discovered a right-angle turn that concealed the entrance to a large cave. The floor inside was cool sand and light filtered down from above, through half a dozen fissures. Unless one was two or three meters away, the entrance was effectively hidden.

They moved Margrit and her nurses to the cave immediately. Fortunately, there were no other patients at the abbey. The women had already packed what they would need to live in the woods. The Abbess inspected the site and declared herself satisfied.

"Thank you, Crowley," she said, in a rare moment of warmth. "You've done well by us."

Satisfied that he had done all he could to keep the women safe, Crowley mounted Cropper and leaned down to take the baby in his arms as one of the nurses handed her up to him. Margrit passed him the water skin full of milk and the linen strips he would use to help the baby feed. He would ride on alone. The other men would follow at their best pace—but that would be nowhere near as fast as the pace Cropper could keep up.

He settled the baby in the crook of his left arm, making sure the shawl she wore was tucked up around her neck and head. The grave little eyes looked up at him, calm and full of trust. Then he wrapped his cloak around her.

"Keep her safe, Crowley," the Abbess said.

"I will," he said. His voice thickened as he spoke, as he thought of the selfless devotion of the baby's mother, and her determination to see the baby born safely. Only then had she succumbed to the weakness that had ravaged her.

He nudged Cropper with his heel and the horse turned away, ready to canter, when the Abbess put up a hand to stop him.

"What is it?" he said, and she indicated the precious bundle in his arms.

"The Queen chose a name for her," she said. "Her name is Cassandra."

22

TRAVEL-STAINED AND WEARY, CROWLEY RODE ACROSS THE drawbridge of Castle Araluen. The sentries on duty, recognizing the Commandant of the Ranger Corps, withdrew to either side at the portcullis to allow him entry.

He checked Cropper with a click of his tongue as he reached the steps leading up to the keep. Carefully, he slipped his right leg over the pommel and, clutching tight to the precious bundle concealed beneath his cloak, he slid down from the saddle. He had ridden nonstop from Woldon Abbey. His knees were weary and his leg muscles ached. He leaned back against Cropper for a few seconds, regaining his balance.

The horse looked as fresh as a daisy, as if he hadn't been cantering smoothly, with only brief rest periods, for the past sixteen hours. Crowley patted his neck with his right hand, then mounted the steps and entered the great hall.

Duncan's chamberlain, who was speaking quietly to two of the castle servants across the hall, looked up and saw the dusty figure just inside the doorway. He hurried across to him, his boots clacking loudly on the bare floorboards.

"Commandant Crowley!" he said. "You're back!"

He glanced curiously, trying to see behind Crowley. Then the significance of the Ranger's early return registered on the Chamberlain's face. The Queen was obviously not with him. But now, as he watched, Crowley eased back his cloak and a small bundle was visible in the crook of his left arm.

Small it may have been, but its lungs were obviously in good condition as it let out a lusty howl. Crowley, by now well accustomed to dealing with the princess's moods, jiggled her gently in his arms and spoke soothingly to her.

"Hush hush, my girl. You're safe now," he said, his voice gentle and reassuring. The words meant nothing, he knew, but the tone was all important.

Gerard, the chamberlain, leaned forward to peer more closely at the red-faced, squalling infant.

"Is that . . . ?"

Crowley gave him a weary smile. "It's Princess Cassandra, heir to the throne of Araluen. Although at the moment, she looks like any other bad-tempered newborn brat," he added, the smile widening.

Gerard, caught unprepared, essayed an awkward bow in the direction of the screaming child. Then, as Crowley continued to rock her, the squalling slowly died away and she nuzzled at one knuckle and emitted a series of burps and grumbles and squawks, sounding somewhat mollified by the Ranger's actions. Then the significance of the fact that Crowley was carrying the child struck Gerard with its full import and the blood drained from his face.

"The Queen?" he began uncertainly, not sure how to continue.

The smile faded from Crowley's face and a look of intense

sadness replaced it. He shook his head. "The Queen passed away shortly after the baby was born."

Tears sprang to Gerard's eyes. He had loved the Queen. More than that, he was a loyal servant to Duncan and he had seen how the Queen brought light and happiness into the King's day, easing the cares and worries that he had to cope with on a regular basis. Her death, he knew, would be a massive blow to Duncan.

As if reading his mind, Crowley asked, "Where is the King now?"

Gerard gestured helplessly at the upper floors of the keep, where Duncan's offices were situated.

"He's in his office," he said. "Shall I have someone tell him?"

Crowley shook his head. "I'll do it," he said. "He'll want to see his daughter." He started toward the stairway in one corner.

Gerard hesitated, then declared, "I'll come with you." He knew that it would be wrong to simply let Crowley walk into the room with the princess in his arms. The King would need some advance notice. He hesitated, looking at the two servants who were now watching curiously. He flapped a hand at them, dismissing them.

"Get on with your work!" he told them, then hurried after Crowley, mounting the stairs two at a time to catch up with him. They left the stairway on the third level and headed for Duncan's suite of apartments. Gerard laid a hand on Crowley's arm, stopping him.

The Ranger looked at him, annoyed. He was tired and dispirited. He had ridden a night and a day without stopping to rest, intent on one thing: to bring the new princess safely back to her father.

"You can't just burst in on him with the baby!" Gerard told him now. "It'll be a terrible shock. Let me announce you. Let me prepare him."

Crowley nodded, seeing the good sense in his words. He had no wish to cause the King any more pain than was absolutely necessary.

"Go ahead," he said wearily, and Gerard, with one last, sad look at the child, turned and knocked twice on the door to the King's apartment. He was one of the King's close confidants and there was no need for him to await permission to enter. After a brief pause, he turned the handle and went in, closing the door quietly behind him.

Duncan was hunched over his desk, peering at a poorly written report from the chief armorer. The armory had been working overtime to manufacture the vast number of arrows that would be needed by the Rangers and the small archery force in the coming battles. The report detailed the numbers currently available.

"What is it, Gerard?" he asked, without looking up. The double knock had identified his visitor.

"My lord," Gerard said hesitantly, "Commandant Crowley has returned."

That caused the King to look up in surprise. Crowley was not expected for at least another week. A puzzled frown crossed the King's face.

"So soon?" he said, rising from his seat and moving round the table. "What's happened?" He knew the Queen could not have traveled so quickly and he also knew that Crowley would never have left her behind.

Gerard shifted awkwardly from one foot to the other. Now he regretted the kindly instinct that had led him to suggest he should break the news to the King. But he saw a look of foreboding growing on Duncan's face and knew he had to go ahead with it.

"He's brought the princess with him, my lord," he said.

Duncan actually staggered a pace, putting his hand on the table to steady himself. Without being told, he already knew the worst. "Is the Queen with him?" Duncan asked, although he knew that was an impossibility.

Gerard shook his head, searching for the right words. Then he realized there were no right words. "The Queen is . . ." He hesitated, then started again. "The Queen didn't survive the birth, my lord," he said wretchedly.

Duncan's lips moved soundlessly, then he found his voice. "She's dead," he said flatly.

Gerard nodded confirmation. "I'm so sorry, my lord."

Duncan drew himself up to his full height and stood for a moment, with his eyes shut tight. The lines on his face seemed to have deepened, Gerard thought—lines carved there by stress and pain and sadness. He seemed to have aged in the past few minutes, as unlikely as that was. He took a shuddering breath as he absorbed the terrible news. Then he straightened his shoulders and his eyes opened.

"Is the baby healthy?" he asked.

Gerard nodded hurriedly. "Crowley says she is."

Duncan nodded once. "Send him in," he said quietly.

Gerard, about to utter further condolences, realized that the words would mean nothing. He turned on his heel and went out through the door, leaving it ajar behind him. Crowley stood waiting in the outer room, the baby cradled now in both arms. Gerard gestured to the half-open door.

"Go on in," he said. "He wants to see his daughter."

Crowley strode into the room, his soft boots making virtually no sound on the floorboards. The King was still standing by
the desk, his back straight and his shoulders squared. His face
was set in stone, but behind the eyes, Crowley could see the
unutterable depths of sadness. He stepped closer to the tall figure and held out the little bundle. Cassandra gurgled once or
twice, seeming to peer up at the figure before her as if, somehow,
she recognized him.

"So this is my daughter," the King said finally. He gazed
down on the tiny face. The eyes were wide-open and they were a
mirror of his own. He reached out one hand to ease back the
shawl around her face, and as he did so, a tiny hand emerged and
seized his forefinger with surprising strength. He allowed it to
stay captured as he gazed at the baby.

"The Queen called her Cassandra, my lord," Crowley told
him. He didn't utter any words of sympathy or condolence. He
knew they would be meaningless. He'd done his duty and
brought the baby safely home to her father—as he'd promised
the Queen he would.

Duncan nodded. "Cassandra," he repeated dully. "That's a
fine name."

"She's a fine girl," Crowley told him. He proffered the little
blanket-wrapped bundle to the King. "Would you like to . . . ?"

Duncan reached gingerly to take his daughter. Like so many
new fathers, he was awkward and clumsy, worried that he would
drop her or hurt her in some way.

Crowley smiled. "Don't be afraid, my lord. She's a sturdy
little thing. She just rode for sixteen hours without complaining." He amended the statement. "Well, without complaining
too much."

Duncan held the baby close. He put his cheek down against hers, marveling at the velvet touch of her skin against his rough beard.

"So soft," he said.

Gently, he rocked his daughter in his arms. Her face lit into a beaming smile and she chuckled—the most magical sound in the world. He looked up at Crowley.

"She laughed," he said.

The Ranger nodded, looking a little proprietorial. "She does that a lot," he told the King. Then he realized that tears were flowing down the King's cheeks as he looked down at the laughing little figure in his arms. He wasn't sure if the King himself realized. And in that moment, Crowley knew that this baby, this tiny scrap of humanity, would be the key to the King's recovery from the devastating tragedy that had struck him and the path to his future happiness.

"Thank you, Crowley," the King said, his eyes still riveted on Cassandra. Then he looked up to meet the Ranger's gaze. "Thank you for bringing my daughter safe home."

Crowley bowed slightly and began to back away toward the door.

"Shall I send some of the women to help you with her, my lord?" he asked. The King's attention had gone back to the laughing baby.

"Yes. Yes, do that," Duncan said softly. He reached for the little face again with his forefinger and once again felt it trapped in the baby's remarkably strong grip.

"But tell them to take their time," he said.

23

TIMOTHY ENTERED THE TENT WHERE HALT SAT AT THE COM-mandant's desk. The temporary commander looked up at the young man, a question on his face. Usually, he didn't like to be interrupted while he was working, and Crowley's clerk knew this.

"Four pigeons have come in, sir," Timothy explained. He held up four tiny message slips that had been taken from the pigeons' legs. Halt gestured for him to hand them over.

The Rangers who had been sent out scouting Morgarath's troop movements all carried messenger pigeons with them. Halt took the tiny sheets of paper and studied them quickly. They had been rolled up in the small metal cylinders attached to the pigeons' legs and they began to furl up once more as soon as they were released.

He noted the locations from which they had come. They were four fiefs to the south and west of Araluen Fief. They would have been the first to be attacked by Morgarath's raiding bands of Wargals.

"When did these come in?" he asked.

Timothy replied promptly, expecting the question. "The first came in twenty minutes ago. The others arrived pretty much all together about five minutes ago."

Halt frowned, placing the message slips side by side and reading them. The wording on the forms were all slightly different, but the message was the same.

"He's gathering his forces," he said.

Timothy frowned. "Sir?" he said, not understanding.

Halt tapped a forefinger on the message forms. "Morgarath's raiding parties are withdrawing from the fiefs they've been attacking. They're all heading for a point south of Araluen. That means he's ready to start coming after us. I imagine there'll be more messages from the other Rangers before too long."

The canvas door flap was pushed aside and Crowley entered, catching the last few words.

"What messages would they be?" he asked, and Halt rose from behind the desk, a huge smile of welcome on his face.

"You're back!" he said. "You have no idea how glad I am to see you." The Hibernian hated the day-to-day paperwork of being in command. He would be glad to hand it all back to Crowley. Then, before Crowley could reply, the smile faded.

"The Queen?" he asked. "Is she all right?"

Crowley looked at the two worried faces before him and slowly shook his head.

"She didn't survive," he said flatly. "It was a very difficult labor and she was too weak."

Halt lowered his eyes, shaking his head as he thought of how devastated the King must be. He and the Queen had been intensely happy together. Now that was over. And, Halt realized, he'd have no time to mourn her properly. Morgarath's forces were on the move. Once they were assembled, they'd come after the royal army with devastating force.

It was left to Timothy to ask the next question. "What about the baby?"

"She's fine," Crowley told them both. "Healthy and strong and fit. She's about the only bright spot in Duncan's life at the moment."

"Well, here's more bad news for him," Halt said, indicating the small pile of message forms on the desk. "It looks as if Morgarath is starting to reassemble his army."

He passed the messages to Crowley. As the Commandant studied them, Halt explained. "I sent Rangers out to scout the fiefs where his Wargals have been attacking."

Crowley nodded approval. Halt may have hated administrative work, but he had good command instincts, he thought.

The Hibernian continued. "These are the first reports to come in. He's seized the harvest for his own army and drawn hundreds of our men away to defend their castles and villages. Now he's ordered his forces to assemble to the south of us. He's obviously planning to attack us before our soldiers can rejoin the army."

Crowley nodded, glancing at the large map on an easel against the canvas wall of the tent.

"Yes. The fiefs will naturally take their time to make sure he's really withdrawn. And then, to rejoin us, the men would have to fight their way through his main force. And they'd be in smaller numbers." He shook his head. "He's a cunning swine."

"We'd better let the King know," Halt said, beginning to move toward the door.

But Crowley stopped him. "We'll take this news to Lord Northolt and Sir David first. They can get the army ready to move. Then we can let the King know what's happening."

Halt nodded. "Yes. We might as well give him a few more minutes with his daughter."

Crowley eyed him sadly. "It may be the only time they get," he replied. Then, as a thought occurred to him, he turned to his clerk. "Timothy, not a word about the princess. Not to anyone."

"Of course not, sir," Timothy replied. His attitude indicated that he thought the caution unnecessary. He never spoke about events discussed in the Commandant's tent. Crowley noted the expression and decided to explain further.

"The fewer people who know about her existence the better," he said. "So far it's the King and his chamberlain and the three of us. Let's keep it that way."

Timothy nodded, a little reconciled to the order. "Of course, sir."

Crowley had a flash of recollection as he remembered the two palace servants who had seen him arrive in the great hall. He made a mental note to tell Gerard to warn them against talking about Cassandra as well. Or to place them somewhere they couldn't talk to anyone.

"Come on," he said to Halt. "Let's find Lord Northolt."

As the three of them exited the tent, they almost ran into a servant hurrying to find them. The man recoiled and apologized. Crowley waved his apologies aside as he saw the message slips in the man's hand.

"Sorry, Commandant. These just came in. I thought you'd want to see them."

He handed the message forms to Crowley, who scanned them quickly, then glanced up at Halt.

"Three more fiefs," he said briefly. "Morgarath's really on his way."

He thrust the message forms into Timothy's hands, then turned toward the castle, striding briskly to find the royal battle master, with Halt a few paces behind him.

The advantage of having a small army was that it took less time to get it mobilized. Within an hour, the tents had been lowered, folded and stowed on wagons, leaving only neat lines of dead grass squares where they had stood. The field kitchen had prepared a meal for the soldiers. Thankfully, the ration situation had improved. The Rangers had brought in deer to supplement the available meat, and a foraging party sent north had returned with bushels of grain, loaves of bread and stocks of potatoes, cabbages and carrots. Some of the latter were old and withered, but they were still edible.

The men sat on the grass by the field kitchens, hurriedly downing the meal. They'd be on the march within an hour and they wouldn't see hot food again until they reached the Ashdown Cut. Lord Northolt planned to have them continue marching through the night, with only a few hours around midnight to snatch some sleep. It was vital that they reach Ashdown Cut well before Morgarath's troops, to give them time to prepare the ground for his attack.

Duncan and his senior advisers ate as well—sharing the same rations issued to the rest of the army. But they ate in the relative comfort of Duncan's office in the castle. Weapons and armor leaned against the walls and the desk, their martial appearance softened by the sight of the tiny crib in the corner by the window.

Halt, Lord Northolt and Sir David had, of course, given Duncan their condolences on the death of his wife. Duncan had nodded his gratitude, his face bleak.

Kings have little time for mourning, Halt thought. There's always something to take their attention.

Yet it became obvious that Duncan had considered the best course to take with the new princess.

"She'll stay here in Castle Araluen," he said. "My mother will be in command."

Crowley frowned thoughtfully. "Have you considered taking the princess with us, my lord? She's a good traveler." He smiled wryly. "I should know," he added.

Duncan regarded him and a slight smile creased his face—a welcome expression amid all the gloom that had befallen him, Crowley thought. But he shook his head.

"All things considered, Crowley, I think she'll be safer here. I'll leave thirty-five men to garrison the castle . . ."

Sir David looked up from the bowl of stew he had balanced on his knees. "Can we afford to leave so many?"

Duncan met his gaze evenly. "Yes," was all he said, and David subsided.

"Normally I wouldn't leave so many," Duncan explained. "But Cassandra is the future of the Kingdom, and she must be kept safe. As must my mother. The walls here are high and strong. There's plenty of food in the castle now and there's a well inside the walls. I think that's enough men to keep Morgarath's beasts at bay until we have the numbers to drive them off."

Halt nodded, shoving his empty bowl to one side. "As you've

said, my lord, Morgarath has no siege towers or catapults. The only way his Wargals could get into the castle would be with ladders."

"Take a mighty long ladder to scale these walls," Crowley put in, and Halt nodded agreement. Castle Araluen's walls were among the highest and thickest in the Kingdom.

"In fact," the Hibernian said, "I'd rather like to see them try. Wargals aren't particularly agile beasts. They're clumsy and their hands have thick claws that wouldn't grip a ladder's rungs too well. I could see Morgarath losing large numbers of them if they tried scaling a long, high ladder."

"In any case," Duncan said, "I'm his prime target and I'm guessing that the first item on Morgarath's agenda is to close with the army and destroy it before we're reinforced. Once he's done that, he can take his time breaking into Castle Araluen."

There was a general mumble of agreement around the room. That was the Black Lord's logical course of action. The army was small and lacking in essential forces like archers and cavalry. The castle was strong, and even a small defending force could make it well-nigh impregnable. Morgarath would be better served attacking the army, and leaving Castle Araluen, and others like Redmont, to wither on the vine. That was his logical course.

There was a rap at the door and Duncan looked up.

"Come," he called, and the door opened to admit one of Lord Northolt's captains. He bowed his head to the King, who acknowledged the greeting with a wave of his hand, deferring to the battle master with a quick gesture. The captain turned his commander.

"Lord Northolt," he said, "the army is ready to move."

24

THE ARMY MARCHED AWAY FROM CASTLE ARALUEN IN THE early afternoon.

Sir David sent out a screen of twenty of the precious cavalry-men to scout ahead. Crowley deployed half a dozen of the Rangers to follow the army as a rearguard and keep watch for Morgarath's forces. Before his command tent in the castle grounds was struck and packed away, he and Timothy prepared messages for the Rangers who were observing Morgarath's forces, ordering them to rejoin the army immediately, at a point halfway to the Ashdown Cut. He sensed he was going to need all his men before much time passed.

Once the messages were sent, he, Timothy and Halt mounted and rode out after the army.

They caught up with them after an hour and a half. From the top of a ridge, they could see the long, winding, snakelike force of men marching across an open plain. The infantry was making good time, marching in four columns, and wearing half armor. Every company had a horse-drawn cart with it, laden with the rest of the men's armor and their heavier weapons.

Weapons and rations were in half a dozen other carts, each

pulled by two draft horses. A small herd of additional horses plodded alongside, allowing the wagoners to change their beasts every two hours, so that the fresh animals could maintain the fast pace set by Lord Northolt at the head of the column.

Out to either flank, the Rangers could see the small cavalry force deployed. As they cantered down the slope toward the plain, they were greeted by the rearguard of Rangers, who seemed to materialize out of the trees and bushes.

"Any sign of Morgarath and his beasts?" called Egon, one of the originals, as they rode past.

Crowley shook his head. "Not so far. But they'll be along, you can be sure of that."

Halt studied the line of fast-marching men ahead of them. He tried to make a mental comparison to the awkward, jogging gait of the Wargals. He suspected that perhaps the mysterious beasts would move faster than Duncan's army. But they had a long way to go before they would catch up.

"Keep your eyes peeled," he called to Egon and the others. The gray-cloaked men nodded grim agreement. Then he and Crowley touched their heels to their horses' flanks and accelerated away from the line of Rangers ghosting in and out of the trees and long grass.

As they neared the tail of the army, Halt could see pale ovals of faces, as the soldiers looked anxiously behind them at the sound of cantering hoofs.

"Keep moving," he said to the nearest men. "No sign of Morgarath and his performing bears yet. Keep up the pace and we'll make Ashdown Cut before they're up with us."

He saw the relieved expressions as the men turned back to the road ahead of them. It must be nerve-racking to be in the rear of a retreating army, he thought. In that position, you'd never know when the enemy might suddenly appear over a ridge or round a bend behind you. You would constantly feel vulnerable.

The two Rangers continued to canter along beside the marching ranks of men, overhauling them easily and reaching the vanguard, where King Duncan, Lord Northolt, Sir David, Baron Arald and their respective staffs rode at ease. Northolt called a greeting and beckoned them to ride beside him. Duncan rode alone, several meters ahead of the small command party. His face was set in grim lines. No wonder, thought Halt. He's in the open with a small army. He's left behind his mother and daughter, hoping that Castle Araluen will provide shelter and protection for them. And in a day's time, he's facing a battle against a vastly superior force.

That would leave little time for small talk.

"Any word?" Northolt asked.

Crowley shook his head. "Not so far. I've recalled the Rangers who were keeping watch on his forces. We've had enough messages to know that he's mustering his entire army into one large force. Then he'll come after us."

"Of course, assembling his forces and getting them on the road will take some time," Northolt said thoughtfully. "We should reach Ashdown in plenty of time to set up a good defensive position." He glanced up at the sun, now low in the western sky. The shadows of the trees stretched out across the ground, elongated and ungainly. So did the shadows of the marching men—seeming to be twice as high as the men who cast them.

"We'll take a couple of hours' rest around ten," he said. Then we'll get moving again once the moon rises. That should be some time after midnight."

The two Rangers nodded agreement. At the start of a grueling journey like this, a few hours' sleep would be enough to refresh and revitalize the men. Later, as their energy reserves were depleted by the constant marching, and the nervous strain of waiting to see if they might be attacked, they would need more time to rest and recuperate.

"Anything you need us to do?" Crowley asked, but Northolt shook his head.

"Just keep marching with the rest of us," he said, glancing sadly at the despondent figure of the King riding a few meters away, his tall form slouched in the saddle.

The army continued to march, eating up the kilometers beneath their nailed boots. Every two hours, Northolt would call a brief halt. The men would break ranks, drink from their canteens and sit in the long grass beside the road, while the wagoners unharnessed one team, then put a fresh pair of horses into the traces. Then the horns would blow along the small column and the march would resume.

As darkness fell, the routine continued. The men were now sunk deep into the cocoon of weariness that affects any body of marching men after a few hours. Feet and leg muscles were numb and unfeeling. Shoulders were rubbed raw where leather straps passed over them, suspending the heavy swords they all wore at their waists. Each man carried his spear, and the outer two files wore their long triangular shields, to protect the column from any surprise attack by archers or slingers. They moved in a daze, almost asleep on their feet, concentrating on nothing but maintaining the plodding, unvarying rhythm, dully anticipating the next short stop and the chance to relax and ease tired muscles.

As night fell, lanterns were lit and carried by every tenth man in the second file, held high on the end of their spears. The screening cavalry moved in closer to the column. To the rear, the ever-watchful Rangers cantered back and forth across the line of march. Occasionally, two or three of them would drop back and find a vantage point from which to keep watch to the rear.

Periodically, one would ride forward and report to Crowley. Each time, the Commandant watched with apprehension as the cloaked figure drew nearer. But each time, he let his shoulders slump in relief as he heard the negative report. There was no sign of the pursuing force.

On one occasion, when Samdash, another one of the originals, reported, Halt gestured out to the flanks of the column.

"Keep watch on the flanks as well," he said. "Morgarath may not come up directly behind us."

Samdash grinned and nodded. "We're already doing that."

Halt shrugged. "Sorry. I should have known. There's no need to teach you your job."

But Samdash's grin widened. "Never hurts to remind us," he said. Then he wheeled his horse around. "Better be getting back."

They marched on. The army plodded up a long slope, men groaning as their calf muscles strained and tightened and cramped. At the summit, Halt looked back. He could see for perhaps five or six kilometers behind them. It was dark, but he could see no sign of a large force following them. Naturally, he couldn't make out the Rangers forming the rearguard. They knew how to remain unseen.

"We might be in the clear," he said to Crowley.

The sandy-haired Ranger considered the statement for a few seconds, then came to a decision. "We'll ride back and check the trail behind us," he said. He apprised Lord Northolt of their decision and the battle master nodded agreement. Truth be told, Northolt would have liked to go back with them. Riding at this constant, unvarying pace was exhausting and mind-numbing, and he was having trouble keeping his eyes open. Of course, he admitted to himself, it was a lot more tiring on the men marching. He glanced up at the stars, searching for the Great Cartwheel. Finding it, he estimated that it was close to nine in the evening. In another hour, he planned a two-hour halt, so it might be a good time to have their back trail checked and cleared.

"Go ahead," Northolt said. "Take care."

"That's what we do," Crowley told him. He and Halt wheeled their horses out of the line and cantered swiftly back down the column.

Northolt watched them go. Those Ranger horses were amazing, he thought. They'd been traveling for hours but showed no signs of tiredness. His own horse was plodding, head down.

A Ranger's life was a good one, he decided. A Ranger enjoyed freedom of action and the opportunity to scout and reconnoiter almost at will. They weren't subject to the strict discipline imposed on the soldiers and commanders of the army. They could urge their nimble little horses out of the line and go and check the situation for themselves.

"Must be nice," he muttered.

One of his captains, riding close by and half dozing in the saddle, jerked upright. "Beg pardon, sir?"

But Northolt made a negative hand gesture at him. "Nothing. Just thinking aloud."

The captain grunted and settled himself more comfortably in the saddle. His head drooped and he dozed off again. Northolt glanced at him enviously. Must be nice to be a junior officer, too, he thought. He can doze off in the saddle, knowing I'm keeping an eye on things.

But this time, he made sure he didn't say it aloud.

It took longer than Duncan had estimated for Morgarath to gather his forces together and set out for Castle Araluen. Bands of Wargals kept drifting into Morgarath's appointed rendezvous area long into the evening. He was tempted to punish his commanders for their tardiness, but realized that there would be no point in it. Assembling a large number of men was always time-consuming. When they weren't men but the brutish, clumsy Wargals, it took even longer.

Then, of course, once they were assembled, they had to eat and pitch their tents. Angrily, he resigned himself to not moving until the following morning.

As a result, it was nearly noon by the time he reached Castle Araluen. His huge army deployed out onto the neat parkland in front of the castle. He rode forward, scanning the walls. He could see men there, manning the catwalks behind the lofty battlements.

But there didn't seem to be too many of them.

He studied the site where the Araluen army had pitched its tents. The field was marked by squares of dead grass where the tents had stood. There weren't a lot of them either, he noted. His plan to raid the fiefs and restrict Duncan's numbers had worked. But now that the threat of the raiding parties had been removed from the fiefs, he knew that the troops would begin to drift north and augment Duncan's forces.

He rode in a giant circle around the massive, soaring castle, accompanied by Stott, one of the human officers who had served under him at Gorlan.

The moat was wide and deep, and the drawbridge was raised. Behind that, he knew, was a massive iron portcullis. There was no easy way in. As Duncan had stated, Morgarath had none of the siege equipment he would need to take such a well-built castle.

And even if he did, he didn't have time to engage in a long siege. He had to move quickly, before Duncan's scattered forces had time to rejoin him and bolster his numbers. At the moment, Morgarath knew all the advantages were on his side. But if he allowed too much time to pass, that equation would change.

They completed the circle and sat on their horses before the drawbridge, staring up at the impossibly high walls.

"How are we going to take this?" Stott asked.

Morgarath glanced at him contemptuously. Was he so stupid that he couldn't see that would be an impossible task?

"We're not," he said.

Then, as Stott went to ask a further question, Morgarath heard an ugly hiss-thud and a crossbow bolt from above slammed into Stott's chest, sending him reeling back out of the saddle, dead before he hit the ground.

Morgarath wheeled his horse and galloped away out of range. Typically, he didn't look back at his fallen officer.

✦ ✦ ✦

High on the battlements, on one of the many turrets situated along the walls, Queen Deborah, the Queen Mother, handed the crossbow back to the sergeant standing beside her. He looked at her in admiration. She was gray-haired, and her face was lined and wrinkled. But she had just pulled off a remarkable shot at pretty much maximum range. He began to understand why her son had left her in command of the castle.

"Good shot, ma'am!" he said, but she shook her head angrily, watching the black-clad figure galloping away to safety.

"Didn't allow enough for the wind," she said. She glared after the retreating former lord of Gorlan. "Don't come back, Morgarath," she muttered. "I won't miss again."

25

THE ARMY REACHED THE ASHDOWN CUT THREE HOURS after sunrise.

The Cut was a valley that sloped uphill. Its sides were steep and rocky, and so heavily overgrown with trees as to be virtually impassable. The Cut narrowed as it followed the slope upward. At the top, it was less than fifty meters wide; at the base, one hundred.

Beyond the top was a downhill slope that led north, with a broad highway twisting through the trees—an easily defensible escape route for the army.

Duncan, Arald and Northolt selected a spot almost two-thirds of the way up the valley, where the slope grew steeper and then leveled out before beginning to gradually climb again. The men were set various tasks to create a defensive position. Some were put to cutting and stripping young saplings to form a barricade of sharpened spikes facing out and down. Others began digging a deep ditch across the valley in front of the spikes. An enemy attacking would have to negotiate the steep slope of the hill, then the deep ditch with its soft crumbling sides, before forcing his way through the thick hedge of stakes facing outward.

And of course, there would also be heavily armed soldiers with long spears behind the earthworks, ready to discourage any would-be attacker.

During the night, all but one of the Rangers had rejoined the company. Berwick had been assigned to a fief in the southwest and had the greatest distance to travel. Crowley expected him to arrive sometime late in the morning. He gathered the Rangers, and their six apprentices, in a small group behind the fortifications.

"We'll split into two groups," he told them, indicating the earthworks being built. "Each group will take up a position at the end of the line. I'll command the left wing, and Halt the right."

"Wouldn't we be more effective in one group?" Robert asked. "There are only twenty of us, after all."

It was a reasonable question and Crowley had considered this option. But he shook his head. "I want to catch them in an enfilade from either side," he said. "If my group shoots first and they turn their shields toward us, they'll expose themselves to Halt's group—and vice versa. Besides, our rate of shooting will make a smaller group seem like a big one."

Robert nodded assent, as did a few of the others. He hadn't been querying Crowley's arrangement to be contentious and he could see the good reasoning behind the plan.

Crowley scanned the line of faces, each one shadowed and grim beneath their hooded cloaks. He found the one he was looking for—Denison.

Since his first brush with Halt, Denison had fallen quickly into line and lost his initial propensity to query and dispute orders from the two young Rangers. He had spoken at length with Samdash, Jurgen and Leander, who were all well-known to him from earlier days. He had been impressed by their whole-hearted endorsement of the sandy-haired commander and his grim, bearded friend.

Now Crowley singled him out because he was one of the most experienced and longest-serving Rangers in their group.

"Denison, you'll be in my ten," he said. "But first I have another task for you." He jerked his thumb back in the direction they had traveled. "I need you to ride back down our trail for fifteen kilometers or so. Find a good vantage point and keep watch for Morgarath's army. The minute you see them, ride flat out back to us and let us know they're coming. That way we'll have plenty of time to get ready for them."

Denison nodded, then made a suggestion. "Can I take Cedric along with me?" he asked. "Two sets of eyes will be better than one, and it'll mean one of us can rest while the other watches. After all, Morgarath could be a few days behind us."

Crowley agreed instantly. "Good idea," he said. He glanced at Cedric. "That all right with you?"

The balding Ranger grinned. He was a cheerful enough fellow, Crowley thought.

"That's fine by me," Cedric said, then added, "Whose group will I be shooting with?"

"Halt's," Crowley said immediately. If anything happened to the two rearward scouts, he didn't want one of the shooting parties weakened by two archers.

Cedric turned his grin toward Halt. "I'll look forward to

that," he said. He had seen Halt demonstrate his shooting skills on the practice range and he was keen to see how the Hibernian accounted himself in a real battle. He expected to be impressed.

"What about the apprentices?" Chase asked now. He was mentoring one of the six apprentices and wanted to know where his protégé would be stationed.

"We'll put them in the middle of the line, behind the barricade. Farrel, can you supervise their shooting?"

The limping Ranger nodded. The apprentices would be using lighter-powered bows and would need an experienced eye to gauge the most effective range for them to begin shooting.

"You won't mind if I take a shot or two myself?" he asked, with a grim smile.

Crowley smiled back. "I'm counting on it," he said. Then he slapped his hands together briskly. "Right, gentlemen, we've got a lot to do. Let's get to it."

The assembly broke up, with Denison and Cedric heading for the horse lines, where their horses were grazing. The rest of the army's horses were tethered to rope lines. The Ranger horses were left to wander free. No Ranger horse would ever stray from its master. As they saddled the two shaggy, muscular ponies, a thought occurred to Denison.

"What's your code word?" he asked.

They were going into a dangerous situation, and neither of them knew what emergency might befall them. It might become necessary for either of them to ride the other's horse, and without the code word neither horse would allow it.

"*Here I come*," Cedric replied in a lowered tone. His horse pricked its ears at the phrase and he slapped it affectionately on the neck. "Yours?"

"*Upsy-daisy-do*," replied Denison, his look challenging Cedric to comment on the phrase. Cedric couldn't prevent that grin of his from spreading across his face. Denison was a good Ranger, but he could tend to be a little pompous. Perhaps the horse trainer, Young Bob, had selected the phrase intentionally, to take some of the starch out of him. Wisely, Cedric didn't joke about it. He merely nodded several times.

"I'll remember that," he said eventually, forcing his face into a deadpan expression.

Denison sighed. "Be hard not to," he replied in a long-suffering tone.

As the two Rangers cantered out of the camp and headed down the army's back trail, Halt and Crowley were sitting on the grass outside Crowley's low field tent, adjusting arrows. Each of the Rangers had drawn forty shafts from the armorer's wagon. They loaded their quivers with a dozen, and kept the other twenty-eight in canvas arrow bags. The arrows had been produced in their thousands in Castle Araluen over the preceding week. They were all made to a standard length, but each Ranger's draw varied, according to the length of his arms. In some cases, the arrows needed to be shortened and have their warheads refitted.

Halt had a standard draw length, so he didn't need to adjust his arrows. Crowley, however, drew his arrows two centimeters less than standard. He and Halt worked in companionable silence now, removing the warheads, cutting two centimeters from the shaft, then resetting the warheads on the shortened shafts. A small pot of glue simmered on the fire between them and they daubed each bare shaft with glue before refitting the warhead.

A shadow fell across them and the two Rangers looked up. Halt recognized the newcomer. He was Wearne, the senior archer from the small company attached to the army—the man who had watched the Rangers practice their shooting.

"What do you want from my men?" Wearne asked, without any preamble. He addressed the question to Halt, as he'd seen him as the commander on their previous meeting. Halt made a gesture to Crowley, deferring to him.

"We're going to be in two groups, one on either wing," Crowley said. The archer nodded. It was a sensible arrangement. "I'd like you and your men—how many do you have, by the way?"

"Twenty-eight," Wearne replied gruffly. "Not many of us, but we're all good shots." There was no boastfulness about the statement. It would be pointless to exaggerate his men's skill at such a time.

"So Halt tells me," Crowley replied.

The archer turned his gaze to Halt again, who shrugged. "I watched you practice after our men left the range," he said. "You all shoot well."

Wearne acknowledged the compliment. He hadn't seen the Ranger watching them. Then he realized that often you didn't see a Ranger, if the Ranger didn't want to be seen.

"I'd like your men in the center," Crowley continued. "About twenty meters behind the army, on the higher ground. Once we start shooting at the front ranks of Morgarath's army, I want you to direct a plunging barrage on their rear."

Wearne considered the idea. Plunging arrows were shot high into the air to come down—plunging, as the term indicated—from a steep angle. It was a skill that Araluen's archers practiced constantly.

"Sounds good," he said. "That way we'll hit them from three directions at once—left, right and above. That should get 'em confused."

"I rather hope it gets them *dead*," Crowley said succinctly.

A humorless smile touched Wearne's rugged features. "That'd be even better," he agreed.

"Just wait for the signal before you start shooting," Halt said. "I'm going to be conducting a little experiment when they start to move up the hill."

Crowley turned an inquisitive eye on his friend. "You are? And what might that be?"

Halt chewed his lip thoughtfully. "I'm going to feint a cavalry attack on their front line."

Crowley frowned. "We don't have enough cavalry for a frontal charge."

Halt made an appeasing gesture with one hand. "That's why it'll be a feint. I'll take thirty troopers and make it look as if we're going to charge. I want to see if the Wargals still react to horses the same way they did when I saw them on the plateau. We won't actually make contact. I'll bring them back before we hit their front line. But while I'm doing that, I don't want the rest of you shooting my backside full of arrows."

Crowley and Wearne exchanged a glance. Both of them smiled.

"We'll do our best to miss you," Crowley assured his friend.

Halt raised an eyebrow. "The way you shoot, that should be easy for you," he said.

26

DENISON AND CEDRIC CANTERED THEIR HORSES TO A POINT twenty kilometers in the rear. As the light began to fade, they selected a tall hill to the right of the trail as their vantage point and urged their horses up to the summit.

From here, they had an excellent view of the surrounding countryside. To the south, the direction from which they expected Morgarath's army to appear, there was a high ridge four kilometers away. Beyond it, they could see the open countryside and the high road.

"There's a lot of dead ground beyond that ridge," Cedric commented. "Maybe we should set up on the ridge itself."

Dead ground was ground that wasn't visible to them, by dint of the fact that it was hidden by the ridge. Denison considered the suggestion, but shook his head.

"We're not sure where they are," he said. "For all we know, they could be just behind that ridge, and I don't want to bump into them. We'll still have plenty of advance warning when they top the ridge itself."

"Fair point," Cedric agreed. They loosened the girths on

their horses' saddles. They didn't want to waste time re-saddling them if the Wargals suddenly appeared.

They settled down in the long, soft grass. Their horses moved to and fro, cropping the fresh shoots. Cedric glanced at the sky and saw that it was clear, with only a few clouds chasing each other across the heavens.

"No need for a tent," he said.

Denison grunted agreement. "I suppose there'll be no fire, either?"

The other Ranger shook his head. "It'd be visible for kilometers if someone's watching," he said. "And you never know when someone's watching."

They had a cold meal of dried meat and fruit wrapped in bread. They washed it down with cold water from their canteens. Luckily for them, they hadn't developed the taste for, and dependence on, coffee that Halt and Crowley shared.

As the sun began to disappear over the western horizon, the evening grew chilly and they drew their warm cloaks closer around themselves, sitting with their knees drawn up, scanning the countryside behind them in silence as the last of the sun's rays faded in the western sky.

Then they became aware of a new light source. It loomed over the ridge they were watching, an orange light that reflected in the sky. The light of hundreds of campfires.

"That's them," Denison said, gesturing toward the sky above the ridge.

Cedric stood up, shading his eyes, and peered toward the south. "Just over the ridge, do you think?"

But Denison shook his head. "I'd say they're a kilometer or

so back. From memory, there's a large open space there where they could pitch their tents."

"Well, at least we know they've stopped for the night," Cedric said.

"True. No sense in our both staying awake. Why don't you grab a few hours' sleep. I'll wake you when it's your turn to watch."

"Sounds good to me," Cedric replied. He settled his knapsack as a pillow, leaned his quiver of arrows against a bush a meter or so from it, then lay down and rolled himself in his cloak. There was a nip in the night air, and he enjoyed the feeling of warmth and comfort that the cloak brought. He kept his bow strung and wrapped in the cloak with him to protect the string from the damp night air. Within a few minutes, he had fallen sound asleep, a skill that all Rangers possessed.

They changed watch halfway through the night. When Denison opened his eyes next morning, he heard the familiar sounds of the horses pawing the earth and cropping the grass. Their harness jingled softly.

He sat up. There was a familiar smell in the air. Cedric, who was standing a few meters away, heard him move and turned to him.

"Wood smoke," Denison said, tossing aside the cloak and standing up. Cedric nodded and pointed to multiple columns of smoke rising into the air beyond the ridge. There was little wind close to the ground and the smoke rose to some height before dissipating in the higher air.

"They've got their cook fires going," Cedric said. "Obviously, they're not in any great hurry."

"They know where we're going," Denison said. It was impossible for an army, even a small one such as Duncan's, to move through the countryside and not leave a clear trail. "If they've got trackers, they probably have a good idea how far ahead of them we are."

Cedric said nothing. Then, after a few minutes, he glanced to where his horse was standing.

"Maybe we should get back and report to Crowley," he said. "We know how far behind us they are."

"Good idea," Denison told him. "You go ahead with that. I'll stay here a while longer. There's something I want to see."

Cedric cocked his head to one side in a question. "What's that?"

"I want to get an idea of how fast they're moving," Denison replied. He gestured to a grove of trees on the flat ground below the ridge. "Would you say those trees—the ones with the really dark green one in the center—are about a kilometer from the ridgeline?"

Cedric squinted, glancing from the grove of trees to the top of the ridge and back again several times. "Close enough to," he replied.

"Then I'll see how long their army takes to pass that point. That'll give us some idea of when they might arrive at the Cut."

Cedric pursed his lips. It was a good idea, he thought. "Of course, they'll move faster this morning when they're rested and fresh. By this afternoon, they'll be slowing up." Denison was studying him with a long-suffering expression on his face, and he realized he had been stating the obvious. "Sorry," he said.

Denison waved a hand, dismissing the apology.

Cedric turned and strode to where his horse was waiting expectantly. He leaned down and tightened the girth straps, then swung up into the saddle in one easy movement. He trotted the horse to where Denison was standing at the summit of the hill, his eyes fixed on that distant ridge.

"I'll be off then," he said.

Denison smiled up at him. "Travel safely."

Cedric nodded toward the ridge. "You too," he said. "And don't leave it too long before you start back after me. Remember, we'll need every shooter we've got."

Denison patted Cedric's horse's neck several times. "Don't worry. I'll be on Sparrow," he said, nodding toward his own horse, who was watching events with her ears pricked in interest. Ranger horses always wanted to know what was going on around them. "She can outrun any band of shambling shaggy bears any day of the week."

"Make sure you give her the chance to do it," Cedric said. Denison had a reputation for being painstakingly thorough when he took on a task. Cedric could see him leaving it too long to make his own escape from the hill, giving Morgarath's mounted men time to overtake him. Then he shook his head. No ordinary horse could match the speed and endurance of a Ranger-bred horse. He touched his heels to his horse's flanks and they trotted off.

Denison watched them go. He preferred to work alone, as did most Rangers. But it had been comforting to have company, especially when he was so close to the enemy, and they were such an unknown quantity. He hunkered down in the long grass and fixed his eyes on the distant ridge.

It was just under two hours before he saw movement there. A group of figures appeared on the crest, spreading out to study the land before them. They were all mounted, and he realized they would be Morgarath's staff and commanders. He counted twenty of them. In the center of the line he could make out a tall figure on a white horse. Morgarath, he thought. Idly, his fingers dropped to the quiver at his side, and he touched one of the arrows nestling there. Of course, the Black Lord was well out of range. But if Denison angled down through the trees, heading toward the high road, he might well bring the enemy general within bowshot.

Then he shrugged the idea aside. Morgarath was no fool. He was an experienced campaigner and he wouldn't expose himself to the risk of a single archer. Besides, Denison had other things to do. He watched as the first of the horsemen started down the slope. Morgarath waited, he noticed. Denison hurried back to his horse and fumbled in the saddlebags for a small sandglass. He glanced back at the enemy, now moving down the slope. The first of the infantry had crested the rise now and dimly, he could hear the tuneless chant that they uttered when they marched. He turned the sandglass and began to measure their progress.

As more and more Wargals appeared over the ridge, he felt his heart rate accelerate. There were a lot of them, he thought. They appeared to outnumber Duncan's small army by at least four to one.

"Well, we're going to have to do something about that," he

muttered. He noted that the last few grains were running through the sandglass and quickly turned it, glancing up to see that the lead elements of Morgarath's army were still well short of the grove of trees he'd selected as a marker.

Big armies move slowly, he thought. They take a long time to muster, and then they're restricted to the pace of the slowest man—or monster.

At least that was something the Araluen army had going for it.

27

"THEY WERE MAKING ABOUT THREE AND A HALF KILOMETERS an hour," Denison told the command team in Duncan's pavilion. "But they've got a big, unwieldy baggage train that will slow them down."

"Probably full of the food from our harvests," Duncan said bitterly. "So we should expect to see them toward the end of the day?"

Denison nodded. "I doubt they'll make it before then."

Lord Northolt rubbed his hands together in a satisfied gesture. "Good! That'll give us time to make a few more preparations—and to get our own wagons started for our next destination."

"Where is that?" Crowley asked.

Northolt deferred to Sir David, who strode to the large map mounted on an easel and tapped a point to the northwest of their current position. "Hackham Heath," he said. "It's a good defensive spot in the fief where I was battle master to Baron Siskin."

"So you know the territory well?" Halt asked.

David nodded. "Yes. Although not as well as my son Gilan. He spent all his time roaming and exploring in the woods and hills."

Baron Arald glanced at him curiously. "How old is Gilan now?" he asked. He recalled meeting the boy at the annual tournament several years ago.

"He's twelve," David replied. "But he's big for his age. Shows a lot of natural talent with the sword. I've had him training with MacNeil for the past year."

Arald raised his eyebrows, impressed. "MacNeil indeed?"

"Who's this MacNeil character?" Halt said in an aside to Crowley.

Crowley suppressed a grin. Only Halt would refer to the Kingdom's legendary sword master as *this MacNeil character*, he thought.

"He's the foremost swordsman in the Kingdom," he said. "An absolute master—and an excellent teacher. He only accepts the most talented young men as his students. Young Gilan must be something special."

"Hmmm," Halt muttered, storing the information away.

Arald asked a question of the room in general. "Do you think Morgarath will attack this evening?"

There was a pause as the others considered the matter. Finally, the King looked to Lord Northolt for his opinion.

"I doubt it," the battle master replied. "They've been marching all day. They'll be tired and hungry—even these indefatigable beasts that Halt has told us about have to rest and eat sometime."

"Plus they'll arrive with the last of the light. If they do attack, they'll soon be fighting in darkness—and that's always risky," Crowley put in.

"Let's not take any chances," Duncan said. "Morgarath has a habit of doing the unexpected. And we know he has little affection for his troops. They're a means to an end. But most likely they'll make camp tonight and attack in the morning, when they have a full day to finish us off."

Northolt rose. "If that's all, sir?" he addressed Duncan. "I have a few tweaks to add to the defenses, seeing we've got some extra time."

Duncan waved a hand in dismissal. "Get on with it then." He looked at the others. "The rest of you, draw whatever rations and weapons you need for tonight and tomorrow from the baggage train. Then get the wagons on their way." With any luck, they all knew, and by dint of traveling through the night, the baggage train would reach their next defensive position at Hackham Heath before dawn and be ready to receive the army as they withdrew from Ashdown Cut.

There was a stir of movement around the table as the meeting broke up, and they all headed back to their respective commands.

"David," said the King, "could I have a word?"

The erstwhile cavalry commander waited as the others filed out of the tent.

"I know you normally command the heavy cavalry," Duncan began.

David's mouth twisted in a rueful smile. "Not that we have any heavy cavalry," he said. "We only have lancers, and precious few of them."

"Precisely," Duncan replied. "That's why I have a new job for you."

David regarded the King with interest. Truth be told, in the absence of any heavy cavalry to command, he had been wondering where he could best serve the army.

"This battle is going to be fought on foot," the King said. He saw David draw breath to speak and, correctly guessing what he was about to say, waved a dismissive hand. "Oh, I know Halt has some far-fetched plan to pretend to attack the Wargals with thirty troopers, but in the main, we're going to be fighting on foot. That means what cavalry we have will fight dismounted, and take their place in the line. Lord knows, we can use them."

David nodded and the King continued. "We're outnumbered. You know that. And it's likely that, at some stage, Morgarath's troops will break through our line. When that happens, I want a fighting reserve ready to plug the gap and drive them back. You, Arald and I are the most skilled warriors in the army. I want the three of us to be ready as a kind of roving reserve. If the Wargals break our line, the three of us will charge in, rally our men and throw the enemy back down the hill."

David nodded slowly. "Sounds like a good plan," he said. "What about Lord Northolt?"

Duncan shook his head. "His job is the overall supervision of the defenses. But he's a little old to be involved in hand-to-hand fighting."

David realized this was true. Northolt was no longer a young man, and this was definitely a young man's job. He smiled.

"I've been wondering what I'd be doing when the fighting starts."

"You'll be doing plenty," the King replied gravely. "We all will."

◆ ◆ ◆

Lord Northolt set men to the task of digging a further ditch forty meters downhill from the main defensive position. This one was lined with sharpened stakes and covered in light branches and grass to conceal it. Two solid bridges were left on either side that would bear the weight of his horses and men as they moved down the hill. Ropes were attached to the bridges so they could be withdrawn when required.

Another party was digging two diagonal trenches, running down the hill in the shape of a V and culminating at the new trench. At the top end of each, the men had placed a large cask of oil from the supply wagons.

Baron Arald was watching all this with interest. "What's the idea here?"

"When it's time for us to withdraw," Northolt told him, "this will give us a little extra time. We'll pour the oil into the two ditches, then set fire to it. With any luck, and if the wind's in the right direction, it'll set the grass burning on a broad front between us and Morgarath. That'll give our men time to fade back over the hill and run like the blazes."

Arald nodded, impressed. He studied the slope below them, visualizing the twin rivers of flame running down the hill, then setting the long grass alight. The smoke and flames would form an effective barrier against their attackers. And they'd conceal that the army was vacating its position and withdrawing over the hill.

"That will give us a start," he agreed. "But will it be enough?"

"Possibly not. But Crowley's Rangers are going to act as a rearguard. They'll set up ambushes at every bend in the road or every narrow valley. Morgarath will have to constantly stop and take up a defensive formation. That'll slow him up."

Arald scratched his chin. "Crowley's a good man," he said. "We're lucky to have him."

Northolt agreed. "Morgarath may have done us a favor without knowing it," he said. "Crowley's more energetic and imaginative that any Commandant I can remember—particularly the fop Morgarath appointed to the position a couple of years ago."

"Halt's no slouch either," Arald commented. "He's been working in Redmont Fief for the past months and I can't remember a better Ranger."

"They make a good pair," Northolt agreed, then he turned to shout directions to some of the men working on the new trenches.

Arald turned away. "Speaking of Halt, I want a word with him," he said, heading back up the hill to where the Rangers were preparing their shooting positions. They had no need of any protective breastworks, as Morgarath had few archers or crossbowmen among his men. But they were building a light screen of saplings and brushwood. If the enemy couldn't see where the volleys of arrows were coming from, it would keep them a little more confused.

Arald found Halt dragging a large bundle of branches and saplings into position and beckoned him over.

"David tells me you're planning a cavalry charge on Morgarath's front line tomorrow," he said, without any preamble.

Halt nodded. "It's a feint. We won't actually make contact. We don't have enough troopers to risk losses in a frontal engagement."

"Then what's the point?" Arald asked, frowning slightly.

"I want to test something I discovered when I was scouting the plateau," Halt told him. "The Wargals seem to be leery around horses. They seem to be the one thing that can unsettle them. I got the feeling that Morgarath was trying to train it out of them and I want to see if he's been successful."

"So if they start looking nervous when they think they're going to be charged by cavalry, you'll know."

"That's right. Could be a handy thing to keep in mind for a later time."

Arald tugged his mustache thoughtfully. "Yes. It certainly could be." He paused, then continued, "Would you mind if I joined in on your mock attack?"

Halt looked surprised, but recovered quickly. "Not at all. The more the merrier," he said. "But why?"

"Well, I thought your little feint might look more convincing if you had a fully armored knight leading it, all shiny and ferocious looking, rather than a shabby Ranger." Arald was smiling as he said it, robbing the words of any possible offense.

"It's a good point," Halt agreed. "I plan to wait till they're assembled and ready to advance up the hill. Then I—or rather you—will lead thirty or forty troopers out in extended line formation and start down the hill. Actually, if you're leading, it'll give me a chance to really watch the Wargals and see how they react."

"Fine. I'll join you first thing then, once the enemy are in place and ready to open proceedings."

Halt nodded several times. He liked Arald. The time he'd spent at Redmont Fief had shown the Baron to be an honest and courageous leader—if a little too fond of good food.

"We'll assemble here," he said, "on this side of the defenses. We'll ride downhill, until we're a hundred meters from the Wargals. Then we'll swing back. If they're still nervous about horses, that'll give us plenty of time to see it."

"And if they're not?" Arald asked.

Halt shrugged. "Well, at least we'll know."

Morgarath's army arrived in the early evening.

They heard them first. The Wargals marched keeping pace to the cadence of a guttural chant. They could hear the sound long before the enemy came into view. Then they could make out the jingle and clash of weapons and harnesses as the beasts moved in their rolling, shambling gait. Duncan's soldiers waited nervously as the noise grew louder and more ominous. They had never heard anything like it and the disembodied sound preyed on their nerves. Stomachs tightened and mouths went dry as the noise grew, ebbing and flowing on the evening breeze.

"Where are they?" someone asked, his voice cracking slightly.

Duncan, standing at the head of his men, turned in the direction of the voice. "Steady," he said, his voice firm and seemingly unconcerned. "They'll be here soon enough."

Then several of the men cried out at once as the first of the Wargal horde came into sight in the indirect light of the setting sun, crossing a low ridge to their front and swarming down the near slope to the beginning of the uphill, narrow valley where the Araluen army waited for them.

A ripple of excited comment swept across the army, then slowly died away as the soldiers became aware of the numbers facing them. The black-furred, shambling creatures came over the ridge in eight ranks—and kept coming.

"There are thousands of them," one of the archers said, his voice a little higher-pitched and a little louder than he'd intended it to be.

Halt turned to face the group of men, leaning on their bows as they watched Morgarath's army deploy onto the level ground at the foot of the Cut.

"Actually," he said, "there are probably fewer than a thousand."

But the archer who had spoken looked doubtful. "That's still plenty more than there are of us," he said.

Halt patted the feathered ends of the arrows in his quiver. "By tomorrow, there'll be a lot fewer of them if we all do our job," he said calmly. His matter-of-fact manner seemed to calm the nerves of the archers, and those of the army who were within earshot.

Finally, the ranks of marching creatures ceased coming over the ridge. They massed in eight extended lines at the base of the hill, facing upward to where the pitifully thin ranks of Duncan's men awaited them. They stood, unmoving, for several minutes, simply threatening the watching men with their numbers. Then a tall black-clad figure rode forward on a white horse and stopped in front of them, facing up the hill to where Duncan and his officers stood watching.

And waiting.

Suddenly, without any signal seeming to have been issued, the assembled ranks of Wargals raised their weapons above their heads and let out one massive shout—a cry of defiance and threat that echoed around the hills. Early roosting birds were driven, chattering, from their trees by the sudden noise.

Crowley, caught unawares by the cry, actually flinched, and cursed himself for doing so.

Then, again without any discernible order being given, the ranks disassembled. Every tenth troop in the front rank remained in place, forming a sentry line and watching the enemy. The others broke up into six-man squads and began pitching camp. Fires were lit and several wagons came up from the baggage train, which was only now beginning to trundle over the ridge, and began preparing food.

In the center of the camp, in the dying light of evening, Halt could make out Morgarath's black-and-gold pavilion being erected. He turned to Crowley.

"Maybe we should slip down the hill and put an arrow in Morgarath," he suggested.

Crowley considered the idea for a few seconds, then rejected it. "He's too wily for that. I doubt we'd get anywhere near that tent," he said. "Look how he's surrounded it with sentries."

Morgarath, with the wealth of numbers at his disposal, had formed a protective screen around his pavilion. Halt studied it and reluctantly agreed. He heard a clatter of plates and pots behind him. The support staff were serving out a hot meal to the men standing behind the palisade. He nudged Crowley with his elbow.

"Let's get something to eat," he said. "We'll need it tomorrow."

28

THE FOLLOWING DAY DAWNED CLEAR, WITHOUT CLOUDS IN the sky. There was a light ground mist lying over the hill leading down to the Wargal camp, but as the sun rose, it burned off.

The enemy was awake. Cook fires were burning once more and their thin columns of wood smoke rose into the air above the lines of low black tents. In comparison to the neatly ordered rows of tents that Duncan's men pitched—although these had been struck and had gone ahead with the wagons the evening previously—the Wargals' tent lines were untidy and haphazard.

Duncan strode along the parapet of the earth rampart thrown up behind the hedge of sharpened stakes. His men were edgy, as was to be expected. They were, after all, about to go into battle with a new and unfamiliar enemy. And they were out-numbered nearly four to one. They had stood to at first light, in case Morgarath tried to catch them napping with a dawn attack. But there was no sense in keeping them tense and ready now.

"Relax, men," he said calmly. "Loosen your armor and take the weight off your feet. They won't be coming for hours yet."

He could see the movement among the enemy lines as the Wargals fetched food from their field kitchen and hunkered down on the earth to eat. Back in the center of the camp, Morgarath and several of his cronies sat at ease around a table, with food and drink being served.

"Eat your rations," Duncan told the men. "No point in fighting on an empty stomach."

The camp cooks, in addition to serving a hot meal the previous evening, had left cold food for the men's breakfast: grilled meat and flat bread. There were fires lit behind the waiting army and one man in eight—the men were divided into eight-man messes—was boiling water and brewing hot drinks for their comrades.

Duncan sensed a relief in the tension as his men sat on the damp grass and loosened their armor, laying aside their heavy helmets and spears and beginning to eat. He realized that he was doing nothing to ease their nerves by pacing up and down the parapet. He saw Arald and David also inspecting the enemy camp below them and called them over.

His orderly had been following him and he turned to the man now. "Bring us some breakfast, Walter," he said quietly, as the other two joined him.

Walter bobbed his head obediently. "Yes, sir. Shall I set up a table?"

Duncan shook his head. He wanted his men to see him sharing the same food and the same conditions they were.

"I think the ground will be good enough," he said. Then, turning to the nearest group of soldiers, he asked with a grin: "What do you say, men? Is the ground soft enough for a royal backside?"

The soldiers chuckled. One of them, a grizzled veteran, rose and walked over to where Duncan and his two senior officers were standing. He made a show of inspecting the ground, brushing aside a few twigs and rocks, then spread out a none-too-clean neckerchief and gestured for the King to sit.

"There you go, my lord. Your royal bum should be comfortable there."

The others nearby joined in the laughter. Duncan grinned at him. "If it's not, I'll have you in the stocks later tonight," he said. "We did bring the stocks, didn't we, Sir David?"

"I'm sure we did, sir," David answered gravely.

The veteran cackled at him and resumed his place among his companions. The three senior officers sat on the edge of the ditch, their legs dangling over it, and munched on the bread and meat that Walter brought them. He also brought a steaming pot of coffee. Duncan hesitated, then looked round to make sure the men had been served with hot drinks as well. Then he took a deep sip and smacked his lips appreciatively.

"Ahhh!" he said. "Nothing like hot coffee in the morning!"

"When do you think they'll be coming, my lord?" It was one of the younger soldiers sitting behind them who asked.

Duncan gave him a reassuring smile. "I should think they'll be a while yet. They're not the most organized troops, or the most disciplined. They'll have to eat, then form up and then advance. I'd say you have a couple of hours. Get some sleep if you can. I'm going to."

And so saying, he stretched his arms over his head, took off his helmet and lay back on the soft earth, hitching his sword around so that he wasn't lying on it. He closed his eyes and spoke to Arald out of the corner of his mouth:

"Keep an eye on things. Wake me if anything happens."

Arald exchanged a grin with David. The sight of the King

sitting eating on the edge of the ditch, then sprawling back and napping, had reassured the men around them. They elbowed one another and pointed, grinning at the reclining monarch.

An hour passed and there was little of note happening in the Wargal camp. Then, as the sun grew higher in the sky, they heard bugles sounding and they could see the black creatures shambling into a loose formation. It took them some time. As Duncan had noted, they weren't the most disciplined or thoroughly drilled troops. But eventually, they formed into four ranks, about fifty across, and began to shuffle forward.

"He's not committing them all to the first attack," David observed.

Duncan opened his eyes, feigned a yawn and sat up reluctantly. In truth, he had been wide-awake the entire time, his nerves trembling like fiddle strings. But to look at him, you'd never know it. He appeared to be annoyed that Morgarath's troops had decided to interrupt his nap. Reluctantly, he rose and turned to the watching troops.

"Get your armor on and move up to the ramp, men. Looks like they're on their way."

The men began to take up their defensive positions. Unlike the Wargals, they were drilled and disciplined and they were in place in a few minutes.

Arald glanced down the hill and gestured to the right-hand side of the line. "I'd better join Halt. We've got a cavalry charge to fake," he said. He shook hands with the other two and strode off, his spurs clinking. His orderly had already led his battle-horse to the assembly point Halt had indicated. As Arald reached the spot, Halt greeted him. There were thirty cavalry troopers mounted behind him in two files.

Arald called to them cheerfully. "Morning, men. Ready to shake up these shaggy black bears?"

There was a chorus of assent. They were glad to be given a job in the upcoming battle. They knew their numbers were too small to waste on direct attacks.

"Remember," Halt told them, "we don't make contact. We'll trot forward to within fifty meters, then I'll give a horn signal and we wheel and come back. Understood?"

The men chorused their understanding.

Halt studied them for a moment or two, making sure they had all grasped the idea. He didn't want anyone to get carried away in the excitement of the moment and charge down on the massed ranks of Wargals. Cavalrymen did tend to get excited, he knew. But he could see from their faces that they all knew this was to be a feint.

"All right. There are two bridges across the second ditch, marked by willow wands. See them?"

The men stood in their stirrups and peered down the hill. The two stripped willow sticks were clearly visible. They assured him that they could see them.

"We'll cross the ditch there. The left file take the far bridge, the right file this near one. Once we're across, form an extended line behind the Baron." Halt gestured to Arald, now looking quite fearsome in his blue-and-yellow armor. "After that, I'll leave it to you, sir."

Arald nodded. "We couldn't just dash down and skewer one or two of them before we turn back, could we?" He gestured with the long spear he was carrying.

Halt gave him a long-suffering look. Arald, after all, was a cavalryman.

The Baron shrugged. "Didn't think so."

Halt glanced down the hill. The Wargal line was finally formed up. Morgarath was riding his white horse across the field behind the fourth and last rank. The Wargal front line stepped out, shields raised before them, spears and swords held to the front. They started up the hill, their shambling, rolling gait, which could have looked comical, now looking ominous.

"Let's go," Halt said, and swung up into Abelard's saddle.

He led the way forward, angling across the hill. He could hear the jingling of harness behind him, and the dull thuds of multiple hoofbeats on the soft grass. He increased the pace to a trot as they neared the two markers. The left-hand file peeled off for the farther marker. Halt pulled his horse to one side as Baron Arald led the right-hand file toward the nearer bridge.

Hooves clattered on the timbers of the bridges as the two files crossed the ditch. Arald marshaled his men into an extended line, circling his spear over his head, then pointing it out to right and left. From the bottom of the hill, Halt could hear the guttural chant as the enemy began to slog their way up the slope. He rode forward, staying out to the right and moving ahead of the line of cavalry so he could observe the Wargals more clearly.

Arald raised his spear and was pointing it down the hill. "Form arrowhead!" he shouted as his battlehorse paced forward, pulling against the reins, eager to come to grips with the enemy. Nobody had told the horse that this was a feint. He was eager to charge headlong into the enemy line.

The troop followed, the two lines angling back to form a V shape as they advanced down the hill. Arald and Halt had discussed this. They had agreed that Arald should put the men into whatever formation he would use for a real attack. Arrowhead was the most effective.

They were still moving at a walk. Halt glanced down at the approaching Wargals. They were in one line, forging their way up the hill. They were clumsy and unbalanced in their marching, and from time to time one of them would stumble and fall. His companions didn't wait for him. A beast from the next rank would fill the gap, treading over his fallen comrade to get there. The fallen Wargal would be left to regain his feet and get back into formation in the second rank.

"Trot!" Arald commanded, raising his spear above his head again, then circling it.

The jingle of harness and weapons and the thudding of hooves grew louder as the V-shaped force began to move faster down the hill.

Halt looked keenly at the Wargals, and his heart leapt as he thought he saw the first signs of hesitation among them. It was only a moment of indecision, but he was sure it was there.

"Canter!" Arald's voice rang out, and the cavalry surged forward, moving from a trot to a canter in the space of one stride.

"Hold your positions!" Arald shouted, as some riders began to move ahead of their neighbors. Troopers hauled on their reins, bringing their horses back into formation. Along the line, the riders held their spears pointing upward, waiting for the order to gallop. In order to conserve their horses' energy, Arald wouldn't give that order until the very last minute. Halt, eyes slitted with concentration, studied the Wargals.

There! He saw it clearly. In the center of the line, half a dozen of the black, shambling monsters slowed and actually began to shuffle back from the horses bearing down on them.

The half dozen became a dozen, then the entire front line was disrupted, either stopped in place or edging back against the following rank. As they bumped into one another and shoved others aside, the line became disrupted, milling in aimless confusion and doubt.

"It's working," Halt breathed to himself. Then he saw a black-clad figure riding forward through the lines, the horse shouldering Wargals aside without any care for their well-being. Morgarath reached the front of the third rank and swung his horse to ride parallel to the disrupted and hesitating front line.

Instinctively, Halt drew an arrow from his quiver and laid it on the string. Then he shrugged. Morgarath was well out of arrow range, he knew. He replaced the arrow reluctantly.

Then he saw the Wargals steady and resume their advance. He realized that Morgarath was goading his troops to return to the attack. The Wargals might have been frightened of the horses, but an enraged Morgarath was a far more frightening prospect. Slowly, they regained their formation and began to march forward once more.

Halt raised his horn and blew a long, descending note—the signal for recall. He saw Arald's right hand go up, holding the long spear high overhead. Then he began to circle the spear in an unmistakable signal. The cavalry halted, and Arald wheeled his horse in place, the riders behind him following in turn until the V formation had reversed its direction and was heading back up the hill again. As they neared the bridges, they split into two files and rode across. The rearmost riders leapt down from their saddles and hauled the bridges back across the ditch. Then they remounted and followed their comrades, riding round the end of the line to take up their position in the rear of the army. They'd be fighting as infantry, ready to reinforce any part of the line that faltered.

Arald saw Halt waiting in front of the ditch and rode across, raising his visor.

"We shook them up," he said.

But Halt shook his head. "Only until Morgarath was able to get among them and drive them on," he said. "If we do that again, we're going to have to take him by surprise."

Arald looked back down the hill. The Wargals had regained their discipline and were moving steadily up the slope, like a malevolent black tide.

"Still," he said, "it's something to keep in mind. We'd better get to our positions."

He urged his horse through the gap at the end of the palisade and swung to the right, heading for the command position in the center of the line. Halt waited a few moments, still watching the indefatigable march of the Wargals, hearing the grunted cadence as they kept in time and the rattle and jingle of weapons and shields.

Then he wheeled Abelard to the left and cantered to his position on the right flank of the line.

The battle that might determine the fate of the Kingdom was about to begin.

29

⌘⌘⌘⌘⌘⌘⌘⌘⌘⌘⌘⌘⌘⌘⌘⌘⌘

"Urrgh! Urrgh-urrgh! Urrgh!"

The guttural chant of the advancing Wargals was getting louder and louder. Some of the men behind the palisade glanced nervously at their comrades beside them. A few of the veterans snarled in response to the Wargals' chant. The sound seemed to put heart back into their less experienced companions.

One gray-bearded veteran looked fiercely at a group of younger soldiers standing beside him, licking dry lips with even drier tongues.

"Let 'em get close," he said, "then let 'em have it. See how their chanting sounds when they're stuck on the end of a spear."

Elsewhere along the line, other experienced fighters were muttering words of encouragement to the younger members of the army. Their savage confidence transmitted itself to the novice soldiers, and they set themselves more firmly, eyes riveted on the black line slowly advancing up the hill.

Mouths were dry; hands were damp. But the soldiers of Araluen stood resolutely, ready to fight for their King against these creatures of ill omen.

Then the Wargals reached the concealed trench, covered by

nets layered with light branches and grass. The first of them failed to see the obstruction in time. When they did and tried to halt, the rank behind cannoned into them, knocking them over the lip and into the trench—where sharpened stakes were waiting for them.

Perhaps twenty Wargals tumbled into the ditch. Five of them were impaled on the stakes and let out shrill shrieks of pain. The chanting stopped, and the steady march was disrupted as the survivors tried to clamber up out of the ditch, shoving at the rank behind them to make room.

On the left wing, a bugle sounded.

Within a heartbeat, a withering storm of arrows flashed across and down the field. Most of the Rangers fired two shots in quick succession. Crowley managed three. All of them were aimed at selected targets, not released haphazardly at the mass of figures on the edge of the ditch. Along the first and second ranks, Wargals cried out in pain and surprise. At least a dozen went down and lay still. Others were wounded, blundering wildly, tearing with teeth and claws at the cruel arrows caught in their flesh.

On the right, Halt's party waited, arrows nocked but not yet drawn.

"Steady . . . ," Halt growled. Then he saw the Wargals identify the direction from which the arrows were coming. Their small shields swung to their right, exposing their left sides and backs to Halt's shooters.

"Now!" he yelled, and let three vicious shafts fly in less than the time it takes to tell about it. His companions shot as well, each of them releasing two shafts. Cedric, trying to match Halt, managed three, but his third was rushed and he snatched at the release, sending the shaft skimming over the Wargal army. He cursed at his own impatience.

Now the shooting became independent, with the Rangers selecting targets at will. Inevitably, several would choose the same Wargal, and many of the black-furred beasts fell with two or three shafts in them.

Another trumpet blast. Halt heard Wearne's rough voice calling orders from the rear of the defensive position, then there was a loud clatter and hiss as twenty longbows released their arrows high into the sky. Before that volley had fallen back to earth, Wearne's men released another. Then the long, barbed shafts began falling almost vertically into the rear ranks of the attacking force. Wargals tumbled and fell, or staggered, clutching arrow wounds in their arms and upper bodies. They blundered into their comrades, who shoved them roughly aside, leaving them to their fate.

Still the Wargals pushed forward, ignoring their losses. Already, almost thirty of them were lying dead or mortally wounded on the field. But the remainder closed up the gaps in their lines and forged forward, picking their way through the obstacles in the ditch, then scrambling up the far side, eyes blazing with hatred and rage, intent on one thing: to reach the Araluen line and strike and strike and strike.

As the first of them scrambled over the uphill side of the ditch, Farrel's little force joined in. The six apprentices shot coolly and steadily. Their lighter bows didn't have the same power as the massive longbows wielded by the senior Rangers, and the shafts often broke or deflected from the Wargals' shields and leather breastplates. But some of them plunged home.

And all the while, the two parties of shooters on the flanks of the army continued to single out individual Wargals in the attack force and kill them.

"More arrows!" Halt shouted. He'd emptied his quiver in the first few minutes. An orderly ran forward with a canvas bag full of shafts. He placed it against a wooden stand by Halt's side and flipped the cover aside. Instantly, Halt began selecting arrows, nocking, drawing and shooting.

And more Wargals fell before the vicious onslaught.

He heard several other Rangers call for arrows. In the heat and confusion of battle, there was no time for tailor-made shafts. Everyone shot standard-length arrows and adjusted their aiming point as well as they could. From the rear, he heard the whooshing rush as Wearne's men released another plunging barrage.

And still the Wargals came on, lurching and chanting, into the storm of arrows that greeted them. There may have been only twenty Rangers shooting, but their ability to shoot rapidly seemed to magnify their numbers. The Wargals had never faced such a deadly arrow storm before. As they had raided across the southwest of Araluen, they had encountered a few archers. But their discipline and rate of shooting was nothing like this. These grim-faced, gray-cloaked figures kept up a nonstop, accurate barrage.

But still the Wargals came on, not knowing what else to do.

And therein lay the weakness of Morgarath's Wargal force. It took the Black Lord some time to outline their targets for them and to set them on a course toward the enemy. They would fight doggedly to attain the goals he set. But they were inflexible in the face of the unexpected. Their minds were blanked by the fury of the battle, and it was difficult for him to penetrate their brutish consciousness with new or revised objectives. Once engaged, they would blindly follow his initial orders and respond only to the simplest changes.

He could set them on a path—order them to attack or to retreat. But he couldn't change the direction or the nature of their attack. He couldn't direct them in intricate tactical maneuvers or give them conditional orders—if Plan A doesn't work, go to Plan B. They were a blunt weapon, and their basic technique was the frontal attack. Once he ordered them forward, they would continue, in spite of the fact that Halt, Crowley and the other Rangers were ripping huge holes in their ranks. The Wargals had been ordered to attack the center of the Araluen line and they would continue to do so until there were none of them left.

They didn't even have the initiative to direct some of their numbers to the flanks where the Rangers were situated. They continued forward, intent only on breaking the Araluen line and killing the King.

Morgarath watched, appalled, as twenty Rangers shot his attack to pieces. Already, he had lost at least a hundred and twenty troops in this attack, and they hadn't yet closed with the main army.

He had no sense of compassion for the Wargals who had died for him. They were nothing more than a tool for him to use. But he knew he couldn't continue to lose troops at this rate for much longer. Already, more than ten percent of his army lay sprawled, dead or dying, on the slope. The grass ran red with their blood.

Another commander might have called them back, ordered them to retreat. But Morgarath watched them advance and die with a pitiless eye. They had less than twenty meters to go before they reached the Araluen defenses. And there were still a hundred of them in the line. Given any luck, they might just break through the palisade and kill Duncan and his senior officers.

He closed his eyes, concentrated fiercely and sent out a mental command to them.

Kill. Kill. And kill again.

As his order reached them, the Wargals surged forward with a new determination, clambering down into the ditch, then up the other side, shouldering their way past the sharpened spikes set to slow them down. They could see the enemy now, and their minds were filled with their commander's order. Some of them lost all sense of the discipline and fighting methods that Morgarath had instilled into them in the past months. They reverted to wild, primitive beasts, casting aside their shields and weapons, and lunged for the defenders, seeking to kill them with their savage claws and massive yellow fangs.

They were met by an impregnable hedge of steel-pointed spears, thrusting at them, tearing into them, then withdrawing to thrust again.

Those who did manage to get past the spears found themselves facing shields and swords and axes as the defenders met them, their blades glittering in the sunshine, then suddenly turning red as they struck home.

But now the fighting wasn't so one-sided. The Wargals might have had no answer to the withering arrow storm that tore their numbers apart as they mounted the hill. But they were fearsome hand-to-hand fighters. And they knew no fear. They struck out at their enemies even as they were dying, knowing only one thing—they were ordered to kill and keep killing.

There were fewer than eighty left from the two hundred who

had set out from the base of the hill. But now they were making their presence felt as the soldiers of Araluen were forced back and battered to the ground. The snarls of the massive beasts filled the air. In a one-on-one contest, they were stronger than most of the soldiers they faced, and what they lacked in skill they made up in brute force.

They were in behind the hedge of sharpened stakes now, and slowly the line facing them began to buckle as they struck and snarled and bit and slashed with swords and claws in a frenzy of savagery and hatred.

Arald saw it first. Saw the line of defenders weakening, saw the uncertainty growing as the Wargals simply refused to give way, refused to die. Many of them had blood streaming from what should have been mortal wounds. But they continued to surge forward, snarling, snapping, striking.

Arald, Duncan and David had been observing the battle from a raised mound just behind the lines, directing reinforcements to points where the integrity of the defenses was threatened. Now Arald realized there was no time to order anyone else forward. He drew his sword, set his shield on his arm and lowered his visor. Then he plunged down from the mound and raced into the milling mass of enemy troops.

His long sword was a glittering circle of light as he swung and hacked and stabbed at the Wargals, cutting them down like a scythe cuts through chaff. Some of them turned to face him. But, fierce and heavily muscled as they were, they were no match for him. He was a champion warrior. He was strong and powerfully built and he was trained to use his weight and strength to best advantage. He plowed into them, hacking and shoving. He used his shield as a weapon, striking with its steel edge at their

faces and necks and arms. When they got inside the shield and
the long sword, he used his helmet, head-butting them and sending them reeling. And all the time, that dreadful sword continued to rise and fall and dart forward.

For a few seconds, he fought alone, surrounded by the black
beasts. Then he felt a movement beside him and Sir David was
there, wielding a terrible two-handed battleax that smashed and
hammered through the Wargals, beating down their defenses,
shattering bones and severing limbs.

The two knights fought shoulder to shoulder, hacking their
way through the Wargal ranks. Then they were joined by a third
juggernaut as King Duncan thrust forward beside them, his
sword never seeming to pause as he slashed and thrust at
Morgarath's troops, cutting them down.

As the soldiers of Araluen saw the three nobles smash into
the Wargal ranks, they found new heart. And when they realized one of the new attackers was the King himself, a veteran
corporal bellowed an order.

"To the King! The King! Help the King!"

And twenty men surged forward, striking the Wargals from
an oblique angle.

The fur-covered, apelike creatures fell and died, struck by the
twin onslaught. But true to their kind, they never gave in. They
never gave way to fear. Morgarath had given them no such
option. Intent on the chance that they might reach Duncan and
kill him, the Lord of Rain and Night kept them fighting to the
last Wargal.

Literally.

The last one fell, fittingly, to a savage thrust from Arald's
sword. As the creature crumpled and fell to one side, the Baron

of Redmont stepped back, swaying wearily, and raised his visor. Around him, the soldiers cheered. They had watched in awe as he fought his way single-handed through the Wargals. He leaned on his sword and scanned the battlefield. Around him, the ground was littered with Wargal bodies. Many of the men of the Araluen army had paid the price as well.

But the losses to Morgarath's forces were horrifying. In one engagement, he had risked—and lost—twenty percent of his forces.

The Baron of Redmont met the King's eye. Arald's face and arms and clothes were covered in the blood of the beasts he'd killed. He smiled weakly, looking round at the carnage that surrounded them.

"I think Morgarath's going to have to change his tactics," he said.

30

As the defenders regained their breath and tended to the wounded and dying, a deathly hush fell over the body-strewn battlefield.

The Wargals were simple-minded creatures and they had been molded by Morgarath's superior intellect to respond without question to his orders. In battle, they were seized by a red rage. They fought without mercy and without regard for their own losses. As Halt had remarked, they would clamber over the bodies of their fallen comrades to reach their enemies. They fought with one overarching idea—to kill the enemies Morgarath directed them against.

In years to come, Morgarath would refine and perfect his mental control over the arcane creatures. But at this time, his dominance over them was clumsy and without subtlety. As long as battle was joined, they would respond to his simple, direct commands—basically, go forward or retreat, and kill or be killed.

But once the rage of battle had died, their traditional attitudes and values reasserted themselves. They were an ancient race, with strong tribal bonds. They had existed and developed far from the sight of man—and from his interference—for thousands of years.

Now hundreds of them had been killed in the space of a few hours. Their simple minds were unable to articulate the fact, but they felt the loss—and felt it deeply.

The close-knit clans and families within their ranks had all lost members during the terrible advance up Ashdown Cut. They sensed the loss—sensed it at the most primitive level. And with that loss they began to feel a distrust for the Black Lord who commanded them. It would take him hours to reassert his control over them. In the meantime, the Wargals shambled about their campsite in a haze of grief. They pushed and prodded at the bedrolls in the empty tents where their companions had been. They asserted their grief in low, deep-throated moans.

Unsure of their intentions, or what their reactions might be to the disaster that had befallen them, Morgarath's human soldiers gave them a wide berth. Early on, several of his subordinate commanders had attempted to shove them into a formation. They were met with snarls and bared fangs and hastily backed off.

Morgarath eyed his bestial troops with suspicion. He sensed he would have to leave them time to overcome their feelings of grief, and their mistrust of him as a commander. He ordered his men to withdraw from the Wargals' tent lines and to wait until their disturbed minds had settled down. Bitterly, he realized that he would have to change tactics in their next attack. He couldn't afford to lose troops at this rate. And if he persisted with his frontal attacks, he risked losing control of his army altogether. Better to wait, let them grieve, let them come to terms with their losses, then reassert his dominance over them. He would start with kindness and understanding, then gradually move to rebuilding a fierce, mindless hatred for the Araluen leadership—in particular, the King.

It would take time, he knew, and he cursed the fact. But it was unavoidable.

And besides, that time would give him the opportunity he needed to plan a new method of attack—one that would nullify the deadly hail of arrows that the Rangers had used to lash his troops.

By mid-afternoon, Duncan's army was ready to withdraw from Ashdown Cut. He was loath to delay their departure, but he had let his men rest in sections, allowing them to snatch several hours' sleep. Although they had been engaged for only a short period, the strain of combat quickly depletes a man's physical reserves.

So the men rested, then rose and ate their cold rations. Their company commanders began to form them up behind the defensive ground they had prepared. The slope of the hill flattened out here and the resultant dead ground hid their preparations from the enemy army on the flat land below.

They had won a significant victory here at the Cut. In all probability, Morgarath would not expect them to withdraw from such a strong and successful position. The command team agreed that it was highly unlikely the Black Lord would attempt another frontal assault that same day. His army had been too badly mauled in the first encounter. Even from their position high on the slope, they could see how disorganized the Wargal army was. The beasts seemed to have lost any sense of purpose. They shambled without purpose through the uneven tent lines and the watchers on the hill could hear their tragic keening as they mourned their dead.

"Fire the hillside," Duncan ordered. Northolt stepped up onto the earth mound behind the palisade of sharpened stakes. At either end of the line, small groups of men were standing by the two large oil barrels. He put his fingers in his mouth and let out a piercing whistle, gaining their attention. Then he made a rolling motion with his arm and the men bent and tipped the heavy barrels on their sides.

Instantly, the thick, glutinous oil began to chug out of the bung holes in the top of each cask. It gurgled down across the packed earth for a meter or so, then found the V-shaped trenches and began to run downhill more rapidly.

As the last few liters ran out, Northolt gave another signal. Two of the men at each post had flint and steel ready. In a matter of seconds, they had a fire burning. They dipped torches into the flames, waited till they caught, then set them into the oil at the top of the diagonal ditches.

The fire flared up, red and angry, with black smoke billowing above it. The flames ran down the hillside from either side of the line, setting the grass beside the ditches alight as it went. It reached the cross ditch, where the first of the Wargals had come to grief, and flared higher as it caught the pooled oil in the base of the ditch. The flames spread from the oil itself to the dried grass and branches that had concealed the ditch, then caught on the grass and bushes on the hillside itself.

Within a few minutes, the breadth of the hill was burning fiercely, and billows of thick, dark-gray smoke rose up as the flames began to eat their way steadily downhill.

"Let's go," said Duncan. He smiled grimly. The towering smoke and the vivid flames would hide their departure from the hilltop. By the time the flames had died down, they would be long gone on the road to Hackham Heath, with Morgarath none the wiser.

Northolt caught Duncan's expression and raised an eyebrow. "Something amusing you, sir?"

Duncan turned to him and urged his horse a little closer so he could speak comfortably to his battle master. "I just had a vision of Morgarath driving his men up the hill again tomorrow, only to find we're no longer here."

Northolt frowned as he shared the thought. "Let's hope he doesn't find out until tomorrow," he said. "There's always the chance that he'll attack again today."

"I doubt it," Duncan said. "His troops are totally demoralized." He paused, then added, "As well they might be."

The twenty Rangers, now riding as a single group, were the last to leave the hilltop at Ashdown Cut. They were to form a rearguard, setting ambushes at suitable locations to delay the pursuing army.

"Let's make every valley, every hill, every bend in the road a potential killing ground," Crowley had told them. "We'll hit and run—five arrows each, all aimed shots. We'll force Morgarath to deploy into a defensive formation, then we'll get out before his men can make contact. That way, they'll start to be wary of every bend, every grove of trees, every spot along the way where we might be waiting in ambush."

With their swift and tireless horses, there was little risk that the ambushers would be caught by Morgarath's forces. They could wait till the last minute, then skip away, rapidly outdistancing any pursuers.

Their first selected spot was a point where the road led

through a heavily wooded forest. The trees grew down to within twenty meters of the road, their densely growing branches providing perfect cover for the camouflaged shooters.

They selected shooting positions either side of the road. The Wargals would pass within forty meters of the concealed bowmen. The party on the left would shoot first, driving the Wargals into cover on the right side of the road, where they would be enfiladed by the second party. Each Ranger would shoot five arrows, then mount and gallop away. If any Wargals or any of Morgarath's human troops followed, the Rangers would wait until they were strung out along the road, then stop and begin shooting again.

"With any luck, we should account for forty or fifty of them," Crowley said.

In fact, their score was nil. The Wargals didn't come.

Puzzled, Crowley sent Berwick and Lewin to reconnoiter their back trail. After several hours, the two Rangers returned, their cantering horses covering the ground at a rapid clip.

"They're still in their camp at Ashdown Cut," Berwick told a surprised Crowley. "They're milling about, making that keening noise. They haven't struck their tents or loaded their baggage train. It'll be hours before they're ready to move out after us."

"What about Morgarath?" Halt asked. "What's he doing?"

"He's sitting outside his pavilion with a group of his officers, just waiting," Lewin told him.

Crowley and Halt exchanged puzzled glances. "Waiting for what?" Halt asked.

Lewin shrugged. "Who knows?"

Berwick rubbed his chin thoughtfully. "Looks like he's waiting for them to settle down," he suggested.

Again, Halt and Crowley exchanged a glance.

"Not much point in our waiting to slow them down," Halt said. "They've slowed themselves down."

"I agree," Crowley said. He glanced around and nominated two more Rangers. "Chase and Bedford, set up an observation point on that small hill to the east. Keep an eye out for them and let us know when they're on their way." He looked around the group. "The rest of you, mount up. It's time we rejoined the army."

Quickly the group mounted and set out, riding in two files. Halt and Crowley, naturally, took the lead. They had gone several kilometers when Crowley glanced curiously at his friend. The dark-bearded Hibernian seemed lost in thought.

"You're quiet. Something on your mind?" Crowley asked.

Halt shook himself out of the reverie that had seized him. "Just thinking about how the Wargals reacted to Arald's mock cavalry attack."

Crowley made a small moue with his mouth. "They didn't seem to react at all, from where I sat."

But Halt shook his head. "I was a lot closer and they definitely reacted. They hesitated and lost their cohesion for a moment. They were still worried by the horses."

"So what happened? They didn't hesitate for too long, as far as I could see."

"No. Morgarath was there almost immediately, and he rallied them quickly." He paused, thinking hard, then added in a quiet tone, "He saw us coming. Maybe we can do something about that."

31

"HE WON'T TRY THAT AGAIN," DUNCAN SAID, AND HIS SENIOR officers nodded agreement.

"Another frontal assault like that and he'll have lost almost half his army," Lord Northolt said. There was a note of satisfaction in his voice.

"Let's not get too cocky," Halt said quietly, and they all turned to look at him. Several of them raised their eyebrows in surprise and glanced at the King. Most rulers didn't take well to being told they were being cocky. But Duncan was watching the bearded Ranger with a questioning look.

"What do you mean, Halt?" he asked.

Halt was sitting on the edge of a table in the tent. He hitched himself up to a more comfortable position. He sensed every eye on him, and as usual, that attention made him slightly uncomfortable. The fact that Lady Pauline was among the group, her clothes muddy and dirt-smeared from riding all night, didn't make him any more comfortable.

"It's just," he said, after a short pause to gather his thoughts, "Morgarath isn't the type to take a beating like that and give up. He's smart. He's ruthless. You can bet he'll come up with a new tactic to counter our arrows. So we should be ready to surprise him."

"Do you have anything in mind?" Baron Arald asked.

Halt hesitated, then committed himself. "I may have. Let's step outside for a minute."

The group of commanders exited from the pavilion, making way for Duncan to go first. Outside, they stood surveying their new position, and the work that was going on to fortify it.

Hackham Heath was an open space covered with knee-high gorse, interspersed with clumps of taller bushes. It stretched for half a kilometer and on either side it was bounded by thick forest. The ground sloped upward, and at the beginning of the slope, the Slipsunder River ran in a huge U-shaped curve. The river widened at the semicircular curve, and the water shallowed, providing a ford. The army had crossed that spot the previous day. Around the ford, the banks were wet and muddy, but by no means impassable. To either side, in the arms of the U, the river ran among thick trees. It was narrower, but much deeper. And the current was fast and treacherous. The ford was the only point where it was possible to cross.

The army was camped on the eastern side of the heath, where the ground rose steeply to form a grass-covered knoll. It was this feature that had caused Lord Northolt to select the site. The defenses—another ditch and palisade—were set in a semicircle, protecting three sides of the knoll. The fourth was anchored against the thick trees. Any attacker would have to labor up the steep sides of the knoll, where he would be confronted by the ditch and another line of sharpened stakes, behind which the defenders would be waiting for him.

The six men and one woman all studied the ground for several minutes. Then Halt pointed downhill.

"We're assuming Morgarath will camp across the other side of the river," he said, "where he'll be protected from any surprise attack on our part. Then, when he's ready, he'll cross the river, form his assault line, and head up the hill." He looked around at the others. "Anyone disagree?"

There was a general mutter of concurrence and he went on. "It seems to me that if we could hit him with a cavalry charge—a real one this time—when his men are halfway up the hill, we could completely disrupt his attack."

David frowned thoughtfully. "But we saw yesterday that the Wargals have overcome their fear of horses—if it was ever there."

"Oh, it was there all right. And they haven't overcome it. I'm sure of it. I was watching them yesterday. When Arald started to canter toward them, there was a definite reaction in the front line. They stopped. They tried to back off. For a few moments, they were disorganized and vulnerable. Then Morgarath rode forward and steadied them. He was goading and threatening them."

Crowley rubbed his beard thoughtfully. "That's certainly the way it looked."

Halt nodded to him. "That's what it was. The point is, Morgarath had plenty of time to order them back into line. He saw you coming"—he gestured to Arald—"then he saw his troops faltering and he rode forward to shore up their confidence. Once he did that, they started forward again."

"Why should it be any different next time?" Duncan asked.

"Because next time, I plan to hit them from the rear. He

won't see us coming and he won't have time to reorganize his troops. They'll be disrupted and surprised. I'm hoping they'll lose confidence and their old fear will reassert itself before Morgarath has time to stop it. Besides . . ." He hesitated.

"Besides what?" Crowley asked.

"Well, I wouldn't be surprised if his mental control over them has been weakened by yesterday's fight. They saw hundreds of their kind killed as they tried to follow his orders. Looking at their camp yesterday afternoon, they were demoralized and disorganized, wandering around aimlessly. If we follow up with a surprise attack from the rear and catch them off guard, we might manage to completely disrupt his hold over them and force them to retreat."

"How do you propose to hit them from behind?" Duncan asked.

Halt gestured to the wide plain at the base of the hill. "I thought I might take what cavalry we have back across the river and hide over in the trees to the south," he said. But even as he spoke, he could see the weakness in his plan.

Crowley articulated it, shaking his head. "Too risky. You couldn't help leaving a trail. You'd have more than a hundred men with you, after all. And their horses. You couldn't move a party that size through that damp ground without leaving obvious signs. And then you could find yourself cut off, facing a thousand Wargals, bent on revenge."

"Eight hundred Wargals," Halt corrected him.

"Eight hundred then," Crowley retorted. "If that makes you feel any better."

Halt opened his mouth to argue. But he knew Crowley was right and he said nothing.

"Perhaps," Duncan said thoughtfully, "you could go north and find another ford, then circle round behind them." He looked at Sir David. "David, you said you were stationed here. How well do you know the terrain?"

David shook his head. "Not well, sir. But my son Gilan knows it like the back of his hand. He'd know if there's another ford within a day's ride."

"Let's have him up here then," Duncan said. He turned back into the pavilion while David sent an orderly to find his son. The others trooped back into the pavilion and took their seats again, waiting on David's young son.

Halt studied the young man as he entered the tent. Gilan was tall for a twelve-year-old, and gangly. But he had a wiry strength to him and intelligent, calm eyes as he looked around curiously. He seemed unflustered to find himself in the presence of so many senior officers. He glanced around the group, nodding greetings as his father introduced him.

He wore a sword slung over his right shoulder and a heavy dagger in the belt around his waist. The weapons were strangely at odds with the young, serious face. Halt shrugged mentally. That was the way of the world these days. Young people grew up fast.

"Gilan," his father said, "do you know of any fords across the Slipsunder? Preferably within a day's ride from here."

The boy considered the question. A slight frown furrowed his brow between his eyes. He answered carefully, not willing to commit himself absolutely.

"There used to be one to the north. I found it several years ago. But . . ." He spread his hands uncertainly.

"But what?" Halt asked quietly.

Gilan turned his gaze on the bearded Ranger, assessing him for a few seconds. "But since then, there could have been floods through that part of the river that might have washed the sand away."

"But you have no evidence that has happened?" Halt asked.

The boy shook his head. "No. I'm just saying it could have."

"We'll assume the ford is still there," Duncan said. He indicated the map on the easel by the tent wall. "Can you show us where it is?"

Gilan crossed to the map, peering at it with that small frown on his face again.

They were interrupted as a messenger knocked on the tent pole by the door and entered. He looked nervously around the King and his advisers, his eyes wide. Then his eyes fell on Lady Pauline, and she beckoned him forward, glancing apologetically at the King. He made a gesture for her to continue. The messenger leaned close to her and spoke in a low voice. When he had finished, she looked at the King again.

"I'm sorry, my lord. I have to attend to this."

The King made the same gesture of permission and she hurried out. They all turned back to Gilan, who had stepped back from the map.

"I can't show you on this," he said flatly.

Halt frowned. "You can't read a map?" He realized he had been rather abrupt and Gilan was, after all, only a boy. He softened his tone. "Or have you forgotten where it is?"

Gilan shook his head, unabashed. "Neither. The map is totally inaccurate. There's no detail—or very little. I couldn't indicate where the ford is within ten or fifteen kilometers." He tapped his finger on the depiction of the river, at a point where it twisted in a series of curves. "This stretch, for instance. I assume it's supposed to indicate the Serpentine Tumbles. But it's nowhere near this spot. It's easily five kilometers farther north. Maybe more."

The boy spoke with confidence and Halt realized he knew what he was talking about. "So you can't show us where the ford is?"

Gilan nodded confirmation. "No." He paused and glanced at his father, then said, "But I could take you there."

"Take me?" Halt said. "You mean come with us?"

Gilan said nothing, simply nodded. Again, he glanced at his father. Halt did the same.

"Sir David," he said, "I'm not sure about this. If he comes with us, I'll be taking him into danger. He's only a boy . . ." Out of the corner of his eye he saw Gilan's face redden.

Sir David glanced at his son, then back at Halt. "He's young, Halt, I'll grant you that. But he's not wearing that sword for decoration. He's faster than me—and more skillful. He can look after himself."

Halt chewed his lip. His previous observation about young people growing up fast in this world came back to him. "I suppose we could always leave him behind once we've found the ford," he said. "Or send him back."

Gilan snorted scornfully, but restrained himself from further comment.

Sir David actually grinned. "You could try that," he said. "But don't expect to succeed."

Halt opened his mouth to reply but was forestalled by Lady Pauline's sudden reappearance. The Courier was smiling widely.

"What is it, Pauline?" Baron Arald asked. She was his senior Courier, after all. Yet Pauline addressed her answer to the King.

"Two drafts of troops have just come in, my lord," she said. "One from Norgate and one from Swinton, in the west. Word is going out that Morgarath has recalled his army and has stopped raiding the fiefs."

"How many troops?" Duncan asked immediately.

"Fifty in all. Thirty of them cavalry," she said, and there was a general chorus of satisfaction. The tide was beginning to turn against Morgarath. And as it continued to do so, more and more troops would join the royal army. The King came to a decision.

"Halt, take the one hundred and twenty troopers we have already, along with the thirty new arrivals. Have Gilan here show you the ford. Then get back here and hit Morgarath where he least expects it."

Halt nodded. "Yes, sir."

Gilan allowed himself a small grin of triumph.

Duncan saw it and addressed him directly. "Gilan, you stay out of trouble and do as Halt tells you. This isn't a game."

Gilan dropped his eyes and muttered an acknowledgment.

The King sat back in the high-backed chair behind the table and looked around the tent. "Gentlemen—and Pauline, of course," he said, "this may be the beginning of the end for Morgarath."

32

By the following morning, there was still no sign of the Wargal army. Crowley had sent a series of two-man patrols out on the high road leading back to Ashdown Cut. They traveled back fifteen kilometers but saw nothing.

"It might be a good time for me to head out with the cavalry," Halt said to Sir David. "I assume Gilan will need some time to locate the ford. And it'll be better if Morgarath isn't here to see us leave."

Accordingly, they mustered the cavalry—the one hundred and twenty troopers who were the original cavalry force and the thirty new arrivals. David and Halt inspected their horses and equipment. Two men were excused from the expedition because their horses weren't in first-rate shape. One was limping slightly as the trooper walked him around. David knelt and gently felt the horse's lower leg.

"Feels a little hot," he said doubtfully. He gestured to an orderly and sent him to fetch Duncan's horse master, Brogan.

The heavily muscled horse master repeated David's examination and confirmed his verdict. "There's definitely heat there. He could well go lame if we send him on a long journey." He glared at the hapless trooper. "Couldn't you see he was having trouble?" he demanded.

The trooper hung his head. "Didn't want to be left behind," he said. "I thought he was just a little stiff and he'd work it out."

Brogan studied him carefully. On the whole, he believed him. The young man was open-faced and guileless and didn't seem the type to intentionally neglect his horse's well-being.

"He'll need rest and treatment," he told the young man. "Bring him to the horse lines this afternoon. Tell the apothecaries that I sent you and your horse is to be looked after."

"Yes, sir," said the young trooper, his eyes downcast. "What shall I do while he's being treated?"

"You can join the army, my boy," David interrupted. "Welcome to the infantry."

The trooper greeted that news with a glum expression. In his world, the infantry was the last assignment one would choose. Infantry walked into battle. Cavalry rode. There was a big difference, both in prestige and comfort.

Brogan was less understanding about the other horse that didn't pass muster. It was a bay gelding and it was suffering from very painful saddle sores—a sure sign that its rider had not been looking after it properly.

As before, Brogan told the rider to take his horse to the horse lines for treatment. The trooper, however, was demoted for not caring properly for his horse and set to cleaning out the horse lines and taking care of the army's latrines.

So it was that by early afternoon, Halt had a force of one hundred and forty-eight cavalry men, all equipped with mail armor, helmets, mail aventails and round shields. Each man was armed with a heavy spear, which could be used as a lance or for throwing, a long sword and a heavy, double-sided dagger. Each man carried rations for three days, and two water skins. Behind their saddles they tied bedrolls and rolled tarpaulins. The latter could be joined with those carried by each man's riding partner to make two-man tents. Sir David had appointed a young captain named Lorriac as their commander.

Gilan arrived at the mustering point half an hour before the due time. He wore a thigh-length mail shirt under a linen surcoat. His helmet was a simple cone-shaped one, with a mail aventail that spread down and protected his neck and shoulders. His sword was now in a scabbard attached to his saddle, alongside his left knee. He had a round shield as well—lightweight but reinforced with strips of brass and with a large central boss made of the same metal. The boy looked eager and enthusiastic about his assignment. Halt inspected him critically, without appearing to do so, and was pleased to see he didn't appear to have any self-doubts about his mission.

"Ready to go?" he asked.

The youngster nodded eagerly. He pointed to the fringe of the trees that delineated the heath.

"We'll stick to the tree line, heading north. Once we've gone about twenty kilometers, I'll be looking for landmarks. Then we'll head into the trees and make for the river."

Halt nodded. "Sounds like you know where you're going," he commented. Then he made a gesture toward the trees. "Lead on."

Gilan hesitated. He may have been confident, but he wasn't sure that he could order the troop to move out. He was concerned that they might ignore him. Or, worse still, laugh at him.

Halt hid a smile and turned to the captain in command of the company. "Move them out, Lorriac."

"Troop, in column of threes . . . trot!" the captain barked. It was a firm, carrying and authoritative command voice. He lowered his raised hand, the signal for the order to be carried out, and the column began to move forward at the trot. Their harnesses jingled and weapons clanked against each other as they headed north. Halt, Gilan and Lorriac rode in the lead. As the column passed the spot where King Duncan and Sir David were standing to watch them go, they all saluted, turning their eyes to right as they came level with their commanders, then snapping them back front again as they passed.

The two senior officers stood watching until the last of the cavalry had passed them. The little column of riders angled up the slope toward the trees, eventually disappearing over the crest a hundred meters away. For a short time, a slight cloud of dust hung in the air to mark their passing. Then it settled and there was no further sign of them.

"I hope that boy of yours knows what he's about," Duncan said.

David glanced at him, seeing the strain and worry on the King's bearded face. "He does," he replied, with a lot more conviction than he felt.

They made their way back to Duncan's pavilion, where his servants had set out a simple meal. They were halfway through the inevitable flat bread, cold meat and dried fruit when Crowley entered the tent.

"My patrol has come in," he said. "Morgarath's on his way."

Suddenly the food seemed to have no flavor. The King and Sir David exchanged a glance, then pushed back from the table.

Duncan drained his tankard of watered wine and the three men stepped outside, hurrying to the earth parapet the army had thrown up behind the protective ditch with its hedge of sharpened stakes, where Lord Northolt greeted them. Most of the soldiers had gathered there to watch as well. Word had spread quickly of the enemy's arrival.

They could hear the rattle of equipment and the guttural chanting of the Wargals as they made their way onto the open ground beyond the river, spreading out to pitch tents in their usual ragged lines.

"There are still a lot of them," Crowley observed.

The others said nothing, then Duncan pointed. "What are they?"

Several of the baggage wagons were loaded with strange wooden frames. Each was about five meters long and fitted with a large, solid wheel at either end. As they watched, teams of Wargals unloaded them from the wagons. There were five of them in all. Then men hurried forward, placing panels made from saplings across the front of the frames and nailing them into position. Each panel was further reinforced by oxhides. The sound of the hammering carried on the wind to where the Araluen army waited.

"Portable barricades," Northolt said after several minutes. "They'll wheel them up the hill, with their troops crouching behind them. That should reduce the effect of our archers."

Crowley nodded, suddenly seeing the purpose of the strange, elongated structures as the battle master explained.

"Why the oxhides?" he asked. "They'll hardly stop an arrow."

Northolt nodded, agreeing. Then he explained further. "They'll soak them with water before they start out," he said.

"It'll stop us using fire arrows to burn the barricades. Morgarath has borrowed the idea from siege towers that you'd use against a castle."

"You said he was no fool," Duncan muttered, his eyes fixed on the structures. They were roughly made and, as a result, not perfectly aligned. But they would be effective in protecting the advancing force from the arrows of the twenty Rangers.

"I'm beginning to wish I wasn't always right," Crowley replied. He glanced at the sun, low in the western sky. "Still, I don't think they'll have time to mount an attack before dark. We may as well get a good night's rest. We're going to need it."

Arald of Redmont had joined them as word went round the camp that Morgarath had arrived. He studied the strange barricades, then looked around the slope of the land and the shallow ford at the base of the hill.

"Maybe we can do something about spoiling their sleep," he said.

Northolt looked at him curiously. "What do you have in mind?"

Arald paused, collecting his thoughts and choosing his words before replying. Then he pointed to the supply wagons, parked on the left side of the Wargal campsite.

"I'm thinking that if I took twenty men later tonight and forded the river quietly, we might raid Morgarath's supply tents and set fire to his food and weapon stores. Then, when he's thoroughly distracted, Crowley and his men might manage to get in among those barricades and burn them." He glanced at the Ranger Commandant, saw the quick nod of agreement, and continued. "Then you and your Rangers could skip back across the river and cover our retreat."

Northolt pursed his lips, considering the plan. He could see that Crowley was in total agreement. But he was the battle master, and he was charged with preserving the King's forces as far as possible.

"It's a risk," he said.

Arald thrust out his bottom lip in an attitude of dismissal. "It's war," he said. "War is full of risks."

"The question is," Duncan put in, "whether the risk is outweighed by the potential benefit." He didn't seem to be making a judgment one way or the other, so Arald continued.

"What's the alternative?" he asked. "We can sit on our backsides here and watch Morgarath push those glorified wheelbarrows up the hill tomorrow until they get close enough to charge."

"You could always use plunging volleys against those things," Northolt said, but Crowley was already shaking his head before he completed the sentence.

"Plunging volleys aren't anywhere near as effective as direct shooting. And they'll be sure to have shields over their heads to protect themselves. I say we try Arald's plan."

Duncan eyed Arald and Crowley for several seconds, then looked sidelong at Northolt.

The battle master shrugged. "It's worth a try," he said. "If they're discovered, Arald and his men can always fight their way out. And Crowley's men will be on hand to cover them."

The King looked at the three of them and saw the determination in their eyes.

"All right. We'll do it," he said. Then he added, in mock desperation, "And here was I, hoping for a peaceful night's sleep."

33

HALT'S LITTLE FORCE RODE NORTH, MAINTAINING A STEADY trot. At regular intervals, they would stop and dismount, leading their horses for several kilometers before remounting and setting the horses to the trot once more.

At three, they halted and unsaddled the horses, letting them graze while the men ate a simple meal. They rested for forty minutes. Halt reclined with his back against the trunk of a tree. He noticed that Gilan was prowling restlessly around the camp and beckoned him over.

"Relax," he told the boy.

Gilan shook his head anxiously. "We should be moving on," he said. "Morgarath and his Wargals could be attacking while we sit here twiddling our thumbs."

"I doubt it," Halt told him. "We had scouts out looking, and when we left, there was still no sign of them. So the odds are they aren't attacking while we 'sit here twiddling our thumbs,' as you put it."

Gilan flushed and looked away.

Halt rose to his feet a little regretfully. That tree trunk was very comfortable, he thought. He dropped a hand onto Gilan's shoulder.

"We have a hard fight facing us in the next few days," he said. "And we need the men in top condition for it, not worn out by rushing around looking for the ford. Even more important, we have to conserve the horses' energy. We don't have remounts, and they'll need to be fit and ready when we charge Morgarath's army. Once a horse is exhausted, it takes a long time for it to recover sufficiently. Fighting is hard work. So when we hit Morgarath's army, I want to hit them as hard as we can. And that means we keep the horses fresh and ready for battle, all right?"

Gilan nodded morosely. "All right," he said. But he sounded only half convinced. He was young and the idea of hastening slowly was totally foreign to him.

Halt glanced at the sun, estimating that they had rested long enough. He gave a signal to Lorriac and the men began to saddle up and remount once more. Gilan was first into the saddle, waiting anxiously for the rest of the men to form up. His horse seemed to sense his impatience. When they moved out, it pulled against the reins, so that the boy had to work hard to keep it down to a trot.

They rode on for several more kilometers. They came to a point where the path led up a narrow defile, fringed by steep rocky cliffs surmounted by thick-growing trees. Halt saw Gilan nodding to himself, a satisfied look on his face. This was clearly a landmark he recognized. But over the next two kilometers, the boy's confidence started to wane and he began to look anxiously from side to side, occasionally standing in the saddle to get a better view of the surrounding landscape. The land had leveled out again and they were in open country and still moving uphill. The heavy forest lay on their right. To the left, there was broken scrub with the occasional clump of trees. None of these looked like old growth. The tallest was barely five meters high.

Gilan pulled his horse to the side of the track they were following and stood in his stirrups again, looking back the way they had come. Halt rode to join him as the troop filed past, the soldiers glancing at them with mild interest. They knew the young lad was their guide, and one or two of them started to comment on his obvious uncertainty.

"Problem?" Halt said quietly.

Gilan turned an anguished face to him. "It's all changed," he said. "It's not the same!" His voice was cracking with the strain of uncertainty. He had been sure he could lead them straight to the ford, but now everything seemed to be going wrong.

Halt put up a calming hand. "Keep your voice down. Don't let the men see that you're not sure what you're doing."

Gilan made an effort to calm down. He took several deep breaths. But then he looked around again and made a helpless little gesture.

"When we came up that gully back there"—he waved vaguely to the rear—"I thought we were fine. I remember that. But now there's no sign of my main landmark. We should have seen it by now."

"What was it?" Halt asked.

"It was a double-trunked pine tree—like a huge V," Gilan replied, the anxiety creeping into his voice once more. "You could see it for miles. It was over there . . . I think." He pointed to the west, toward the new growth Halt had noticed.

"But now it's gone," he repeated desperately. He was very

conscious that he had led them here, away from the main battle. And now he had managed to get himself, and the cavalry, lost. He was also aware of the pivotal role that the cavalry had to play in the coming battle.

"We'll lose the battle," he said. "And it'll be my fault."

"Get a grip," Halt told him crisply. He was just a boy, and Halt could see his confidence ebbing away. But he needed to be brought up sharply. This was no time for soft words. Halt urged Abelard toward a clump of low trees. "Let's take a closer look." He turned back to the captain. "Halt the column, Lorriac."

"It's not there," Gilan told him as the column came to a halt, horses stamping and snorting, then lowering their heads to crop the fresh grass underfoot. "We'd see it if it was. It was ten meters tall, for pity's sake." But he urged his horse to follow Halt.

The Ranger allowed him to come level with him, then spoke again.

"Trees can fall down," he said. "Particularly big, old ones. Or they can burn in a forest fire. Or be struck by lightning."

They reached the section of new growth, a tangled mass of young trees, festooned with vines. He edged Abelard forward, peering into the jumble of branches that faced them.

"There," he said, pointing. Concealed in the tangle of greenery, they could make out an old, splintered stump. It had once supported a massive pine, but its edges were blackened, a sign that it had taken a lightning strike.

Looking farther afield, they saw the charred remains of the V-shaped tree it had once supported, lying in the long grass, overgrown with creepers. More charring was visible on the old timber.

"There's your V-shaped pine," Halt said calmly, and he saw the relief flood into Gilan's young face.

"So it is. So it is," the boy said, his confidence returning with a rush. He looked eagerly up the slope to the crest.

"What do we look for next?" Halt asked.

Gilan indicated the higher ground ahead of them. "At the ridge, we should be able to see two mountains to the west. If we line them up, they'll show us the way to the ford."

He began to trot up the hill. Halt allowed Abelard to follow him.

"Well, at least *they* won't have been struck by lightning," Halt murmured.

They reached the crest of the ridge and looked west. Immediately, Halt could see two large hills—hardly mountains, he mused. Gilan seemed to echo his thought.

"They seemed taller when I was young," he said.

Halt smiled. "That's often the way. I used to think my father was a giant, and he was actually quite short. But they are the mountains you spoke about?"

"Oh yes," Gilan said, nodding emphatically. "I remember that bare white patch halfway up the nearest one." He pointed and Halt could make out a white scar among the trees on the distant hill. Probably chalk, he thought.

"So now," Gilan said, concentrating, "we line up the crest of the first hill with that U-shaped gap in the second one . . ." He urged his horse forward until he had the alignment fixed. "And that's the direction to the ford."

He turned in his saddle to look behind him, checking once to make sure he was looking along the line indicated by the two hills. "So we go into the forest right beside that very dark green tree. Then, if we keep heading east, we'll come to the river—and the ford."

Halt regarded the young man for a few seconds. He was handling this situation very well for someone so young, he thought. Then he glanced back and forth several times, getting the alignment and the direction set in his mind. Once they were in the trees, he knew, it would be all too easy to lose their direction. But he had a way of preventing that.

"How long before we reach the river?" he asked.

Gilan considered his answer. "An hour," he said. "Maybe a little longer."

Halt looked at the cavalry troop, sitting at ease a hundred meters down the hill. It'd take a lot longer with nearly one hundred and fifty riders pushing through the closely set trees, he thought. And that meant it would be getting on for dusk by the time they reached the ford—assuming they found it without any further delays. He came to a decision.

"We'll leave the men here and go on alone," he said. "Once we find the ford, we'll come back for them. But realistically, I don't think we'll get them all across the river before dark."

He cantered down the hill and apprised Captain Lorriac of the plan. As the men dismounted and began unsaddling their horses, Halt cantered back up the hill to the spot where Gilan was waiting for him. They rode into the trees together, Gilan leading the way.

Instantly, Halt realized that he'd been right to leave the men behind while they found the ford. The trees grew closely together so that he and Gilan had to wind their way through them, riding single file. And it was dark under the heavy leaf canopy. He knew it would be almost full dark under here in an hour or so.

"There used to be a game trail," Gilan called back to him as he edged his horse round the trunks of three trees growing closely together, then resumed his course on the far side, shoving saplings and lighter growth aside and trampling the knee-high undergrowth. Thankfully, with the thickness of the overhead leaf canopy, there wasn't a great deal of underbrush. Halt followed him, but his innate sense of direction told him they were straying from their course. He reached into his belt pouch and produced his Northseeker—a magnetized steel needle balanced on a slender pin in a brass case. The needle always pointed north–south. He let it steady, then saw they were heading slightly north of east. He pointed his arm in the right direction as he studied the little instrument.

"That way," he said. "Swing back to the right a little."

Gilan complied, glancing with interest at the instrument in Halt's cupped palms. "That's very handy," he said.

They continued in that fashion for the next hour, with Halt pausing at intervals to correct their course. Every five meters, he drew his saxe and cut a long notch in a tree, marking their course for the following day.

Eventually, Gilan drew rein and waited for Halt to force his way alongside him. He was frowning.

"We should have reached the river by now," he said.

Halt glanced around at the dark forest surrounding them. "Was the growth as thick as this last time you were here?" he asked, and Gilan shook his head. "That's it then," Halt continued. "We're having to force our way through, and we're making detours around the bigger trees all the time. Stands to reason we're taking longer than you used to."

Gilan opened his mouth to reply, but Halt held up a hand for silence. He leaned forward in his saddle, listening, his ear cocked to the east. "Listen," he said. "What's that?"

They both listened. They could hear the birds chirping in the forest, and the occasional rustle of small animals moving between the trees. Then they heard another sound—a musical ripple of running water.

"That's the river," Halt said. Without discussing it, they both urged their horses forward, heading for the sound. After thirty meters, they saw the gleam of light on water through the trees. If the last of the day's light was reaching the water's surface, Halt thought, that meant there must be a sizable gap in the forest canopy. And that meant the river widened at this point.

And that usually indicated the presence of a ford.

They rode out of the trees onto a level, sandy bank. The river gurgled past them, widening to around fifty meters. To the left and right, it narrowed down to around fifteen, with the current flowing rapidly between the banks, and the water dark and deep. But at the wider part, they could see the sandy bottom. Gilan rode forward for ten meters. The water barely rose to his horse's belly. He turned and grinned at Halt.

"I knew I could find it!" he said triumphantly.

Halt raised an eyebrow. "Of course you did."

34

"READY?" ARALD SAID IN A LOW VOICE. THE MEN AROUND him all replied in hoarse whispers that they were and he gestured down the hill. "Then let's go."

He led the way out from behind the palisade, crossing the ditch on a temporary plank bridge that would be withdrawn as soon as he and his men were on their way. The moon had set half an hour ago and the land was dimly lit by starlight. Scudding clouds rode the wind across the sky, sending their shadows rippling over the ground and making it all the harder to pick out the movement of the small group as they headed downhill.

Behind him, a man slipped and fell on the long, smooth grass, hitting the ground with a slight rattle of his sword in its scabbard. The party froze, waiting to see if the enemy had heard the slight noise. But they were still a long way from the Wargal camp and it seemed to have gone unnoticed.

To his right, Arald heard a single owl hoot and glanced across the slope. At the far side of the palisade, he could just make out Crowley and his party of Rangers as they ghosted out of the armed camp and slipped away to the right. He shook his head in admiration. The Rangers were skilled movers, and even though he knew where they were and where they were heading, he was hard put to see any sign of them. Occasionally, a dim form might be fleetingly visible above the long grass. But then it was gone again, melting into the land, using the moving cloud shadows as cover.

He wished his own group could move with such skill. But then he realized they were a diversion. They were supposed to be seen by the enemy to draw their attention from the real threat— the Rangers intent on burning the wheeled barricades.

Still, he thought, it would be nice if his men didn't bump into one another and utter muffled curses. And it would be better if they didn't allow their weapons to clatter as they moved and their equipment to creak quite so loudly.

He led them obliquely down the hill, until they were hugging the tree line on their left. As they became more accustomed to the terrain and the lack of light, he was glad to hear that they moved more stealthily. From time to time, he halted them, gesturing for them to sink into the long grass while he studied the enemy camp, looking for any sign that they had been seen.

So far so good, he thought, as they stopped for the third time. There was no reaction from the Wargals. He could see their sentries patrolling, but none of them seemed to be alarmed. He looked across the hill again to where he knew the Rangers must be. He thought he saw a slight blur of movement. Perhaps it was one of Crowley's men. Or perhaps, more likely, it was a cloud's shadow moving across the grass or the grass itself rippling under the wind.

"Come on," he whispered, and started off again, heading for the eastern end of the ford. On the far side, the bank was a vertical drop about half a meter high. It would give them better cover than the sloping beach that formed the main part of the ford.

They reached the river and he held up his hand once more for his men to stop. They sank to the ground, lying prone. Crowley had given them a briefing earlier in the evening.

"When you stop, resist the temptation to move. It's movement that the eye notices first. So just lie still, even if you think you've been spotted. Chances are, you haven't been. But chances are, if you move, you will be."

The little band of raiders wore no armor or helmets to make noise or reflect the light. Each man had a war belt, with a sword and a heavy dagger in scabbards on their left and right sides. They were all dressed in dark clothing—overshirts and trousers—and had black scarves wound round their heads. Their faces were blackened in irregular patches—another of Crowley's dictums, to prevent their faces showing as pale ovals or regular shapes under the starlight.

At the edge of the ford, a thick clump of bushes grew down to the water's edge. They would use this as their entry point into the water. Arald belly-crawled toward it, grunting softly as he did so. It wasn't the most comfortable way for him to move. His belly tended to get in the way.

Have to do something about that, he thought, then mentally shrugged. He'd been saying that for years—usually at the urging of his wife, Lady Sandra.

He reached down and unclipped his scabbard from the belt. Glancing back, he gestured for his men to do the same. He couldn't wade across the river with the scabbard dangling around his legs. He'd hold it horizontally, above the river surface.

He heard the subdued clinks and rattles as his men released their own scabbards. Then, turning side on, he edged his way into the slow-flowing water of the ford, crawling on one hand and both knees until the water grew deeper, then rising into a crouch to continue. Finally, as the water reached its full depth, he stood erect and forced his way against the sluggish current as the river rose to his chest.

He glanced behind and saw other dark forms entering the river, gradually transforming into heads and shoulders as the men found their feet on the sandy bottom. He heard movement on the far bank and, looking up, could see the dark shape of a Wargal sentry shuffling along the bank in that rolling gait they all shared. He froze, standing still in the water, bending his knees until only the upper part of his head was above water, his nostrils just brushing the surface.

The beast went past, barely paying any attention to the river surface, uttering those small, almost percussive grunts that the Wargals seemed to make when they were moving. Arald waited until the sentry had reached the end of his beat and turned to go back the other way. Once it was past him again, he resumed his movement. He felt desperately exposed out here in the water. The bank was only twenty meters away now and he was tempted to cover the last of the distance in a rush. He suppressed the urge to do so. Speed meant noise, he knew. And noise was something he couldn't afford.

Slowly, infinitely slowly, he continued to forge his way through the black water, even though every instinct was urging him to rise to full height and run. He glanced once to the west, looking for some sign of Crowley and his little force.

Of course, there was none.

* * *

Crowley and nine of his Rangers flowed down the hill like the wind that stirred the long grass. They were all experts at silent and unseen movement, and there was no need for Crowley to give them any instruction.

Like Arald, they resisted the temptation to move quickly. But in their case, it was second nature borne of long practice, not something they had to force upon themselves. They had discarded their cloaks—the long garments would be too cumbersome crossing the river, and once they were soaked, they would be too noisy, with water dripping out of them. Instead, they wore their dull gray-and-brown overshirts and woolen trousers, tucked into soft, calf-high boots. They had dark scarves wound round their faces, and like Arald and his men, their faces were streaked and smeared in irregular patterns with dark coloring.

Robert and Jurgen carried flint and steel and an assortment of combustibles, secured in waterproof wrapping. Each man had his bow and quiver, which they left on the bank of the ford as they entered the water. They would need them to provide cover for Arald's party as they made their way back across the ford. Naturally, they all wore their double scabbards, with their saxes and throwing knives held snugly against their left-hand sides.

As he reached the water, Crowley took stock of the situation. There was a sentry at this end of the ford as well, with another patrolling the middle section. Crowley waited until the Wargal was shambling back toward the middle of the ford, then slid into the water, crawling initially, then rising to his hands and knees and finally to a crouch as the water rose. Behind him, the others entered the river. Only Leander remained behind, his bow in hand, waiting to take care of the sentry once they heard Arald's diversion.

Keeping an eye on the sentry, Crowley slid through the water, stopping and sinking lower as the beast came back into view. He didn't need to check that the others were doing the same. They'd all been trained in the same hard school.

Earlier that evening, Morgarath had summoned one of his lieutenants, a man who had served under him at Castle Gorlan for the past ten years. The Lord of Rain and Night sat outside his black pavilion, drinking deeply from a silver tankard filled with wine, staring up at the hill opposite them, where the campfires of the Araluen army twinkled in the dark night.

His subordinate approached carefully, wondering if he had done something to annoy his leader. You never knew with Lord Morgarath, he thought. The man was capable of flying into a tearing rage at the slightest provocation—or at none. It paid to make your way carefully until you ascertained his mood.

"You sent for me, my lord?" he said deferentially.

Morgarath didn't reply for several seconds. When he did, he didn't look at the man. Instead, he gestured with his tankard at the Araluen camp. "You see those men, Trask?"

For a moment, Trask thought Morgarath had actually seen someone on the hill. Then he realized he was referring to Duncan's army in general. He nodded carefully, still unsure what Morgarath had in mind. The silky, low-pitched voice gave no hint.

"Yes, my lord," he said.

Again, Morgarath paused before replying. Perhaps it was an

intentional gambit, designed to keep his men off guard and uncertain. Or perhaps he was just thinking carefully. Trask realized he'd never know.

"I know those men," Morgarath said at last. "Duncan. Arald. Crowley. And Halt—especially Halt." There was a note of pure hatred in his voice as he repeated the Hibernian Ranger's name.

Trask sensed that some kind of reply was necessary. "Yes, my lord," he said. His reply was as noncommittal, as nonjudgmental as he could make it.

"They're clever men," Morgarath said. "Clever, *clever* men. And they'll be making a clever, clever plan."

Trask hesitated. A further *Yes, my lord* didn't seem appropriate. He held his tongue and waited for Morgarath to continue.

"They'll have seen our wheeled barriers. And they'll have worked out what they're for."

"Do you think so, my lord?" Trask asked, with a note of surprise creeping into his voice. He had been puzzled by the strange wheeled contraptions until their purpose was explained to him.

Morgarath turned a basilisk stare on him. It didn't do to question the former Baron of Gorlan. "Yes. I do," he said carefully. But behind the simple words was a dire warning. *Do not question me again.*

Trask swallowed. His throat was suddenly dry and he found the action difficult. He dropped his gaze from his commander's.

Morgarath noted the subservient action and nodded. It was all to the good to keep his followers in fear of him. "As I say, they are clever men and they'll be up there, scheming, thinking of a way to try to destroy my machines. They'll creep down the hill tonight, cross the river and try to destroy them. I can sense it."

"Shall I double the sentries along the riverbank, my lord?" Trask asked.

Morgarath looked at him once more. It was the typical sort of nonthinking answer to a problem that he had come to expect from the men who served him. Extra sentries might drive any prospective raiders away. And he saw this as a chance to rid himself of some of the men who faced him. Particularly the Rangers. He expected that they would be the ones assigned to try to destroy the barriers. With any luck, Halt himself might be among them. Or Crowley. It would be a good night's work if he could kill or capture one of them.

"No. I don't want to stop them. I want to kill them. Let them cross the river, then kill them. Take thirty Wargals and form a perimeter around the machines. Stay hidden and, when the Rangers come, let them get close, then cut them off from the river. And kill them all."

"Yes, my lord. Will thirty be enough? I could take fifty of the beasts."

Morgarath shook his head. "No, no. It'll be dark, and if you have too many you'll be blundering around getting in each other's way. I doubt they'll send more than half a dozen men, so thirty will be plenty. Just stay hidden and be ready for them."

Trask hesitated to ask the next question, but knew he had to. "My lord, how will I know they're coming?"

Morgarath smiled. He'd wanted the question because it gave him a chance to show how he could outthink the enemy. It was important that he maintained a certain reputation for ingenuity.

"Because they'll stage a diversion to draw us away from the machines," he said. "Probably on the far side of the camp. It will be noisy and obvious and you will not respond to it. Understand?"

"Yes, sir. I understand." There had been an unspoken threat in that last word of Morgarath's. Unspoken but very clear.

"When you hear an uproar somewhere else in the camp, stand fast. Stay hidden and wait for the Rangers to come."

Now those unblinking eyes bored into Trask's once more. He wanted to drop his gaze but realized that, if he did, it would only fan Morgarath into a rage. He swallowed again. And Morgarath smiled. A thin smile that touched only his lips as he spoke.

"And when they come, kill them."

35

THE WARGAL WAS COMING CLOSE AGAIN ON HIS REGULAR patrol. Arald crouched below the low step of the riverbank, listening as he heard the creature's feet approaching, then stopping directly above him. His men crouched on either side of him, hard up against the bank so that the sentry couldn't see them.

Arald felt for the heavy club that he carried on a leather thong around his neck. They had debated the best way to deal with the Wargal sentry, with the minimum of noise. A knife had been suggested, but they were all unfamiliar with the Wargals' physical shape. It might be difficult to hit a vital spot with one thrust. One could always muffle the sentry's cries with an arm around his face and mouth. But Wargals were equipped with powerful fangs, making that alternative an undesirable one. Nobody would want to put their arm or hand close to those massive yellow teeth.

All in all, a club seemed to be the best solution.

Now, as the sentry passed the point where Arald crouched beneath the bank, the baron thrust himself up and out of the water, the club drawn back and ready to strike.

His movement made noise, of course, as water cascaded off him, out of his soaked clothes and back into the river. The Wargal began to turn, but Arald knew speed was his ally. He may have been slightly overweight, but he was an expert warrior, trained to strike swiftly. The sentry's head was only halfway round to him when the club thudded down onto its head, crushing the flat leather cap it wore and knocking it senseless. Arald was poised for a second strike if it was necessary, but the massive, shaggy beast uttered a low moan and collapsed on the soft ground of the riverbank with no more than a dull thud.

"Let's go!" the Baron of Redmont said softly, and his men rose from the river, dripping water, and swarmed onto the bank.

Arald took a moment to get his bearings. They knew the supply wagons were on their left-hand side, set back behind the first of the tent lines. He shoved the club inside his jerkin, drew his sword and hurried in that direction. His men followed him, their boots squelching as water was forced out of them.

At first he was worried about the noise. But then he realized that the Wargals were anything but silent sleepers. The night around them was filled with groans, grunts and yips—as well as the occasional shattering fart. A little bit of dripping water would hardly cause any notice.

Moving in a crouch, they reached the far edge of the tent lines and started toward the wagons and supply dump. Arald picked his way carefully. The tents were pitched in haphazard lines—not neat, geometrical lines like those in the Araluen camp—and there was a constant danger of catching one's feet in the guy ropes that stretched out in the darkness, difficult to see and to avoid. He turned to the men following him and whispered a warning.

"Watch out for the tent ropes."

A few of them nodded. Then, inevitably, one of them caught his foot in a rope, windmilled his arms wildly, and fell onto the side of one of the black animal-hide tents, collapsing it and landing on a sleeping body inside.

The Wargal gave a startled grunt and thrashed around to free itself from the collapsed tent. One of the other men seized the fallen raider by the arm and hauled him off the half-collapsed pile of black leather. Then, with a flurry of movement, the Wargal who had been so rudely awoken scrambled out of the entrance, rising to its feet and glaring around, bewildered and still half asleep. It saw the dark forms of the men crouching close by and began to utter a challenging snarl.

Arald lunged and ran it through, and the creature staggered, clutching at the blade through its middle until Arald could withdraw it. Then it tumbled over, falling back onto the ruined tent and shrieking in pain.

All around, they heard the snarling cries of the other Wargals as they came awake, lumbering out into the open, and onto the swords of the small party who had infiltrated their camp. The supply tents were only a few meters away and Arald gestured toward them with his sword.

"Burn the supplies!" he ordered. "Three of you stay with me and hold them off."

As he spoke, he hacked down at another Wargal, dropping it to the ground. But more and more of them were scrambling out of the tents, searching for the source of the commotion. Then one of the men in Morgarath's army started shouting.

"Alarm! Alarm! We're being attacked! Sound the alarm!"

And suddenly the night was filled with snarling, snapping

Wargals, some armed, some unarmed, lurching toward Arald and his party as they recognized them as interlopers. The Baron cut down another two of them in quick order. The soldier beside him stopped a third.

There was a flare of fire from the supply tents as Arald's men tossed oil onto the canvas and then struck flint and steel to set the combustible liquid aflame.

The Wargals were barking and snarling in alarm as more and more of them rushed to the site. Arald glanced around. His men were still standing. Those who had fired the supply tent were back behind him.

"Get to the river!" he shouted, and led the way, the others following him with pounding, squelching feet. The darkness was their ally—as was the large number of Wargals who had rallied to the supply tents. They actually were fighting with each other in some cases, and most of them had no idea where the sudden attack had come from, nor where it had gone.

But before long, the dark, running figures were spotted, and Morgarath's bestial soldiers lurched and lumbered in pursuit.

Two of them were closer than their brothers. Arald glanced back and saw them leaping and bounding after his men. He moved to one side, letting his raiders pass him, then stepped in front of the two Wargals.

These two were armed. One had a short spear and the other a sword. Arald parried the spear thrust, engaging the shaft and whirling his sword in a fast, circular motion that tore the spear from its owner's grip. Then he thrust at the bulky figure, feeling the point go home, hearing the beast shriek in agony as it fell.

The second Wargal aimed a massive overhand cut at him. Had it gone home, it would have split him from shoulder to waist. But Arald swayed to one side, feeling the wind of the blade as it just missed him, then struck the ground by his feet. He hammered the hilt of his sword into the off-balance Wargal's head, then, as the beast staggered, he cut at its neck with a carefully controlled movement.

He didn't wait to see it fall. He turned and ran for the river once more. Dark shapes blundered out of the tent lines in front of him, and he cut them down with a ruthless efficiency before they could register that he was an enemy.

"Into the river!" he shouted, although, as he heard the sound of violent splashing, he realized the order was unnecessary. In front of him, a man staggered and fell as a spear took him squarely in the back. It was an obviously mortal wound, and Arald had no time to waste checking on him. He ran on, hearing the sounds of pursuit close behind him, and blundered into the river, throwing a curtain of spray high in the air.

On the far side of the enemy camp, crouched in the shallow waters of the ford, Crowley heard the sudden outbreak of shouting and saw the vivid flare of flames in the night. He turned back to see Leander, no more than a dark shape crouched on the far bank, bow ready, and waved his arm.

Leander rose to his feet. He already had an arrow nocked. He drew back, sighted and released, in one smooth continuous motion. The arrow took the Wargal sentry in the middle of his back. The creature gave a low grunt of surprise and pain, then fell to the sandy bank, already dead.

Instantly, Crowley was on his feet, leading the rest of his men into the Wargal camp and heading toward the spot where they knew the wheeled barricades were stored. As they came level with the dark, bulky structures, he beckoned Robert and Jurgen forward. Jurgen was already striking flint and steel together, letting the sparks fall into an oil-soaked torch that he carried, and blowing on the tiny sparks until they suddenly flared into fire. Robert was carrying a large bladder of oil. He unslung it from his shoulder, ready to throw it over the barricades.

And at that moment, the night erupted with dark shapes, snarling, grunting and yipping as they rose from their hiding places behind wagons and tents, and the barricades themselves. Crowley heard a human voice yell, "Attack!" and he drew his saxe, cursing the fact that he had left his bow on the far bank.

One of the Wargals lumbered toward him. He slipped under its wild roundhouse swing, hearing the sword whistle over his head. Then, without pausing, he stepped forward and drove his saxe into the heavy body. He heard a grunt of surprise, then pain, and the Wargal staggered back, nearly ripping the saxe from his grip as it went.

All around him, he heard the clash of weapons and the grunts and snarls of the Wargals as they ambushed his small party. He didn't know how many of the enemy there were, but he knew his men were badly outnumbered.

There was no way they could carry out their mission. Their only mission now was to survive and escape.

"Back to the river!" he shouted. "Retreat!"

Hopefully, Leander would be ready to provide covering fire once they made it back to the water. He parried another sword stroke, cut at the Wargal's hand and saw the sword fall from its nerveless fingers. Still the beast came on at him and he thrust with the saxe, taking it in the throat and killing it instantly.

Then, a few meters away from him, he saw Robert whirling the bladder of oil over his head, then releasing it to spill its contents over a small group of Wargals who were preparing to charge. They recoiled as the oil sprayed them, then realized it was harmless and started forward again.

Which was a mistake. Jurgen hurled the burning torch after the oil bladder and it fell among them, catching instantly in the highly combustible liquid.

There was a *WHOOSH* of flame, and three of the beasts were engulfed in fire. The fourth leapt back, its arm and hand burning. It beat at the flames, snarling in terror.

It was enough to give the Rangers the opportunity they needed to escape. As one, they wheeled and ran for the river. After a moment's hesitation, the Wargals followed them. Crowley could hear their human commander yelling orders at them, urging them to pursue the fleeing raiders.

He looked around, eyes slitted in the uncertain light. The flames that had engulfed the Wargals were still burning fiercely, and now there was a vile smell of charred fur and burning flesh in the air. Finally, he saw the commander, standing to one side, sword drawn, and shouting at his troops until his voice cracked.

Crowley slid his saxe back into its scabbard and drew his throwing knife. His arm went back and forward again in one smooth action and he sent the knife spinning across the open space between him and the Wargals' commander.

"Don't let them get—" the man was yelling as the knife came spinning out of the darkness and struck him in the chest. He staggered a few paces, looking down stupidly at the hilt that protruded from his body. He clutched at it with both hands, trying to withdraw it, but somehow he didn't have the strength. Then his knees gave way and he sank to the ground, finishing his command in a barely audible whisper.

". . . away."

Then Crowley was splashing through the shallow waters of the ford, along with his men. The Wargals hesitated as Trask went down and his voice fell silent. They weren't good at directing themselves in battle. As the leading group stopped at the river's edge, Leander began shooting from the far bank.

"Rangers! Stay down!" he yelled, and they needed no second bidding. Crowley, crouched low in the water, heard the air-splitting hiss of Leander's shafts as they whipped overhead, barely a meter above him. He heard the dull thuds as the arrows went home. The first four Wargals went down in rapid succession, with barely a heartbeat between them. Those behind them hesitated for a second or two, waiting for Trask to issue more orders. It was a fatal few seconds. It gave Crowley and the first three of the Rangers time to scramble ashore and take up their own bows. A volley of arrows flashed across the river, killing or disabling another half dozen of the enemy.

The Wargal ambush had started with thirty troops. Now they were down to less than half that number, in the space of a few minutes. Leaderless, they milled about uncertainly. Then, as more shafts flashed out of the night and killed two more of them, they turned and took cover from that relentless arrow shower.

"They're not following!" Crowley shouted. "Get along the bank to cover Arald and his men."

They followed him at a run. But where there had been nine of them originally, now there were only eight. Crowley looked around desperately, trying to ascertain who was missing. But in the darkness and the general confusion, he couldn't make out the faces of his companions.

As the far side of the ford came into sight, they could see the dark shapes of Arald's men pushing through the waist-deep water toward them, pursued by more dark shapes as the first of the Wargals plunged in after them.

Realizing that they were about to be caught, Arald turned in the waist-deep water, facing his pursuers, and shouted at the two men closest to him.

"Hold them back!" he yelled.

The men, swords drawn, pushed back through the water to join him. He parried a blow from the leading Wargal, then cut sideways, nearly severing its head from its body. The beast went over with a massive splash, its blood staining the water for meters around them, looking black in the flickering light that illuminated the scene. His nearest companion deflected an ax stroke from a second Wargal and Arald's sword darted out like a striking death adder—fast and lethal.

But more and more Wargals were pushing into the river, fanning out to encircle the three men protecting their comrades' retreat.

"Where are those damn Rangers?" Arald's second companion demanded, as he parried and cut desperately with a huge, powerful Wargal.

Then they heard the now-familiar *hiss-thud!* as multiple arrows rained down over them, dropping the Wargals like wheat before the scythe.

Suddenly, the river was clear of the beasts. There were another dozen hesitating on the bank, and they took the brunt of the next volley. Five of them toppled over in less than two seconds. The others, not yet controlled by the mad killing rage that Morgarath could incite in them, retreated a few paces. Then, as more arrows fell among them, they sought cover from the pitiless scourge.

"Let's get out of here!" Arald said gratefully, and the small raiding party waded quickly back to the far bank and ran up the hill.

"I lost three men," Arald said bitterly, as they convened in Duncan's tent to assess the results of the raid.

"And we lost Jurgen," Crowley added. His voice was low. He hated losing men and to lose a Ranger was almost unthinkable. In his eyes, each Ranger was worth at least five normal troops.

Duncan glanced at him, sympathy in his eyes. "How did that happen?"

Crowley gave vent to a deep sigh. "He and Robert saved us. They used the oil and a torch to break up the first Wargal attack—when they took us by surprise. Robert hurled an oilskin over a group of them and Jurgen dashed forward with a burning torch to set the oil on fire—and the Wargals with it. It gave us the time we needed to regroup and withdraw. But it left him exposed and one of the Wargals threw a spear and hit him in the side."

The men fell into a depressed silence. Then Crowley spoke again, his voice bitter. "It wouldn't be so bad if we'd actually achieved something. But they were waiting for us and we never got near the barricades."

Arald nodded gloomy assent. "We didn't even do much damage to their supply dump," he said. "Morgarath out-thought us from the word go. He knew we'd be coming and he was ready for us."

Duncan noted the sunken shoulders of his two commanders, and their downcast eyes.

"Morgarath is no fool. We know that," he said softly. "We can't expect to win every battle against him."

Crowley and Arald looked up at the King and saw the steely determination glittering in his eyes.

"We just have to make sure we win the last one."

36

HALT CALLED AN EARLY START THE FOLLOWING DAY, PLAN-
ning to get the troop through the forest and across the ford by
midmorning. They ate a quick breakfast in the predawn darkness. There was no enemy in the vicinity, so Halt permitted the
men to light cook fires. This wasn't done entirely from selfless
concern for their comfort. A cook fire meant that water could
be boiled, and boiled water meant coffee. Halt hated starting
any day without coffee.

He sipped appreciatively on a steaming cup while he discussed the order of march with Lorriac. Gilan paced the campsite, full of nervous energy and anxious to be on the move. Gilan
was always anxious to be on the move, Halt thought, although
there was no point in starting out before daybreak. In the darkness under the trees, men would become lost and disorientated.

"Gilan and I will lead the way to the ford," he told Lorriac.
"We'll have the men ride in single file. The trees are too close set
for them to travel any other way. I've blazed the trail on trees
every five meters or so, so there should be no problem with people getting lost."

Lorriac nodded understanding. "Where do you want me?"

"You bring up the rear and keep any stragglers moving," Halt said. "I expect that we'll get strung out. That always happens when you have a single line of riders moving through difficult country."

"True," Lorriac agreed. "But as more and more riders follow the path, it should become a little easier for the ones at the rear."

Halt hadn't considered that. As a hundred or so men traveled the narrow, winding trail he and Gilan had followed to the ford, the undergrowth would become progressively beaten down, saplings would be forced aside and the trail would widen. The last fifty men would be able to move more easily through the trees.

"Nevertheless, keep the pressure on them," Halt said.

Lorriac swallowed the last of his breakfast. He took a swig from his canteen—he was no coffee drinker—and strolled off to organize his men as they struck camp.

Halt drained his coffee, considered making another cup and then glanced at the sky in the east. The sun was beginning to show over the treetops and he reluctantly decided there was no time. He tossed the dregs of his cup into the campfire beside him and made his way to where he and Gilan had pitched their one-man tents the previous evening.

Anxious for something to keep himself occupied, Gilan was there before him, striking the tents and rolling them into tight bundles that would sit behind their saddles. Halt nodded his thanks.

"Good work," he said, and Gilan grinned at the praise. Must remember to do that more often, Halt thought. He recalled his own younger days, when words of praise were few and far between and his days were shadowed by his twin brother's resentment and plotting against him. He rolled his bedroll into a tight cylinder and fastened it with the leather ties that would keep it in shape. He had used his saddle as a pillow the night before and now he clicked his fingers to Abelard.

The little horse ambled obediently to him and stood while he lifted the saddle onto his back and tightened the girth.

"Wish my horse would do that," Gilan said enviously. His pony was displaying all the fractiousness of its kind in the cold early-morning air, prancing and dancing, stepping sideways as he tried to settle the saddle in place, then taking a deep breath to expand its belly as he went to fasten the girth. Halt pointed a warning finger. If Gilan didn't nip that in the bud, his horse would exhale when he had buckled the girth strap and it would become loose. But Gilan was up to the horse's tricks.

"I know," he said. "He always tries that on."

He pulled the horse a little closer and firmly drove his knee up into its belly, forcing it to let the pent-up breath go. Before the horse could breathe in again, he pulled the cinch tight and buckled it.

"You'd think he'd understand that I'm onto that trick by now," Gilan said.

Halt grinned. "They all like to try it."

Gilan raised an eyebrow. "Even Abelard?"

"Not anymore. He tried it for the first few weeks I had him. But he's smart enough to realize that it's a lost cause." He patted the horse's velvety nose affectionately. Abelard blew out a cloud of steam as he snorted in acknowledgment.

"I'd love a Ranger horse," Gilan said, eyeing the sturdy little beast.

"Have to become a Ranger first," Halt told him easily. He was joking, but Gilan took him seriously.

"Is that possible?" he asked.

Halt was taken aback by the swiftness of his reply. "Well . . . yes. Of course it is," he said, not sure how much he should encourage this sudden interest. "You'd have to apply to Crowley first. He'd assess you."

"I don't imagine there'd be any trouble there," Gilan said. "After all, my father is a battle master."

A slight frown creased Halt's forehead. "Doesn't matter who your father is when you apply to become a Ranger. Or what he is. It's who *you* are that's important."

Gilan flushed. "I didn't mean to sound as if I'm privileged or anything," he said. "Or that I'd have a better chance than someone else because of who my father is."

Halt said nothing. But he smiled quizzically and raised an eyebrow.

Gilan said nothing for a few moments, then dropped his gaze. "Actually, I suppose I did mean that, when I come to think of it," he admitted.

"Well, as long as you admit it," Halt said, hiding a smile. Then he swung up into the saddle and Gilan followed suit. But now the idea had been raised, the boy wanted to pursue it further.

"How old would I have to be?" he asked.

"I believe most apprentices are fifteen," Halt told him. "So you have a couple of years to wait."

"Oh. Right." Gilan considered that for a few seconds. "Are you planning on taking an apprentice?"

Halt sat straighter in the saddle, surprised by the question. "Not if I can help it," he muttered. He touched his heels into Abelard's sides and cantered to where Lorriac had the troop formed up in three files. Gilan followed a few strides behind him, sensing that the subject of his becoming a Ranger was now closed.

Lorriac nodded as Halt drew up to one side. The captain was slouched comfortably in the saddle, facing the assembled troop.

"Ready, Halt?" he asked. Halt made a gesture for him to proceed with his briefing and he raised his voice so that those in the rear of the troop could hear him.

"We'll travel single file," Lorriac said. "The Ranger and the battle master's son will lead the way."

"His name is Gilan," Halt said quietly, and Lorriac hesitated, then realized that by referring to Gilan as "the battle master's son" he might be diminishing the boy's sense of individuality. He corrected himself, with a nod to the Ranger.

"The Ranger and Gilan, our guide, will lead the way. We'll follow in this order. Left file first, then the middle file, then the right. I'll bring up the rear. Sergeants and corporals, keep the men moving. Don't let them get separated."

Lorriac had formed the troop up with his best and most reliable men in the left and right files. The shirkers, potential troublemakers and the thoughtless individuals who were always present in any group, he had placed in the center rank. That way, they would be sandwiched between the more reliable troops in front and behind.

"Stay closed up. Don't cause delays. The trail is marked every five meters by blaze marks on the trees, at eye height." He glanced at Halt to confirm that this was correct. The Ranger indicated that it was and Lorriac continued. "We want to be through the trees and across the ford within the next two hours. Chances are, Morgarath's army will attack today and our comrades are going to need us. So if the rider in front of you is slowing you up, poke his horse in the backside with the butt of your spear to get him moving. If that doesn't work, poke the rider with the point." There was a muted chuckle from the troopers. He paused, glancing along the triple line of faces. "Questions?"

One trooper raised his hand. "When we reach the ford, do we push on across, or do we wait for you?"

Lorriac glanced at Halt and indicated that he should answer.

"Gilan will cross first," Halt said, raising his voice, "to make sure there are no deep holes or problems with the ford. Then I'll wait on the bank on this side while the rest of you go across. There's more open space for you to form up on the far side." He glanced at the left-hand file and singled out a sergeant. "Sergeant, you take charge forming them up on the far side. By the time the last man is across, we want to move off."

They paused, scanning the ranks to see if there were any more questions. Three lines of faces stared back at them. Lorriac raised his right hand and pointed to the forest.

"Ranger, Gilan, lead us out, please."

Halt and Gilan tapped their heels into their horses' ribs and cantered toward the trees. Behind them, they heard the jingle of harness and weapons and creaking of saddle leather, as the men began to follow them in a long, snaking file.

They rode into the dimness under the trees. The sudden loss of light caused Gilan to hesitate for a moment, then he made out the first of the white slashes Halt had made in the bark of a tree and his confidence returned. He headed toward it, saw the second marked tree slightly to the right, and urged his horse forward. Halt followed a few strides behind him.

The men grew silent as they moved into the forest, following the slightly zigzag path laid out by their guides. There was no real reason for them to maintain silence, but the dimness and the close presence of the trees tended to inhibit idle conversation.

Halt glanced back over his shoulder. He could see the first ten men behind them, then the irregular path they were taking, and the lack of light, made it difficult to see any farther. But he could hear the noises of horses shoving their way through the undergrowth and the jingle of harness behind him.

"Keep closed up. Keep moving," he called. Already, he could see that the first few men behind him were leaving greater spacing between them than was necessary. He assumed it would be the same for the men behind them. As he called the order, he heard the sound of voices urging the horses on and the line closed up a little. In the near distance, he heard a sergeant calling the same order.

He was glad now that he'd thought to mark the trees along the path. Using the Northseeker would have been time-consuming and awkward. This way, Gilan could move confidently from one marker to the next, his eyes searching the shadows for the white marks in the darker bark of the trees.

They moved on. Gradually, the sun rose higher, sending its rays slanting down through the forest canopy. Birds began to sing in the trees and the day grew hotter. Halt wiped the perspiration from the back of his neck. The close-growing trees allowed no breeze and he thought that soon he would have to take off his cloak.

Still Gilan moved on, aided by the marks on the trees, and the line of men moved steadily toward the river, twisting first one way, then the other as the track avoided the thickest growth of trees. But always it came back to that constant easterly path.

They came to a small clearing and Gilan paused, looking round the open space for the sight of the next blazed tree. Halt urged Abelard up beside him and smiled encouragingly.

"How are you doing?" he asked.

Gilan was frowning in concentration. Then his face cleared as he saw the next mark and pushed forward. He glanced round at Halt and smiled quickly.

"Fine," he said. "We should be there soon."

Halt realized there was no need for him to stay with the lad. Gilan was having no trouble finding the trail. He edged Abelard to one side and let the following men move past him. They were keeping good formation, with only a few strides separating each man from the one following. Then there was a longer gap and he assumed he had reached the beginning of the middle file—the slackers and woolgatherers who would lose concentration and allow the column to get ahead of them.

"Pick it up!" he called abruptly, and the first few men reacted as if they had been stung. He realized that, wrapped in his green-and-gray cloak, sitting astride his unmoving gray horse, he had faded into the background and they had no idea he was there until he spoke.

The startled troopers urged their horses to close the gap between them and the men in front. Halt smiled grimly and remained where he was. Ten men went past, then there was another gap as a trio of riders, having lost sight of the men preceding them, ambled away off the path.

"Wake up!" he snarled, and had the same reaction of sudden surprise. "Keep the line closed up! There's your next marker! There!" He urged Abelard forward a pace to block their sideways movement and pointed to the next marked tree. Hurriedly, the riders corrected their course and began moving in the right direction. But there was still too big a gap between them and the riders ahead.

"Pace it up!" he snapped at them. They hurried to obey and

the men behind them, hearing the anger in the Ranger's voice, needed no urging to follow them. Halt watched them go, gradually closing up the line, and shook his head in disgust.

"We'll be in this damn forest all day if they don't lift their game," he said. Then, without even checking that he needed to, he snapped once more. "Come on! Close it up!"

Again, the urgent voices of the troopers and the sudden increase in the speed of the horses' movement told him that he had been right to give the order.

With Halt chivvying and driving the middle of the column and Gilan keeping a good pace at the head, they reached the bank of the ford just after two hours had passed.

By the time Halt had caught up with the head of the column again, shouting curses and admonishments at the slower riders as he forced his way past them, Gilan had ridden across, testing the ford. Thirty of the troopers were already across with him, forming up under the eye of the sergeant Halt had detailed for the job. As the Ranger had told them, the close-growing trees thinned out somewhat on the far side of the ford. They could see open country beyond.

Gilan had left a trooper by the edge of the river to pass on directions. As Halt began to walk Abelard into the water, the man warned him.

"There's a deep hole eight meters out from the bank. It drops away quickly, but your horse will manage it. Just be ready for it."

Halt nodded and rode forward. The men behind him hesitated, giving him a chance to move clear, then followed him into the river. At the point indicated, the water suddenly rose up past Abelard's body, coming higher than the saddle. Halt held his bow high above him, keeping the string clear of the water. He felt Abelard hesitate, then urged him on. The horse found firm footing and moved with more confidence. Then the bottom of the river rose and he was clear of the water once more, the horse shaking himself violently.

Halt rode up the far side of the ford to where Gilan sat astride his horse, watching anxiously. The Ranger gave him a nod of approval.

"Well done, Gilan. That's a good morning's work."

The boy glowed under the words. Once again, Halt remarked to himself how a few words of praise could do wonders for a young man's confidence. He dismounted, sat on the ground and took off his boots, pouring the water out of them, then hauling them back on again.

As the men continued to cross, the sergeant chivvied them into formation. Finally, Halt saw Lorriac bringing up the rear. The trooper Gilan had detailed for the job warned him about the deep hole, then followed him into the river. Lorriac rode up the firm sand and glanced at the men, assembled in three files once more, the wet horses steaming under the sun.

"Everyone here?" he asked the sergeant, and received an affirmative answer.

"Then let's head south again," the captain said, and trotted his horse to the head of the column, signaling for the front rank to follow him.

With the now-familiar jingle of equipment and harness, the troop rode out.

37

Late in the morning, the Wargal army began to assemble on the flat ground on the far side of the ford.

They formed up in three ranks, each consisting of one hundred and fifty troops. Morgarath was committing over half his remaining force to the attack, and the defenders on top of the hill knew this would be a fight to the death. There would be no carefully planned tactics used here. It would be a simple, brutal frontal assault. An attack designed to bludgeon their meager forces and smash its way inside the defensive position.

The command party watched as groups of Wargals lumbered to the wheeled barricades and carried them across the ford. They were easy to handle in the water, as it bore a great deal of their weight. The barricades were placed end to end, with a slight gap between each one. Set that way, they stretched across a front of nearly forty meters.

Once the barricades were across, the rest of the attack force followed, moving in line abreast, and taking their positions behind the barricades. The Wargals who had carried the devices across the river now lifted them again and began to jog up the slope, the ranks of warriors behind them, ready to take shelter behind the protective barriers. The watchers on the hilltop could hear the nerve-grating chant of the Wargals as they advanced.

"Urrgh, urrgh, urrgh-urrgh-urrgh!"

It was repeated over and over, without variation. Crowley fingered an arrow in his quiver, but the enemy was still out of range.

"Wish they'd learn another song," he said. "I'm tired of this one."

"It's certainly not very tuneful," Arald said. "Why do you suppose they do it?"

"Probably to keep in time. It's a cadence so they all move together," Duncan said.

Crowley stared down the hill through slitted eyes. Most of the ground cover on the slope was long grass, slippery underfoot—although the Wargals, with their heavily clawed legs, seemed to have no trouble finding a firm footing. He had marked a small scrubby bush sprouting out of the grass a hundred and twenty meters below them. When the Wargals reached that point, they would be well within range. They were five meters short of the bush now. They were still in open formation, those directly behind the barricades marching upright, so their heads and shoulders were unprotected. As they came level with the bush, and trampled it underfoot, he nocked an arrow, raised his bow, found a target and released. He heard two of the other Rangers shoot as well and silently berated himself for not organizing a full volley from all of them. His shaft hit the target, sending the Wargal he'd selected staggering back down the hill, clutching at the heavy arrow in its throat.

Then the barricades moved together and the Wargals carrying them lowered them until the barricades were rolling on the heavy wheels at either end. The troops massed behind them dropped into a crouch, so they were completely concealed. The grunted cadence became slower and more deliberate now as the barricades rolled forward at a slow walking pace. The archers, under Wearne, released a volley, but the shafts smacked harmlessly into the soaked hides covering the timber frames.

"Save your arrows!" Crowley called.

Wearne repeated the order to his men, then ran forward to speak with the Ranger. "Will we try a plunging volley?" he asked.

Crowley considered the suggestion, frowning. He pointed to where the rear ranks of the advancing Wargals had produced shields and were holding them over their heads for protection against such a ploy.

"Save your arrows until they're at close range," he said. "They'll have to show themselves sooner or later."

The art of shooting nearly vertically and letting the arrow plunge back to earth with devastating speed was a difficult skill to master. All archers practiced it, but it was usually employed against a static target. With the Wargals moving forward, even slowly, it meant the range was changing all the time. And the downhill slope didn't help. The arrows would come down not vertically, which was their most devastating angle, but obliquely, which would cause them to skip off the tilted shields.

Wearne nodded, studied the inexorable approach of the Wargal army, then hurried back to his own men. Crowley saw a gap between two of the barricades widen momentarily, exposing a Wargal behind them. He raised his bow and shot. The Wargal screamed and fell.

"Good shot," Arald said beside him.

"We're not getting enough chances for them," Crowley said

bitterly. His men could kill the occasional enemy warrior with shots like that, but they couldn't match the devastating volleys they had released at Ashdown Cut. Their shots were mere pin-pricks against the massed forces.

He shaded his eyes, searching the hill for Morgarath. If they couldn't kill the Wargals in large numbers, perhaps he'd manage a shot at their leader and controller. He scanned the advancing army and finally saw Morgarath off to his left. His black armor and white horse should have made him stand out, but he was surrounded by a group of riders, all carrying long, kite-shaped shields. Crowley could see only occasional glimpses of him. His head was above the shield barrier, but he was wearing a full-face jousting helmet and not even a Ranger longbow could send a shaft to penetrate that.

Arald had followed the direction of Crowley's gaze. "He's no fool," he said.

Crowley laughed bitterly. "More's the pity. He's certainly out-thought us this time."

"Keep an eye on him," Arald said. "He may get careless."

Their conversation was interrupted by a sharp command from Lord Northolt. "First squad! Stand to!"

There was a rustle of armor and equipment, and forty men moved to the first defensive position. They stepped up onto the waist-high earthwork, standing above the deep ditch, with the pointed stakes between them, angled down and designed to funnel the attackers into set channels. Each of the soldiers was armed with a heavy spear and a triangular shield of wood reinforced with metal strips. They all wore armor—mainly a knee-length tunic of hardened leather with brass scales riveted to it. Their helmets were simple iron caps, each one with a nasal—a protective strip that came down over the nose, guarding the nose and face from attack. They wore long swords at their belts and heavy-bladed daggers. But in this first engagement, the spears would be their most effective weapons.

"Second squad! Stand ready!"

Another forty men moved forward and stood behind the earthworks. They'd take over when the first squad tired, bringing fresh muscles into play.

The enemy barricades were thirty meters away now, and the chanting was almost deafening. It grated on the nerves of the waiting men, a bestial, inhuman sound. Hands clenched and unclenched around spear shafts as the Araluen soldiers waited in silence.

Crowley leapt up onto the earthworks and scanned the enemy lines. He saw another Wargal raise his head to peer over the barricade toward the enemy. It was the last thing the Wargal did. Crowley's arrow hit him on the forehead, below the iron peak of his metal skullcap.

Then they were a mere ten meters away and a horn sounded. The barricades swung open like gates and the Wargals behind them surged forward, growling and snarling their battle cries. As they did, Crowley's men, who had been waiting for this opportunity, released a volley and twelve of the beasts went down. Not all were dead, however. At least half of them, some with more than one arrow in their bodies, scrambled upright and continued to charge for the ditch.

The Wargals swarmed down the far side of the ditch and pushed forward. Now the defenders were close to them and the Rangers couldn't continue to shoot, for fear of hitting their own men in the snarling, struggling mass.

Duncan's troops stabbed down at the black shapes below them, their spears taking a terrible toll. For a moment, the first Wargals into the ditch faltered. Then a second wave poured in behind them, pushing them forward, grabbing their comrades and lifting them up to help them scale the far bank of the ditch. They slashed and hacked with spears, swords and clubs, attacking the legs of the men standing above them. And now the defenders began to fall as well, and their comrades behind them dragged them back and replaced them in the line, even as they called for the healers to come and take care of them.

One Wargal, mortally wounded, dropped his sword and shield and reached up for the leg of the man who had just speared him. His clawed hands fastened round the leg, and even as the soldier beat frantically at him with the shaft of his spear, he dragged him, screaming in terror, into the ditch. A host of black-furred bodies swamped the man, hacking and stabbing until his screams grew silent.

A Wargal clambered up from the ditch onto the earthworks, snarling hatred and defiance. He was promptly spitted on the end of a spear and sent crashing back onto his comrades. But now more and more Wargals made it out of the ditch, urged on and boosted by their comrades. As the defenders turned to repel them, they left gaps in the line, which allowed still more of the terrible beasts to clamber up the earth slope and drive their way forward.

Crowley, finding a clear spot from which to shoot, cut down half a dozen of the beasts in a matter of half a minute. But more of them came to take the place of their comrades and, slowly, the line of defenders was thinning. Gaps were appearing and men began to take their first tentative steps backward. They gave ground slowly at first, but that rearward movement could become a panic-stricken retreat at any moment.

King Duncan, standing back several meters on a raised earth platform, saw the line begin to fade back. He drew his long sword, turned to Arald and David, standing beside him, and pointed to the spot where the defenders were faltering.

"Come on!" he shouted, and dashed forward. The other two drew their swords as well and followed him, setting their shields more firmly on their arms as they went.

Duncan hit the Wargals like an armored battering ram. Swords clanged harmlessly off his helmet or were deflected by his shield. His own sword rose and fell and swept and thrust with deadly efficiency as he mowed down the clumsy enemy troops. And right behind him, at either shoulder, Arald and David joined in, their own swords flashing in the early afternoon sun, the blades at first bright-burnished silver, then slowly becoming stained with red.

The three expert warriors were unstoppable, hacking and cutting and stabbing as they forced their way into the Wargal ranks. A sword caught Arald a glancing blow on his left shoulder, tearing through the mail armor there. The steel links held firm long enough to prevent any serious injury, although blood began to cascade down his arm, mixing with the blood of the Wargals he had killed.

In the heat of battle, he didn't even notice the wound. A Wargal rose in front of him, fangs bared in a snarl, and Arald slammed his shield into the beast, using the reinforced center boss to smash bones and the force of his lunging body to send the Wargal toppling back into the ditch. He fought like a man possessed, the sheer speed and power of his sword strokes carving great gaps in the Wargal ranks.

David was more clinical in style. Lacking Duncan's and Arald's size and massive strength, he substituted speed instead, lunging with the point, withdrawing it instantly, then lunging at a new target. Where Arald smashed and battered and hacked his way through the enemy, David fought coolly and precisely, seeing a gap in a Wargal's guard and darting his sword point out like a striking death adder.

And, like a death adder, his strikes were fatal.

The three warriors, each one a champion in his own way, broke the impetus of the Wargal attack and rallied the defenders to go forward once more. Then, from his vantage point on the mound, Northolt bellowed an order.

"Second squad! Forward!"

The second squad, standing ready behind their comrades, had been waiting for this moment. Fresh arms and legs thrust forward into the Wargal ranks. Now the Wargal line began to bend backward, the rearward movement gathering speed and momentum.

From the left, they heard a horn blast, and the enemy began to retreat. But it wasn't a wild rout. Defeated for the moment, they fell back to the barricades and formed behind them, as arrows rattled and quivered against them. Then, under Morgarath's mind control once more, they retreated down the hill.

Over a hundred of their comrades lay dead or seriously wounded, sprawled on the earthworks or tumbled together in the ditch. Morgarath had paid dearly for this attack.

But forty-three of the defenders lay dead as well. And

another fifteen were seriously wounded, carried back to the healers' tents.

There was no question of pursuing the Wargals down the hill. They were still in relatively good order, and the men of Duncan's army were exhausted—and their numbers seriously depleted.

Crowley, his quiver empty, joined the senior commanders as they leaned on their swords, breathing deeply. All of them were wounded, and all three were stained with the blood of the Wargals they had killed.

Duncan shook his head wearily and watched Morgarath's troops receding down the hill.

"We can't afford another attack like that," he said.

David wiped his hand across his forehead, leaving a smear of blood there, some of it his own.

"There's not much we can do to avoid it," he said.

38

THE EXHAUSTED ARALUEN SOLDIERS DROPPED TO THE ground where they stood, draining the last few drops of lukewarm water from their canteens. Fighting like this set a man's thirst raging and they reacted gratefully as stewards moved among them with full water skins.

The water skins themselves had been soaked on the outside, then hung from tree branches in the morning breeze. As the wind evaporated the water from the exterior of the skin, the contents inside became cooler. For the last hour or so, when they'd had time to gulp a mouthful of water, the soldiers had been drinking slightly leather-flavored warm water from their canteens. The cool, fresh water was deeply appreciated.

Other servants moved among the fighting men, handing out food—flat bread wrapped around dried meat, cheese and pickles.

Still others carried baskets of crisp, juicy apples on their hips, handing them out as they passed. Duncan crunched appreciatively on one of these, feeling the tart juice spring to life in his mouth, quenching his thirst and overcoming the metallic taste of battle.

"This was a stroke of genius," he said, looking appreciatively at the glossy fruit. "Who thought of this?"

"My man Chubb," Arald told him. "He's the young kitchen master at Redmont."

"Kitchen master? What's he doing with the army?" Duncan asked.

Arald shrugged. "I tried to leave him behind but he can be downright disobedient at times."

"Good for him!" Duncan said, finishing the apple and sucking the last juice out of the core before he hurled it aside. "I might steal him from you when this is over."

Arald's smile disappeared. "You could try," he said, a warning note in his voice. Duncan raised his eyebrows, but said nothing. One rebellious baron at a time was enough for him.

"Someone's coming!" one of the sentries shouted, and the men stirred, some climbing wearily to their feet and reaching for their weapons.

Duncan stood up on the parapet and looked at the valley below. "Relax," he called. "It's one man. And he has a flag of truce."

The Wargals had withdrawn as far as the near side of the ford, setting the rolling barricades down in position there and sitting on the grass to rest and recover. A single horseman was pushing through their ranks, urging his horse up the slope. He carried a white banner on the end of a spear, waving it from side to side as he came.

As the men saw him and heard Duncan's words, they relaxed. Those who had stood sank gratefully back onto the soft grass. Duncan took his sword from where he had placed it, point down, into the earth as the Wargals withdrew. Now he slid the blade back into its scabbard and stepped up onto the earthwork, an audible groan escaping his lips with the effort. Every muscle in his body was aching. The multiple flesh wounds that he had received during the battle, hastily bandaged by a medical orderly, throbbed painfully.

"Give me something white," he called back over his shoulder. One of the soldiers stepped forward and handed him a white surcoat taken from a wounded comrade when the healers had begun to work on him. The King glanced at it, wrinkling his nose at the blood and dirt smeared on it. Then he raised it over his head and waved it slowly from side to side.

Morgarath's messenger paused momentarily, then rode another twenty meters uphill. He was now well within arrow range and Crowley fingered a shaft thoughtfully. Maybe Morgarath would come as close, he thought.

"Lord Morgarath offers a parley," the herald shouted, his voice just carrying to them.

Duncan straightened, filled his lungs and bellowed back. "Tell Morgarath to come ahead," he called, intentionally leaving out any title.

"Will you respect the flag of truce?" the herald shouted.

Below and behind him, Duncan heard Crowley mutter, "Right up until the moment I shoot him."

The King glared at his Ranger Commandant and spoke out of the corner of his mouth. "Touch that bow, Crowley, and I'll cut you down myself. You will not dishonor my word."

"As you say, my lord," Crowley said. But his tone was rebellious.

Duncan caught Arald's eye. "Arald, keep him from doing anything stupid."

Arald nodded. "Aye, my lord." He eased his dagger out of its scabbard. He stepped closer to Crowley, and the Ranger felt the point of the weapon poke into his ribs. "Do be sensible, Crowley," he said.

Crowley shrugged and set his bow down on the grass. "All right. But we're making a mistake," he said. I've been spending too much time with Halt, he thought.

The herald sat his horse uncertainly, waiting for Duncan's answer. The King hurriedly shouted it.

"Tell Morgarath he's safe. We'll respect the white flag," he said.

The herald nodded and raised a silver whistle that he wore on a lanyard around his neck. He placed it to his lips and blew a long, trilling blast. From the ranks of Wargals and human troops below, a black-clad figure on a white horse detached itself and began to ride slowly up the hill.

"And here he comes," said Crowley softly.

Morgarath's white horse paced deliberately up the slope. The black-clad former Baron was in no hurry, content to let his enemies' speculation about the subject of the parley take hold. He passed his herald and continued riding uphill for a further twenty meters, finally reining his horse in thirty meters from the earth rampart. Still he said nothing. He sat impassively, letting the silence drag out and, by his silence, forcing Duncan to open the discussion.

Duncan was having no part of Morgarath's mind games. When they had confronted each other at the tournament at Gorlan, he had been caught out by the former Baron's smooth tongue and honeyed words, and his way of twisting the truth ever so slightly, so that it suited his own purposes.

Now he simply turned his back and stepped down from the earthworks, disappearing from Morgarath's view.

"Tell me when he feels like talking," he muttered to Arald and Northolt.

Morgarath cursed. This wasn't what he had expected. He rose in his stirrups, trying to catch sight of the King. Finally, he was forced to speak first.

"Duncan!" he called, and waited as the King slowly remounted the earth barrier.

"You had something to ask me?" Duncan asked. The wording was intentional. It implied that, in this scenario, Morgarath was the supplicant. It was only a small point, but parleys like this were made up of small points, with each participant trying to gain the ascendance.

Morgarath's forehead contorted in an angry frown. In the past, he had become accustomed to besting the King in these verbal confrontations. It seemed Duncan had learned quickly. He decided to do away with petty one-upmanship and get straight to the point—which was what Duncan had intended.

"You're defeated!" he shouted now, the anger obvious in his voice.

Duncan smiled. "Yet here I am. And there you are below me," he replied smoothly.

Morgarath gestured to the lines of Wargals at the base of the hill. "You're outnumbered. You can't possibly win."

"So you say," Duncan replied smoothly. "Yet I'm still inside the palisade here and you and your men are still outside." He gestured to the bodies of the Wargals who had died assaulting his position. The army had taken in its own dead and wounded, of course, and had laid them out for treatment or burial behind the defenses. The lack of any of their bodies emphasized the fact that so many Wargals had died.

"Don't bandy words with me—"

But Duncan cut Morgarath off, his voice rising in volume to shout over the top of the enemy general. "Morgarath, when a person calls for a parley, it's usually to make some kind of offer— not make meaningless threats. Say what you came to say or ride away."

There was another silence. Morgarath swallowed his anger, allowed his breathing to steady and slow. Then he spoke in a deliberate tone.

"I'll offer you a chance to surrender," he said. "One chance and one chance only. In spite of your prevarication, you know your situation is hopeless. You don't have the numbers to continue."

"As a matter of fact," Duncan said calmly, "we're expecting reinforcements from three of the northern fiefs any day now."

Morgarath's laugh was harsh and scornful. "*Any day* will be too late for you. You won't last another day. Do you want to hear my terms or not?"

Duncan shrugged. His claim about the imminent arrival of reinforcements was more wishful thinking than fact. Lady Pauline, riding frantically between the neighboring fiefs to engender their aid, had been given assurances of support. But assurances were one thing. Troops were another matter entirely. Duncan was convinced that many of the barons, without actually declaring for Morgarath, were standing by to see how matters transpired here at Hackham Heath.

"Go ahead," he said, keeping his tone as matter-of-fact as possible.

"Your soldiers can lay down their weapons and walk away— back to their farms and villages. I'll do nothing to stop them," Morgarath said. "Your commanders' lives will be spared. They'll be banished from Araluen, of course. I can't have them here fomenting another rebellion against me."

Duncan smiled mirthlessly, noting the way that Morgarath had typified their present conflict as a *rebellion against him*.

"My commanders?" he asked. "Whom do you include in that?"

Morgarath nodded toward the small group standing behind Duncan. "Arald, David, Northolt and Crowley. Naturally, they'll all have to swear an oath never to return and try to create an uprising against me."

Behind him, Duncan heard Arald snort scornfully.

"What about the other Rangers?" Crowley demanded, stepping forward a pace.

Morgarath studied him calmly. The red-haired Ranger's face was flushed with anger. He shrugged. "They can continue in the Corps," he said. "So long as they swear allegiance to me. Otherwise, they will be banished with you."

"Does that include Halt?" Crowley asked.

Morgarath's eyes narrowed as he scanned the faces behind the earthwork barrier. "Where is Halt?" he demanded suddenly.

Crowley bit his lip, wishing he hadn't raised the subject.

Arald stepped smoothly into the gap. "He's in the healers' tent. He was wounded in the raid last night," he said.

Morgarath nodded in satisfaction. He had no idea who had taken part in the failed raid, but it stood to reason that Halt would have been among them.

"Let's hope it's nothing trivial," he said viciously. "But I'm afraid the offer of amnesty doesn't apply to Halt. He's caused me too much trouble." The black-clad former Baron had a special antipathy to Halt. The Hibernian had refused his offer of a place in his army—and had then gone out of his way to thwart Morgarath's plans for seizing the throne.

"And what do you have in mind for me?" Duncan asked.

Morgarath studied him for a few seconds before replying. "You know I can't afford to let you live, Duncan," he said. "You'd be a rallying point for rebellion against me as long as you were around. But I'll guarantee you your execution will be as quick and as painless as I can manage." He paused and shrugged diffidently. "You know I have to do it."

Duncan slowly nodded. It was no less than he expected. "I'll need time to think about it," he said.

Morgarath gestured for his herald to ride forward. He held out his hand for the spear the man carried, then leaned down and scraped a groove in the ground, before planting the spear at the end of the groove.

"I'll give you until the shadow of the spear reaches that mark," he said. "That should be about two hours. If you accept my terms, wave a red flag. Otherwise, no quarter." He turned abruptly and spurred his horse away down the slope. The herald, caught unawares, hurried after him.

Duncan stepped down from the parapet and faced his comrades. "Perhaps we should consider it," he said. "There's no way we can defeat him and there's no reason for all of you to die."

"He'll kill us anyway," Crowley said, and the other two muttered agreement.

Duncan shrugged his shoulders. He agreed with them.

Morgarath was a liar and a cheat and a murderer. The King had no faith in his word.

"I say we fight on, sir," Northolt said. "We're not beaten yet. And Halt may well turn up any moment."

Duncan sighed. "Ah yes. Halt. I wonder where the devil he's got to?"

The two hours passed quickly. The shadow of the spear seemed to race around the ground until it was level with the mark. As it crept past the shallow groove cut by the spearhead, they heard a rattle of armor and equipment from the base of the hill.

The Wargals were lifting the wheeled barricades once more and beginning to set out toward the small group of defenders huddled behind the palisade. As before, they moved in time to the toneless chant that had become familiar to Duncan and his men.

"How many would you say?" Duncan asked.

Northolt pursed his lips thoughtfully. "Two hundred. Maybe two-fifty."

Duncan sighed. "And we have ninety-three to face them."

Still the Wargals came on. But then the defenders saw something new. The remainder of the Wargals across the river began to form up in ragged lines and march into the ford, splashing and lurching in the waist-deep water. On and on they came, until the camp was empty and the entire force was moving up the slope—nearly seven hundred in total. Morgarath was committing everything he had to this last battle.

A low murmur of despair went round the beleaguered army as they saw the numbers facing them.

Northolt turned and called an order. "Still!" he shouted, and the murmuring died away. But the sense of doom continued to hang over them all. They could see their fate lumbering up the hill toward them—implacable, unstoppable, unbeatable.

"They'll stay out of range until the first group have closed with us," said Duncan. "Then they'll charge and swamp us with sheer numbers."

The air was filled with the ominous chant of the Wargal army as they continued up the hill. Crowley and the other Rangers began shooting whenever they saw a target. But the opportunities were rare.

"Maybe we should have accepted his offer?" Crowley grinned. "Do you think it's too late?"

As before, Morgarath was out to the left, just behind the rolling barricades, and protected by a ring of riders bearing shields. From close behind his troops, he was mentally urging them on, exhorting them with one simple message: Kill and kill and kill again.

Then Crowley, in the act of nocking an arrow to his string, stopped and looked more closely at the deserted camp on the far side of the river. A long line of armed riders had emerged from the trees behind the camp and were threading their way through the lines of deserted tents. They were led by a gray-cloaked Ranger on a small gray horse.

"It's Halt," said Crowley. "He's made it in time."

39

Aside from a few support staff—cooks, orderlies and servants—who fled into the trees at the sight of the grim-faced riders, the Wargal camp was deserted. The great majority of its occupants were marching ponderously up the hill to the redoubt where Duncan's army waited for them.

Halt led the troops through the empty, irregularly spaced tent lines, halting them in two extended files on the edge of the ford while he consulted with Lorriac.

"How do you plan to do this?" he asked.

The cavalry officer twisted his lips in thought as he considered the situation. "We'll go up the hill in three wedges of fifty men, echeloned to the right. I'll lead the first squad. We'll hit the rear of the Wargal line, drive into them, then withdraw. As we get clear, the second wedge will hit them ten meters to the right. They'll hit and run, then the third wedge will follow. When they withdraw, we'll go in again." He paused, then glanced at the Ranger. "It's a standard maneuver. We practice it constantly."

Halt nodded agreement. Cavalry's best weapon was the crushing force of the charge as it hit home against infantry. The horses' momentum and weight would smash into the enemy ranks, scattering them and leaving individuals vulnerable to the troopers' lances and longswords. But once the speed and impetus of the charge dissipated, as the cavalry became entangled in the milling scrum of enemy fighters, that advantage was lost. The maneuver Lorriac was suggesting meant the Wargals would be subjected to a continuing series of thundering assaults along their line.

Halt glanced around. The cavalrymen were formed into a long line along the edge of the ford. He rode out ahead of them, then turned Abelard to pace along the line.

"No noise," he told them. "No cheering. No bugles. Keep quiet for as long as you can. We want to take them by surprise. That's our best chance of panicking them. They'll have their eyes on the battle at the top of the hill."

Their faces turned to follow him as he rode past. Here and there, a man nodded, but for the most part they simply set their lips and gripped their spears more tightly, occasionally glancing up the hill at the advancing enemy army.

Halt turned to Lorriac, who was riding slightly behind him, and gestured toward the hill. The captain gave a hand signal and wheeled his horse toward the ford. The troop followed him forward, splashing through the shallow water. Horses tossed their heads at the sudden contact with the river, but kept going. The men stopped on the far bank, the horses twitching and shaking themselves dry.

Lorriac called out his two senior sergeants and told them the plan of battle. Then he rode to the left wing of the line and called softly, "First squad, on me. Wedge." He supplemented the verbal order with a hand signal, then began to walk his horse forward.

The first fifty men formed on him as he did, creating an ever-widening wedge behind him.

Halt, seeing that all was in hand, cantered out to the left wing of the force. He saw Gilan hesitating, wondering whether he should join the cavalry. "Gilan!" he called. "With me."

Gilan urged his horse alongside Abelard. He looked slightly disappointed. "Aren't you going to charge with them?" he asked.

Halt shook his head firmly. "I'm not equipped for it," he said. "And neither are you. Our horses are much smaller than cavalry horses."

Glumly, Gilan had to admit that what Halt said was true. Much of the smashing impact of a cavalry charge came from the cavalry's riding tall, heavy-boned animals that could crush the enemy beneath their weight. Gilan's own horse, and Abelard, were both small and agile. They didn't have the sheer mass of the cavalry mounts. On top of that, a horse needed to be specially trained to take its place in the battle line. A rider relied on his horse to cause injury and confusion to the enemy—biting, kicking out with iron-shod rear hooves and rearing high over an opponent. A trained, seasoned battlehorse was deadly to the enemy. An untrained horse could be just as deadly to its rider, panicking in the noise and confusion of battle, rearing without warning and throwing its rider off, leaving him vulnerable to the surrounding enemy troops.

"No. You're right," Gilan said.

Halt brought Abelard to a stop some ten meters to the side of the advancing line of troops, and thirty meters ahead of them. He studied the formation keenly. The horses were trotting and their riders had formed into the three wedge formations Lorriac had ordered, with each wedge to the right of and slightly behind the preceding one. Halt could hear the jingle of harness and the rattle of weapons, along with the soft thud of trotting hooves on the long grass. He glanced uphill anxiously. So far, Morgarath's troops had no idea there was a force to their rear. The Wargals lumbered upward, the lead group still crouched behind the rolling barricades, the second wave safely out of range of the defenders' bows.

Any minute now, he thought. He looked around the enemy formation, searching for Morgarath. Finally, he saw him, surrounded by his small group of shield bearers, out on the right wing. His head was bowed as he concentrated on sending orders to his troops, committing them to the coming battle.

Then the rolling barricades were flung to the side, opening like gates to release the first Wargal assault group as they plunged forward up the hill. The Araluen force waited in place as Crowley and his Rangers released a killing barrage of arrows onto the charging Wargals. Once the Wargals were at the palisade and fully engaged, Halt knew, the major part of the force would advance and roll over the defenders, sweeping them aside with their crushing numbers. He looked across at Lorriac and waved his arm forward.

"Now!" he yelled. He saw the cavalry captain nod, then turn to the bugler behind him.

No need for further stealth. Now was the time to shock and surprise Morgarath's fighters. The bugle rang out. Two long blasts followed by two short. Then the first wedge began to canter forward, the noise of their approach increasing with their speed.

The bugle sounded one long sustained note now and the horses went to a gallop, their hooves pounding, nostrils flaring, harnesses creaking and jangling. The troopers' spears came down level, forming a bristling hedgehog of steel around the wedge, then the lead riders smashed into the Wargals' rear ranks with a rolling thunder of noise.

"Stay with me!" Halt yelled at Gilan. He urged Abelard forward, nocking an arrow to his bow as he went.

He stopped fifty meters from the Wargal line and began shooting. Each arrow slammed home and dropped a Wargal to the turf. At the same time, Lorriac's force were smashing their way deep into the Wargal formation, thrusting with spears, slashing with their longswords, smashing into the Wargals with the massive weight of their horses, hurling the black-furred creatures to either side.

They bit a deep, V-shaped hole into the Wargal ranks, then, as their speed began to drop off, the bugle blared again and the leaders turned inward, reversing the V as they withdrew, still striking out to either side and leaving broken, slashed bodies behind them as they went.

They didn't get off scot-free. Some of the riders went down and were engulfed by the enraged beasts. But their comrades quickly closed up to seal any gaps in their line. Then Lorriac's men were cantering into the open, and as the last of them emerged, the second wedge slammed into the Wargals' rear rank.

The Wargals—at first surprised, then infuriated by this unexpected attack—were now overcome by a new feeling, as the first stirring of their ancient fear of horses was awoken. They began to look around fearfully, losing their formation and concentration as the second wedge struck them. It didn't happen immediately. It was a gradual cancer of fear that spread progressively through their ranks, beginning with those closest to the horsemen and spreading out like the ripples on a pond. Some of them began to turn away, seeking to escape from the terrible pounding hooves and snorting nostrils.

Out on their left flank, Halt's hands flew from quiver to bow as he nocked, drew and released, sending a stream of deadly shafts hissing across the battlefield, every one finding its mark and either killing or wounding one of the bestial warriors.

The second wedge crashed home, thrusting, hacking and cutting. Then they were clear, and the third wedge began to repeat the action. Halt's hand went to his quiver and came away empty. He'd used all his arrows.

"Look out, Halt!"

Gilan's voice cracked with tension as he called the warning. Halt twisted in his saddle and saw three Wargals only a few meters away, lumbering across the long grass toward him. They were among the first to leave the strictly formed ranks of the attacking army, slinking away to the side. Now they sought revenge against the solitary rider before them. His horse wasn't plunging and kicking. It stood calmly while its rider loosed arrow after arrow, and in their brutish minds, they saw an opportunity to kill.

As they came on, Halt tossed the useless bow aside and drew his saxe, but he was in serious trouble. The Wargals were armed with swords, and one of them had a long-hafted ax. Too late, he realized he should flee, but that would leave Gilan alone.

He touched Abelard with his knees and sent him dancing backward, away from the danger of that long ax and the swords. The thought of exposing his horse to those cruel weapons sent his mouth dry. The Wargals, encouraged by the fact that the horse was retreating before them, snarled viciously, baring their cruel yellow fangs at him.

Then a gangly figure darted between Halt and the three vicious beasts, Gilan's sword catching the light as he took guard in front of them. Halt took a breath to shout at him, realized that he might distract the boy if he did so, and slipped from Abelard's back to help him.

But Gilan needed no help. The first Wargal swept his sword down in a brutal overhead cut. The boy swayed slightly to his left, and the massive blade hissed past him, missing by centimeters, then burying itself in the soft earth. As the snarling beast tried to withdraw it, Gilan thrust off from his left foot and lunged under its arm, driving his sword through its leather breastplate and deep into its chest cavity.

The Wargal gave an anguished roar, staggered and fell.

Its comrade lumbered forward clumsily, the long-handled ax sweeping in a deadly horizontal arc that would have cut Gilan in two at the waist.

If it had connected. The young fighter saw the ax coming and, a split second before it caught him, hurled himself forward in a somersault. The ax passed harmlessly above him, and as he rolled to his feet, he was safely inside the ax's reach. Again, he thrust out with the razor-sharp sword, taking the Wargal in the middle of its body. The beast gave an unearthly shriek, fell to its knees and crumpled forward.

Which left one remaining enemy. Gilan withdrew his sword from the body of the second Wargal and took a guard position. The Wargal lunged at him, striking forehand and backhand in short, savage strokes. Gilan's blade met the blows without any seeming effort. Knowing that the Wargal was putting all its weight and strength into the blows, he didn't try to block them directly. Rather, he deflected them, letting the creature's heavy blade slide off to either side without making solid, arm-wrenching contact.

He retreated a pace, and the Wargal, encouraged, surged forward. Only to be struck by Halt's saxe, thrown with all the Ranger's considerable strength.

The heavy knife slammed into the beast's throat and it staggered back, dropping the sword and clutching in vain at the knife that was buried hilt deep. It let out a gargling scream, then its legs gave out and it toppled sideways onto the grass.

Gilan looked around, surprised. He had been so focused on the fight that he had forgotten Halt's presence. Now he saw the Ranger a few paces behind him and grinned at him.

"Thanks," he said. "But I did have his measure."

"Well, forgive me for spoiling your little fight," Halt said. He was somewhat amazed by the boy's skill and speed. "Your father said you're quite useful with a sword."

Gilan shrugged. "I have a good teacher," he said. Then he turned toward the Wargal army, advancing up the hill. He pointed his sword.

"Look at that!" he said.

40

IN LATER YEARS, WHEN HE RECALLED THE BATTLE OF HACKham Heath, Halt would be convinced that he saw a physical tremor run through the ranks of Wargals.

The third wedge of cavalry had just smashed into the rear of Morgarath's army. Lorriac's first squad was wheeling round to strike again as soon as the third squad withdrew.

The Wargals, already unsettled by the cavalry attack, stopped moving uphill at their steady, inexorable pace. They began to move in haphazard directions, all cohesion gone from their formation. They blundered into one another and struck out at their own comrades.

One of them began to retreat down the hill, then three. Then a dozen. Then the hillside was covered with hundreds of Wargals, running blindly from those terrible horses, panicking, terrified by the resurgence of that old fear that had been ingrained in them for so long.

Lorriac and his men withdrew to the side to let them go. Their horses stood, heads down, sides heaving, nostrils flaring as they drew in great, shuddering breaths.

At the palisade and ditch, the initial assault group sensed that something was wrong. They looked back to see their brothers in full retreat, sensing the panic and terror that was in their minds. Morgarath, on the right wing of his army, tried to hold them in his control, but it was an impossible task. His mental orders were drowned by the ancient panic that seized Wargals when they encountered horses. He realized that he had lost control and wheeled his horse, galloping down the hill, passing his own troops as he went.

On the earthen mound behind the palisade, Duncan saw the enemy troops hesitate as their leader deserted them. He recognized that this was the pivotal moment in the battle and turned to Sir David and Baron Arald on either side of him.

"Come on!" he roared, and charged forward, shield raised and sword flashing in the sunlight. The two armored knights followed him and plunged into the Wargals' faltering ranks. Forty of the defenders—those still unwounded—followed them, yelling battle cries and challenges. Some of them just yelled—inchoate cries wrenched from the gut in the moment of triumph.

And the Wargals broke.

A score of them died under that first charge. The others gave way to the terrible sense of panic that was sweeping through their ranks. Within minutes, the entire remaining force was streaming downhill, without formation or control. Some stumbled and fell on the smooth long grass. Their comrades trampled over them. They hit the river and spray flew high in the air as they fled across it, and kept going.

Duncan raised his sword and halted his small force. He watched the retreating army below them and shook his head wearily. For the moment, the Wargals were routed and terrified. But he had no idea how long that state would continue and there were still hundreds of them. At any moment, Morgarath might regain control and turn them back against the Araluen army. If that happened, all they had achieved this day could be lost.

"Do we go after them, my lord?"

It was Sir David who asked, but Baron Arald answered before the King could.

"With what?" he said. "Our men are exhausted and we're still outnumbered. Halt's cavalry have ridden over fifty kilometers in the past day, then pulled off one of the finest cavalry charges I've ever seen—riding uphill to do it. Their horses are spent. The riders are exhausted."

"But . . . they're running!" David said, gesturing toward the Wargals far below. Tactical wisdom said that when your enemy broke and ran, the best course was to pursue them. To harry them. To give them no rest.

But tactical wisdom didn't allow for the fact that your own men might be exhausted, wounded and their numbers decimated. That your cavalry might be at the end of its tether. If they went after Morgarath and his army now, the Wargals might recover and turn back on them. And the weary soldiers might be overwhelmed by a sudden resurgence.

If that were to happen, the Wargals' confidence would soar and the victory might be reversed. Perhaps it wasn't likely. But it was possible.

"We'll go after them tomorrow," Duncan said. "We'll chase them back to their dark, rainy mountains and bottle them up there."

He glanced up as two riders walked their horses up to the small command group. Halt and Gilan slid down from their saddles. The boy embraced his father. Halt nodded at David.

"He did very well," Halt said. "Killed two Wargals who had me cornered."

"Halt killed the third before I could," said Gilan, still a little aggrieved.

Halt hid a smile. "Well, I did apologize."

The King stopped further conversation. He stepped forward and embraced the bearded Ranger. "Good work, Halt. You saved us today," he said.

Halt sighed. "Pity we missed Morgarath."

The King glanced down the hill at the enemy army, streaming across the plain and disappearing over the distant ridge.

"We'll get him next time," he said. "I think we need a few reinforcements before we take that lot on again."

All around them, men were stripping off their helmets and mail shirts, sinking wearily to the ground, unable to believe that they had secured a victory when everything had seemed lost. Baron Arald's indefatigable cook had his orderlies out once more, passing out cold water, apples and bread and meat.

Crowley pushed through the crowd and joined them. He embraced his fellow Ranger, then stepped back, grinning. "Did you have a nice little ride in the country while we were here doing all the fighting?"

Halt glanced down at his friend's belt quiver. Like his own, it was empty.

"Lost your arrows somewhere, did you?" he said, and the two of them laughed. Crowley put an arm around Halt's shoulder.

"Come and see the others," he said. "They're all keen to hear what you've been up to."

Halt glanced at the King, who made a gesture to indicate that the two Rangers had permission to withdraw. Duncan turned to Northolt.

"We'd better do a roll call," he said. "We need to find out

how many men we have left. We'll have to fight again in the next few days. Then I want to visit the wounded and thank them." He left unsaid that they faced another, grimmer task: the burial of those who had given their lives in the battle.

Northolt nodded. A commander's work was never done, it seemed. Once the battle was over, the soldiers could rest. But the leaders had to make sure they would be ready to fight again when needed.

The two Rangers had gone half a dozen paces when Halt stopped and turned back. He eyed Gilan keenly. "You did very well, Gilan. I owe you my life."

The boy flushed at such praise, particularly as it was delivered in front of his father and the King. Before he could reply, Halt continued. "If you still want to be a Ranger, come and see us in a couple of years."

A huge grin spread over Gilan's young face. His father regarded him curiously. This was the first he had heard of Gilan's desire to join the Rangers. The boy bobbed his head in gratitude.

"I'll do that, Halt," he replied.

Halt hid his answering smile, maintaining a deadpan expression.

"I'll put in a good word for you," he said. "I have a certain amount of influence with the Commandant."

Crowley raised his eyebrows in surprise. "Is that so? It's the first I've heard of it."

Halt slapped him on the back. "You're always the last to know things," he told his friend.

As it turned out, the army was called upon to fight again over the ensuing days, in a series of bitter engagements with the retreating Wargal army. Once he had put sufficient distance between himself and Duncan's forces, Morgarath managed to regain partial control of his troops, although it would be years before he managed to reclaim the complete dominance he had enjoyed over them at the start of the campaign.

While Morgarath headed back to the Mountains of Rain and Night with the bulk of his army, his Wargal forces set ambushes and made surprise attacks on the royal troops as they doggedly pursued the rebel baron.

The army fought half a dozen skirmishes, all of which served to delay them while Morgarath made his escape. Crowley had his men out scouting and reporting on his progress. There came a day when Berrigan rode into camp, dust-covered and weary.

"He's made it back to Three Step Pass," he reported, and there was a general chorus of anger from the command group gathered in Duncan's tent.

"We can't touch him there," Northolt said bitterly.

The King nodded. "His time will come," he said. "In the meantime, we have a hundred Wargals camped a few kilometers away. Tomorrow, we'll have to fight them."

"They're the last of the troops he set to cover his retreat," Crowley said. "After tomorrow, we'll be rid of them."

"And after that, we'll need to set a force to contain Morgarath in the mountains," Northolt said.

Duncan nodded agreement, then smiled.

"I'll leave that in your capable hands, Northolt," he said. "After tomorrow, I'm heading back to Castle Araluen. I have a daughter I want to get to know."

EPILOGUE

~~~~~~

IT WAS LATE AT NIGHT IN CASTLE REDMONT. ONE BY ONE, the windows in the keep went dark as the occupants retired to their beds. One light remained burning.

Halt and Lady Pauline sat in comfortable chairs in the parlor of her suite of rooms. On the floor between them lay a large basket, holding a small infant, wrapped in blankets. His alert brown eyes peered over the top of the covers, swiveling between them as they spoke in lowered tones.

"His father saved your life?" Pauline said.

Halt nodded. "Without a doubt. It was the last skirmish with Morgarath's Wargals, south of Hackham Heath. I was knocked down and I thought I was done for. I *was* done for, to all intents and purposes. Then he was there."

His eyes had a faraway look as he thought about that day. Pauline said nothing. After a traumatic event like that, a person often just needed to talk—to relate what had happened, to exorcize the mind-numbing fear that could leave one helpless and exposed.

"He leapt over me, armed only with a spear, and fought them off. Then one of them smashed the head of his spear and he used the shaft like a quarterstaff, knocking them senseless, sending them reeling left and right. Then he ripped a sword away from one of them and struck out again." He shook his head over the memory. "Bear in mind, he wasn't trained as a swordsman. He was a simple soldier—a sergeant, as it turned out. I was dazed and not seeing too clearly, but I figure he killed a dozen of them before they eventually brought him down.

"Then the other soldiers reached us and drove the Wargals off. But they were already beginning to back away, even as Daniel fell."

"Daniel. That was his name?" Pauline asked.

"Yes. He managed to tell me that. And he made me swear to find this little fellow and his mother and see that they were safe. Of course, I promised I would. Then he was dead."

"What became of the mother?" she asked.

Halt sighed unhappily. "It took me days to find out where they lived. When I finally reached their farm, she was being attacked by two of Daniel's so-called comrades. Seems they specialized in robbing the homes of soldiers who had been killed during the battle.

"There was a fight. One of them dragged me down, and the other was about to stab me. Then the mother threw herself on him and gave me a chance to fight back." His face set in grim lines as he remembered the scene. "But he killed her before I could stop him. As she was dying, she told me the boy's name: Will."

They both fell silent, looking down at the little person in the basket. As before, the lively brown eyes switched back and forth between them, watching them. Pauline reached down a hand to touch the baby's face. Instantly, a tiny fist emerged from under the blankets and seized her forefinger. The baby smiled and gurgled happily at the contact.

"He's a cheerful fellow," she said, jiggling her hand. The baby clung tightly to her finger, refusing to release her. His smile widened.

"He is," Halt agreed. "He was no trouble at all on the trip here." He paused, then sighed once more. "The question is, what do I do with him now?"

"You can hardly look after a baby," she said. "You're always away."

"I know," he said despondently. "And even if I could, it might not be the best thing for him to be associated with me."

She raised her eyebrows in an unspoken question and he explained.

"You know how people feel about Rangers. They trust us to a certain degree, but they do have suspicions about us. Some of them even think we're wizards. They're frightened of us, more often than not."

She made a small moue. "I'm not. Nor are any of the people here in Redmont."

"Not the Baron or the knights or their ladies," he agreed. "But the common folk definitely want to keep their distance from us. The people in the villages are only happy to talk to us when they need us."

"I suppose that's true," she said. "Mind you, the Rangers have done a lot to encourage that attitude. It adds to your sense of mystery."

"I know that. But I wouldn't want him to grow up facing that sort of prejudice. *Oh, there's the Ranger's boy,*" he said, in a fair approximation of a countryman's accent. "*Don't get too close to him. You can't really trust them.*"

"I can see that might be a problem," she said, and another silence fell over them. Then she frowned and said suspiciously, "You weren't hoping that I'd take care of him for you, were you?"

Halt threw up his hands in surprise, rejecting the suggestion. "Lord no! You have your own career, and you're away nearly as much as I am. More, sometimes."

The suspicion cleared from her face and she relaxed. She jiggled her finger again, but the baby resolutely refused to release her. She smiled at him. There was something endearing, something trusting, in the warm grip around her finger.

"What about the Ward?" she said eventually. "The Baron set it up to look after the orphans of parents who died serving the Kingdom. He'd be well treated there. He'd be educated and trained. Eventually, he'd be able to choose a career path for himself."

Halt was nodding as she spoke. "I was thinking about that."

Pauline took his hand in both of hers. "It's a perfect solution," she said. "It's a happy place and the children are loved and cared for. Arald keeps an eye on it and takes a personal interest in the children raised there—as does Lady Sandra."

He rubbed his beard thoughtfully. "They couldn't know that I brought him there," he said. "People mustn't know I have any involvement with him or the stigma will apply to him."

She nodded. "Of course. You'd need to leave him there anonymously." She rose and went to a small writing table by the window. She rummaged in the drawers and produced a plain sheet of paper, took up a quill that was resting in the inkwell, then hesitated, searching for the right words.

Halt gently took the quill from her hand and wrote rapidly, speaking the words aloud as he did. "His mother died in childbirth." He looked up at Pauline. "That's not strictly accurate, of course."

She considered the point, then dismissed it with a hand gesture. "You're right. But the full details of her death are too complicated. People would ask questions and your involvement could be revealed."

"I suppose so," he said slowly. He continued writing for a moment.

"His father died a hero," he said softly as he added the words, "Please care for him." He weighed the sheet of paper in his hand, then placed it in the basket, tucking it in at the foot of the blankets, away from Will's questing little hands.

"Seems like that's the answer," he said. "And of course, I can keep an eye on him as he grows older."

She grinned, finally securing the release of her forefinger. "Who knows, you might even train him to be a Ranger one day."

But Halt shook his head. "Not me. I'm not the type. I don't have the patience for it."

"You might surprise yourself," she said.

Halt rose and made his way to the window. The castle outside was dark, the courtyard deserted. The three-story building that housed the Ward was opposite Pauline's room. There was an oil lamp burning over the front door, but the rest of the rooms were in darkness.

"I may as well take him there now," he said, "while there's no one to see me."

He picked up the basket and headed toward the door. Pauline held up a hand to stop him.

"I'll check and make sure there's nobody in the corridor who might see you," she said. She started toward the door, then stopped beside him and smiled down at the little face on the pillow.

"Interesting, isn't it?" she said. "We've been through so much death and destruction and yet here he is, a brand-new life."

"Just like the King's daughter, Cassandra," Halt said.

Pauline nodded. "Yes. Life keeps renewing itself, doesn't it?" She gave a little laugh. "I wonder if he and the princess will ever meet?"

Halt shook his head. "A princess and the orphan son of a farmer? How could that happen?"

Turn the page for a look at

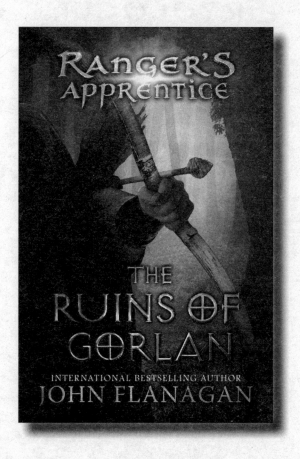

PROLOGUE

MORGARATH, LORD OF THE MOUNTAINS OF RAIN AND Night, former Baron of Gorlan in the Kingdom of Araluen, looked out over his bleak, rainswept domain and, for perhaps the thousandth time, cursed.

This was all that was left to him now—a jumble of rugged granite cliffs, tumbled boulders and icy mountains. Of sheer gorges and steep narrow passes. Of gravel and rock, with never a tree or a sign of green to break the monotony.

Even though it had been fifteen years since he had been driven back into this forbidding realm that had become his prison, he could still remember the pleasant green glades and thickly forested hills of his former fief. The streams filled with fish and the fields rich with crops and game. Gorlan had been a beautiful, living place. The Mountains of Rain and Night were dead and desolate.

A platoon of Wargals was drilling in the castle yard below him. Morgarath watched them for a few seconds, listening to the guttural, rhythmic chant that accompanied all their movements. They were stocky, misshapen beings, with features that were halfway human, but with a long, brutish muzzle and fangs like a bear or a large dog.

Avoiding all contact with humans, the Wargals had lived and bred in these remote mountains since ancient times. No one in living memory had ever set eyes upon one, but rumors and legends had persisted of a savage tribe of semi-intelligent beasts in the mountains. Morgarath, planning a revolt against the Kingdom of Araluen, had left Gorlan Fief to seek them out. If such creatures existed, they would give him an edge in the war that was to come.

It took him months, but he eventually found them. Aside from their wordless chant, Wargals had no spoken language, relying on a primitive form of thought awareness for communication. But their minds were simple and their intellects basic. As a result, they had been totally susceptible to domination by a superior intelligence and willpower. Morgarath bent them to his will and they became the perfect army for him—ugly beyond nightmares, utterly pitiless and bound totally to his mental orders.

Now, looking at them, he remembered the brightly dressed knights in glittering armor who used to compete in tourneys at Castle Gorlan, their silk-gowned ladies cheering them on and applauding their skills. Mentally comparing them to these black-furred, misshapen creatures, he cursed again.

The Wargals, attuned to his thoughts, sensed his disturbance and stirred uncomfortably, pausing in what they were doing. Angrily, he directed them back to their drill and the chanting resumed.

Morgarath moved away from the unglazed window, closer to the fire that seemed utterly incapable of dispelling the damp and chill from this gloomy castle. Fifteen years, he thought to himself again. Fifteen years since he had rebelled against the newly crowned King Duncan, a youth in his twenties. He had planned it all carefully as the old king's sickness progressed, banking on the indecision and confusion that would follow his death to split the other barons and give Morgarath his opportunity to seize the throne.

Secretly, he had trained his army of Wargals, massing them up here in the mountains, ready for the moment to strike. Then, in the days of confusion and grief following the king's death, when the barons traveled to Castle Araluen for the funeral rites, leaving their armies leaderless, he had attacked, overrunning the southeastern quarter of the kingdom in a matter of days, routing the confused, leaderless forces that tried to oppose him.

Duncan, young and inexperienced, could never have stood against him. The kingdom was his for the taking. The throne was his for the asking.

Then Lord Northolt, the old king's supreme army commander, had rallied some of the younger barons into a loyal confederation, giving strength to Duncan's resolve and stiffening the wavering courage of the others. The armies had met at Hackham Heath, close by the Slipsunder River, and the battle swayed in the balance for five hours, with attack and counterattack and massive loss of life. The Slipsunder was a shallow river, but its treacherous reaches of quicksand and soft mud had formed an impassable barrier, protecting Morgarath's right flank.

But then one of those gray-cloaked meddlers known as Rangers led a force of heavy cavalry across a secret ford ten kilometers upstream. The armored horsemen appeared at the crucial moment of the battle and fell upon the rear of Morgarath's army.

The Wargals, trained in the tumbled rocks of the mountains, had one weakness. They feared horses and could never stand against such a surprise cavalry attack. They broke, retreating to the narrow confines of Three Step Pass, and back to the Mountains of Rain and Night. Morgarath, his rebellion defeated, went with them.

And here he had been exiled these fifteen years. Waiting, plotting, hating the men who had done this to him.

Now, he thought, it was time for his revenge. His spies told him the kingdom had grown slack and complacent and his presence here was all but forgotten. The name Morgarath was a name of legend nowadays, a name mothers used to hush fractious children, threatening that if they did not behave, the black lord Morgarath would come for them.

The time was ripe. Once again, he would lead his Wargals into an attack. But this time he would have allies. And this time he would sow the ground with uncertainty and confusion beforehand. This time none of those who conspired against him previously would be left alive to aid King Duncan.

For the Wargals were not the only ancient, terrifying creatures he had found in these somber mountains. He had two other allies, even more fearsome—the dreadful beasts known as the Kalkara.

The time was ripe to unleash them.

1

"TRY TO EAT SOMETHING, WILL. TOMORROW'S A BIG DAY, after all."

Jenny, blond, pretty and cheerful, gestured toward Will's barely touched plate and smiled encouragingly at him. Will made an attempt to return the smile, but it was a dismal failure. He picked at the plate before him, piled high with his favorite foods. Tonight, his stomach knotted tight with tension and anticipation, he could hardly bring himself to swallow a bite.

Tomorrow would be a big day, he knew. He knew it all too well, in fact. Tomorrow would be the biggest day in his life, because tomorrow was the Choosing Day and it would determine how he spent the rest of his life.

"Nerves, I imagine," said George, setting down his loaded fork and seizing the lapels of his jacket in a judicious manner. He was a thin, gangly and studious boy, fascinated by rules and regulations and with a penchant for examining and debating both sides of any question—sometimes at great length. "Dreadful thing, nervousness. It can just freeze you up so you can't think, can't eat, can't speak."

"I'm not nervous," Will said quickly, noticing that Horace had looked up, ready to form a sarcastic comment.

George nodded several times, considering Will's statement. "On the other hand," he added, "a little nervousness can actually improve performance. It can heighten your perceptions and sharpen your reactions. So, the fact that you are worried, if, in fact, you are, is not necessarily something to be worried about, of itself—so to speak."

In spite of himself, a wry smile touched Will's mouth. George would be a natural in the legal profession, he thought. He would almost certainly be the Scribemaster's choice on the following morning. Perhaps, Will thought, that was at the heart of his own problem. He was the only one of the wardmates who had any fears about the Choosing that would take place within twelve hours.

"He ought to be nervous!" Horace scoffed. "After all, which Craftmaster is going to want him as an apprentice?"

"I'm sure we're all nervous," Alyss said. She directed one of her rare smiles at Will. "We'd be stupid not to be."

"Well, I'm not!" Horace said, then reddened as Alyss raised one eyebrow and Jenny giggled.

It was typical of Alyss, Will thought. He knew that the tall, graceful girl had already been promised a place as an apprentice by Lady Pauline, head of Castle Redmont's Diplomatic Service. Her pretense that she was nervous about the following day, and her tact in refraining from pointing out Horace's gaffe, showed that she was already a diplomat of some skill.

Jenny, of course, would gravitate immediately to the castle kitchens, domain of Master Chubb, Redmont's head chef. He was a man renowned throughout the kingdom for the banquets served in the castle's massive dining hall. Jenny loved food and cooking, and her easygoing nature and unfailing good humor would make her an invaluable staff member in the turmoil of the castle kitchens.

Battleschool would be Horace's choice. Will glanced at his wardmate now, hungrily tucking into the roast turkey, ham and potatoes that he had heaped onto his plate. Horace was big for his age and a natural athlete. The chances that he would be refused were virtually nonexistent. Horace was exactly the type of recruit that Sir Rodney looked for in his warrior apprentices. Strong, athletic, fit. And, thought Will a trifle sourly, not too bright. Battleschool was the path to knighthood for boys like Horace—born commoners but with the physical abilities to serve as knights of the kingdom.

Which left Will. What would his choice be? More importantly, as Horace had pointed out, what Craftmaster would accept him as an apprentice?

For Choosing Day was the pivotal point in the life of the castle wards. They were orphan children raised by the generosity of Baron Arald, the Lord of Redmont Fief. For the most part, their parents had died in the service of the fief, and the Baron saw it as his responsibility to care for and raise the children of his former subjects—and to give them an opportunity to improve their station in life wherever possible.

Choosing Day provided that opportunity.

Each year, castle wards turning fifteen could apply to be apprenticed to the masters of the various crafts that served the castle and its people. Ordinarily, craft apprentices were selected by dint of their parents' occupations or influence with the Craftmasters. The castle wards usually had no such influence and this was their chance to win a future for themselves.

Those wards who weren't chosen, or for whom no openings could be found, would be assigned to farming families in the nearby village, providing farm labor to raise the crops and animals that fed the castle inhabitants. It was rare for this to happen, Will knew. The Baron and his Craftmasters usually went out of their way to fit the wards into one craft or another. But it could happen and it was a fate he feared more than anything.

Horace caught his eye now and gave him a smug smile.

"Still planning on applying for Battleschool, Will?" he asked through a mouthful of turkey and potatoes. "Better eat something then. You'll need to build yourself up a little."

He snorted with laughter and Will glowered at him. A few weeks previously, Horace had overheard Will confiding to Alyss that he desperately wanted to be selected for Battleschool, and he had made Will's life a misery ever since, pointing out on every possible occasion that Will's slight build was totally unsuited for the rigors of Battleschool training.

The fact that Horace was probably right only made matters worse. Where Horace was tall and muscular, Will was small and wiry. He was agile and fast and surprisingly strong, but he simply didn't have the size that he knew was required of Battleschool apprentices. He'd hoped against hope for the past few years that he would have what people called his "growing spurt" before the Choosing Day came around. But it had never happened and now the day was nearly here.

As Will said nothing, Horace sensed that he had scored a verbal hit. This was a rarity in their turbulent relationship. Over the past few years, he and Will had clashed repeatedly. Being the stronger of the two, Horace usually got the better of Will, although very occasionally Will's speed and agility allowed him to get in a surprise kick or a punch and then escape before Horace could catch him.

But while Horace generally had the best of their physical clashes, it was unusual for him to win any of their verbal encounters. Will's wit was as agile as the rest of him and he almost always managed to have the last word. In fact, it was this tendency that often led to trouble between them: Will was yet to learn that having the last word was not always a good idea. Horace decided now to press his advantage.

"You need muscles to get into Battleschool, Will. Real muscles," he said, glancing at the others around the table to see if anyone disagreed. The other wards, uncomfortable at the growing tension between the two boys, concentrated on their plates.

"Particularly between the ears," Will replied and, unfortunately, Jenny couldn't refrain from giggling. Horace's face flushed and he started to rise from his seat. But Will was quicker and he was already at the door before Horace could disentangle himself from his chair. He contented himself with hurling a final insult after his retreating wardmate.

"That's right! Run away, Will No-Name! You're a no-name and nobody will want you as an apprentice!"

In the anteroom outside, Will heard the parting sally and felt blood flush to his cheeks. It was the taunt he hated most, although he had tried never to let Horace know that, sensing that he would provide the bigger boy with a weapon if he did.

The truth was, nobody knew Will's second name. Nobody knew who his parents had been. Unlike his yearmates, who had lived in the fief before their parents had died and whose family histories were known, Will had appeared, virtually out of nowhere, as a newborn baby. He had been found, wrapped in a small blanket and placed in a basket, on the steps of the ward building fifteen years ago. A note had been attached to the blanket, reading simply:

> *His mother died in childbirth. His father died a hero.*
> *Please care for him. His name is Will.*

That year, there had been only one other ward. Alyss's father was a cavalry lieutenant who had died in the battle at Hackham Heath, when Morgarath's Wargal army had been defeated and driven back to the mountains. Alyss's mother, devastated by her loss, succumbed to a fever some weeks after giving birth. So there was plenty of room in the Ward for the unknown child, and Baron Arald was, at heart, a kindly man. Even though the circumstances were unusual, he had given permission for Will to be accepted as a ward of Castle Redmont. It seemed logical to assume that, if the note were true, Will's father had died in the war against Morgarath, and since Baron Arald had taken a leading part in that war, he felt duty bound to honor the unknown father's sacrifice.

So Will had become a Redmont ward, raised and educated by the Baron's generosity. As time passed, the others had gradually joined him and Alyss until there were five in their year group. But while the others had memories of their parents or, in Alyss's case, people who had known them and who could tell her about them, Will knew nothing of his past.

That was why he had invented the story that had sustained him throughout his childhood in the Ward. And, as the years passed and he added detail and color to the story, he eventually came to believe it himself.

His father, he knew, had died a hero's death. So it made sense to create a picture of him as a hero—a knight warrior in full armor, fighting against the Wargal hordes, cutting them down left and right until eventually he was overcome by sheer weight of numbers. Will had pictured the tall figure so often in his mind, seeing every detail of his armor and his equipment but never being able to visualize his face.

As a warrior, his father would expect him to follow in his footsteps. That was why selection for Battleschool was so important to Will. And that was why the more unlikely it became that he would be selected, the more desperately he clung to the hope that he might.

He exited from the Ward building into the darkened castle yard. The sun was long down and the torches placed every twenty meters or so on the castle walls shed a flickering, uneven light. He hesitated a moment. He would not return to the Ward and face Horace's continued taunts. To do so would only lead to another fight between them—a fight that Will knew that he would probably lose. George would probably try to analyze the situation for him, looking at both sides of the question and thoroughly confusing the issue. Alyss and Jenny might try to comfort him, he knew—Alyss particularly since they had grown up together. But at the moment he didn't want their sympathy and he couldn't face Horace's taunts, so he headed for the one place where he knew he could find solitude.

The huge fig tree growing close by the castle's central tower had often afforded him a haven. Heights held no fear for Will and he climbed smoothly into the tree, continuing long after another might have stopped, until he was in the lighter branches at the very top—branches that swayed and dipped under his weight. In the past, he had often escaped from Horace up here. The bigger boy couldn't match Will's speed in the tree and he was unwilling to follow as high as this. Will found a convenient fork and wedged himself in it, his body giving slightly to the movement of the tree as the branches swayed in the evening breeze. Below, the foreshortened figures of the watch made their rounds of the castle yard.

He heard the door of the Ward building open and, glancing down, saw Alyss emerge, looking around the yard for him in vain. The tall girl hesitated a few moments, then, seeming to shrug, turned back inside. The elongated rectangle of light that the open door threw across the yard was cut off as she closed the door softly behind her. Strange, he thought, how seldom people tend to look up.

There was a rustle of soft feathers and a barn owl landed on the next branch, its head swiveling, its huge eyes catching every last ray of the faint light. It studied him without concern, seeming to know it had nothing to fear from him. It was a hunter. A silent flyer. A ruler of the night.

"At least you know who you are," he said softly to the bird. It swiveled its head again, then launched itself off into the darkness, leaving him alone with his thoughts.

Gradually, as he sat there, the lights in the castle windows went out, one by one. The torches burnt down to smoldering husks and were replaced at midnight by the change of watch. Eventually, there was only one light left burning and that, he knew, was in the Baron's study, where the Lord of Redmont was still presumably at work, poring over reports and papers. The study was virtually level with Will's position in the tree and he could see the burly figure of the Baron seated at his desk. Finally Baron Arald rose, stretched and leaned forward to extinguish the lamp as he left the room, heading for his sleeping quarters on the floor above. Now the castle was asleep, except for the guards on the walls, who kept constant watch.

In less than nine hours, Will realized, he would face the Choosing. Silently, miserably, fearing the worst, he climbed down from the tree and made his way to his bed in the darkened boys' dormitory in the Ward.

DISCOVER THE DAYS WHEN AN APPRENTICE BECAME A MASTER

RANGER'S APPRENTICE
THE EARLY YEARS

THE INTERNATIONAL
BESTSELLING PHENOMENON

READ
THE COMPANION SERIES

BROTHERBAND CHRONICLES